Crimson Sand, Crimson Snow

By Craig Gallant

Crimson Sand, Crimson Snow
By Craig Gallant
Cover design by Michael Nigro
This edition published in 2019

Winged Hussar Publishing, is an imprint of

Pike and Powder Publishing Group LLC
1525 Hulse Rd, Unit 1   1 Craven Lane, Box 66066
Point Pleasant, NJ 08742   Lawrence, NJ 08648-66066

Copyright © Craig Gallant
ISBN 978-1-945430-86-2
LCN 2019951594

Bibliographical References and Index
1. Fiction. 2. Fantasy. 3. Action & Adventure

Pike and Powder Publishing Group LLC All rights reserved
For more information on Pike and Powder Publishing Group, LLC,
visit us at www.PikeandPowder.com & www.wingedhussarpublishing.com

twitter: @pike_powder
facebook: @PikeandPowder

Prologue

Thunder rolled across the valley, echoing hoofbeats crashing back from the high, rocky hills to either side. War cries rose into the clear sky; the host charged as if destiny rode with them, each warrior grinning fiercely, imagining the songs and sagas that would follow them the rest of their days. Eyes shone with absolute faith in their victory as they rushed toward the distant ford.

The philosophers of the Empire of Kun Makha would no longer sneer at their fyrdar neighbors. Astrigir would claim its rightful place as an equal of the empire once the last strength of Vestan and Subraea was broken. The Broken Kingdoms would be united under the leadership of King Einar Jalen once more, ending more than a hundred years of bloodshed.

The fyrdar were an ancient warrior race, and their blood flowed through Einar's veins. It filled the warriors of his elite honor guard, the saemgard, with fire as they charged the peaceful ford over the river Merrick.

King Einar was young, the old king barely a year in his grave, but he had learned from the old tales well. Once the fyrdar kingdoms were united, Kun Makha would have no choice but to treat with him as equals, and the jarls of Astrigir would enjoy the power and authority that had been denied them for so long. Iver of Vestan was too weak. Old Jerrick of Subraea was a coward. But Einar remembered the sagas, better than either of the other kings. The time had come for the warrior race to reclaim their place in history; to redeem the dishonor of their flight from the terrible Utan so many centuries ago.

His strategy had been agreed upon by the greatest warriors of Astrigir. The wisest men and women of the splintered fyrdar realms had guided his hand. His father's most trusted advisor, Chogan, himself a son of the proud Empire of Kun Makha, had shown himself nearly the equal of the vanished wizards of the old tales as he wielded alliances, threats, and promises to position Astrigir for its final rise to power. Everything was in position; nothing would stop Einar from taking his rightful place alongside the lords of the empire.

The saemgard were the flower of a generation of Astrigir's warriors; each a proven fighter, fiercely loyal to the king and his vision. Trained in the ancient forms of combat and clad in the traditional furs and leathers of their fyrdar forebears over the hard steel of the king's armories, they wielded the deadliest weapons Einar could provide. The massive maekre blades, a brutal combination of sword and axe, wielded to best effect in two hands, whirled over their heads as they howled the ancient war cries.

At the head of the charge rode the newest member of the saemgard, a towering youth whose loose mane flowed behind him like a banner. Eirik Hastiin, youngest to ever complete the training and take the oath, was the king's closest friend. Orphan of a landless thane, Eirik had been raised as a ward of the old king, earning first the friendship and then the trust of the prince. He now acted as the king's eyes and ears. Lord Chogan had insisted King Einar stay behind in the Bhorg, the labyrinthine citadel in the heart of his capitol at Connat. Einar was a warrior as well as a king, and nearly defied his advisor. But in the end, he relented, under the condition that Eirik be given the honor of leading the charge at Merrick Ford.

The other warriors were proud of their youngest brother, and happy to give him his day. The greatest heroes of the age reined in their eager mounts, urging the ice-eyed fighter forward, the crimson wing of his father proud on his round shield, ceding to him the honor of first splashing into the cold, autumnal waters of the Merrick.

The main body of the Vestan army was far to the south, thanks to Lord Chogan's artifice. Einar's scouts had seen Iver's own hearth guard leading the defenses of the border forts; there was no doubt that this ford, remote and lost in the folds and twists of the deep valleys, had been left nearly undefended. The saemgard of Astrigir would sweep across, follow the river south, and catch the bulk of Iver's armies from behind. The battle would be over in minutes, reducing Vestan to vassalage. Only old, fat Jerrick would remain to stand in the way of Astrigir's ascension.

The shining spear tip of King Einar's army thrust into Vestan, splashing across the Merrick River, the warriors grinning fiercely as the lonely border guards, realizing their plight, dropped their weapons and staggered back toward the red-mantled trees.

Laughing, Orrik Ashkii was the first to fall. One of the oldest saemgard, his easy smile and booming laugh had filled the Bhorg since the days of Einar's father's youth. A massive bolt, as thick around as the big man's thumb, struck him in the neck, plunging through leather gorget and fur mantle, slamming him from his rocking charger as a look of pained bewilderment swept across his face.

Young Eirik was too far ahead to notice the terrible blow, but others were forced to wrench their mounts away from Orrik's horse as it stumbled. The big man fell to the ground spraying dark blood over the pale autumn grass.

More bolts flashed into the charging warriors, striking out from the forests on either side of the narrow path on the other side of the ford. Shields were raised, maekre blades sheathed or dropped as the saemgard attempted to defend themselves from the hail of death.

War cries turned to shouts of pain and dismay as the charge faltered. Rogar, jarl of Loftsthon and thane of the saemgard, growled, rising in his stirrups to urge his brothers and sisters onward.

More of Einar's warriors fell, sending their blood swirling down the Merrick as horses screamed in panic, a surging barrier of flesh that churned in the center of the ford, barring the way for those coming on behind.

The heavy bolts could only mean one thing: King Einar had been betrayed.

The Vestan forces had been warned that the saemgard would attack the ford. Siege bows were heavy, they could not be shifted and deployed on a whim. It would have taken Iver's fighters days to get the big weapons into position. Yet there they were, in lethal ambush.

But the massive bows were slow to fire, each requiring two trained men to work them. There could not be that many. Already, the initial volley had died away; individual bolts slashed out now, only as quickly as the different crews could load them. If the saemgard could rally and push through, there was still hope of forcing their way across the ford.

As Rogar shouted, waving his heavy blade, Eirik reigned in, alone on the far bank. The Vestan archers had concentrated their fire on the main body of the saemgard, ignoring the lone, impetuous figure at their head. But that grace would soon end as the attacking formation dissolved under the withering fire. The young fighter scanned behind him, shock twisting his face. Everywhere, riderless horses milled about, some screaming terrible cries of agony all their own. To remain still would mean death for them all. To run would be to betray the destiny of the moment.

Eirik tore at his reins and brought his mount back around. He drove it mercilessly toward the nearest arm of forest, toward the men moving beneath the trees. The surviving saemgard surged around him, allowing the momentum of their charge to carry them past the dead and dying, toward the prepared Vestan forces.

Rogar's cries were silenced as two bolts struck him in the chest, knocking him into the swirling water. But the angle was growing more difficult; bolts were flying wide as the saemgard clambered out of the river, readying their charge.

A shout rose up from deeper within the woods; a wave of leather-clad fighters rushed out, axes high, pushing through the foliage with their round, pale-blue shields.

Eirik sneered. Barely a step above peasant conscripts, these kerns were hardly the equals of the saemgard of Astrigir. The young fighter shrugged his shield into position as a small axe hurtled out of the oncoming mob. With a dull clang, the weapon flicked off into the shadows, but several more followed.

A soft grunt beside him brought his head around just in time to see Gyda Knoton, hero of Belnath Peak, take an axe to the side of the head. Her horse shied away as the wave of enemy warriors swept into them. The hero was dragged from her saddle, axes rising and falling above her.

Eirik swept his heavy maekre blade through a swath of peasants charging him from the right, clearing the forest around him and driving his horse backward a few steps to make more room. Over half the saemgard were down, but that left more than two hundred still milling through the forest amidst many times their number of peasant fighters. The battle was by no means lost if the saemgard could only regroup, combine their strength, and bring it to bear against the poorly equipped Vestan levies.

But the siege bows continued to sing out, sending bolts whistling through the dappled shadows whenever a target presented itself. Grey-haired Othay Verun, rallying a group of saemgard, was struck in the back of the head. His helm rang like a bell as it flew off into the trees, his body tumbling into the leaves.

This could not be happening. King Einar and Lord Chogan had been planning this day for over a year. Every piece was in place; Iver could have had no warning. Even the saemgard had not known their true target until they left the Bhorg the night before. Eirik bellowed in frustration, reaching out to lop one foeman's head off with a lazy swing of his axe-like sword.

Something flashed in the corner of his eye; he ducked around, his shield rising just in time to catch a glancing blow from a siege bolt as it flew through the branches. He grunted as he was thrown into the dirt. He gasped; his lungs stunned by the impact. A shadow staggered over him, iron and fur marking him as a saemgard even as a trio of ragged men drove at him, axes raised, out of the shadows.

"No!" the man growled, throwing down his splintered shield and taking up his maekre blade in two hands. It might have been mighty Gnoton Lyth, it might have been sour Kare Findu. It was impossible to tell with the blood streaming from beneath the man's helm, one half of his face a glistening red mask.

The warrior swung his heavy blade, sweeping across the enemy's advance and catching the lead man in the side. The foe was dashed to the dirt, blade lodged halfway through his ribcage, but his companions jumped over his twitching body to beat the saemgard down into the muck.

Eirik pushed himself to his feet with a grunt and rushed the men. By the time he reached them, he was too late for anything but vengeance. A flashing blow of his own blade broke one man's spine, while the return slash caught the last man in the jaw as he turned, open mouthed, to watch his companion fall. Eirik himself collapsed to one knee in exhaustion, his blade falling beside him.

Everything was chaos. Shouting, screaming, and the pitiful sounds of terrified, anguished horses echoed through the trees. Throughout the forests on both sides of the ford the branches lashed and whipped as if they were alive, concealing the fury of Astrigir's greatest warriors and the Vestan conscripts who had been set in their path.

A small cohort of saemgard broke out of the surrounding soldiers, those still mounted reaching down to pull their stranded brothers up behind them. The odd siege bolt whistled out, but most of the heavy bows had been silenced. It appeared as if they might make it back across the ford.

A terrible slithering sound rose up over the cries and moans and screams. The arrows were much smaller this time, coming down like a sudden, heavy rain, but they peppered the tightly packed formation without mercy. Horses shrieked and bolted, dumping many of the armored riders into the river. Men and women slumped from saddles, grasping at shafts that had penetrated layers of leather and fur. One saemgard thane, his blue eyes wild, mouth red with blood, screamed back over his shoulder as he fell, arrows trembling in his back and legs.

A smaller wave of foot soldiers, these wielding vicious little short bows, stepped out from the woods. They began to plod across the torn ground, sending their arrows flashing into any saemgard showing signs of life. The forest was filled with the dead and the dying. Far more of the bodies sported splashes of Vestan blue than the iron and fur of the saemgard, but there was no question as to who had won the day.

Eirik watched, gasping, as the line of archers made their slow, steady way through the spreading silence. Every few moments there was a quick whik-thud, and another gasp or cry or moan would be cut short.

The line was only a few paces from where Eirik lay, buried in a pile of ruptured enemy, when another fur-clad figure surged up out of the carnage in the face of the line of archers.

"Run, lad!" It was Othay, his gray hair matted with blood, rising like an avenging fyrdar god from the wreckage of the battle. The old man held his fierce maekre blade clenched in one hand, a long-handled axe in the other. "Einar must know what happened here!"

Eirik's grey eyes went wide as he watched the old man stagger forward, arrows striking like hammer blows against his thick armor. "Betrayal! Treachery!" Othay lurched into the battle line, sword and axe striking in a whirling storm of iron that smashed Vestan fighters away in every direction. Casting a wild glance over his shoulder, he saw Eirik frozen in place and snarled.

"Now, boy! Go!"

Eirik shook himself, and he Looked around desperately for his maekre blade. He could not find it amidst the carnage. He bent to grab one of the long-handled Vestan axes.

An arrow struck his shoulder, ringing off the armor and sending him staggering over a drift of bodies. He flung one hand out to catch himself, snarling as he rose, looking for the archer who had hit him, but Othay had beaten him to the strike. The old man was wheeling down the line of archers, sending them screaming and jumping out of his path. There was no clean shot as he danced among them, any attempt as likely to hit a friend as to find the crazed, grizzled saemgard. Others, with clumsy knives and axes, were trying to drag the hulking old man down before he could do more damage.

Othay was screaming like a wounded bear as he surged from one knot of enemies to the next.

"For the king, boy! This isn't for you, it's for the king!"

Eirik paused. Somehow, all of the king's plans had been ground into dust. Astrigir would be all but defenseless. King Iver's hearth guard could very well be cutting their way into Connat at that moment to murder Einar. To murder his friend.

With a hopeless scream, Eirik hurled the axe at the closest archer. The haft struck the man in the head and sent him toppling back into the carpet of the dead and dying. He turned, with one last glance at Othay, and then forced his legs into a slow, unsteady jog toward the river.

An arrow struck him a glancing blow to the back of the head, forcing his helm down into his face and his knee into the bloody mud. Another shaft struck him in the shoulder, this time finding a chink between steel and leather. He groaned, prying a throwing axe from the cold hand of a corpse, and pushed himself back up to his feet.

Turning, he watched as the towering figure of Othay finally succumbed to the press of filthy bodies. The old man gave out one last defiant cry as he fell.

The soft sounds of the river were at his back. But it might as well have been a thousand leagues away for all the good it was going to do him. The Vestan men were turning now, toward him, the last member of Einar's saemgard standing upon the field.

They were wary. They moved forward with a hunched, hunted look, rather than victorious warriors. Their hesitation gave Eirik a moment to breathe. He surveyed the field, outside of the woods and beneath the clear, autumn sky.

The saemgard were dead. Whether they had each and every one breathed their last or if they were now wounded or unconscious beneath drifts of bodies, these peasants would see them to the other side before sunset. But King Einar's finest warriors had not spent their lives cheaply.

Despite the treachery, despite the perfectly laid trap, the heavy siege bows, and the waves of infantry, Vestan had been sorely wounded as well. There had to be over a thousand dead and dying across the field. There was no glory here; nothing would change in the Broken Kingdoms. Power would remain balanced between the three fyrdar realms, and Kun Makha would continue to dominate the land from the northern plains.

Something within Eirik's chest broke. He gave a small cough, a bubble of blood forming on his lips, and he looked up to see the line of men, having gathered what courage remained, starting to move toward him. Bows were rising, arrows glinting in the cold sun.

Without even thinking, the youngest man ever to take the oath of the saemgard dropped his gaze toward the men who came for him. He took a staggering step, and then the world around him lurched. He had reached the river after all. The muddy embankment beneath him shifted and gave way. He toppled into the river.

The cold water shocked him to wakefulness as it closed over his head. He surged back up, reaching for the light and gasping for breath. He struggled in the grip of his steel, sodden leather, and fur, the armor dragging him toward the bottom. With a last burst of strength, he writhed free, letting his precious war gear settle into the muck as he relaxed, gasping for air, the river carrying him downstream.

Arrows began to fall all around him, but he could only stare up into the shivering canopy of crimson leaves sliding by overhead. A shaft found his leg, but he gave no sign he felt its impact. The water around him swirled with his blood.

He floated, the arrows slowed, and then finally he was alone, drifting beneath the blazing autumn leaves.

Chapter 1

Tyr pondered the sad pile of dull coins in his palm with a cold, distant calm. All around him, the rickety stands were filled with farmers, merchants, and others eager to satisfy their ancestral sense of bloodlust, once removed, for the last time of the season. The tournies were the most sought after entertainments among the fyrdar. Most towns and villages squeezed as many into each season as they could manage. Overhead, the clouds were heavy and dark, promising more cold late-autumn rains.

All of which seemed to give the coins in his hands just that much more weight. His brow furrowed. No, it was his need that had grown heavy, not the coins.

He needed more coins.

Around him, the crowd muttered quietly to itself, peasants and merchants tearing into greasy chunks of meat, quaffing mead and ale in liberal doses. These tourneys never varied; whether they were being held on the outskirts of Burlin, the coastal ports of Subraea, or the borderlands of Astrigir, they were always the same. Locals of all levels of society flocked to nearby fields dotted with tents and pavilions of every color and shape; farmers, merchants, jarls, and thanes took their seats on the temporary stands erected by the squires and servants of the tourney warriors. Even thralls were allowed time from their lives of endless drudgery to attend the tourneys. It had seemed a glorious adventure to him as a child, when he had found the gall to convince his father to hand over his carefully-hoarded apprentice's fee to one of the most glorious, mysterious tourney warriors in the Kingdoms. Sadly, that was many years ago, and the shine had quickly worn off the lifestyle and his master both.

He sighed. He wished they could spend more time in Astrigir. He could barely remember his home, he had been so long away. But his master had had good reason to avoid the kingdom when Tyr had first joined him, and time had only hardened that resolve.

On the muddy field, two massive warhorses moved slowly into position, and the crowd settled down to watch the next match. A quick glance told Tyr everything he needed to know, and he went back to his brooding. Neither Jorunn Tizoq or Ove Chu'a were real contenders for the day's prize. Both had been active in the ceaseless border skirmishes between the fyrdar nations when they were younger, but those battles were far behind them now.

That thought brought a bitter sneer to Tyr's face. Both of the men readying their mounts were younger than his master.

If these two men were both fading lights on the tourney circuit, what did that make the old man?

The two fighters urged their mounts forward to a ragged cheer from the crowd. The horses were nearly as old and tired as their riders, and the charge lacked the implacable force of the younger warriors.

The two men brandished their heavy swords, weaving slightly in their saddles as they prepared the single blow the pass would allow. Many poorly-matched tourney fights would end with a single pass, as an unskilled or out-of-practice warrior mistimed his blow, or missed entirely, opening himself up to a battering return slash that could easily knock him from his saddle. Most, even among the more gifted warriors, seldom lasted three or four passes. The heavy blades were huge and cumbersome, unforgiving of error and exhausting to wield for any length of time.

Tyr closed his fist around the coins as the clatter from the tourney field announced a heavily-armored figure crashing to the ground. A quick glance revealed that Jorunn Tizoq's star had fallen even lower. A smattering of boos, hisses, and pungent suggestions peppered the man as he staggered to his feet, attempting to reclaim his heavy sword while throwing rude gestures at the laughing crowd. At the far end of the field, Ove roared like a champion from the ancient sagas, pumping his sword over his head as if he had just vanquished a mighty dragon.

Tyr felt his gorge rise. He had less and less tolerance for this life with each passing day.

With a grunt, he pushed himself up off the rough plank bench and began to ease his way through the crowd. With vague smiles, nods, and an occasional muttered apology, he moved through them with as little fuss as possible. At the bottom, he glanced around, found Torben Hurit huddled with several other men and women of business, and moved toward them.

Torben was the resident ring-leader for the circuit's unsanctioned wagering circle. Although most of the warriors who fought in the tourneys did so in the hope of earning a share of the prize purse, most hedged their bets by placing wagers on the other matches. The locals, however, provided the bulk of Torben's business.

When the gruff older man saw Tyr approaching, he made no effort to hide the look of exasperation that rose to his proud, copper-skinned face. Men and women of oyathey descent were not entirely common within the Broken Kingdoms, preferring to keep to the more civilized, refined provinces of Kun Makha to the north. The man's jet-black hair was streaked with white, blowing in the chill, rain-heavy wind.

"Lad, I don't have the time—" The rich tones of Kun Makha rolled across the diminishing space between them, but Tyr waved the words away.

"You've already got our money, Hurit." He tried not to smile at the flash of annoyance in the older man's face. The other businessmen stepped back, willing to let the little drama play out. It was something a man in Torben's line of work had to deal with on a fairly regular basis.

"It won't hurt you any to take a little more." Tyr pushed the fistful of coins toward the Oyathey wage-keeper.

Torben's eyes narrowed as he saw the small pile. When he looked up again, his regal face was not unkind, which made Tyr's jaw clench more than anger or dismissal might have.

"This is all you have for the winter?" That set the younger man back. It wasn't all they had, but it was closer than he liked. And if he lost it, the cold months would be lean indeed. But there would be no feasts either way, and Tyr was tired of living the life of a pauper.

"We're good for it." He shook the money. "You know that. I don't want special treatment. Just put this with the rest, at the same rate."

Torben shook his head. "Special treatment? Just by the way you say it, I know you lie. Like some great fyrdar lord granting me some boon." The expression hardened. "Your master doesn't draw the crowds he used to, Tyr. He's not the man he was. Hell, he's not even half the man he once claimed to be!"

Tyr felt his lips tighten; his fists clenched. But Torben raised a hand. "There's nothing personal, here, Tyr Wayra. I couldn't take the money if I wanted to. Your master's up next, lad. The book's closed on this one. I'm sorry."

But he didn't look sorry. Tyr looked more closely at the man, who flinched just a little under the scrutiny. "You've taken my money later than this before. What's going on?"

Torben glanced back at the field, where several grooms were trying to lure Jorunn Tizoq's mount away, and shrugged. "Have you seen him today?" Another shake of the head. "I would not suggest you throw any more of your coin down that path today, son."

Tyr started to speak, but the older man's face hardened and he turned back to the others. "I'm trying to be kind. You'll soon have more worries than my opinion of him. Keep your money, you'll need it in the months ahead. Perhaps Vestan or Subraea will be kinder? They may yet have a tourney or two, before it gets too cold." The last words, thrown over the man's fur-clad shoulder, stung worse than all the other. "Astrigir's an ill-omened land for him, I think."

Tyr watched Torben walk away, wrestling with the need to follow, to continue the argument, and the rising urgency of finding his master and discovering what, exactly, the oyathey had been talking about.

In the end, years of habit won out and he spun, moving quickly toward the staging area behind the tents. If it wasn't too late, he might be able to convince the master of ceremonies to shuffle the schedule a little bit and give them some maneuvering room to settle the issue with Torben. The coins made a pathetically weak chinking sound as he dropped them into his pocket pouch, forcing himself to a nonchalant pace. It would not do to appear nervous before a match, especially with such a tenuous reputation in the local circuit.

But before Tyr reached the gateway to the staging area, Torben's words proved prophetic; a massive, black-clad charger bulled passed him, nearly knocking him into the frigid muck.

"Master, wait!" Tyr reached up for a rein, but with an angry grunt, the massive old warrior pulled the leather strap out of his reach, tossing something away with his other hand. The squire followed the trajectory long enough to identify the object, then cursed under his breath.

A mead horn.

Throwing a scowl back toward Torben Hurit's enigmatic shrug, Tyr tried to catch up with his master knowing full well that it was far too late. Was he swaying in his saddle more than usual? He was pulling at the enormous sword with one gnarled fist while the horse, confused, neighed angrily and stomped in a tight, aggressive circle.

Tyr cursed again and dropped all pretense at calm, running for the border fencing as if there was anything more he could do.

The big man was clad all in black, as befit what had once been called a runn warrior. Before the end of Einar's dreams, warriors who had somehow dishonored themselves or their jarls in battle would resort to fighting in the tourney circuit, shorn of their names and sigils, hoping eventually to reveal themselves as champions and redeem their reputations.

As the bloody stalemate between the Broken Kingdoms dragged on, and Kun Makha's indifference remained unwavering, the practice had fallen out of favor. There were enough border skirmishes, raids, and petty squabbles to provide that kind of man with all the honor he could ask for. If a man ran from one battle, or was bedeviled with some plague of ill luck, he could merely move on to the next camp that would have him and continue the fight. The concern for honor and glory, with the weight those words had once carried, was long gone.

Except, it would appear, for Tyr's master. The man had never once shown his sigil or claimed an infamous name in all the years the squire had served him, nor during the many, many years before that.

What had once been a noble cloak of glamorous mystery had become little more than a joke to the other warriors on the circuit, and soon even the rustic audiences had grown tired of the charade. But none of them knew the one thing that Tyr had learned the hard way.

For his master, this was no pretense.

The sigil hidden behind the black fabric shroud on his shield was very real. It had been one of the most recognized symbols in the kingdom, once. And today, it could well be enough to get the man bearing it killed out of hand.

Tyr's master truly believed that this was the best he deserved from the world. The brooding was no act. The passing years should have proven that to even the most skeptical provincial. In fact, most of the men and women involved with the circuit had come to accept his master as an honest eccentric, and although his identity was one of the most coveted secrets on the circuit, no one had made any real attempt to force the issue in years. In fact, most of the warriors, squires, and servants on the tourney circuit merely called him the Ruun. And for years, facing the Ruun in a tourney had always made for a good spectacle.

But what was unfolding before him now had become more and more common over the years, and Tyr didn't know how much longer he wanted to be responsible for picking up the pieces from what would follow.

Tyr spat as he saw his master's match, Knoton of Vestan. Knoton was a younger man, one of the new warriors who saw more advantage and advancement in the circuit than in the endless little wars ravaging the Broken Kingdoms. And he was good.

Tyr shook his head, fighting the urge to look away. There was a time when no young puppy like Knoton would have been able to challenge the Ruun. But those days were far gone. A loyal voice in his mind screamed at that thought; his master was still skilled in battle. When he wasn't addled with drink, there were few warriors who could claim to be his equal. There were whispers that at one time, no man or woman in any of the kingdoms or the empire to the north could make such a claim.

But that was before he had forsaken his name and sigil for the black of the Ruun. Something had driven the big man onto the tourney trail, where he eked out an existence on the fringes of society, leaving whatever life had known before behind.

Tyr ground his teeth. There was no doubt in his mind: his master was swaying. The horse was doing its best to compensate. They had only owned the big black for a year or so, but already it was sadly accustomed to taking the field with an unsteady rider. His master had refused to name the beast, so Tyr had taken to calling it Hestir, the old fyrdar word for horse. At first he was using the term sarcastically, trying to goad his master, but over time the name had stuck, and even his master used it when he didn't think anyone was listening.

With a shouted challenge, Knoton dug his spurs into his mount's flank and drove it directly at the Ruun, shield raised. The big man in black seemed to be tangled in his reins and shield as he cleared his own heavy sword. There was something different about the weapon, something indefinable that set it apart from the tourney swords the other fair weather warriors used. Despite its heavy solidity, it was of finer make, with a sort of grounded elegance that the other slabs of iron lacked.

Not that it was going to make much difference in this fight.

Knoton's mount pounded across the ground with a grace that belied the animal's weight and size. The entire match looked like a foregone conclusion as the crude sword rose for a single crushing blow that would send his master flying into a pile of leather, fur, and steel.

But at the last possible moment, the Ruun weaved to the side and the blade sailed harmlessly past. Whether it had been a conscious maneuver or blind, drunken luck, he could not have said; but Tyr knew that all they needed was one good counter blow as Knoton galloped past, and their winter would be set.

The slash snaked out, glinting in the cold light, but it was wild, undirected, and whistled past the other man's retreated back without making contact.

As Tyr's master drew up nearby, the crest of wild, gray-blond hair rising from the stubbled scalp bobbing wildly, he saw that the man's icy grey eyes were wide and vague. How much mead had he downed? Tyr scowled. And who had given it to him? The other warriors knew he would drink himself blind if given half a chance; there was an unspoken agreement among them to keep the drink away on a tourney day. It was in no one's interest for the locals to be given anything less than a decent showing for their pennies.

Knoton had pulled up on the far side of the field and turned, not willing to give the lucky old drunk another chance, and was already driving his mount back up to charging speed before Tyr's master could set himself. But a cold look came over the black-clad warrior, and Tyr felt hope surge in his chest again. There was awareness there. Not just awareness of his situation, but awareness that Knoton was trying to take advantage of the situation.

As the other warrior charged, Tyr's master kicked at Hestir's flank, driving the beast forward to meet him. The ground shook as the great chargers pounded across the cold, clammy field. The Ruun rose up in his stirrups, shield cast careless at his side as his gleaming sword rose. He was still swaying, but the effort seemed to compliment his mount's movement, and each shift in Knoton's approach was matched, clearly frustrating the younger man. And then the great sword was coming down; the cheers rose to a painful crescendo. That only showed how little they knew about fighting. For the blow, great and grand and dramatic, had come several seconds too early.

The big sword crashed off Knoton's upraised shield, knocking the wooden circle away and forcing a grunt from the younger warrior. But a savage grin flashed from within the man's tangled beard despite the pain. The Ruun's shield was out of position. He was off-balance as his massive sword was sent angling downward. And his mount, trying to shift beneath him to compensate for a rider already sliding farther and farther to the left, slid directly into the path of Knoton's horse.

The two beasts came crashing together. The man known as the Ruun began to fall before his opponent's sword even landed. When the slash struck home, it only sped up the inevitable, dashing the older man out of his saddle and into the mud.

Hestir rolled beneath Knoton's mount's, screaming as he tumbled. The fallen warrior crashed to the earth like a kitchen's worth of ironware crashing off a high shelf, his grunts and cries lost in the madness.

And then it was over. Knoton and his mount thundered past, leaving his vanquished opponent rolling and moaning on the cold earth. Hestir struggled back up, snorting in disgust. Tyr felt one tight knot in his chest loosen; at least the horse seemed to be okay. The other knot was only getting tighter as he moved out onto the field to help his master up and back to their tent under the insults and laughter of the crowd.

*****

Like almost everything else in their life, the tent's best days were long behind it. It had once been black, of course. Now, it was a faded, washed out gray. Clothing and supplies were piled up along the sides, with the master's armor a dented, stinking heap in one corner.

The man himself lay on his back, one hairy arm thrown over his pale eyes as Tyr mopped at the blood still seeping from his mouth.

"You've got no one to blame but yourself." He made no attempt to keep the bitterness from his voice.

"Silence." The word was a brittle croak, echoing the dizziness of drink and the shock of the day's defeat.

"You knew how things have been." He twisted the bloody water into the bowl and dropped the rag after it. The worst of the bleeding had stopped. "You'll understand better when we've run out of money for drink before midwinter."

The big man grunted, waving at the boy with one weak hand. "Enough."

Tyr shook his head, looking down at the man he had once thought a legend. Defeat had broken something inside the Ruun. There was almost nothing left of the man who had been the youngest warrior to pick up one of the famed maekre blades in over a hundred years.

Although the name was no longer spoken outside of this ratty tent, Tyr knew he served Eirik Hastiin. He had discovered the truth years ago, following a conversation with the drunken fighter outside of his home village. Eirik had denied it, but Tyr had believed, with all his heart. And fueled by that belief, he had convinced his father to give the man all of the coin they had saved for his apprenticeship to the local smith.

Tyr had known that Eirik's destiny had not yet run its course. He had truly believed that greatness still lay within the man, only waiting to be reborn. Tales were still told of Eirik Hastiin and the saemgard from the earliest days of Einar's reign. Despite his youth, the man had been one of the greatest fyrdar warriors in generations.

Little was known about the Battle of Merrik Ford; even less about the young champion who had led the ill-fated charge. What should have been the greatest moment in fyrdar history had been the greatest defeat since they had fled from the mythical Utan across the vast oceans to the shores of Kun

Makha in days lost in time. The king's rage at the defeat was said to have known no limits, and the age of bloodshed and chaos that followed had left no time for reflection or relief.

Most assumed Eirik Hastiin had died that day with all the others. Some whispered that the boy had survived through some cowardly trick, to live on in exile or take his own life in shame. As far as Tyr knew, no one knew the Ruun's true identity, or how he had come to join the tourney circuit all those years ago.

Tyr had been born on lands gifted to the young warrior before the battle. After, when Eirik had disappeared, the king had reclaimed the fiefdom, holding it as a domain of the crown ever since. The people of the area had kept the memory of their brief former lord alive longer than most others. Tyr had seen the Ruun for the first time at that tourney just outside of town, fighting from within an enclosed helm and behind a blank black shield, a glimpse of red barely visible behind a small, ragged tear. His curiosity had been aroused, and he had followed the mysterious warrior through the encampment, sneaking away from his father and spying from the shadows long into the night. To this day, he could not say where he had found the courage to approach the huge stranger, now a battered and aging tourney warrior, but the flicker of recognition he saw in those icy eyes when he called the man by his name would never leave him.

He sat back on his haunches, staring down at the wreck before him. He was beginning to fear that he would live to regret convincing his father to part with the apprenticeship fee all those years ago.

The years had ground past, and he was no closer to helping Eirik Hastiin reclaim his place in Astrigir. The old man claimed King Einar wanted him dead, that agents searched for him wherever he went. And although none of these agents had ever manifested themselves where Tyr could see them, his master did get into more than his fair share of brawls. They spent a great deal of their time in midnight escapes, galloping off to the next stop on the circuit before the winners of the last were even announced.

When Tyr had first joined Eirik, the drinking had been minor, and the man won far more matches than he lost. Due to his fear of Einar, they spent most of their time traversing Vestan and Subraea, but they did well enough for themselves. Over time, the mead and the ale seemed to have taken a larger and larger share of their winnings. Each night was spent deeper and deeper in the cups of desperation.

It had been a long, slow slide ever since.

Tyr took the coins from his pocket and dropped them on the battered camp table that dominated the center of the small space. Two rickety chairs flanked the table, draped in clothing, rags, and furs. Scavenging through the rest of the tent, he accumulated a slightly larger pile. Scattered among the copper and silver were even a few coins of old, dark gold. A single shining Kun Makha golden disk shown in the middle, the pride of the collection.

"We're going to starve before spring." Tyr stared morosely down at the pile. Even if he ignored such things as blame and fault, the prospect of scrimping their way through another frigid winter was almost more than he could bear.

Eirik squinted from beneath his forearm up toward the table. From that angle, there was no way he could see the little pile, but he knew better than to question Tyr when it came to their finances. "We might catch a last tourney in Vestan." The tone of voice, almost that of a wheedling child, was nearly enough to send Tyr screaming from the tent.

"That's what Torben said." He muttered the words, knowing they might set his master off and not really carrying.

"What?" Eirik surged upward for a moment before sinking back onto his furs, face tight with pain. "What did that bastard cheat say?"

Tyr shook his head. "He wasn't cheating me. In fact, I tried to put our last reserves on you just before your match and he wouldn't let me." He glanced at the prostrate form of his master and made no effort to hide the bitterness in his voice. "I think he felt bad for me and didn't want to see me throw good coin after bad."

Eirik spat. "Damned sun-worshiper." Tyr paused but decided to let it go. Up in Kun Makha, the old emperor had declared the spirits of the oyathey and the gods of the fyrdar to be as one decades ago. After fifty years of such preaching, even in the Broken Kingdoms most people now saw the sun above as the physical manifestation of the All-father's single, unblinking eye.

But Eirik had never had much faith in gods or spirits, or all of them together bunched up in the sun for that matter. And come to that, neither had Tyr.

"We need to decide what we're doing next." Eirik sagged back down, a constant, low-grade moan coming from beneath the crook of his arm as Tyr continued to speak. "The chances of us catching a last tourney are slim at best, even if we leave tonight." The moan got louder, and Tyr grinned. He hadn't figured they'd be leaving tonight either way.

He hesitated and then coughed. "There's always the vernal faire out-side Connat. We could make that—"

"No!" Eirik glared at him over a shaking hand. "We're not going near the Bhorg."

Tyr shrugged. "Then we'll go hungry." He stood and began to putter around the room. "If we sell some of these things, we might be able to make it." Even as he said the words, he knew it didn't matter. He would not be with Eirik Hastiin come spring. Either the old man would drink himself to death on cheap rotgut, or Tyr would lose the last of his patience and walk away. Either way, this was the beginning of the end.

It weighed heavily upon him, but there came with the realization a feeling of sad calm as well. Perhaps his father could give him a loan. He could gather enough equipment to join the circuit himself. If he started small, he could probably work his way up into the prize circles before too long. The gods and spirits knew he had to have picked up some skills, watching one of the greatest warriors of the age lose all of his.

"No!" Eirik said again, but this time there was a sober, angry power behind the word, and Tyr looked down to see what he had picked up. It was the heavy sword in its leather sheath. The thing was as heavy as stone, and might be one of the last maekre blades left in all of the Broken Kingdoms. Although not the weapon he had sworn his oath upon, it was nonetheless the only thing Eirik seemed to truly care about in the entire world.

"We're not selling the sword!" Eirik threatened to surge up onto unsteady feet, and Tyr quickly lowered the weapon.

"Of course not." The treacherous daydream faded away, reinforcing the realization that this part of his life was over. "I was just going to clean it."

"You can clean it tomorrow." The old man sank back into the furs. "Now leave me. I'm in no condition to deal with anymore of your nonsense tonight."

Before Tyr could respond, the sounds coming from beneath his master's elbow deepened into guttural, air-shivering snores.

He shook his head and dragged himself into one of the chairs, careful not to break it as he settled down. He stared at the pile of leather and furs, not knowing what to do. It seemed like he should be recognizing the occasion somehow, marking the end of this misguided phase of his life.

"Excuse me?" A gentle voice whispered from the darkness outside the tent, and Tyr jumped despite its mild tones. The folk of the tourney circuit knew better than to come to the Ruun's tent after a day like today.

Tyr sat still, staring at the flap, wondering what he should do. If someone woke Eirik up, there would be several levels of hell to pay. Maybe they would just go away?

"Excuse me, may I come in?"

The voice was soft and warm. But somehow, despite that, there was a strength behind it that put ignoring its bearer out of the question.

Tyr cast one last look at the snoring warrior on the ground and then moved to the tent's opening.

"I'm sorry, but—"

Tyr stopped. The man standing patiently outside the tent was ancient; definitely not one of the circuit regulars. His hair was almost entirely white, with only a few wisps of darkness at the temples. A simple bone necklace of oyathey design fit snuggly around his neck, and his pale clothing made him seem to float in the evening gloom like some kind of spiritual being, while the old, worn bag slung over one shoulder conjured up images of a mystical messenger of the gods from the old tales.

"I am sorry, but my situation is urgent, and I was hoping to speak with you and your master before he turned in for the night." The man spoke with a kind, reassuring smile whose warmth almost touched the growing darkness in Tyr's chest. He tossed a look back into the tent before turning reluctantly out to the old man.

"I'm sorry, but you're too late. I'm afraid he's not feeling well."

The old man's smile widened, dimples forming in the wrinkles beneath his cheeks. "Well, I would be surprised if he was feeling anywhere close to well, after the day he's had!"

Tyr felt an answering smile cross his own face, but then forced it down. He didn't know this man, and he didn't like the slightly mocking tone of the comment. "As you say. If you'd like to speak with him tomorrow, I'll tell him you stopped by when he wakes. Perhaps—"

"No, I don't think so." The old man bent beneath Tyr's arm and swept into the tent without another word. He spun, grabbing for the intruder, but the little white figure moved dexterously aside, spinning to stand by the table, taking everything in with one piercing gaze.

"Hey, look!" Tyr's angry words hissed as he tried to keep from waking his master. "You can't come in here! He can't talk to you anyway, and I don't know who you are! You'll have to—"

The dark eyes were soft with compassion, but there was an edge there he had not seen before. "My son, I understand the position in which you find yourself, but there is little choice. Events are moving at their own pace, and we can either attempt to keep up or be overwhelmed."

Tyr shook his head. "I don't know what that means, but it doesn't even matter." He gestured to Eirik's still form. "The Ruun is asleep. You won't be able to talk to him now anyway. And again ... who are you?"

The old man shook his head, staring at Eirik's still form. "I know who he is, boy. This is Eirik Hastiin, last member of the saemgard of Astrigir, and contrary to all current signs, much more than that besides."

Tyr tried to take that in, but before he could even begin to make sense of it, the old man turned back to look directly into his eyes. "As for me, I am just an old man trying to make right something that went wrong a long time ago. You may call me Tsegan, if you wish."

Tyr cocked his head to one side. "Tsegan ... so you're from Kun Makha? What do you want with Ei— What do you want with my master?"

The old man bowed his head. "I need to speak with your master, son. Please don't be alarmed, but there is no other way; we have run out of time."

Before he could step between the old man and Eirik's prone form, a thin, aged arm reached out and a wizened, spidery hand unfolded above the sleeping warrior. The air within the tent grew suddenly warm and dry, and Tyr found himself struggling to swallow as all the moisture in his mouth disappeared.

"What—?" He tried to speak, but all that emerged was a parched croak.

Eirik's body snapped into a rigid, painful arch and an animal snarl of pain and confusion tore from his mouth. He made several gagging noises, writhing beneath the furs as a terrible, greasy sweat rose up on every inch of exposed skin, only to be whisked away by the thirsting air.

"Gods!" Eirik surged up out of the furs, grey eyes as wild and clear as they had ever been. "What in the name of all the frozen hells ... Who the hells are you?!" He lurched menacingly toward the old man, who raised his outstretched hand in a sign of peace, taking a few quick steps back to the wall of the tent.

"We must speak, Eirik Hastiin." The voice was calm and mild, but carried an undeniable authority, even as the little old man sagged against a tent pole. But Tyr was paying less attention to the man's voice, and more to his master as the warrior stood rigidly in the center of the tent, chest heaving, as sober as a eulogy.

The terrible, dry heat had dissipated, the cold autumn night leaching once more through the thin walls of the tent. But there was no denying the brutal force that had filled the space only moments before. It seemed to have leached every drop of mead from his master's blood.

"Tsegan..." Tyr muttered, and Eirik's grizzled crest of hair whipped around as the warrior turned to face him.

"What?" There was no slur to the snarling growl now. Tyr could not remember when his master had been so frighteningly sober.

And he had been utterly insensate only moments before.

"Tsegan Aqisiaq? From the legends?" A cold chill swept over his flesh as he said the name.

The smile was back, although overshadowed with a weariness that had not been there before. "I made no such claim." He shrugged. "I told you that you may call me Tsegan, if you wished."

Tyr pointed at his looming master, who, despite his sudden sobriety, was clearly having a hard time following the conversation. "How did you do that?"

The old man looked sad for a moment, his smile melancholy. "What? I'm sure I don't know what you're asking."

"What did you do to me?" Eirik's eyes narrowed, swinging between his squire and the stoop-shouldered stranger. "And who the hells are you?"

The old man cocked his head as if hearing something outside, and then squared himself against Eirik.

"Your people need you, Eirik Hastiin of the saemgard. Forces are in motion, and there is only one path to peace now left to us." The old man moved around the tent, looking at the door as if expecting someone to charge through at any moment. "The most devout wishes of your youth are within your grasp. The spirits and the gods alike have chosen you, and without you, there can be no hope. Astrigir will fall."

The words felt heavy to Tyr, loaded with ominous power that he didn't understand. How had this strange little man returned his master to his senses? It seemed like something out of a children's tale. A mysterious stranger arrives, and with a wave of his hand all of their troubles were gone?

But were they? Eirik was more sober than he had been in months; of that Tyr was certain. But as for all the rest? How could Eirik Hastiin save anything?

The old man's dark, oyathey eyes hardened and he seemed to grow a little taller. "I had assumed you would rise to the occasion, Saemgard. I had assumed you would sense the truth in my words and heed the call." He gestured toward the little table with its sad pile of coins. "But perhaps you have a better plan for your winter?"

That got under his master's skin. The big man's rugged, drink-ravaged face tightened. "I don't see how our plans are any concern of yours. I think you should—"

The kindly smile slid into a cruel smirk.

"Heading east into Vestan, maybe?" The old man's voice was light, but his gaze bored into Eirik's with a silent challenge. "Maybe push south, hoping to catch one more little mock battle, scrape together a little more silver before the snows fly?"

Eirik's beard writhed with his intended reply, but the old man waved him off. "Certainly won't be staying in Astrigir, though. Wouldn't want Einar's Shadows to track you down."

The words, so close to his earlier thoughts, brought Tyr up short. His master seemed to shoot him a strange glance but then shook his head.

"Get out, old man. I have no need of your nonsense or your insults. If you don't—"

A small bag sailed through the air and landed with a ringing chime on the table, scattering their meagre coins. "That will get you to where you need to be." The little man produced a tight roll of parchment and placed it beside the bag. "And this will tell you where that is."

Neither Eirik nor Tyr said a word as the white-haired phantom moved back to the tent's entrance. "You can take the money and disappear, hide from the king's agents for a little while longer, or you can meet me there and see what you shall see. There is a safe winter refuge at the end of the map, if nothing else. Spend the dark season with me, listen to my words, hear my arguments. Come spring, if you have not been convinced, you can rejoin your glamorous little life without delay."

Tyr and his master watched as the man lifted the tent flap. Eirik's eyes flashed from the stranger to the bag of coins and back. As his shoulder slipped out into the cold night, however, the little man stopped, turning back inside. His face was solemn, and when he spoke, his voice seemed much deeper and more powerful than it had been before.

"You may disbelieve, Eirik Hastiin. You may cast my words and my warning away without a thought. But I beg you, take this chance, this last chance. The world you know, such as it is, cannot long survive. If you have no faith in me or my words, have faith in the old songs of fate. There is more truth there than you know."

The flap slid closed and a heavy silence fell within the tent. Tyr looked to his master, to the heavy pouch, and back.

The night seemed to grow colder around them.

Chapter 2

Outside, the winds of late autumn rattled the heavy shutters and tore the last of the leaves from the tall, skeletal trees. The guesthouse and its attached tavern were old buildings; they had survived nearly a hundred such winters and would probably stand for as many more. But on an evening such as this, the patrons were glad for the big hearth with its roaring fire and the thick, leaded glass that kept the warmth from fleeing out into the deepening gloom. Harvest was done. The farmers, field workers, tradesmen, and thralls had completed their annual back-breaking, weeks' long labor and earned a short respite before the long tasks of surviving the winter began. And as was always the case at this time of year, the tavern was nearly full.

There were still rooms available in the guesthouse, of course. Baedr was a small township in southern Astrigir, one of the last villages on the road toward the looming White Mountains. Aside from the occasional merchant or peddler, the beds at the House of the Fallen Oak were not nearly in as high demand as the warmth, the mead, and the company.

Maiara snorted under her breath at the last thought. She, at least, could well do without the company.

She weaved her way through the throng with a cluster of clay cups in either hand, readily avoiding lurching drunks, grasping hands, and one old man who lost his footing in the rushes and stumbled into her path with a cackling laugh.

She deposited the cups with a practiced, empty smile and moved on without stopping. Vali, the host, would not care to see her linger overlong, whether she wanted to or not.

She definitely did not want to.

The men and women crammed into the Fallen Oak were as familiar to her as her own family would have been, had she had family. She had grown up in Baedr, in the tavern. She had lived in that attic garret for nearly all the eighteen years of her life. She knew every face, every voice, and every opinion by heart. She knew that Stur and his friends in the corner would spend the night complaining about their taxes and the king crouched beneath the Bhorg in high Connat. She knew that Brandt and the other young men by the fire would be expounding upon King Einar's fascination with Kun Makha, completely with whispered conspiracies of a secret alliance with the empire, flooding the high mountains with oyathey workmen.

Maiara moved up to old Achak's table, smiling slightly as she collected empty cups. Achak and his companions were the elders of the village and carried what passed for ancient wisdom this far from civilization. They had nothing kind to say about the king's new farming initiatives and the various ways the king's representatives were suggesting they change their techniques for better yields and stronger crops, dismissing it as Kun Makha hoodoo.

Maiara moved away, her hands full, and shook her head. She could have told them why the king's men were urging them to make such changes, but no one here would ever care what she had to say on such things. She had only memorized an entire almanac when she was ten. Why should that matter?

She tried to summon a genuine smile for Kustaa as the boy carried a heavy load of firewood through the crowd, but knew she did a poor job of it. In her honest moments, she knew that Kustaa was the only real friend she had in Baedr, but Turid Sayen, Vali's wife, had had nothing good to say about boys in general, and the boys of Baedr in particular, for as long as Maiara could remember. It was hard, on a busy evening when she was already feeling sorry for herself, to give anyone the benefit of the doubt.

She saw Vali shooting her a grim look over the milling crowd; she ducked her head to avoid his gaze, finding another table to clear before he called her over to give her another lecture on the duties she owed the man and woman who had given her a home.

Sometimes it was more than she could bear, dealing with the grasping old couple who had provided her with a roof, food, and learning, if no sense of a family. She could feel the thick air closing in around her, recognizing the onset of one of the rare dark moods that plagued her during the long winter months.

Before she could be roped into further duties, Maiara pushed through the throng and out a small side door into the frigid cold. The sun had disappeared behind the mountains; the sky was a deep purple stretching toward the spangled blackness of the east. It was beautiful. And her inability to appreciate that beauty only made her mood worse.

"Oh, hey, Mai." She jerked a little, and then relaxed as Kustaa moved past her toward the enormous woodpile behind the guesthouse. "Getting a bit much in there, eh?"

She smiled despite herself. "Well, if I have to hear Stur curse the taxmen one more time, I won't have any option but to brain the man with a pitcher."

The boy laughed. "I would have thought for sure it was Brandt's oyathey fantasies that had driven you out into the cold."

She watched as Kustaa pulled logs from the pile. He was not as brawny as some of the other village boys, but he had no trouble managing the armload of heavy wood.

She smiled again. For most of her life, she had had only Turid and Vali Sayen for company, and the small pile of dog-eared manuscripts they inexplicably kept in her small attic room. When they had taken Kustaa on as a servant last year, she had thought things might get better. And they had. A little, anyway. She was no mooncalf, with no understanding of the inter-action between boys and girls. She watched the children of the village, fol-lowed their lives, their relationships, and their petty feuds from a distance. But Turid and Vali had always seemed determined to keep her separate; her childhood was filled with little moments when, just as someone reached out in kindness or thoughtfulness, one or the other of the Sayens would swoop in and pluck her away, throwing her back in her little room with her books and her paper, almost as if they were afraid she was going to break some law or taboo, and the ultimate price would be theirs to pay.

Which left only Kustaa for her to talk to, when she could. And they watched him like a hawk as well, at least where she was concerned.

"Kustaa, do you ever miss the farm?" She had asked him that before, and he always declared that nothing would be able to convince him to return to the dirt. But she never tired of hearing him talk about his dreams. At least Kustaa had dreams, and he was trying to make them happen.

"That dirty trap?" His smile was wide as he came back up the steps, arms piled high with wood. "Why would I miss a filthy pig sty like that?"

She shrugged. "Well, if not the farm, your family, at least? Your broth-ers and sister must miss you."

He thought about it for a moment and then nodded. "I do miss them, sometimes. But there's nothing stopping them from coming in for a drink if they wish."

Kustaa was determined to open his own guesthouse, somewhere on the road between Baedr and Connat. He always had a moment to spare her, but otherwise his days and nights were spent learning as much as he could from the Sayens, doing all their dirtiest tasks and never seeming to regret a thing.

She sighed. "But they're out there. And you know that. And they know that."

He stopped, looking into her eyes. "It's not the same, I know, Mai." He looked away, and she knew what was going to come next. This conversation always followed the same pattern. "You know, when I go ..."

She started to answer, but the door behind them slammed open and Turid's red face peered out of the warm heat. "That wood won't pile itself, boy!" The gaze settled on Maiara's face, and her eyes widened before tighten-ing, her scowl deepening as well. Maiara suddenly realized that she was very cold. "And you. Mooning about over wizards and trolls? Back inside before you catch your death."

Maiara bit back a sharp reply. Turid and Vali had always mocked her childhood interest in the fairy stories from her dog-eared old book of tales. She shrugged, scooting past Turid and back into the common room.

The sounds weren't as loud as they should have been, and Maiara knew by the feeling of the air that something had changed. Turid pushed past her and moved toward the plank bar, where a nervous-seeming Vali was trying to complete some business with a local farmer. But the host's gaze was fixed on the front door. A space was quickly clearing around a small figure wrapped in a light-colored winter cloak, the ratty bag of a messenger slung over one shoulder.

A lifetime of observation told her that her guardian was unsettled as he watched the man close the door behind him and turn to survey the common room. She could almost convince herself that she was imagining things as a look seemed to pass between the white-haired newcomer and the taverner. As Vali's eyes widened, she turned back to the door, trying to see what about the short little man might have blanched Vali's ruddy face like that.

There was nothing particularly special about the newcomer as far as Maiara could see. Long hair mostly white, face wrinkled in a well-used, friendly sort of way. His eyes were the deep black of the oyathey, but even this far from the empire, that wasn't as strange as it might seem.

Despite the deep lines around the man's mouth, he wasn't smiling now. He scanned the room, nodded to the innkeeper and his wife, and then, without hesitation, the dark eyes speared into Maiara, evaluating her like a farmer looking to buy livestock. They roved over her face, and when they met her own, they widened.

Maiara felt her spine stiffen, her chin rise. She was not used to such direct appraisal, and she found she did not enjoy the sensation.

The man began to move through the crowd as if expecting it to part of its own accord. Much to Maiara's surprise, it did. The farmers and workers seemed to melt away from the man, staring at him as if King Einar himself had swept into the room. Not that most of the peasants standing gape-mouthed in the Fallen Oak would have recognized the King of Astrigir if he walked through the door, a bitter voice in her head muttered.

The man approached the plank bar where Vali Sayen crouched. The host nodded his head with a jerky motion, looking around desperately for his wife. Glancing back, Maiara was surprised to see Turid leaning behind one of the large kegs in the corner, her wide eyes reflecting the distant fire with a feverish shine.

"Vali, my friend." The man's voice was soft and warm; hardly a voice to instill such fear in her guardians. And yet there was no doubt Vali had flinched at hearing his name. "Do you think I could have a drink, before we get down to business?"

Vali's chin wobbled as he nodded, but he made no move toward the cups or kegs.

The little white-haired man smiled wider and turned to Maiara. "My dear, perhaps you could help an old man to a cup of mead? I've also got a friend out in the cold that might like a mug of warm cider, and a couple of horses that could use some oats and water."

Maiara looked to Vali for guidance, and the man nodded quickly. But as she turned to grab a cup, the strange little man held out one hand. "Maybe the boy can see to my friend and the horses? We will need you close by, I think."

That caught Maiara short, and she shot a quick glance at her guardian, then at the strange little man at the bar, before she moved over to where Kustaa was watching through narrowed eyes. With quick, whispered words, she passed on the instructions, pushing the boy toward the row of kegs while watching the pair at the bar. Neither of them spoke while she was away, but the white-haired man turned to scan the room with an amiable air of indifference while waiting for her to return with his mead.

"Thank you my dear." He nodded his thanks and then turned back to the host. "Now, I think we probably want some privacy for the rest of our conversation, friend Vali, do we not?"

Vali's eyes widened and jerked out over the bustling crowd. The House of the Fallen Oak was a lucrative business, easily the most successful in Baedr. There would be plenty more nights like this before winter closed its frosty grip on the town, keeping folks closer to home most nights. Even so, she knew it would be like twisting a knife in his neck for Vali to see so much custom walk out the door this early in the evening.

"Come now, Vali." The small man leaned against the rough planks of the bar. "Let's not make this more dramatic than it needs be?"

Kustaa came in through the small back door carrying a bucket heavy with water and moved through the crowd, his sharp gaze locked on the three of them. He didn't look happy, and Maiara wished she had a better grasp of what was going on.

Vali nodded, but as if he was in some kind of nightmare. He was not in the habit of closing his doors until the last penny had been squeezed free, the last drunken local staggering back to his bed.

The newcomer heaved an exaggerated sigh. "Very well, then. Allow me."

Maiara didn't see what the old man did, but it appeared as if he tossed his hand toward the large fire across the room. She felt, rather than heard, a soft surging, and then the fire billowed suddenly as if someone had sprayed spirits into the air above it. Burning light filled the common room as an angry roar echoed off the walls. The heat spiked, higher even than the snarling flame could explain, and pin pricks of sweat stitched themselves across her scalp and down her spine. A part of her was terrified at the flare of light and the wave of heat, but another part, deeply buried, welcomed the sensations as if they were old friends. Half remembered dreams of heat and dust rose in her mind, and her confusion deepened.

The men and women nearest to the fire jumped back with screams and shouts, while the rest pushed away toward the far walls to escape the fury and the heat. They looked around, bewildered, but the fire had already died back down to its usual fitful glow. Aside from the marked heat, everything had returned to normal.

"My friends, please attend?" The little man raised his hands, his voice carrying even over the muttering crowd. "I am afraid that our kind hosts must close their fine establishment early this evening. Please finish your drinks and retire."

The mumbling rose into an angry surge, and the man patted the air with his raised hands again in a calming gesture that was more effective than it should have been. "Please, friends. Don't worry about payment. That has been taken care of, as well as a first cup for each of you tomorrow."

That got their attention, and Vali's as well. The host stared at the little man incredulously, only slightly mollified when a small leather pouch appeared, tossed onto the bar with an unmistakable jingle.

The crowd milled around for a moment longer, but their greed got the better of them, and the prospect of leaving with their tabs unpaid saw cups upended, cloaks and coats swept from chairs and hooks, and soon the last of the locals, old Achak and his crew muttering darkly about oyathey agents and a king who didn't know what was best for his people, stumbled out into the darkness.

As the last old men left, Kustaa came back in, fighting against the tide, a confused look on his pale face. Maiara could only shrug as she rushed around collecting cups and plates, and he moved to help her, leaning in to ask a question as the old man, now wandering around the room with his vague smile back in place, coughed.

"Young man, has my companion received his cider?"

Kustaa muttered an oath and ducked his head, moving back to the big stove where he had put up a pot, thin wisps of steam rising into the hot air. He carefully poured the cider into a clay mug and stalked back out into the cold, giving the stranger an ugly look as he passed.

"Now, why don't we all sit down and get reacquainted, yes?" The man's voice was again calm and kind, the lines around his mouth deepening with a warm smile as he gestured toward one of the large tables in the middle of the room.

Maiara looked from the stranger to Vali and back, an unspoken question in her eyes. In the corner, Turid had still not stirred, which Maiara found perhaps the strangest part of the entire event so far.

"Yes, yes." Vali turned away to pour himself a brimming glass of strong spirits before moving around the bar toward the table. "Maiara, join us please."

She moved tentatively to the table, feeling as if the ground might shift beneath her at any moment. Neither Vali nor Turid had ever included her in any sort of meeting before, and she was unsure why she was being invited to sit down now. But the stranger gave her a reassuring look and a friendly nod, gesturing to one of the chairs across from him before settling down himself, taking another sip of his own drink.

"Your wife can join us, if she wishes, Vali. But of course, there's no particular need, if she's more comfortable hiding in the corner."

The host ducked his head in a meek nod that only served to add to Maiara's disquiet.

Turid stayed where she was, and that was even worse.

The door slammed open and Kustaa rushed in as if launching himself into the middle of a battle. His jaw was thrust forward, his hands bunched into tight fists, feet spread apart as if ready for a fight.

The stranger gave the young man one look over his shoulder and smiled. "I trust Chagua is doing well? He doesn't particularly care for the cold. Of course, most islanders don't." He turned back to Maiara and leaned forward as if sharing a secret. "I think the weather up there thins their blood, to be honest."

Maiara felt her gaze flick toward the door. She had never met an islander. Mysterious travelers from the far north, where it was said snow never fell and winter's grip was unknown. And there was an islander outside, right now? The evening continued to grow more and more strange.

"Yu— um ... yes." Kustaa's voice cracked, his lips tightening in anger. "Yes. He's fine."

"Good, good." The white-haired man nodded, turning back to the table. "Then I think you may leave, young man. Your master will not need your services further this evening."

The edge of dismissal was unmistakable, and even more pointed for all that it seemed so casual. She looked back to where her friend stood by the door, eyes wide.

"But—"

"Vali, I am pressed for time." The warmth was gone, and as the stranger glanced placidly down into his cup, it was clear his mind had moved on to other things.

"Kustaa, go." Vali growled, not looking at the boy.

"What? Wait, no! You can't—"

"Now, boy!" Vali stabbed a finger back at the small door behind Turid. "I won't hear another word!"

Maiara shrank away from the tone. Vali had a famous temper and could rise to anger without a moment's notice. At such times, he treated both Maiara and Kustaa worse than the meanest thralls. But there was more than anger in his voice now. He was afraid.

Behind them, after another awkward moment, Kustaa stormed toward the small door. He tried to get Maiara's attention, but she refused to watch him go.

What was Vali afraid of?

"Now, Vali, down to business, as they say, yes?" The stranger settled back in his seat as Vali lowered himself into a chair between the newcomer and Maiara, resting his overfull cup before him with exaggerated care. His head was bowed and he would not look up.

"We entered into a business arrangement nearly eighteen years ago this autumn, did we not?" The man folded his hands before him on the table, not giving his mead a second glance. He was staring at the top of Vali's head, his gaze implacable.

Without a sound, the innkeeper nodded.

The stranger nodded in return. "Yes. Yes we did. And it looks very much as if you kept up your end of the bargain!" The man's eyes rose to give Maiara another assessing glance. It felt as if he was staring directly into her head, and she forced herself not to look away.

A strange shadow crossed the old man's face, and he turned back to the host. "Her eyes ... they never darkened?"

It was hard to tell from her angle, but the question seemed to surprise Vali. He shook his head after a moment, and the newcomer shrugged.

"Well, no matter. It appears as if you have done excellent work. Excellent, really, Vali. Although I assume Turid was involved as well."

Maiara would have sworn she heard the older woman suck in a sharp breath.

"You are truly beautiful, my dear." The smile was back, warm and caring. The face glowed with gentle mirth, and the head tilted slightly as if sharing a quiet joke. "But then, we knew you would be, didn't we? Blood will out, as they say." His eyes lingered on hers, and she looked away at last.

All the strangeness seemed to come tumbling down upon her. What was this all about? Blood? She did not care at all for the proprietary light she thought she saw in the man's eyes.

She folded her own hands on the table before her. "Sir, I do not know you, and although I thank you for the kind words, I would rather not be the subject of further assessments while you conduct your business."

The smile widened, and the man rocked back in his seat, applauding gently a couple times before settling forward again. "Excellent! Better than I could have hoped." He cocked his head to one side. "You can read?"

She shot a glance at Vali, who continued to stare at the scarred tabletop. Reading was not a common skill in Astrigir outside of the merchant class; but Vali and Turid had taken special pains to see that she could read at an early age. She had never wondered too much about it, as it was essential for the running of the guesthouse.

She nodded. "I can."

That seemed to please him and he sat back again, rubbing his hands together as if the common room wasn't already stifling. "Brilliant. And what is it that they have you reading?"

She looked at Vali again before answering with a shrug. "There is an old almanac up in my room, as well as a book of children's stories." She looked back at Turid, but the woman would not meet her gaze. "And I help keep the house's accounts in order, as well."

The stranger nodded, shooting a quick glance at Vali. "Curious choice of materials, but excellent. Truly excellent. There will be a great deal more for you to learn, but you are well on your way. Yes, well on your way."

Again, she had the unmistakable feeling that she was being judged. The discomfort and the strangeness of the evening all began to work within her, shifting from confusion to anger. "Who are you?"

She was not accustomed to being so direct with folks who came to the Fallen Oak on business, but with no help or protection from Vali or Turid, and Kustaa sent away, she would be damned before she allowed this man to make her feel like a cow on the auction block in her own home. Or, anyway, in the building where she had grown up.

The smile didn't shift, although there was a bright glimmer deep in those dark eyes. "You may call me Tsegan."

She nodded, looking back at the fire. She still didn't know how he had done it, but at least she was catching on to his game now. "Tsegan. As in Tsegan Aqisiaq, from the stories?"

The man shrugged casually, not seeming bothered by the doubting tone in her voice. "It is an old name, an honorable name. I could do worse, I think."

"So you'd have us believe you are a magician, stepping out of the ancient sagas to ... to do what, exactly? Are you here to defeat some terrible troll or dragon? Are you here to rescue me from my awful situation?"

The smile never wavered. "Well, I would hope that your situation here has not been entirely awful. I would feel horribly guilty otherwise, as it was I who brought you here in the first place."

She looked at Vali, who seemed to shrink in on himself.

"Yes, my girl. I brought you to Vali and Turid, to be raised away from the world, where no one would think to look for you. They kept you safe at my direction. All looking forward to the day when I would come and take you away once more."

That was wrong. As soon as she heard the words, she knew it was wrong. How often had she wondered about her parents as she grew up? How many hours had she stared out over the fields and forests, wondering where she had come from, or who her family had been?

She had come to the conclusion long ago that these must be common thoughts for an orphan. Fantasies of great destinies, or deep, mysterious pasts and tragic separations from loving parents were probably the dreams of every child raised by strangers.

She had decided long ago that such stories were no more true for her than they were for anyone else.

This stranger's words struck a note deep within her, but it was not a pleasant note. It was a song she had long since turned her back upon. A refrain she had long outgrown.

And this man, offering her exactly that, could be nothing but a fraud.

She shook her head. "So, you come here, bully Vali and Turid, throw some powder into the fire, and toss around some old name from the stories, and what happens next? I leave everything here behind, and join you on the road?"

His face softened as she spoke, and as he looked at her, she could see nothing but sympathy there. She wanted none of that.

"I have a good life here, sir Tsegan, if that is what you wish to be called. I am needed here, and I don't believe I will be following you anywhere." Behind her she heard Turid stifle a sob, and then the small door slammed shut. Vali jerked at the sound but did not glance up.

The white-haired man leaned forward, but there was still nothing but kindness in his eyes. "Maiara, these are trying times. Dangers you cannot even begin to imagine bear down upon us even as we sit here. There is but one hope, and you are it. You have always been the last, best hope for Astrigir; for all the fyrdar realms, in fact. A terror worse than the ancient Utan approaches, and only you can save us. I cannot explain the rest here, but I will not drag you away from your home against your wishes. However, have you given any thought, in these last few rushing moments, that perhaps Vali and Turid might be done with you?"

She looked again at the man who had done his best to raise her, but his stare was locked on the clear liquid in his cup.

"They are sad creatures, in their way. They have been compensated well for their services, but have they showed you any particular warmth over the years? They were singularly venal creatures, all those years ago. They kept you isolated and alone, yes? You have moved through the village of Baedr like a ghost, never truly belonging? Never truly part of anything beyond the walls of this house?"

"That was because of you! You told us–!" Vali's head had snapped up at this litany, and Maiara was shocked to see an anger boiling there, burning at the edges of the fear that had held him down. "We followed your instructions!"

The man who called himself Tsegan nodded slowly, his face sad. "I did. And you followed those instructions to the letter, I know." He turned to Maiara. "Down to my least instruction, my dear. No sense of love or nurturing, but only following the orders of the man with the coins. Tell me, did you feel that lack of love?" His eyes shone, and she was shocked to see the honest sorrow there. "There was no other path that I could see. It was the hardest decision I have made so far in this entire endeavor, to leave you with people capable of raising you, but incapable of loving you so that you would, in the end, be willing to leave it all behind."

She looked from Vali's, to the stranger, and back again. A coldness had replaced her anger. Vali would not meet her gaze. For some reason, the man looked small, defeated and ashamed.

The stranger was not Tsegan Aqisiaq, obviously. There was no such thing as magic, there hadn't been in over two hundred years. None of the creatures from her little storybook existed any longer. But just as obviously, Vali and Turid had been doing this man's bidding from the moment she had come to the Fallen Oak as a babe almost eighteen years ago, and the strange, isolated childhood she had known was a direct result of his instructions.

It was equally clear that no compunctions of parental affection or caring had gotten in the way of their work, either.

She could feel tears stabbing at the back of her eyes as she looked around, taking in every detail of the common room. The man was right. She had known nothing but this squat little building all her life. She had never belonged anywhere else, she had never been welcomed into any of the village homes, made friends with the girls or boys of Baedr. In fact, she had been kept separate like some kind of rare specimen her entire life.

The anger and isolation she had felt earlier in the evening, never far from her mind in the dark, cold seasons, came rushing back. But was it enough to drive her to leave with this strange little man with his tricks and mild manners?

She shook her head, pushing away from the table. "No, I'm sorry but—"

"You have to go!" Vali slapped his palm with a crack on the table, still not looking up. "Don't you understand? We don't have a choice! You don't have a choice! You can't stay here!"

A sound by the back door made her think that perhaps Turid had not run away after all, but there was no further movement there either.

"I don't understand." She shook her head. "This is all foolishness! I don't want to—"

"It doesn't matter what you want! You can't stay!"

She was staring at the top of Vali's head, unable to believe what she was hearing despite everything that had happened.

"No, that's not true." The man using the ancient sorcerer's name broke in, shaking his head slightly. "It does matter what you want, Maiara." He reached out to touch her hand, and she was too numb to pull away. He leaned toward her, his dark stare delving into hers, and spoke with all the weight of the world behind his voice.

"Come with us for the winter. Let me explain what is happening, and why you are needed. Let me show you why you and you alone can stop the coming storm." He shrugged, his kind smile returning. She thought she heard that strange surge again, but the fire continued its gentle dance, failing to leap back up into the air. "If it turns out I'm just a crazy old lunatic, or you do not believe what I have to tell you, you may return here in the spring."

Another sharp noise from the door almost made her turn around, and finally Vali straightened in his chair to stare incredulously at the old man. And the stranger nodded again. "She can return, and you will be clear of any debt to me that remains. I will leave you to your own devices, and you will never hear of me again."

Vali looked at Maiara, then back to the stranger. "You'll bring her back?"

He nodded. "I will."

Maiara could not look away from the dawning hope in Vali's face. She had no idea what the history was between these two men, or why the prospect of her returning in the spring had suddenly brought the landlord back to life, but there was no denying the newfound energy he showed. He looked at her, and there was more genuine warmth there than she could ever remember seeing in him before.

"Maiara, go with him. Hear his words, spend the winter with him and his people. And come spring, return to us." He grabbed her hands and she felt tears sting her eyes for reasons she could not have said. "Come home to us."

The stranger nodded. "Come with me, Maiara, and come back to them in the spring."

She looked from one to the other, and before she could analyze her emotions further, or cast more doubt into her own mind, she nodded.

She rose, thinking to collect her clothes and what few possessions she owned from the attic room, but the old man reached out one hand to stop her. "We have everything you need, Maiara. We need to go."

"But, my clothes?"

"Will not be appropriate where we are going. I have all the clothing you will need. And other things besides."

But she didn't want to leave everything behind. Was there nothing she could call her own, that she could take with her into this mysterious future? "What about my books?"

His smile warmed. "You will not lack for books, I assure you."

She nodded absently, her eyes unfocused, as two bustling forms came up behind her, wrapping her thick winter cloak around her shoulders. Vali and Turid were pushing small packages into her hands, food, a wineskin, a small portfolio. She saw Vali wink as he slipped the old book of children's tales into the satchel, and almost cried again.

"You will come back to us, child." Turid muttered, and Maiara almost couldn't recognize her voice. "You will come back to us, and all will be well."

She nodded, allowing herself to be led to the door. This was all so strange. What had caused their treatment of her to change so drastically?

Outside it was full dark, and they moved down the long staircase to the courtyard below. A strange, heavily-laden cart was waiting there, two big draft horses in the traces, a large man sitting at the front, watching with eyes that flashed black in the darkness. Halfway between the guesthouse and the cart, a tall shape loomed out of the shadows.

Kustaa, a long, straight stick in his hands, blocked their path. "No! You don't even know who this man is, Mai! You can't go with him!"

"Out of the way you fool." Vali moved forward to push Kustaa away, but the boy wouldn't budge. "Kustaa, move, or you will lose your position with us this night!"

Still Kustaa wouldn't move. She was alarmed to see the hopeless look on the boy's face. He was shaking, but she knew it was not from the cold. His breath came in ragged puffs of fog that were whipped away by the rising wind.

She could feel the old man coming down the stairs behind her and had no idea how he would react to Kustaa's latest foolishness. But she wanted to be gone, she wanted to leave, before she had time to entertain any further doubt.

"Kustaa, it's alright. I'm coming back, I promise." She owed him no promises, no grand gestures, but she needed to see her way clear of this moment, to what might lay beyond.

He shook his head, but had no more words to say. His gaze was pleading with her in the night, but she had no idea what he was begging her for.

"Son, things don't have to go this way." The white-haired man moved around Vali and Turid, placing one gentle hand on Kustaa's back and moving him farther into the courtyard, away from the house and the cart. "Please let me speak with the boy, we'll be right back."

She felt a spike of fear for Kustaa and could see the innkeeper and his wife tense beside her, but although he was in a daze, allowing himself to be led away, Kustaa did not seem to be in any danger.

The white-maned man took the boy out into the darkness and they spoke for several minutes. There was no shouting or violence, no confrontation of any kind.

Maiara found herself a little disappointed there was no sudden flash of flame.

When Kustaa and the old stranger returned, the boy was holding something tightly in one fist, the long branch loose in the other hand. His face was rigid, under strict control, and his eyes were locked on Maiara's.

"Come back." He muttered the words in a harsh voice, and after one long, last look, he spun away and hurried off into the night.

She watched him go, her brows drawn tight, and then looked to the old man.

"We really must go. We have a long ride ahead of us, but there are plenty of blankets and furs in the back. Chagua is a wonder of stamina and strength. He'll drive through the night, and then take a rest as we take our turns tomorrow."

She looked back at the wagon, taking a closer look at this man, Chagua. He was bundled up beneath layers of heavy cloaks and blankets. Almost nothing could be seen beneath his hood except for several long coils of hair that gleamed in the cold light of the stars.

This was truly the strangest night of her life.

But as she climbed onto the wagon, watching Vali and Turid cling to each other as the hulking drover urged the horses out through the main gate, she could not help but feel she would not see them again, no matter how many times she had promised to return with the spring.

Chapter 3

The place looked like a thousand other run-down guesthouses he had seen in his life. Geir sneered as he rode his horse through the main gate and into the cluttered courtyard. He sat higher in his saddle as he caught the looks from the peasants and thralls he passed. He knew he cut an intimidating figure for provincials this far from civilization. His leathers were of the highest quality oyathey craftsmanship rather than the fyrdar rags of the Broken Kingdoms. The clothing was dyed a rich, deep black to match the three braided twists of his long, elegant beard and the stubble of his shaven scalp; intricate tattoos swirled over his head. Silver glittered at his cuffs and collar. He was obviously a man of means and importance. A pathetic little settlement like Baedr wouldn't see such a figure once in a year.

Geir knew that as a simple fact. There were not many men like him. He was a Shadow of King Einar, with the skills, bearing, and aura of a man who knew how the world really worked, and had spent his life bending it to his will.

These peasants had no idea what kinds of things were needed for a kingdom to thrive. And they especially had no idea what kind of men and women were needed to keep a kingdom like Astrigir free in the face of the treachery and barbarism that surrounded it. The farmers and thralls who tilled the soil, grew the food, and saw that it made it to where it needed to go continued their work blissfully unaware of the kinds of things agents like Geir needed to do every day. And he sneered to think of it.

He looked up at the small sign hanging by the large doors. "The House of the Fallen Oak." He muttered under his breath. Looking around, he could see no oaks, fallen or otherwise. He moved his horse toward the barn off to the side of the courtyard and gave the boy who took the reins an imperious nod as he slid down. A single coin flipped through the air followed by a single eyebrow raised in warning. The boy nodded with a smile, pocketed the silver, and led the horse to the barn.

Geir surveyed the yard again. The place wasn't very busy, but then it was the middle of the day. Autumn was winding down, the harvest was in, and most folks were preparing their homes and stores for winter. It was typical of the small settlements that dotted the plains, and would most likely make his simple task here even easier.

Geir had served Astrigir for most of his adult life, although he had never met his king in person, nor even set foot within the Bhorg. To rule a kingdom properly, there were things that needed to be done that were not fit for a king's personal attention. The wheels of governance were in constant need of greasing, and that was the responsibility of Geir Muata and agents like him, the Shadows of the King who roved the land taking care of problems that defied King Einar's mundane power.

A cold chill swept down the man's back and he pulled his riding cloak more tightly around himself. There was blood on his hands, he knew that and accepted it as necessary. He was more than willing to perform the duties that were required of him to allow his king the freedom to lead in these dark times. He knew agents who enjoyed their work, who reveled in the moral latitude Drostin, the king's Lord of Shadows, allowed them while on the king's business. Geir did not share their feelings, but he did the work nevertheless, confident in the knowledge that he was working toward the greater good of the kingdom.

He was just glad to have returned from the mountains. For more than a year now, he had been combing the peaks and valleys of the White Mountains in search of some phantom Lord Drostin was convinced was stalking the land. Strange wanderers from Kun Makha had been moving through the mountains for years, but none of the king's Shadows had ever been able to puzzle out who they were or what they were about. Geir had only returned from the glacier fields a month before, returning to the capital to report that he was no closer to breaking the mystery. It had been frustrating; he had even captured three of the bastards himself. But no matter how sharply he questioned them, they had not talked, and eventually each had expired giving him nothing at all.

Lord Drostin had been vexed by the lack of progress, but not overmuch. Agents had been combing the mountains for years with no more success than he had found. And so he had been handed this latest task, much simpler and more direct. Hopefully there would be more work for him on the plains and along the borders, and he could avoid the mountains, at least for the winter.

He would rather not head back down into the mountains so soon after returning.

Maybe Drostin would send him, once again, chasing the phantom of the traitor of Merrick Ford.

The wooden steps up to the guesthouse's common room creaked beneath his heavy boots. Above, the sky was dark with the promise of snow, and he found himself wishing he could stop here for the night. Unfortunately, by the time he completed his task, that wouldn't be possible. The next village was many hours' ride to the south. He would end up in a tent, under the snow, yet again. He knew it.

The thought did nothing to improve his disposition.

Pushing open the heavy door, Geir stopped just inside and surveyed the room. It was dank and ratty in the daylight washing in from the big windows to either side. A huge hearth in the center of the room contained only a small fire, tracing smoke upward into the scooped chimney above.

A couple of the rough tables were occupied by men and women whose clothing marked them as a slight cut above common farm workers. They cast vaguely curious gazes at him before turning back to their tables and their talk.

A long plank bar was set off from the back wall, with kegs and several stoves lined up behind it. A short man stood behind the bar, his paunch straining at the stained apron wrapped around his waist. He was lining up a collection of cups, inspecting them and wiping them down before shifting them to a shelf behind him. That would be Vali Sayen, the landlord and host. The man gave him a cursory glance before returning to his work, and Geir found himself mildly annoyed with the lack of acknowledgement for a newly-arrived guest.

Provincials.

Geir was not here for the man, though, or for his fat wife, although Turid Sayen was nowhere that he could see.

No, Geir was here for a very specific purpose, one of the less pleasant duties he was called upon to perform from time to time. The sooner he found her and was done, the better he would feel. He would need to return to Connat for new instructions, although he was thinking that maybe he would not rush back as quickly as he should.

The description of the girl had been quite detailed; it shouldn't be too difficult to find her. And girls from little villages like this were notoriously easy to lure away with the promise of a gold coin, a kind smile, or an escape from their mundane lives.

Then, a couple minutes in the woods off the trail and he could be on his way. Endure one night in his little tent, and then back to civilization; at least for a little while.

But first, the girl. He continued to survey the room, looking for anyone who matched the description. She was said to have the long straight black hair of the oyathey, with refined features that would make her stand out in a little village like Baedr. The most recent dispatch from Drostin had said the girl's eyes would reveal her identity, however; shifting between bright gray and blue, his letter had said they had the texture of polished crystal, as if made from some precious stone.

Geir liked eyes. It was one of the first things he noticed about a person, and the description had caught his imagination. He had spent hours on the ride down from Connat wondering what it would be like to look into such eyes. It would make his task a little more difficult, he knew, but he was a professional, and in the final analysis, nothing would stop him from performing the duties King Einar required of him.

Of course, in order to do that, he needed to find her.

And that was going to be a problem, because no girl even close to that description was present in the common room.

There was a tall blond boy, a typical fyrdar peasant, bustling about, collecting dirty dishes, checking in on the various guests, and tidying up the area around the hearth. The boy looked surly, clearly unhappy to be there, and had not been included in the packet of information Geir had received about the Fallen Oak.

But he was about the same age as the girl, and obviously familiar with the place. He might know where she was, or why she wasn't in the common room.

He sighed. He always hated it when easy jobs became complicated. In his mind, he was already halfway back to Connat, looking forward to the comforts of the capital. But he was going to have to track this tavern wench down first.

A comforting thought occurred to him, and he moved toward an empty table. He might as well have a half-decent meal while he waited. He could conduct his inquiries afterward, if she failed to make an appearance while he ate.

He waved the tall boy over and ordered something hot off the stove. A blank face and a sullen glance back at the host did not bode well for the order. A vague shrug closed the deal.

"We've only got the stew during the day."

Stew. Of course. What else would he expect, so far into the hinterlands? This little village was tucked into the eaves of a small forest, among the first foothills of the White Mountains, as if someone was purposely trying to hide it from the rest of civilization.

He nodded and ordered a bowl of stew without asking what was in it. In a place like this there was no telling, and it wasn't like he had any other choices. Several of the other patrons had empty stew bowls by their elbows and didn't seem to be suffering any ill effects, so he figured he was probably safe enough.

He settled back in the shaky chair, taking a deeper look around. There were hundreds of places just like this scattered throughout the kingdom; probably hundreds more in Vestan, Subraea, and maybe even in Kun Makha itself, although he imagined there the architecture would be a bit more inspired, and there might be more than a single stew on offer.

It looked almost as if someone had set out to construct a typical guesthouse and tavern from the ground up: building every last join, rafter, and stick of furniture to elicit a feeling of homely sufficiency. The place was what it was, and it didn't pretend to be more.

Geir shook his head. He was forever a man trapped between worlds. He longed for the sophistication of the capital, or maybe even Kun Makha itself, but his duties and talents saw him forever cast either into the deepest wild or scouring the scattered settlements of Astrigir, pursuing his king's enemies no matter where they might hide, or what danger they might pose.

The enemies of a kingdom were many, Geir knew. And intent mattered not at all. Often those enemies seemed harmless, merely men and women with ideas that, if allowed to spread, would endanger the kingdom and the countless thousands that it kept safe within its borders.

That was how Geir slept at night, when the shadows of his past deeds crowded in. Next to the throngs of subjects protected beneath the king's peace, the men, women, and even children he had been forced to slay over the years were a mere trifling handful.

Sometimes it helped.

The stew was dropped before him and he forced himself to nod politely as the boy moved away. No need to surrender the niceties merely because one found oneself in a mud hut surrounded by pigs. Much to his surprise, the stew was quite good, and the meat was almost definitely lamb. Or maybe pork. A sip from the cup revealed smooth, rich mead, and he decided his afternoon was looking up.

By the time he had finished the food and drink, the girl had still not made an appearance. He settled back and raised a finger for another cup. Until he found the girl, there was no pressing need for him to leave the warmth of the guesthouse.

But by the time he finished his second cup, his prey was still absent. The landlord's wife, Turid, had arrived, moving in the kitchen area, checking on the stew, and speaking in quiet tones to her husband. But then she was gone again, with not so much as a peek from beneath her frosted red bangs at the elegant stranger in black.

He hated not being noticed.

Maybe the girl was ill? That would make his task both easier and more difficult at the same time. He took in a massive chest-full of the warm air and expelled it in a mighty sigh. He couldn't really justify waiting any longer. It was time to find this girl, look into those strange eyes of hers, and move on.

When the boy came back around to collect his bowl, not asking if he'd like another, he reached out and grabbed a sleeve. The gesture stopped the boy in his tracks, earning a vicious little look colored with too much pride and not enough fear.

Geir forced himself to smile through the annoyance. "Easy, lad. Just have a quick question for you ... Is there a girl who tends to patrons here? Pretty, long dark hair?"

The pale eyes narrowed even further as the boy pulled his arm away. "What?" It was more of a bark than a question, and Geir had to struggle once again to keep his rising annoyance in check.

"A girl. There's a girl who serves here? Daughter, or some such, of the landlord and his wife?" He tilted his head toward the bar, where the fat man continued to count his cups.

The boy's gaze shifted between Geir and the barkeep, his head shaking slightly before he began to talk. "I don't know what you're talking about." He ducked his head and turned away, moving toward the bar faster than he had moved since Geir had arrived.

This was a fairly common occurrence, when things were starting to shift against him, and the king's Shadow rose smoothly behind the boy and stalked after him with a casual, easy grace. None of the other patrons noticed anything amiss, and the boy certainly had no idea he was being followed.

The landlord looked up with an empty expression, but his eyes widened immediately as he saw Geir. The boy didn't have time to turn around before the agent closed the remaining distance between them and pushed him gently but firmly against the bar. From farther than a table or two away it would look as if he had his arm around the boy's shoulders in a friendly fashion.

But there was no way the boy could move, despite the fact that he was much stronger beneath the rough spun shirt than he had seemed.

"No need for any trouble here." He forced a smile, the kind he knew was most likely to cow provincials like these when coupled with the rough whisper of his voice. "I just have a couple questions, and there won't be any need for unpleasantness. Now, when I ease back, we're all friends, right boy?"

He waited for the boy to nod with a stiff jerk, the old man's look disbelieving, and then he backed off on the pressure, letting the boy move away to stand by the bar, hands tensing at his sides.

Geir looked back out into the common room. No one had taken any notice, which was just as well. He wouldn't want to have to silence the entire establishment, if things got out of hand. He saw a flash of the room around him bursting into flames, and he shuddered. He would have no choice if he lost control of the situation now. He couldn't take a chance of others knowing an agent of the king had slaughtered a tavern full of farmers.

He never liked it when he had to resort to such crude measures. Burning down buildings to hide his tracks reminded him too much of the barbarous sagas of his people's distant past. After centuries of the civilizing influence of the oyathey, they were above that, or should be. And he certainly considered himself to be better than some ancient fyrdar raider, expecting a demonic Utan to jump out of every shadow.

He smiled again, reassured by the dull fear in their faces. "I just want to ask you a few questions about the girl."

The old man glanced at the boy sharply before assuming a clownish look of exaggerated disinterest. "What girl?"

This was going to be a long afternoon.

There was a small side door leading out into the back area behind the guesthouse. The wife had come through there a little while ago, and if things didn't start to clear up soon, he would need to speak with her anyway. He indicated the door with a tilt of his head.

"Why don't we take this conversation outside, lads, eh?" He reached to his belt, his hand sliding over the cruel length of steel riding on his hip. But then he grabbed the pouch hanging beside the dagger and it made a soft metallic sound. "I'm not above compensating you for your time."

Usually that worked in places like this. Here, however, he watched as the landlord's face hardened. "I don't know what you're talking about, and you're welcome to leave before I have to ask you to go."

A quick hiccup of a laugh escaped Geir's lips. He was used to the entire array of human responses to threat and danger, and had seen the smallest of men resort to threats when their back was against the wall. And yet people could still surprise him in moments like this. Who was this girl, that this coward of a man would threaten him, rather than betray her?

But she was important enough for the king to have taken notice, or Lord Drostin, anyway. And so obviously there was more moving beneath the surface here than some scullery maid. Perhaps he shouldn't be so surprised after all.

"Old man, I'm not here to cause trouble. I need to see this girl, to ask her some questions, is all. Is she here?"

He watched the churn of thoughts behind the man's eyes. He saw denial, and defiance, and above all, he was happy to see fear. The host was smart enough to fear a man like Geir, anyway, and that meant there was hope.

"Let's go out back and have a calm conversation like civilized men. I'm only going to ask a couple questions, you men can have your say, and I'll be on my way." He raised both hands, keeping the reasonable smile on his face, and once against gestured to the door. "Please?"

The boy and the fat man exchanged another quick glance, and then the landlord nodded. He waved the boy toward the door and then followed. He did not look back at Geir.

Through the door was a small yard, a large pile of stacked wood, and a path over to the rooming house on the other side. There was no sign of the old woman; that would be one more thing he needed to worry about if these two couldn't help him.

The air was cold, and their breath hung about them like ghosts looming above their heads. "Now, if we can just relax, I only want to know where the girl is."

The boy's chin rose defiantly, but the old man could not hide his own fear. "Who are you? What do you want with her?"

This was more like it. Even when defiant, people who started to ask questions like these were not far from being convinced to say what he needed them to say. Now it was just a question of which path would lead to the quickest results.

He kept his hand away from the long knife, but stood so it was plainly visible. It would help if neither of these men forgot where this could go.

"She is your ward, yes? You've raised her here, from when she was a child?" He had not been given a great deal of information; he seldom was for such tasks. He was given a mark, enough information to find them, and then left to his own devices. Usually, that was enough.

The old man made to answer, but the boy shoved himself forward, not willing to be dismissed so easily. "Before we say anything, we asked you a question. Who are you?"

Geir nodded easily, acting as if this was an entirely reasonable request. Under the rules of civilized human interaction, it certainly would be. And there was no reason these two should think that the normal rules did not apply here. Yet.

"My name is Geir. I was asked to find her, to make sure that she was well." He raised his hands again. "That is all. There are people in Connat who wish to see that she has not been mistreated."

That got a rise out of the old man. "Who says she was being mistreated?" He spat the words and realized before their echoes faded what he had done.

Geir smiled. "Exactly. She lives here, she works here. Is she nearby? I only need to speak with her briefly."

"Well, she's—"

"She's gone!" The boy interrupted, ignoring the fat man's enraged look. "She's gone, and you won't be able to find her!"

That stopped Geir for a moment. He hadn't even allowed for that possibility. Usually, when a person was brought to his attention, his prey was unaware of their situation. Few of them ran before he arrived on the scene. Most never even knew they were in any danger at all.

"Gone where?" He kept his voice steady, although he could feel his control beginning to slip.

The two fools exchanged a look, the old man angry, the boy defiant. But there was a flicker of uncertainty in both of their faces that Geir did not like at all. No matter how talented he might be at persuasion, even he could not convince people to tell him something they did not know. And if this girl had run away...

"Where is she?" He repeated the words, making sure his voice carried just enough serious weight. He allowed his hand to slide casually to the hilt of his knife as well. His sword and axes were on the horse, in the barn. That was going to be a long walk if he suddenly needed them.

He sized these two up again. He shouldn't need anything more than his knife.

Both of the men looked back with caged looks he had seen too many times in his life. He recognized it. He knew there were agents who immediately turned to bloodshed when faced with such looks, but he seldom found such responses helpful.

"You don't know where she is." His words were flat, and he made no effort to hide his annoyance. Both men flinched from the tone. He didn't care.

"She's gone, and you don't know where she is." Geir sighed as a simple task became infinitely more difficult before his eyes. Was he now going to have to hunt down a girl who had run off with a peasant lover? Was she angry with her guardians, running off after some strange notion of freedom? He eased his back against the guesthouse wall. He was going to have to track this daft girl off into the looming storm, far from the warm comforts of even this broken down little inn. He was going to be out here for days, now, he felt certain.

He looked back up at the old man. "When did she leave? Was she alone?" He might as well get started. The sooner he got everything these two knew, the closer he was to finding her, and putting this all behind him.

The landlord stared at him, thin-lipped. Despite the fear and ignorance in his eyes, his face was hardening into a look that promised Geir some heavy work before he was able to continue on. He looked away and took a cleansing breath. Maybe he was going to have to burn the place down after all.

"We don't know who she was with." Again it was the boy who spoke, in defiance of the old man's obvious wishes. But this time he shrugged and continued. "She went with two men, an old oyathey who called himself Tsegan, or something, and an islander."

Well, that was something new. "An islander?" The dark-skinned northerners were vanishingly rare in Kun Makha, and almost entirely unheard of in the fyrdar realms. "When did they leave?"

The old man seemed to deflate, defiance running out of him like sand from a slit bag. "Four nights ago." The words were whispered, but he had no trouble hearing them. And he believed them, too. There was too much empty despair in the man's face for this to be a ruse. Country folk were, as a rule, not sophisticated enough for that sort of ploy.

"How did they leave? What direction did they go in?" If they had been gone for four days, he wasn't going to catch them today, even if he pushed his horse to its limits. The snow would fly before dark, he was certain, and then he would be plodding through the darkness and the cold, apt to miss the most obvious trail in his own miserable hell.

This time the boy shrugged, suddenly unwilling to tell him more. His fingers fluttered to a pocket in his shirt, but veered away before Geir could think too much about it. The old man's resolve had been broken, and Geir didn't even need to brush his knife's hilt to get the rest.

"South. Their wagon headed south out of the gates. It was heavily laden. Two horses."

So. Three people on a heavy wagon, loaded with supplies and pulled by two horses. But with the storm fast approaching, there was almost no way he was going to be able catch them. He would have to follow behind, stop at every crossroads he came to, and hope for the best.

But that was not the worst of the news he had just received.

South. They were headed south.

Toward the damned mountains.

Of course, they might be headed to Connat, or any of the cities located among the heaving foothills.

But that wasn't how Geir Muata's luck generally ran. They were headed to the mountains, and he had no choice but to follow.

Who was this peasant girl that Drostin needed her to die so badly? He would do almost anything to avoid returning to the mountains so soon.

He sighed, sagging more heavily against the building. He fought off the momentary urge to burn the tavern and kill the peasants out of a fit of general pique. But what would that accomplish? And Drostin would not appreciate if word got back to the king that one of his shadows had slaughtered his subjects for no reason beyond personal frustration.

But there was a brighter side to this sudden revelation.

Geir looked up into the ominous sky and a slight smile returned to his face. "I think we can go in now, boys. No need to spend any more time out here in the cold."

He pulled the pouch off his belt and allowed several coins to spill into his palm. "How much for the warmest room in the House of the Fallen Oak for the night, friend?"

Chapter 4

Eirik looked up into the gray sky and felt his lips curl. There was a steady, low-grade pounding behind his eyes that would not go away. It had dogged his step ever since the strange old man had dragged him from his sleep in the ratty tent.

Being out in this frozen wasteland was not helping his disposition, either. By now he could have been ensconced in some little tavern for the winter; drinking away the frozen months, waiting to pick up the circuit in the spring. It was a path he had followed for more years than he cared to count, and he had long ceased giving any thought to changing it.

Except that he had changed it, hadn't he? He snarled, hawked, and spat into the frozen grass of the greenway. He was not accustomed to dancing to another man's tune. Part of him wanted to blame Tyr. The boy took too much upon himself. Eirik might have to take a hand to him if this ridiculousness didn't end well.

All around them rose the sharp peaks of the White Mountains. Tyr claimed the old man's directions had been very specific, strangely so, and had led them up through the central plains, past the hill cities, and into the mountains of central Astrigir. Eirik had demanded they steer well clear of Connat, which had added days to their journey, but Tyr had made no arguments. The boy had merely nodded at his proclamation at the crossroads and followed after his master without complaint.

Neither of them had spent much time in the mountains before. The tourney circuit did not often venture from the main arteries of commerce and supply that ran through the fyrdar kingdoms. In fact, Tyr had probably never been this close to the glacier-crowned peaks.

Eirik had, of course, but that seemed like another lifetime.

The greenway stretched before and behind them for as far as they could see. It wasn't really green at the moment, autumn having long ago given up its battle with the oncoming winter this high up. It was instead a rather parched yellow dusted with white. The snows had wasted no time, and the two of them had already been caught twice in vicious early-season squalls that had seen them hunkering down in their little road tent, bundled up beneath all the furs they possessed, entertaining third, fourth, and fifth thoughts about this entire affair.

The old man's coins had run out sooner than Eirik had expected. The map had made it clear they could only take the greenway so far before venturing off the ancient road and into the winding tracks of the deep mountains; and although his horse would probably be okay, he would never ask the charger to carry them both. And so, some of the money had gone to buying Tyr a mount of his own.

The boy was a sentimentalist, as always, and was excited to find that the beast came ready with a name. Vordr wasn't the youngest horse ever to trod the greenway, and he probably wouldn't be winning any races, but he was steady, and tough, and more than able to carry the supplies they would need to make the trek south. Eirik knew the lad had chosen the horse because its heavily-muscled build made it look like a charger if you squinted. He didn't have the heart to tell the boy it was just a farm animal, a draft horse that had probably seen too many winters to guarantee it would survive another. It was more than sufficient, however, to carry the boy and the supplies they had managed to gather.

In fact, although he would never admit this to the lad, his reactions reminded Eirik of his own, the first time he and Einar had been given mounts of their own to care for. The novelty had soon worn off, but he still remembered the emotions well.

The supplies Tyr had purchased had taken up the rest of the old man's coins, and probably eaten into their own meager savings besides. Getting ready for the journey had been a constant battle, with Tyr ceaselessly dictating what they should buy, as if he were the master and Eirik the hapless servant. It had been a struggle, but he had managed to wrest enough coins from their dwindling wealth to ensure that he would not lack for drink on the journey. He could only hope there would be more when they arrived at their destination. He was trying to limit himself to the evenings and dispose of the little bottles where Tyr wouldn't see them, to avoid the silent looks of disappointment he knew the boy would send his way. As it was, he could tell from Tyr's glances that somehow, he knew anyway.

The sour twist to his lips tightened. Their journey was proving to be one of the most challenging tasks he had undertaken in years. Every day was a struggle, and he had to force himself not to dip into his dwindling supply of little bottles until after Tyr went to sleep. That made for long, boring, and awkward days as he rode for hours, thinking of little beyond the blessed numbness that awaited him that night.

Tyr was a little tyrant, forcing him to assist in making camp, preparing meals, and caring for the horses each day. At night they needed to keep a watch; Eirik knew that. The rising foothills were lawless territory, and deadly for anyone who did not take their strange inhabitants seriously. But as darkness descended each night, and silence settled over their camp, it was all he could do to wait for Tyr to sleep so he could open one of his bottles once again.

Tyr had started taking the first watch, and Eirik knew the boy was staring at him the entire time he pretended to sleep. And when his squire woke him up and curled over into his own blankets and furs, he knew the boy stayed awake as long as he could manage. A small voice in his head assured him he should feel ashamed at this behavior, but he had a long history with that voice and had learned how to ignore it years ago.

Once they had past the high Connat road, there had been fewer travelers on the greenway, and Eirik had started to relax. He knew that meant those men and women they did meet were more likely to be the rough and tumble sort, but the road had been empty for days, save for two small parties who had kept to themselves, traveling higher into the mountains on foot. They hadn't seen anyone else, and he started to feel more comfortable with his nocturnal drinking. Bandits and highwaymen did not often stalk the high mountains; not enough prey to make it worth their while.

He rode on in his accustomed silence, trying to remember how many bottles remained of his little collection, when he heard Tyr click his tongue behind him, urging his horse forward.

"So, what would be your best guess, then?"

The conversation, if you could call it that, seemed to have been dragging on for eternity. Tyr would bring up the question, Eirik would grumble, growl, and bark, and then the squire would ease up, allow his master to move several spans ahead, and they would ride in a silence that would last for miles. It had happened several times a day.

Eirik had no interest in discussing the old man. The man who had called himself Tsegan Aqisiaq had somehow convinced them to ride off into the wilderness, abandoning the circuit and their planned winter respite in the north, with an ease that Eirik found suspicious. But his memories of that night were muddy. In fact, they felt almost like a dream, or some fantasy his mind had conjured up during a long ride. Tyr had described what he had seen and how it had felt. Eirik knew how much he had drunk that day, but he had laughed off the boy's fears of potions or magic. The pouch of coins had done more to convince them to follow the man's instructions than the fading effects of drink or the disappointments of the day.

There was no magic. He knew the sagas claimed there had been, once, long ago, when the fyrdar had first arrived in Kun Makha, fleeing the Utan, the old stories claimed. But that was hundreds of years ago. He had never seen magic, and no one he knew had ever seen magic. There were many stories about Tsegan Aqisiaq, both in the histories and in the more wild fairy stories and sagas. In the histories, he had been a great man who had helped unite oyathey and fyrdar, and then worked tirelessly to the betterment of both people. In the fairy stories, he was the last great wizard, a master of incredible powers and enchantments that rivaled those of the spirits and the gods. Why would anyone give that name to strangers? Did he expect them to think he was the great man, or some descendent of his, who had inherited his mystical powers?

It had to have been some trick in the tent that night, some medicine he had slipped to Eirik earlier or while his squire was distracted. Or maybe the mead had not been as strong as he had believed. That had happened before, when his own mind, exhausted from battle or from struggling with his own demons, would succumb to the drink, only to have the blessed numbness suddenly flare away, leaving him cold and lucid in the light of his own failures.

He shook his head. It hardly mattered now. They were in the mountains, following the old fool's map to the gods alone knew where, and they hardly had the supplies to turn around now.

That brought him up short. What if it was all a ruse? What if, when they arrived in this hidden valley, it was empty? They would starve to death up here, and no one would ever know what had become of them.

Maybe this was all some elaborate scheme of King Einar's, to remove the last stain of his greatest failure without risking the ire of the gods.

But if that happened, would it be so bad? Tyr would be a loss, no doubt. The lad was keen, and kind, and far too trusting of old stories and songs. But he didn't deserve to die such a lonely, unsung death. But then, the boy was also resourceful. He would be able to take care of himself, to hunt and forage as he made his way back down to the plains.

That might be the best outcome for all involved, in fact. For a while, now, he had felt the lad would be better off without him.

"Master? What do you think? Of the old man?"

Eirik had forgotten Tyr was riding beside him and scowled over at the eager face. "I don't."

He watched Tyr frown then looked up into the hazy sky. How long before he could declare they would stop for the night? Against all rational thought, he could feel the bottles in his saddlebags, wrapped in furs, blankets, and spare clothes. He needed a drink, just a sip, more than he could ever remember needing anything before. But if he indulged himself, the silent agreement with Tyr would be broken, and he would have to endure the looks, the sighs, and the sharp comments for the rest of their journey, if not for the rest of the winter and beyond.

He settled back down, wrapped his furs tighter about his shoulders, and kicked at his horse's flank to gain a little distance from that even stare.

Tyr let him go, as he almost always did.

When Tyr spoke again, sometime later, the boy's voice broke into his sullen reverie with such sharp tones that he almost barked again. Then the words sank through the pain in his head.

"What?"

"I think we leave the greenway here." Tyr had the map out, and was pointing to it with one gloved hand. "Marker forty-three." Eirik saw an old granite post, half buried in dry, brown vegetation, off to one side. It had something carved into its length that might be numbers if he cared to get closer. "There should be a path off to the left."

They looked and eventually saw the narrow track leading deeper into the forest. It looked less than inviting.

"We will be able to follow this for a few days before the path becomes trickier. There will be a trading post that we'll have to avoid." By Tyr's voice, it was clear the boy was thinking beyond their next stop. From this point, their journey would be far more difficult, as the mountains and the winter ranged against them. That was a far more direct threat than any peasant bandits that might have struck lower down the greenway. The thought of passing up a warm bed and some rowdy companionship was not something Eirik would consider lightly, and he knew that Tyr was nearly as desperate for warmth as he was. But the old man had been insistent that they avoid anyone on their journey into the mountains, and if they were going to do this, Eirik and his squire had both agreed that they would follow the strange little man's instructions completely, rather than take a chance of spoiling whatever endeavor they had decided to join.

Besides, he reasoned, he was getting used to the cold, right?

He remained singularly unconvinced by his own reasoning.

The horses were not eager to penetrate the heavy shadows, but with a little coaxing from Tyr and one sharp blow of Eirik's fist to the side of his own mount's head, they pushed onward. The forest was thick here, and the shadows deep. Eventually, after an hour or so of steady riding, they broke through into a clear area. The trail meandered down into a long, shallow valley, a murky tarn dominating the central span. The water was black, reflecting the sullen sky like a dark mirror, and the bone-white trunks of drowned trees reached up into the air like hands pleading for help that had never come.

The trail wound around the tarn and rose back up the forest on the other side. There were several places where it had been covered over by the spreading wetlands. This was going to be an unpleasant passage.

"We need to stop. That's far enough for one day." He reined the big warhorse in and cast a glance around. The trail was narrow, the forest looming up behind them. This far into the mountains, most of the trees were evergreens, their dark pine-laden bows only adding to the gloom. Plenty of skeletal hardwoods, their own branches bare of all but the most tenacious leaves, skulked within the shadows as well, however, lending the forest a haunted air.

When they were still in the north, fresh out of the foothills, they had been pitching their little road tent farther back among the trees, away from the ancient road. But here, the forest was much thicker, harder to push the horses through, and he didn't relish the idea of putting camp together in the twilight, his head pounding and the bottles weighing heavily on his mind.

"Let's just put the tent under the eaves right there." He pointed one gloved hand to a likely spot. "I don't imagine we'll be seeing anyone tonight, now that we've left the road behind."

He could tell Tyr disapproved from the echoes of his silence, but he didn't much care. They hadn't seen anyone in days. No bandit would be up this far. Why would they? There were several small trade settlements tucked into the sheltered valleys of the high mountains, giving the trappers, woodsmen, and those few others who hacked their living out of the winter forests a place to gather and do their business. But there were not nearly enough people in the winter mountains to supply a thriving criminal community.

He thought tonight might be a night for an entire bottle. They'd be safe enough, and there was no way they were going to get warm with yet another storm on the horizon.

Tyr slid down from his horse and began to unbuckle its tack. The saddle and other gear settled on the crackling grass, and a nonchalant glance over his shoulder burned a slight sense of guilt into Eirik's mind to see that he took care of his own mount before doing anything else.

The tent went up quickly, a fire was set, and they were soon settling down to a dinner of broth and hard bread. He was fairly certain there was still some meat somewhere about, but Tyr was being difficult, and he didn't feel like battling with the boy over a hank of chewy dried cow.

Besides, with the fall of darkness, the sweet little bottle wasn't far away.

As the light faded from the sky, things above them progressed steadily from one ominous shade of gray to the next. He watched the illumination fade on the surface of the tarn below. It was an eerie sight, reminding of him of more than a few of the darker sagas, those most often used to frighten unruly children. He could imagine a troll or troop of evil elves marching out of the forest opposite, coming down to the water for some unholy rite.

"Maybe he needs a fighter."

Eirik looked up from his musings, a scowl on his face. "Who?"

Tyr ignored his surly, willfully ignorant response with a shrug. "Maybe the old man needs someone to fight for him, to protect him, or something." Eirik snorted and went back to watching the tarn fade into the dark of night. "Or maybe he needs someone to listen to his stories, to believe his lies; an audience for some minstrel show he plans on weaving around himself."

Tyr shook his head, stirring the fire with a long stick. "No, it's more than that. You didn't see..."

Eirik smiled. "I'm not sure there was anything to see, lad. And neither are you. But we'll find out soon enough, right? We can't be too far from this mysterious little valley. A few more days; maybe a week? Then we'll know. Why don't you rest? I'll take the first watch. You need the sleep."

Tyr gave him a sharp look. "No, I think I'll take the first watch. You go to sleep. I'll wake you when it's time."

It was exactly what he had come to expect, but it annoyed him all the same. "I don't think so, boy. Who's the squire here, eh? Who's the master? Go to sleep. I'll watch."

"We can both stay up, then, if you'd like." The edge in Tyr's voice struck just the wrong chord. Who did he think he was, with his condescension and high handedness?

Eirik stood. He wasn't afraid of the boy. He refused to live like a sneak thief, some petty criminal fearing his own shadow. No child was going to tell him how to act or what to do.

Besides, they were far enough from civilization, they had nothing to fear.

Eirik moved to the pile of bags beside the tent and knelt, rummaging around until he found what he was looking for. He unwrapped the little bottle and held it up into the light of their fire, making sure Tyr could see it.

"Want a sip?" He grinned and then pulled the cork out with his teeth. The fumes clawed at his sinuses and made him jump. Knowing they would have limited space, he had forgone his favored mead and procured as many hard spirits as he could find before they left. The drinking wasn't as pleasurable as it might have been, but the results came faster, and for less weight in the pack.

Tyr just watched him, his gaze flat, as he took a slug of the potent brew.

He forced down the cough that rose up his burning throat, and the satisfaction of rubbing the little pup's face in this was almost as sweet as the slow burn he could feel spreading out from his gut. Already the headache was fading, and he felt more at peace with the world than he had in a long time.

With that peace came a mild sense of shame. "Just the one sip, Tyr, that's all."

He stoppered the bottle but, instead of putting it back in the bag, he slipped it into a pocket in his heavy cloak.

One sip, for now.

Tyr watched him for a moment longer and then stood smoothly and moved to the tent. He glanced around the camp one last time, avoiding his master's look, and ducked in without a word.

Eirik watched the tent for a moment, but there was no further movement there, and he shifted around to look out over the dark valley below. He settled his back against a rock, near enough to the fire to enjoy the warmth but far enough away to preserve his night vision.

There was no need for another sip. He could show Tyr he was able to keep watch and would awaken the lad at the proper time, as any veteran campaigner could. Then he would have another sip or two when his watch was done, and he was safely alone in the tent, shielded from the damned boy's prying eyes.

*****

There was a sharp crack, and Eirik surged to his feet, glaring blearily around. The first thing he noticed was that it was dark. It was far, far too dark. The fire had collapsed into a sullen red heap of darkening cinders that did nothing to illuminate the trees around them. The second thing was the clinking of an empty bottle resting by his boot.

He had finished the bottle and fallen asleep. He knew it the moment he saw the fire. And something out in the forest had awoken him. A light snow was falling; the moon invisible behind the shroud of storm clouds overhead. He had no idea how late it was, but the fire could not have burned so low before he should have summoned Tyr to his watch.

Now, if he woke the boy, he'd know that his master had fallen asleep. He had no desire to face that judgmental gaze again so soon.

Eirik slowly spun about, doing his best to pierce the darkness all around. There was no movement in the deep shadows, no sounds that might indicate danger of any kind. Animals would avoid even this low a fire, and he still believed there would be no danger of bandits or such this far from the towns and villages.

He stopped but dragged his blade closer to him, patting its worn leather sheath as if for reassurance. One of the last maekre blades in Astrigir, it made perfect sense that it would comfort him. Almost as comforting as a second little bottle.

*****

Again it was a snap that awoke him, but this time it was accompanied by the rushing, crunching sound of hurried footsteps across the dry grass of the verge.

Eirik was barely conscious before he was up, roaring defiance, sweeping his blade from its scabbard. A dark figure dashed across the clearing toward him, an axe waving over its head.

"Foes!" Eirik's voice echoed across the valley and he heard, with what small part of his mind was left to notice such things, Tyr grunt from within the tent.

Eirik felt like a god as he crashed through the remains of their own fire, now little more than ash. Fire filled his veins, his mind was clear and cold, and he was ready to face a hundred brigands who might attack out of the cold of the mountain night.

He felt as if he were young again, with the clear lines of battle before him. There were enemies, there was him and the boy, and the tourney circuit and its rules and wagers were a hundred leagues away.

This was what he had been made for.

And then he tripped. Whether it was a root or the traitorous circle of stones around their fire, he couldn't tell. One moment he was gliding through the night, his mind afire with deadly intent, and then he was crashing forward, all sense of balance lost, straight for the shadowy attacker.

For some reason, as he struggled to bring his feet back beneath him, to recapture his sense of balance, his mind refused to work with him.

Luckily, his misfortune surprised the enemy as much as it surprised himself, and he crashed into the man's chest with all the force of his berserker charge, bowling the man over with a startled cry, and sending his axe flying into the darkness.

"Master?" Tyr's muffled voice was confused, muzzy with sleep but tinged with fear.

"Arm yourself!"

Beneath him, Eirik could feel the enemy struggling to pull a dagger from his belt. The maekre blade was too heavy and unwieldy now, so he dropped it as he made a grab for the man's wrist, his other hand scrambling for a handhold around his neck. The man's blue eyes were wide, his mouth writhing within the red beard.

Four other shadows moved in the darkness now, more cautious or intelligent than the first. They were spreading out to come at the camp from different directions.

There was a flash behind him, and one of the shadows faltered with a startled scream. It stumbled, almost falling, grabbing at a bloody gash glistening on its neck. Its massive axe drooped as one hand rose to clasp hard against the wound.

Tyr ran past before the other attackers could gather their senses, a fighting axe in either hand, and took the two attackers sweeping in from the left at the same time.

Eirik felt his own opponent's dagger sliding from its sheath and spat. His fingers were clumsy, all feeling of godhood disappeared, and he cursed the drink that fogged his mind.

He clenched thick fingers around the man's neck. The attacker began to thrash desperately, beating at him with his free hand. A thumb slid across his cheek, seeking for his eye, and he craned his neck back and away, pressing down harder to end this before he was blinded.

Arching away from the man on the ground beneath him, he saw Tyr exchanging blows with his two opponents. Each of them was fighting with a single long-handled axe, and the squire was dancing around them, a weapon in either hand, catching a blow on the shaft of one axe before slicing toward an attacker with the other. Eirik had not realized how proficient Tyr had become; the two-handed fighting style was terribly difficult to master. The boy could have easily stood in a tourney melee with the best young champions of the season.

Beneath him, the man was bucking and heaving, choking on his last breath, but he was taking too long to die. Two more shadows were moving around from the right, circling behind Tyr to take him from behind. It wouldn't matter how fancy the boy was with his axes at that point; four to one was enough to topple even the most seasoned fighter.

Eirik rose up higher, putting all his weight on his attacker's throat and surging down over and over again, spittle spraying into the man's darkening face as he screamed down at him to die, die, die!

There was a wet crack and the body beneath him went limp all at once. But Eirik had seen warriors feign death before. He slipped the man's dagger out and slid it into his neck, just beneath the jaw.

Eirik didn't wait to see if the wound bled. He surged to his feet, grasping for his long blade, and swung around to face the attackers moving through the camp toward Tyr's back.

A man and a woman, both dirty, their hair in disarray, furs and leathers wrapped around them against the winter chill, they had rubbed dirt on their faces to better blend with the night. When they saw him rise they stopped, looked at each other, and shifted their approach.

Eirik smiled.

A maekre blade was not an elegant weapon. It was a heavy weight of steel with a razor's cutting edge along one side; heavy enough to knock an armored man from his horse ... Or to cut a man in fur and leather in half with a single blow. In tourneys he fought with a leather sleeve laced over the blades edge. That sleeve had been removed long before they began their journey south.

He might not be as fast as he once was, and he might have forgotten more about wielding the blade than most would ever know, but he still had his bull's strength, and the wind in him to swing.

With the roar of a wounded bear, Eirik charged forward, the blade swinging wide and then slashing back in toward the man on his right. With the force of both of his arms behind it, and enough room this time to swing, there was almost nothing a warrior could do to counter a maekre blade but to avoid the blow.

This fool tried to meet the attack with the haft of his axe.

The heavy sword crashed into the wood, cutting a great divot from it before continuing through to smash against the brigand's ribs. The axe handle probably stopped the maekre blade from cutting him in half, but that was precious little mercy as the man's spine snapped and he was thrown bodily into the woman rushing forward beside him.

The woman screamed as she was hit and went tumbling across the grass, tangled up with the whimpering body of her companion. Eirik let the momentum of his mighty swing bring the sword back around to the ready and stalked toward her.

She was not an ugly woman, although a hard life was written across her face in lines and scars, and her sandy hair, hacked short, was streaked with gray. She glared up at him from beneath her fallen friend, the man still moaning and shaking with the shock of his terrible injury.

Eirik looked down at the woman with flat grey eyes, and she looked back with equal defiance.

Tyr's cry shattered the moment. The squire had been holding off his two assailants admirably, but one had finally moved around and gotten a solid blow in from behind, too far around for Tyr to parry with any strength.

The axe had forced its way past the squire's guard and laid a bloody gash across the back of his left biceps. The sleeve glistened with blood in the winter dark.

Tyr whirled around, waving the axe in his right hand at eye-height, keeping his two attackers at bay. He was snarling, his left arm low, the axe across his body for defense, as his high axe wove back and forth as a warning.

But the boy was tiring. Already, his high axe drooped as it moved. Soon, he wouldn't be able to keep the two away.

The woman at Eirik's feet had begun to snake her way out from beneath the dying man, her hand reaching for a fallen weapon, when he looked back down at her. Without a second thought, he put a boot into the angle of her neck and pressed down with a sharp jerk that snapped the delicate bones beneath.

As he approached the last two bandits, he was gratified to see Tyr sink his right-hand axe into the neck of his wounded opponent, opposite the side of his earlier injury. The man fell writhing, clutching at the spurting wound, but Eirik's pride was short lived as he watched the boy follow his enemy to the dirt. The last remaining brigand brought his long-handled axe back for a massive over-hand blow that would crush Tyr's skull.

There was no growling cry this time. He hardly had the breath, never mind the time.

The maekre blade caught the last attacker in the side, just beneath the right arm, and cleaved through fur and leather, flesh and bone. The force of the blow threw the man sideways, his axe spinning in the air to land with a dull sound in the grass as he rolled to a stop against a tree several paces away, a horrific wound nearly separating his head and shoulders from the rest of his body.

Eirik fell to one knee, gasping for breath. What was wrong with him?

A moan from the shadows brought him back to himself and he stumbled over to fall to his knees beside Tyr, who was curled on his side cradling his wounded arm.

"I'm sorry."

The boy's voice was vague and feverish, but it was strong enough that Eirik's fear abated; at least a little.

"Nothing to apologize for, lad. You held them off plenty long enough." He looked around for something to bandage the wound, and eventually stripped the woman of her cloak on the assumption that a woman might keep her clothing cleaner than a man; even in the mountains.

He slashed at the fabric, tearing the cloak into strips, and then cut Tyr's sleeve away so he could better see the wound. It was deep, but the cut was with the muscle and should heal cleanly if it wasn't infected.

After cleaning the wound with some of his precious spirits and binding it with the dead woman's cloak, Eirik began to move around the camp trying to sort some order from the mess. He laid a new fire, stoking it high and hot, then began the tiring work of dragging the bodies away from camp, kicking dirt over the worst spills of blood and offal. It was cold enough that they wouldn't start to stink before Eirik and Tyr were on their way.

He cursed under his breath the entire time, a tremor in his hands rising from the depths of his anger and fear. He massaged one rough hand with the other, staring into the fire, but nothing would soothe the trembling away.

He felt the weight in his pocket and slowly drew out another bottle. With a guilty glance at his unconscious squire, he dashed a solid dram into his mouth and choked down the cough. Then he went back to cleaning up the encampment, gathering anything useful or valuable from the bodies. As he moved around camp, he continued to sip at the bottle, lost in the minutia of tasks that seemed to get more complicated, rather than less, as the night wore on.

"Master, no..." The voice was weak, and when he glanced down at Tyr from the corner of his eyes, he could see the boy already fading back into sleep.

He shrugged. They had done what needed doing. Five against two, with the five having every advantage, a single slashed shoulder was more than a fair price for victory under such circumstances.

He told himself he couldn't have done much better in his prime.

He wrestled the unconscious boy into the tent and settled down by the fire with the remains of the second bottle, his eyes dark and narrow as he stared into the flames.

Not long after, the small bottle rolled from his loose fingers to join its brother in the cold, churned dirt of the forest floor.

Chapter 5

"So, how much longer do you think we'll be traveling?" The words were as casual as she could manage, but she knew there was still a slight edge in her voice. As she thought about it, she wasn't sure why she cared.

The dark-skinned islander didn't even glance up at her question, continuing to stare out over the two horses and the greenway stretching before them. As they made their way up into the mountains, each day was colder than the last, but the big man always wore his hood down during the day, as if hungry for any hint of the sun. His hair, twisted into long, tight rolls, hung loosely over his shoulders, the fitful wind tugging them this way and that.

His silence was nothing new, however; she hadn't heard him speak since she had first met him in the courtyard of the Fallen Oak. In fact, coming from the gregarious environment of a tavern, even under the care of such a cheerless couple as Vali and Turid, the nearly silent journey was taking a terrible toll on Maiara's peace of mind. But even that was better than being alone with the equipment and supplies in the back.

The old man, Tsegan, he still asked to be called, had had a horse of his own at a stable in a small crossroads village a day south of the House of the Fallen Oak, and had left them soon after that on some errand of his own. He promised to join them again before they left the greenway, but she had no idea when that might be, so the thought carried little comfort.

She had spent the first couple of days idly going through the contents of the wagon as it creaked its way along. Her feelings of propriety had faded quickly, once she realized the big dark skinned man was going to ignore her no matter what she did. She figured she should be able to divine something from the contents, since no further information seemed to be forthcoming from any other source.

The packs and boxes had been singularly unenlightening. There were barrels of dry goods, grains, dried meats, and such. There were furs and bolts of cloth, common tools such as sledges and axes. But there were also stranger tools she barely recognized as stoneworker's implements from her visits to Baedr. There were several sacks of a dusty powder that might have been dry mortar; if she was right about that, there was some serious construction or repairs in someone's future.

It was less than reassuring, if such heavy work was ahead of them.

She had found three small tents that she interpreted to mean that each of them would be sleeping alone. That had removed one of her most pressing fears, but did nothing for her sense of growing isolation. Each time they stopped for the night, Chagua would set the fire, light it, and put up the tents. He had prepared the meals as well, their first two nights, until she had demanded she at least be allowed to do that before she lost all sense of usefulness.

Once all of their tasks were completed, their meals cooked and eaten, the dishes cleaned and replaced in the wagon, they would sit in silence, staring at the flames for whatever remained of the day. Occasionally, she would catch Chagua glancing toward the cart, toward a crate she knew contained nothing but piles of books; but when she asked him what he was looking at, he glanced at her in silence, of course, then back to the fire. Inevitably, she would give up and retreat to her tent to stare at the canvas wall, usually paging slowing through her collection of fairy stories by the soft glow of the fire beyond until she fell asleep.

She often experienced strange, vague dreams of heat and dust that never seemed in keeping with her waking life. But as they moved higher into the cool mountains, with snow threatening every day, the dreams were becoming more and more common. Often, now, she woke up choking on a dry, acrid taste that faded even as she bolted upright.

She didn't know if Chagua slept at all. Usually, when she finally faded off to sleep, he was sharpening the blade of a strange, thin sword. The weapon was long, nearly as long as she was tall, with a slight curve that made it look weak to her. She had not seen many weapons at the Fallen Oak, of course. Farmers seldom had need of such things that far from the borders. But she knew that the fyrdar folk favored axes or straight, heavy swords; while the oyathey of Kun Makha, she had read in the almanac, used heavy, weighted weapons with no edge at all, like weighted balls on heavy sticks. She wasn't sure why that was, but in the stories in her children's book it seemed to mean they killed monsters less often than scaring them away.

More often than not, when she awoke in the morning, he was either preparing breakfast, putting the horses into harness, or once more caring for the sword. For nearly two weeks, she had not seen him so match as swing it through the air, but the way he handled it, she was fairly certain he knew how to use it.

She looked out over the land around her once again. On either side, the great southern forest loomed, and beyond that she could see the gleaming white crowns of the mountains thrusting up in the distance. Those glittering mantles were glaciers, she knew from her readings, often many feet deep. They never melted, even in the heat of high summer, although the records also spoke of the glaciers retreating in recent years. She had often wondered what could cause that, and what it might mean to anyone trying to carve a living out of the frontier lands between the plains and the peaks.

"You don't even have a guess as to how long we'll be riding?" She knew he would not respond, but hopelessness was no defense against the boredom that pushed down on her like the heavy clouds overhead.

"Well, I'd imagine we'll be leaving the greenway in the next couple of days, personally." She went on in a conversational tone as if he had responded. "We'll be well and truly in the mountains, then, and the almanac says there really isn't much up there anymore. Fyrdar forts from the early invasions, when they still feared the Utan were following. Maybe a castle or two tumbled down into ruins, but—"

It all slotted into place with a click she could almost hear. The tools, the materials... They were going up into the mountains, where the only real shelter would be ...

In the middle of winter, with nowhere to live but tents, they were somehow supposed to make a tumbled-down old fyrdar ruin habitable again.

"I don't know how to set stones, you know." She looked out the corner of her eyes and watched for a reaction. There was none.

She sighed and rested against the backboard of the driver's bench. "Well, I hope the old man gets back soon, if we're going to be turning off. There can't be much left of the old roads to those forts, and I don't know if just the two of us will be able to manage on our own." She smiled as her mind continued to work. "Of course, I'm not sure how much help an old man like ... Tsegan ... is going to be with a pair of draft horses and a big wagon."

The horses continued to plod up the grassy sward, the mountains growing imperceptibly taller with each heavy step. She smiled, rested her elbow against the backboard to bring her face around closer to Chagua's and summoned her most casual tones.

"I guess he could use magic, maybe."

Was there a flicker in those black eyes? It was hard to tell, but she almost thought she had seen something. Of course, after days of such effort, she could have easily imagined it.

She sighed, straightened back around to face the horses, and took a deep breath of the cold mountain air.

Fleeing from the Fallen Oak with the old man and the dark islander had turned her entire world on its head. But it had its advantages. The air never smelled so sweet in the common room of the old guest house.

They hadn't seen anyone in days, but she had heard many stories in the tavern over the years. Tales of brigands and killers wandering the hills were a favorite around the big fire; evil men waylaying innocent travelers and perpetrating all sorts of terrible things upon them. In fact, she had learned years ago that there was a certain type of man who took an unkind glee in telling such stories to young girls, and so she had heard more than her fair share.

They hadn't seen any bandits themselves. Although she had to admit to a secret, thrilling curiosity, to see how Chagua might fare against a brigand or two.

They had seen one party of dark-haired travelers at a distance one day, but the group had moved off onto a side trail soon after, and there had been no further sign of any others sharing their improbable path.

She had another thought, and spoke without worrying about whether Chagua would respond or not. "Do you think there are monsters in the mountains?"

He might have reacted, she wouldn't have known. She was just speaking now to accompany her own thoughts, to hear a human voice, any human voice, in the void.

"I don't think there are such things as monsters." Although a certain kind of man, often the same with the grotesque stories of the robbers, would tell any little girl who might listen, that there were monsters in the mountains as well. "I mean, no real monsters; trolls, changelings, or things like that. There are probably bears up this far, and the gods and spirits know they probably get big out here."

She had seen a bear head once. A trader traveling through town had stayed at the Fallen Oak and tried to sell it to Vali. The landlord had wanted nothing to do with the thing, saying it was a sad, flea-bitten specimen; but it had looked vicious to her and made quite an impression.

"But as for the creatures in the fairy stories? The ones who supposedly followed the fyrdar, like the trolls or dwarves, or the ones who were here long before, like skinwalkers or horned serpents?" She shrugged, enjoying even the charade of a conversation. "I don't think they're real." She sighed. "Although I have to say, it would be a brighter world, I think, if some of those things existed, don't you agree?"

She looked at him with a wide smile, taking an unkind joy in the stony rigidity of his face. Although ... did she see just a slight glimmer of a smile on that dark face?

"I mean, I'd hate to think that we already know all there is to know about the world." She settled back with a smile, content, for the moment.

Several days later, Maiara was brooding in the back of the wagon, sitting on one crate, her back braced against another, furs and blankets piled high around her, when she heard Chagua whicker to the horses, flick the traces slightly, and the constant creaking of the wheels slowed.

She stood up, brushing down the fall of her skirts, and turned to look to the front of the wagon. Over Chagua's shoulder she could see the slight form of the old man riding toward them.

Riding toward them. From the south. Which meant that somehow Tsegan had managed to loop around through the thick southern forests to get in front of them.

There was certainly more to the old man than met the eye, magician or not.

Chagua brought the wagon to a halt in the middle of the greenway and waited for Tsegan to approach. As always, the old man's face was wreathed in a smile well-suited to its natural lines and shadows. He raised one hand and hailed them as if he was riding out of a saga.

"Hail, friends, on the long and lonely road!" The little man brought his horse even with the wagon and wheeled it around, smiling broadly. "How have you fared while I was away? Did you miss me?"

Maiara's hands went to her hips; she was surprised to find herself taking one of old Turid's most belligerent stances, but she didn't relax it.

Tsegan, however, seemed undaunted.

It took all the energy out of her righteous anger, and she suddenly felt like a petulant child.

"He wouldn't talk to me." It came out more a mutter than the ringing accusation she had intended, and her hands slipped off her hips, one sliding up to hold the opposite elbow before she realized what her traitor body was doing and forced it back down, tightening both into angry fists.

Beside her, Chagua did not shift on the drover's seat, sitting at casual attention as he always did. The old man gave the islander a dramatic look of shock and leaned over his horse's neck.

"Chagua Emeru, is this true? You left the young lady wrapped in your sullen silences for days on end?"

The islander did not flinch, merely returning the old man's black-eyed stare.

Tsegan chuckled. "Well, I should have known. To be honest, my dear, he's not much of a talker. Not really his strong suit, I'm afraid."

He brought his horse around so that it was facing south once again and gestured for Chagua to bring his own horses back up to speed. "The road ahead is clear; nothing much to worry about from here to the high mountains. Although it looks like we'll be getting more snow soon, so that should keep things lively for the next little while."

Maiara fought against the rocking of the wagon for a moment before dropping back to her improvised seat, struggling to keep the pout off her face. She was aware of Tsegan bringing his horse closer to the side of the wagon, but she refused to look up.

"My dear, you can't stay annoyed forever."

The smile in the voice was enough to stir up her frustrations anew, and she shot him a look. "Why am I here?"

That damned smile again. "Well, mainly because I have spent the better part of the last twenty years seeing that you would be here, my girl. A lot of time and effort went into that, I assure you. I would have been most put out if that had all come to naught."

She huffed, nearly overwhelmed with the urge to hit something. "But why? Why me?"

He sighed, and she straightened her shoulders. There was no way he was going to make her feel guilty.

"Maiara ... may I call you Maiara, for now?"

That was odd enough to get her attention. For now?

"Call me whatever you want. Just tell me why, in the names of all the gods and spirits, I'm rolling up the greenway into the mountains with two strangers!"

There was nothing normal or sane about any of this. She couldn't understand why she had agreed to come with this strange pair in the first place; although there was a sense of adventure to the whole arrangement that she had never felt before. And she didn't remember, if she was going to be honest, being given much of a choice in how things went that night.

"Maiara, all will be revealed in time, I promise you. For now, is it not enough to know that the world is far wider than the House of the Fallen Oak? And that your place in it is far, far more significant than that of helpless waif, tavern girl, or the wife of some future innkeep?"

She shrugged, not wanting to look at him. That last had reminded her of Kustaa, of course. She knew the boy fancied her. And in a way, much like any girl will fancy the boy she is forbidden to look at, she liked him as well. She cared far more for him as a friend, as perhaps the only friend her strange childhood had allowed. But still, she knew that marriage, future marriage, someday far, far from this one, had been somewhere in his mind.

She had not given much thought to that herself, taking each dreary day as it came. But when she did, she was far more likely to imagine herself taking the place of the heroes and heroines of her tattered story book rather than standing beside any man, even one as kind as Kustaa.

"As I said the night we met, Maiara, there are momentous events afoot. Dark forces rise up against the kingdom; against all the fyrdar kingdoms. Only one path will allow the people to see the light on the other side. Your assistance is essential to the navigation of that path." His voice was warm and reassuring, but heavy, too. He was trying to convince her that this implausible, fantastical, and above all vague story was true.

But she knew herself. She knew what she was, and who she was. She had a firm, practical grasp on her abilities. She could cook, clean, and do the counting books for a guesthouse at least as well as Turid. She was a voracious reader, devouring anything she could get her hands on. She could often see the outcome of an argument or negotiation in the common room of the Fallen Oak long before the men and women involved.

But none of that seemed to indicate anything particularly momentous. What did she have to offer the fates of kings and kingdoms?

He reached out and grabbed the side railing of the wagon, leaning toward her, his gaze intent. "Please have faith, Maiara. All will come clear very soon now. We have nearly reached our destination. When we arrive, when I have gathered the last remaining pieces of the puzzle together, you will know everything. I promise you."

She stared into his eyes, trying to find even the shade of a lie or half-truth in the luminous blackness there. But she saw only warm sincerity and friendship. And friendship was something she had had too little of during her life.

She grunted, trying to keep a hold of her pique. "Where have you been?"

He smiled, sensing the imminent thaw, and settled back into his saddle. "There are a great many moving parts in this grand drama, I'm afraid. It is a thankless, exhausting task, keeping the various plates spinning, making sure the entire edifice does not come crashing down around us all."

"That wasn't very enlightening. What were you doing?"

He frowned, his face tightening. "Maiara, I don't know that I care for your tone. I have labored longer than you have been alive to prepare the fyrdar kingdoms for this looming threat. I assure you: everything I do, I do for the greater good of all."

For some reason, managing even this slight crack in his composer made her feel a little better. With a grin she made no effort to hide, she tossed her head back toward Chagua. "So, does he talk at all? Or did you leave me with a mute?"

Tsegan rode on for several paces in silence, and then gave her his own slight smile. "That wasn't kind, Maiara. Chagua is more than capable of speech when he wishes." The old man's eyes darkened for a moment and he glanced at the islander. "I often think his silence is his way of asserting his own brand of ... independence."

She looked at the old man at that. She didn't think he was feigning the annoyance that colored the edges of his words. As for Chagua, he looked straight ahead and didn't acknowledge that they were talking about him at all.

She shook her head. She was going to have to accept that this strangeness was her new, normal world. If she was going to survive with any appreciable share of her sanity intact, she would have to accept it for the winter, at least.

Camp each night, after Tsegan rejoined them, was a far more pleasant experience. She thought she detected an added energy behind the old man's stories, his smiles, and his laughter. He was obviously trying to compensate for their companion's stoic silence.

She noticed that Chagua never so much as glanced at the crate of books after Tsegan had joined them, however.

Most of Tsegan's stories were variations on the old sagas. Most, she noticed, dealt with young warriors, wizards, and the like, who found themselves in implausible situations and won through to save the day against all manner of terrible beasts, monsters, and evil men. Each tale was lighthearted and amusing, and they kept the evenings lively. She found herself laughing out loud on more than one occasion, and she thought she saw gratified relief in the old man's face.

By the time she retired to her tent, she was tired, relaxed, and found sleep within a matter of moments; the book of fairy stories all but forgotten. The strange dreams, however, only got worse. Each morning she awoke drenched in sweat, gasping silently for breath.

Three days after Tsegan had rejoined them, they reached a rough trail that plunged into the shadows of the forest to their right. It was nowhere near as wide as the greenway, but the cart would fit, barely. And it was just smooth enough that the contents were not spilled out across the forest floor. But the ride was far too rough for her to enjoy spending any further time with the supplies. Even the drover's seat was not a pleasant ride, and she soon found herself walking beside the cart, often with one hand on a horse's neck, enjoying the warmth of the physical contact.

The new trail wound down from the greenway, past several small mountain lakes and wide fields of tall, waving grasses, yellow with the passing of autumn. The snows they had been getting were not accumulating yet, despite their passing fury. But the temperatures were plunging, especially at night, and she found herself more and more thankful for the furs and blankets from the wagon.

They had been on the new trail for three days when they stopped to make their camp beside a small, rushing stream. The trees were thick all around, forming a nearly-impenetrable wall about ten paces beyond their clearing. Chagua gathered the supplies they would need for the night while Tsegan took his horse to the side to remove its saddle and harness. With fresh water so close, she knew how she could help without asking. She pulled a heavy pot from the wagon and made her way down the steep slope to the stream.

The water was freezing, of course. A shoreline of golden needles tracked the flow on either side, but the water of the little river itself was crystal clear, and plenty deep enough to get the pot in to scoop it full to the brim.

She was turning to negotiate the incline back up to camp, the pot an ungainly weight dragging at her arms, when a ferocious roar erupted directly behind her, sending terrifying echoes bouncing through the trees.

Maiara screamed, dropping the pot and spinning to face whatever had made the terrible noise. There was nothing there, whatever had made the sound hidden in the shadows on the far side of the stream. Low branches thrashed against the darkness, and another roar struck her like a physical blow. She fell back against the slope, striking a rock hidden beneath the leaf mold, and cried out as the pain overcame her terror.

Chagua's answering roar startled her all over, his long sword gleaming in his hands as he rushed past her, hitting the bank of the river running, and leapt over the water in a single stride. The tails of his hair waved wildly behind him.

A part of her dazed mind realized that it was the first sound she had ever heard him make, other than tisking at the horses.

Tsegan scrambled down the hill beside her, his dark eyes scanning the shadows. There was still no sign of whatever creature had made the noise, and Chagua had stopped just short of the wall of trees, his sword at the ready, peering into the darkness, his shoulders heaving, and the steam of his breath wreathing his head in a halo of misty white.

"Is it a bear?" Maiara asked as she cradled her hand to her chest. "What is it? Was it a bear?"

Tsegan continued to look out in the darkness, shaking his head. "I don't know, child. It sounded like no bear I have ever seen."

Whatever it was, it gave another thunderous bellow, and they both shrank back. Chagua, with a low growl of his own, plunged into the shadows, sword flashing upward.

"Run!" The man shouted over his shoulder as he disappeared into the shadows, his accent so thick Maiara almost didn't understand the word, but Tsegan pulled her to her feet, still watching the forest where the islander had disappeared, and shoved her up the slope.

"Go, girl. I need to make sure Chagua is alright."

She wasn't about to argue, the old man's stories heavy in her mind, far darker than they had seemed around a campfire. But part of her was confused by his words. If the big islander wasn't alright, what was the little old man going to do about it?

"Wait, what?" She stopped moving, half turning around.

"Just go!" He shoved her again, and then turned to skip down to the river's edge. He moved with far more grace than a white-haired old man should be able to muster.

Once she reached the top of the hill, she turned, the fire at her back, and watched Tsegan hop from stone to stone across the river. The burbling of the water seemed horribly out of place now, as she waited for some monster, Chagua's blood dripping from its maw, to emerge from the darkness.

It was no monster that emerged, however, but Chagua himself, flying horizontally as if thrown by some impossible force. The islander's slender sword spun through the shadows with him to clatter among the rocks along the near edge of the river as the man landed with a heavy grunt in the needles and fallen leaves on the far side. Chagua rolled to a stop against a line of stones, groaning and rocking back and forth, holding his ribs, his white teeth flashing in a pained grimace.

Tsegan, standing near the fallen islander, knelt, muttering something Maiara couldn't hear, and then eased himself upright again, hands to either side, and moved toward the shadows.

"No!" She reached out as if she could stop him. "What are you doing?"

Tsegan never turned to her, but patted the air behind him with one gentle hand. "No fear. All ... will ... be ... well ..."

His last words were low and came with a strange, slow pace, as if he was readying himself for some great exertion.

She never could have explained what she felt next, because she had never felt anything like it before. Even back in the Fallen Oak, when Tsegan had done ... whatever he had done to the fire, she had not felt this.

It was as if she could hear a heavy, whispering roar that she knew was not there. She felt the air around her warming, even though she could still feel the freezing cold of winter on the skin of her face. She felt, for just a moment, as if the entire forest had faded back and she was somehow standing in some vast flat space, with nothing but the roaring of a burning wind all around.

A flash of her haunting dreams erupted in her mind, then faded away. Below, it looked as if Tsegan was pushing on something with his arms, although there was nothing there. His shoulders shook with the effort, his arms rigid before him, his fingers splayed.

The shadows before the old man churned as if it was some thick, substantial mist or fog. The darkness seemed to take on the texture of something rough and shifting, like sand or dust. The moist mountain air around her seemed suddenly dry and harsh. Again, she thought of her dreams.

From the deep blackness beneath the trees came a scream of such indescribable pain that she crouched down, her hands over her ears.

The trees thrashed, several crashing down around the old man. The scream went on and on and on, rising in pitch until she could only crouch there, her eyes clenched shut, fists thrust against her ears, and pray that it all would end.

When it did, abruptly and without warning, the shock was almost as deep as when it had first begun. She opened her eyes in time to see Tsegan stumble back, reaching out one hand to grasp a tree for support. Before him, the forest was dark and still.

Maiara moved to return down the slope but stopped when she saw Chagua rise with a sharp grunt of pain, moving quickly to the old man's side. As she watched, Tsegan allowed the islander to ease his way across the stream, both of them seeming to support the other, moving slowly back up to camp.

"What was that? What happened?" She dropped down beside Tsegan as the old man settled by the fire, almost screaming at him as she clutched at his sleeve. "What did you do?"

Tsegan shook his head, reaching back for a small skin of water and gulping deeply.

Maiara stood and turned to Chagua, who was standing at the edge of camp, holding his ribs gingerly, looking down into the silent shadows. She took his shoulder without thinking of it, and fell back a step as he spun on her.

"What was it? Is it coming back?" She held her hands up in a calming gesture.

He shook his head and looked back down. "I don't know."

Again, his accent made the words hard to understand, although they flowed with a pleasant, almost singsong lilt.

He pointed. "I need my sword." He headed back down, at a slow, careful pace, before she could respond.

At the bottom, he crouched with another grunt of pain to pick up the blade, then rose, his eyes fixed on the dark forest before him. He glanced back at her, and then eased his way between the thick trunks, disappearing into the shadows.

"What are you doing?" She screamed, but then winced at the sound of her own voice, and repeated, much more softly, "What are you doing?"

Chagua emerged moments later carrying something that gleamed in the reflected light of their fire. It was the size of a large pumpkin, and something about it unsettled her even before he brought it back into their camp. He laid it wordlessly beside Tsegan near the fire and took a step back. Maiara could not tell if the strange look on his face was respect or fear.

It was a massive skull, the basic shape and details unmistakable. There were eye holes, and countless jagged yellowed teeth cut the darkness within into sharp triangles. There were many gaps where teeth were missing.

There was no lower jaw. The flesh had been completely flensed away. It shone in the firelight as if it had been polished. In fact, it was pitted and worn, like a relic that had lain in the woods for a hundred fierce winters, not the remains of a beast that had been threatening them only moments before. It was deformed as if by some horrible blast, so that the original shape of the thing was almost impossible to discern.

"Is it a bear?" She asked in a whisper, her eyes flickering to the old man and then back to the skull. "What is it?"

Chagua shrugged, shaking his head. "I do not know. It could be a bear."

Or it could be a troll, or a skinwalker, or a giant striding out of the sagas to terrorize her dreams for the rest of her life.

"It doesn't matter what it is." Tsegan dismissed the thing with a wave of one tired hand. "It is no longer a threat. I need sleep."

He did not look up as he rolled over, rose with a grunt, and disappeared into his tent without another word.

She looked at Chagua, burning with a thousand questions. "What ...? How ... ? I ..."

He shrugged, wincing, and moved around to settle beside the fire with a sigh. He unsheathed his sword and began to inspect it, she assumed, for any possible damage.

She sat, staring at the malformed skull, for longer than she could have said.

Chapter 6

Geir stared morosely into the flames, his hands wrapped around what the place billed as a mug of warm, mulled cider. It tasted more like urine and looked like dishwater, but it was warm, and that had to be worth something this deep into the spirits-forsaken mountains. Outside, through cloudy, leaded glass nearly opaque with frost, snow swirled in a thick, fluid stream that obscured what little vision the windows might have allowed.

The air within the Bjornstad trading post was thick with smoke and a dizzying array of smells that would have been enough to drive a dog back out into the cold. This far south, civilization was hard to come by. The trappers, woodsmen, hunters, and their thralls who frequented a place like Bjornstad, lost amidst the clouds atop the White Mountains, were long on hair and foul looks, short on hygiene, fashion, and common decency.

Still, he found himself in places like this far more than he could have desired. And it wasn't as if he didn't fit in, whether that fact made him proud or not.

He had followed the little girl's wagon across the plains, weaving past the larger towns and villages, leaping from crossroads to crossroads. He knew from his conversations in the tavern that she had left traveling with two men, a large fellow who remained bundled up whenever he was around strangers, and an old man who looked more oyathey than fyrdar. That was intriguing, but the king's Shadow had only grown more and more frustrated with the entire affair as it dragged, and now he only wanted to track the girl down so he could finish the job and get back to Connat.

He hated the mountains.

But that was it, and he knew it. He wanted to spit, but refused, knowing that no one nearby would condemn him for it. The animals.

He had lost his quarry on the greenway. He hadn't even seen any of the small oyathey parties he was normally tracking through this region. With winter closing things down south of the foothills, no one was moving around in the mountains but the usual folk, following the game trails, logging tracks, and secret paths they had been following for generations.

All of which led back to Bjornstad, or places like it. There were a few other posts higher up. If he wanted to really do a thorough job he could have gone straight up to Gnaefa, the highest post, and looked down on all the earth.

Hells, from up there he probably could have spotted the damned wagon himself.

If he didn't freeze to death first.

Drostin would most likely be cross with him for stopping in Bjornstad, but when he was so far from the capital, he admitted to himself that he didn't much care what the Lord of the king's Shadows might think. He would find the girl eventually, he knew, and then he would demand an assignment down on the plains. He needed time to thaw before king and kingdom sent him back up to freeze his tender bits off in the name of duty once again.

He took another sip and was immediately reminded that the mug served best to warm his hands.

He coughed to hide his reaction to the cider and kicked his boots a little closer to the fire. He liked them to be just on this side of burning when the wind outside was rattling the heavy storm shutters and seemed to find every chink between the rough-hewn logs of the walls.

He looked into the far corner where the musty old head of an ancient black bear gaped out over the assembly with milky glass eyes. It was a terrible example of taxidermy, which was a damned shame, really, as the specimen itself had probably been ferocious in life.

A lot like him, he thought, and straightened out the braids of his beard over his broad chest.

He felt his thoughts turning dark and wished there was something stronger than this cat-piss to be had. He was not ashamed of the work he did for the king. The Shadow agents of Lord Drostin performed essential tasks; the king himself knew of his work. He had sent his thanks through clandestine channels often enough that Geir had no doubt of that.

Somewhere behind him, a table of rough men and women were discussing a group of mountain mercenaries that seemed to have disappeared. He shifted in his seat, eager for any sort of distraction, but there were no real details to be had. Four men and a woman, apparently, had gone out on the usual routes, looking to maybe pick off a few lone mountain folk before winter truly locked things down. Mercenaries did that on occasion, but they were usually quiet about it when they were taking shelter in a trading post.

These folks seemed nervous enough that they weren't being nearly as discrete as usual.

Often, when bandits were caught by the mountain folk, they were either paraded back to a trading post for public execution or they were killed on the road, and trophies brought back and displayed as a warning to others. It didn't pay to prey on the men and women who made the mountains their home, and the occasional reminder was seen as a good thing by those who shared the high places.

But this party seemed to have disappeared without a trace.

For five armed bandits to vanish like that was certainly an oddity. Surely this could not have anything to do with his prey?

He hoped not. He couldn't secure many more fighters with the coin he carried with him, and a king's bill of debt didn't carry too much weight this high up. If the cart driver and the old man had been able to kill five mountain thugs, he might need more swords than he could currently afford.

He sighed with a vague grin. It couldn't have been them. Still, it gave him something to think about. The current weather had lasted for days, and he could feel himself starting to lose his grip. He needed to get back out onto the trail before this stinking little rat trap drove him insane.

Sitting in this dung-pit for days on end while the winter winds howled across the poorly-glazed windows, and the faces around him, also trapped in the low, foul-smelling hovel ... it was always times like this that his mind turned to those darkest corners of his memories, and he knew all too well what would happen if he indulged himself in such rough and ready surroundings.

He kicked the chair of the man beside him and leaned forward. "Vidhar, set up the board."

He pushed the king's table game board toward the other man, the small pieces rattling within the tiny wooden walls. The rest of the men and women sitting at the table groaned dramatically, many moving away to other tables in search of less cerebral entertainment. Geir let them go. The only thing worse than having a game of king's table with a second-rate novice was having a game of king's table with a second-rate novice while a crowd of disinterested muscle watched, making inane comments.

Vidhar snorted awake, jerking upright and looking back at Geir owlishly before leaning forward to sort the pieces into their appropriate squares. There was plenty of room at the table now that the others had moved away.

"I'll take defender, give you a fighting chance." Geir nearly took another sip of his cooling cider but caught himself in time. He placed the mug on the table, off to the side where it would not get in the way of the game.

King's table was a game popular throughout the fyrdar realms. Tradition said they had brought it with them across the seas when they had first invaded Kun Makha. Although it was popular with all manner of men and women, highborn and low, and most of the folks stranded in Bjornstad with him would know the rules well enough, Geir knew the chances of him getting a decent game this far out into the wilds were slim.

Vidhar was one of that singular class of fighter that haunted posts like Bjornstad and Gnaefa, nursing their dwindling purses until a job, any job, came along. They would lug furs down from the high places, guard caravans, make and break camps for the higher class of trader who would rather not do the scut work themselves. In short, they were desperate mercenaries with almost no qualms against any job you might name. The crew that had abandoned their table moments ago were all the same. He had secured their services for his hunt with a few drinks, a coin or two, and promises of more once the job was done. They wouldn't be worth much in a standup fight, but he didn't expect a young girl with a drover and an old man for company to give them too much trouble.

Geir always found it helpful, as soon as he arrived in a place like Bjornstad, with a task like this before him, to put together such a crew against any possible needs he mind find along the way. There were too many smaller trails and paths, including several wide enough for a cart, for him to track down every one on his own. Among his current team were several local trappers who had spent their lives in the mountains. They knew every hidden valley, warm spring, and tumbled down ruin that could shelter his quarry.

It might take all winter, but he would find them.

As Vidhar finished putting the pieces in place, a shout behind them rose up from a crowd of furriers in a far corner. Geir looked over, trying to gauge what was happening and if it was going to impact his afternoon. He would be the first to admit that a good brawl could be just as diverting as a middling game of king's table.

A woman had stood up, swaying slightly, to glare down at one of her companions with a look of outraged disbelief. Geir settled in, turning his chair so he could watch, while making no move to get any closer. The situation was a familiar one, and not something an outsider would be wise to enter.

Being a woman on the fringes of civilization came with a slew of added problems that most men seldom had to confront. One of those, perhaps the most annoying to Geir's mind, was the unwanted attention of their, usually male, compatriots. You had to be a tough person to make a go at living this far from the towns and villages, and most of these folks developed a sense of self-preservation and pride early on or they didn't make it.

The woman's reddish hair was as wild as her eyes as she continued to shout into the man's face. Geir's view of the man, facing away from him, was mostly blocked by a bushy beard, but he didn't seem to be overly concerned about the accusations, turning to another furrier with a shrug.

Until the woman punched him in the side of the head, a stoneware mug still in her fist.

The furrier went over onto the floor, limp as a corpse, and the other men at the table surged to their feet. Soon the patrons around nearby tables were rising also. Fists were flying, men and women were being pushed and kicked and knocked cold with mugs whose contents made them far better weapons than drinking vessels, and as Geir watched, the violence began to tumble toward his table.

He raised a single eyebrow.

Under normal circumstances, he would be in no danger in a place like Bjornstad. He had spent too much time in the mountains, had left too many bodies to the bears, to be taken lightly. But this had turned into a full-out brawl. There were no allies, no friends. It was a bloody free-for-all as often happened in the middle of a blizzard in places like this.

For a moment, Geir entertained the idea of joining in. It would keep him warm, wouldn't leave a nasty aftertaste, and would be worth an afternoon's diversion between the actual fighting, the winding down, and the laughter-filled retellings afterward. He was warmed to see that his own hired blades were faring well in the fighting.

But no. He had his heart set on king's table, so king's table it would be.

A man came sprawling out of the melee, reeling from a blow to the head and flailing around with balled fists, spinning violently when Geir brought him up short.

"The fight's over that way, friend." He forced a smile and nodded toward the rowdy fracas.

The man stared at him for a moment, then cocked one fist back to strike.

Geir's smile never wavered as he snapped a quick punch into the man's nose. The wild eyes crossed, surprised, and then the belligerent drunk started to topple forward. Geir caught him by the fur collar, steering his slow fall away from the table and its game board, and then settled back down in his seat as the man thumped to the dirty floor.

He watched as Vidhar finished preparing the board, eyeing the fallen man and the chaos beyond. With the fight winding down, they leaned into the game, Geir knowing that the mercenary wouldn't be offering much of a challenge.

King's table was a game of strategy and planning. One player took the role of the king, whose fortress and defenders were represented on the grid of the board with markings and small stones. His goal was to escape off any board edge. The attacker was trying to kill the king, his encampments and troops represented by similar markings and different colored stones. It was generally accepted that the defender had the harder task, with a fixed position, a vulnerable central piece, and roughly half the forces of the attacker.

But aside from the fact that Vidhar was only a mediocre player at best, Geir liked to take the role of defender. It reminded him of the duties that moved him in his real life. And it reminded him how difficult guarding a king was, and what kind of odds were always going to be stacked against him.

Vidhar opened, as he almost always did, by sliding one of his attackers all the way from the edge of the board to a space adjacent to one of the defenders. There was little finesse about Vidhar's play, despite the fact that he had been the most gifted gamesman Geir had found in Bjornstad. The attacker's role in the game was to capture the king, that was true enough. And the only way to do that was to eliminate the defenders by catching them between a pair of attacking pieces. The problem, as was always the case with such straightforward thinkers, was that as long as Vidhar came directly at the center, he was telegraphing his every move, and so made it possible for Geir, with fewer pieces, to outmaneuver him long enough for an opening to form and the king to escape.

As the inevitable conclusion faltered toward them, and the last combatants behind them tumbled to the ground, Geir allowed his mind to wander. Slowly, as he watched the situation on the board develop, the pieces shifted in his perception. He ceased seeing the large king piece as King Einar. In his mind, it became a young girl with long black hair and shining, crystalline eyes. The attackers ceased to be traitorous Vestan soldiers, and instead became sad little duplicates of himself, moving clumsily through the mountains in a fruitless search.

And as he slid his king off the table to the accompaniment of Vidhar's muttered curses and the cruel snickers of his returning cutthroats, he thought of a wagon disappearing into the mountain mists.

He muttered a curse himself.

Without a word he spun the board around and began to replace the pieces.

"Chief? You want another game?" Vidhar looked confused. Geir usually lacked the patience for a second game against the hired blade; especially after a game that had ended so quickly.

"Yes." Geir didn't look up from preparing the board. "You'll be defending this time."

It wasn't the best test of his theory, but it was better than just sullenly brooding over it as he nursed another mug of swill. The fighting was all done, those able to stand collapsing into seats, ordering another round of cat's piss. Already, the tales were starting, laughter taking the place of the shouting and screaming of a moment ago.

When the board was prepared, he pushed it toward the middle of the table and Vidhar leaned in to survey his position. The defender's situation was always the same, but a player of Vidhar's questionable ability never seemed to realize that.

Geir reached out and placed a single finger on one of his pieces. Without lifting it at all, he pushed it across the board. It bumped slightly as it slid over each carved grid line. He left it, against the far edge, nowhere near the beleaguered king's position, and thus not threatening any of Vidhar's defenders.

The mercenary looked up at him in confusion, then down at the board again. As he puzzled his way through Geir's opening gambit, the Shadow rested back against his chair and stared down at the small stone king and his array of defenders. The key, he thought, if he was right, was to watch all the pieces, rather than merely try to break through to get to the king.

Vidhar slid one of his pieces into a new position and Geir nodded.

Several turns later, Geir had still not made a move on the central position, merely shifting his attackers around the edges of the board. Each time he moved a piece away from one area, he reinforced that area with his next move. Vidhar, seeing no opening, was forced to decide upon his own avenue of escape, just as Geir had intended.

And as the defenders shifted, Geir began to see the board as a shifting plane of darkness and light. As the defenders moved toward a new area, it would grow brighter in his mind, while the area left behind would darken.

He smiled as he watched Vidhar's strategy, for what it was worth, unfold.

By watching the board, Geir saw entire areas that were being ignored by his opponent's developing strategy, and thus he could afford to ignore those as well. There was no way he could know where the king was going to try to break out; there was no way he was going to be able to tell where the king might be, several moves from now.

But, by watching all of the pieces, he could tell where the king wasn't going to be. And, with superior numbers, it was simple to shift his pieces to bring an overwhelming advantage to bear against those few remaining places Vidhar's moves had limited him to.

When the mercenary finally made his move, the game was over in a matter of moments. Defenders surged into what appeared to be an open area to make an avenue for the king, and Geir's attackers, striking at a vulnerable flank left open by the shifting pieces, broke through with ease and captured the king.

Vidhar sat back muttering again and tossed off the contents of his cup. Geir smiled, knowing the man had no idea why he had lost. To the untrained cutthroat, every game seemed different. He didn't remember patterns or strategies from one session to the next. The only thing that stayed the same was the outcome, and so to Vidhar, this was just another loss to the dour man in black who was paying him to sit on his ass in the warm trading post.

But it had worked out exactly as Geir had expected. By watching the pieces, he had figured out where Vidhar had to be.

Through patience and observation, he had seen exactly where the mercenary was going to move himself, and so he was ready.

Geir's smile widened. He wasn't going to head out into the mountains tomorrow after all.

The mountains might be nearly devoid of human settlement, but there was a community up here, even so. The few people who carved a living from the forests and glaciers were scattered up and down the White Mountains, and not the kinds of folks who generally relished companionship.

But as scattered as they were, they did form a community. They moved through the valleys even in deepest winter, and they saw everything that occurred. Someone would see something, and word would spread from post to post, and eventually it would reach Bjornstad, the largest and lowest trading post in the mountains. And when that happened, Geir would head out, with Vidhar and the others, and he would make quick work of the girl.

A nagging voice in his mind reminded him of the years he had spent in the mountains scouring the valleys and peaks for the oyathey wanderers plaguing the high places of his king's domain. He had dashed back and forth in all seasons, never closer to finding the truth of that particular mystery.

But still. This was one girl, young and inexperienced, with a large wagon full of supplies. She had no woodcraft, no way to fade into the trees without a trace. How hard could it be to find her?

He had Vidhar put the pieces back within the raised board and set the game aside. He would wait for word, wait for the situation to develop as he collected information about abandoned fortresses and empty valleys, narrowing his scope. Then he would take out his merry little band of cutthroats and see the job done.

But as he sat, trying to relax with a cup of water the barkeep had grudgingly boiled, his mind kept going back to king's table, and the defense of the king. His theory had worked quite well against a clumsy oaf like Vidhar, and he believed it would work well even against a more advanced opponent, like this mysterious old man. But he couldn't help but feel that there was an even deeper concept at play, scratching at the back of his mind, demanding to be heard.

He stared at the stacked board from beneath heavy brows, knowing the game had some further secret to tell him.

Chapter 7

Maiara had drifted into a hazy sense of half-sleep, bundled in the warm blankets and furs, lulled into oblivion by the steady rumble of the wagon wheels on the rutted road. The track looked as pitted and uneven as any of the others they had traveled down since leaving the greenway, but for some reason, the ride was much smoother. It was almost as if the illusion of a rough, eroded track had been laid over a much smoother surface, to hide it from prying eyes.

But she shied away from that thought. Ever since that night by the stream, she had looked at the old man differently. She was still bothered by the dry, distant feeling of power she had felt surge through the forest as he killed ... whatever it was that had threatened them. None of the tales of magic she had ever heard had spoken of such raw, destructive power. Even in the fairy stories from her book, magic was something from the natural world; a gentle power emanating from water, wind, fire, and the natural strength of the forests and the mountains. What she had felt in the clearing had felt alien and intrusive.

She was starting to fear that magic might be real after all. And it might be nothing like the benign forces from her stories. And yet, she couldn't shake the sense that the power Tsegan wielded didn't even fit the admittedly childish concepts she had encountered in her old book. Could he weave an illusion over a long, open road?

The wagon gave a bump that jolted her upright, and she looked around at their new surroundings. They had come up over the lip of a small valley, and as she turned to look over Chagua's shoulder, she couldn't help but gasp.

It was an old fyrdar border fort, sure enough. The ancient stones had blended into the background colors and textures of the valley over the centuries; moss, grass, and trees half-obscuring its tumbled down lines as the structure was slowly drawn back into the earth. It clung to the sides of a tall hill in the middle of the valley, a shallow rivulet curving around from behind, hugging its base, and then meandering off into the forest beyond.

She noticed that, although snow was piling up on the slopes rising above them, somehow, the valley was completely clear. Steam seemed to curl up from behind the hill, and she wondered if there were hot springs there, keeping the valley warmer than the surrounding area.

A single tower rose out of the huddled mass of stone by the hill. It was slightly canted to one side as if a drunk man was doing his honest best to stand. And she could see, as she shielded her eyes against the harsh winter sun, that there was what looked like new stonework around the top of the tower, recreating a wider chamber that must have collapsed down into the valley long ago.

It reminded her of nothing so much as a picture out of her little book.

And yet, although the wrecked fortress looked ancient and worn down by time and weather, there was a sense of something even older crouching over the valley. She had a brief thought that something was laid over the vision of the toppled stonework and straight, majestic trees; an awareness, or a power, that was almost older than the mountains rising all around them.

With a jerk, the wagon lurched up and over the crest of the valley's edge and started a slow, shaky descent. Chagua rode the break all the way down as the big draft horses, skittish with such a heavy weight behind them, shied back against the slope of the hill.

Beside them, Tsegan gave a warm, tired smile and urged his own horse onward, taking the hill at an odd, sideways gait that kept his mount steady despite the incline. There was a structure of recent construction at the base of the hill, built from the remnants of the old fortress. Tsegan pulled up beside that and leapt down, wrapping the reins once around a stone post and then, craning his neck up at the tall tower, moved around the ruin.

The bulk of the old wall was roughly one story. It was hard to tell, as it had clearly been taller, once. The basic shape of the keep could be guessed at, but what was left of the original walls was mostly covered by tumbled stones from higher up. Windows could be seen through the wreckage, the darkness of the forest beyond glaring out at them blindly.

As they approached the old fort, a bitter chill settled into her chest at the thought of spending the winter huddled in this slumped-down wreck. Judging from the jagged tops of the wreck, there wouldn't be much of a roof. The new, low structure was clearly solid, but as she came closer she realized it was a stable, with only room for five or six horses, and they had three. Was she going to be sharing a horse stall all winter?

The fairy tale that had been in the back of her mind since leaving the Fallen Oak had been battered and bruised in the time between, but this wreck was definitely the worst blow of all.

Tsegan eased his mount into the low stable, where it moved directly into a well-appointed stall of its own, and he disappeared into the shadows at the back. The wagon had pulled up in front, and she looked around to see what Chagua was going to do. The big man leapt off the drover's seat, wincing only slightly, and immediately moved to the back of the wagon. He pulled one of the crates of supplies forward and hefted it with a grunt of effort. He turned to make his slow way into the stable. She jumped down to follow him and found that there was a wide storage area in the back, burrowed into the hill. The ceiling was low, and as Chagua bent down to drop his crate and push it into the recess with one booted foot, she could easily see there wouldn't be any room for them to sleep there once the rest of the wagon had been unloaded.

It was all too much.

"Where are we going to sleep?" She tried to keep her tone light, despite what she was afraid might just be rising hysteria.

He gave her a look that seemed not entirely unsympathetic, but then moved back to the wagon to grab the next bundle.

"I mean it, Chagua, where are we going to sleep? Are we staying in the tower?"

That made the most sense. It had been finished at some point and probably had enough room for the three of them. In fact, as she thought about it, she could feel herself relax a little. That had to be it. She had been overwhelmed by the wreckage, and the hopeless, tumbled-down state of the place, but the tower was probably plenty big enough for the three of them.

Chagua looked at her, shook his head, and turned back toward the stable with a heavy roll of cloth.

"What?" She could definitely detect hysteria in her voice, and she didn't care. "What's the tower for, then?"

Already she could see lights gleaming from the windows in the top chamber. Chagua looked up, pointed to the windows, and then ducked into the stable.

She stood there under the cold winter sky for a moment, staring up at the looming tower, and then rushed in behind the big islander. "Wait! So ... where are we going to be staying?" She whirled amidst the stalls. "Here? With the horses?"

He emerged from the shadows and looked around at the stalls. Five of them had troughs filled with water and a stand of fresh hay, with blankets hanging from hooks on the side of each. Chagua smiled, but shook his head.

She didn't try to hide the relief. It would have been a terrible blow, to have given up her private attic room at the guesthouse for a frozen stable stall. But still, as she looked around again, she didn't see better, either.

"So, where?" She demanded, standing before him as he tried to move around her, back out to the wagon.

Chagua glanced at the wagon, then at the sky, where the light was taking on a distinctive afternoon slant. This high up in the mountains, evening would come swiftly, she knew. Then he shrugged, sighed, and turned back toward the darkness, gesturing for her to follow him.

They went back to the storage area, but then Chagua turned down into the shadows off to the left. It was nearly pitch black beneath the eaves, but he moved with a surety that made her wonder if he could see in the dark. There were all sorts of strange stories about the northern islanders; although seeing in the dark wasn't one she remembered.

She hesitated, but then followed quickly as his broad back disappeared into the gloom.

At the end of a small passage, a stairway led down into deeper darkness. Chagua waited for her at the top and then moved on down. After a moment's hesitation, and a glance back at the gloomy light of the stable, she hurried after.

At the bottom, she was surprised to find a small amount of light filtering in through cracks high up along one wall. They were in a cellar, which sprang into focus when Chagua lit a small lantern that had been set on a table near the doorway at the bottom of the stairs. Obviously, this room had been cleared out some time ago. There were supplies piled along the wall opposite the cracks, and stacks of blankets and furs. A door led into total blackness, unrelieved by the islander's lamp.

But what caught her attention as she scanned the cellar chamber was a set of shelves in a back corner, as far from the cracks as possible, and near the dark doorway.

They were almost completely filled with books.

She felt her jaw drop as she moved toward the shelves, reaching out to touch the spines without pulling them down. She read title after title after title. Nearly all of them appeared to be about civics, leadership, and history. She turned, her mind stuttering with awe, to stare at Chagua, who had crossed the chamber with her. His dark gaze locked on the shelves, staring hungrily at the various titles.

"Are these for Tsegan?" She asked in a quiet voice. She had never seen so many books in one place before. This was amazing. There seemed to be hundreds of books here. And not one of them was about children's stories.

Chagua shook his head, not looking away from the shelves.

"Well, who are they for, then?" She reached out and touched one, half expecting the islander to slap her hand away. But instead he looked at her, and then his hand slowly rose up to point to her chest. There was a look in his face that she found hard to decipher. For a moment, looking into his face, it didn't register that he was pointing at her.

Then she nearly fell over.

"Me?"

He shrugged and turned away, nodding.

She shook her head. "But that makes no sense. Why would anyone want to give me a stack of books like this?" She had worked for everything she had ever gotten in her life, except for those two ratty books. Books cost a fortune, and the number of books she saw before would have been a thane's ransom. She doubted there were this many books in Einar's library in the Bhorg.

Chagua looked at her again, his dark face blank, and then turned to place the lantern on a short stand at the end of the shelves. He straightened, gestured over to the stairs, and moved away.

"Wait!" She raised a hand as if she was going to grab his shoulder, but then stopped in mid gesture, letting her hand fall. She looked around at the cleared chamber. Aside from the books, the stacks of supplies along one wall, the two small tables, and a small collection of chairs in another corner, the room was empty.

He stopped at the doorway and turned, giving her a questioning look.

"Is this where we're going to sleep? Both of us in this chamber?"

The floors were stone. They looked to have been swept, but it was freezing. There was no place for a fire, and nothing resembling beds.

He looked around for a moment and shook his head. His hand came up again to gesture toward the far doorway.

She looked, then looked back at him. "Through there? Are there more rooms back that way? Are those the sleeping chambers?"

He sighed, his shoulders slumping slightly, and bowed his head. When he looked back up at her, she didn't know if he was smiling slightly from some sense of amusement, or grimacing at her out of frustration and annoyance.

"This is the only chamber prepared at the moment." The words alone were a shock. Again, she found his accent, although sometimes hard to interpret, to be soothing in its sing-song cadences. "We will need to unload the wagon, and then finish preparing this chamber. I will need to build a fire pit, using some of the cracks in the walls for ventilation, and stop up the others so that the heat will not escape." He gestured back at the dark door. "There are chambers beyond that we will, eventually, be able to make our own."

He looked at her again, eyebrow raised as if daring her to ask another question, and then turned back to the stairs.

"Wait!" She had never been one to shy from a challenge. "Is Tsegan staying up in the tower? Is it finished up there?"

Again, Chagua sighed. "Master Aqisiaq's chambers are in the tower, yes. I have not been inside since I completed the construction, so I do not know to what extent he has furnished them himself."

He turned before she could ask another question and took the dark stairs two at a time, disappearing up into the gloom.

Maiara stood at the bottom of the stairs for a few silent moments, turning back to look at the cold, dank chamber. This was not what she had had in mind when she left the Fallen Oak. Her gaze slid to the bookshelves, and she sighed. She had never had anything more exciting to read beyond the sad, tattered examples at the guesthouse.

She rushed back up the dark stairway after the islander.

He was heaving a stack of grain sacks onto one shoulder, sweat starting out on his broad, dark brow, and rolled his eyes when she came rushing out of the stables.

"I don't understand. Why are we here? What are we supposed to be doing? We don't even have rooms yet?"

Chagua glanced up at the tower looming above them. A thin line of smoke was rising from a metal chimney in the shingled, conical roof. Somehow, the smoke was coming out in thin streamers rather than a thick column, as she would have expected on such a windless day.

The islander looked back down at her, jounced his heavy load into a more comfortable position, and moved around her toward the storage area. "Miss, I do not know why you are here. My place is not to ask questions, but to perform whatever tasks are laid before me."

With a grunt, Chagua dumped the sacks onto the earthen floor and stood up, straightening his back with a grimace. "Since arriving in Astrigir, I have built the stables, rebuilt the tower, and cleared out the cellar. I have no doubt, when time serves, I shall prepare the lower chambers as well. Now, please, can I finish unloading the cart?"

She let him pass and stood uncertainly in the middle of the stable, looking at the stalls. Six stalls. Five of them prepared for horses. Tsegan's mount was already in one, munching contentedly away at the hay placed there. The pair of horses that had drawn their cart up into the mountains would take up two more...

Maiara turned back to the entrance as Chagua came in with another sack. "There are more people coming?"

He ducked past her without answering, moving straight to the pile he was building. This time, when he straightened, his hands pressed to the small of his back, he gave her a flat, empty look. He turned, taking in the furnished stalls, and shrugged. "Master Aqisiaq bid me prepare five of the stalls. Five stalls are prepared."

He moved past her without another word. It was easy to forget, watching the man work, that only a few days before he had been thrown violently into a tree. She was impressed, watching him ease yet another heavy burden onto his shoulder. She had carried such sacks back at the guesthouse, and knew exactly how heavy they were. She could barely lift one. Vali prided himself on his strength, but never attempted to carry more than one, claiming that he had no need to impress anyone. Kustaa would carry two sometimes, although by the time he got them to where they were going, he was pale and shaking. She had noticed, too, that he only tried that trick when he knew she was about.

The thought of Kustaa made her pause, and her eyes stung. She had never been gone from the Fallen Oak for more than a day before this ridiculous journey. Now she had been gone for weeks, and winter was only just beginning. She missed it all, but she was a little surprised to find that she missed Kustaa the most.

The boy was always frustrating, never letting her do her own work, always getting in the way, trying to help. But he had always been there. Always a friendly face, a smile, even when Vali and Turid were at their worst. And he was gone now, with all the rest.

She sighed. This entire adventure still confused her, but she would be damned if she was going to sit around and let things happen to her without at least trying to take part.

As Chagua marched past into the stable once again, she made way for him, following his progress. She had thought he was carrying two sacks, but she saw that, this time around, anyway, he actually had four swaying above him.

He was always bundled up, the cold always bothering him more that she thought it should. She found herself wondering what he must look like beneath the layers of wool.

What was he here for? Drover, manual laborer, nursemaid? The islanders were famous for their scholars, philosophers, and traders. The islands were several weeks journey north by the fastest ships; few islanders made the trek south, beyond traders and an occasional curious scholar.

There was no denying Chagua's fascination with the books, both in the wagon and on the shelves in the basement chamber.

But that sword of his was wicked; and he kept it terribly sharp. He had rushed in to face the bear-thing in the forest without hesitation and seemed to have escaped being thrown through the forest without serious injury. And now, carrying such prodigious weight on his shoulder ... the man had to be incredibly strong.

She shook her head. Just one more small mystery among so many hardly seemed to matter, she thought.

"Can I help?" She fell into step beside him as he returned to the wagon.

Chagua looked sideways at her, and she felt her chin rise all on its own. "I can lift things. I'm not helpless."

He smiled, shrugged, and then pointed at one of the sacks. She felt her shoulders slump as she realized there were still several more. She looked at him, sighed, and then maneuvered one off the wagon bed and onto her shoulder. She refused to grunt and stood carefully, denying her body's demands that she collapse beneath the weight, and forced herself to walk at a calm, sedate pace toward the stable.

She almost made it before she felt her back giving out and had to bow under the weight, stumbling forward. She managed to dump the sack with a dusty thud near the others but had lost all hope of keeping her balance in the process, tumbling onto her shoulder in the dirt beside the pile.

She gave the smiling but silent Chagua a flat look, and then moved back to the wagon for something maybe a little lighter.

*****

Maiara watched as Chagua worked, constructing the hearth and chimney for their fire pit. Tsegan had not come down from his tower, and the islander had lapsed into his accustomed silence. She was bundled up in several layers of fur and wool, staring at the big man as he built a stone flue that would lead the smoke up to various cracks in the foundation that he had left open when he covered the rest with his first batch of mortar.

It was a strange affair, twisting and convoluted, compared to the hearth he had already laid down. Despite that, they were going to have a very nice fireplace, if they didn't freeze to death before he was finished.

When she realized what he was doing, she asked why he wasn't simply leading the smoke up to a single, larger crack and letting it vent there. She got another of the islander's looks, and then a brief lecture concerning 'Master Tsegan's' instructions that smoke from their fires be dispersed as much as possible.

So, they were hiding. She wasn't sure who they were hiding from, but she had figured that much out, at least. Tsegan, whether improbable, all-powerful wizard or eccentric old man with too much gold and time on his hands, would not have retreated up into the mountains if he was eager for neighbors to stop by.

Although the twisting, elaborate flue seemed a bit much, if she was going to be honest.

Maiara had placed the deformed skull from their encounter on one of the small tables. None of them had seemed to know what to do with it. She thought perhaps they could put it up on a wall when Chagua was done with the fireplace. Unless the islander thought Tsegan would want the skull for his own, up in the tower?

She took a lantern into the back rooms and decided, after peeking into the first one, that she would let Chagua take the lead on preparing them. The one she looked into was half-filled with debris, the ceiling shattered by the collapse of the keep above. There were broken splinters of ancient, rotten wood scattered about with the tumbled stones, probably what was left of the original furniture.

The room was small, and when she backed out into the cluttered passageway beyond, she saw rusty iron bars over the small window situated high up on the heavy door.

She quickly grew bored of the cramped hallway and moved back out, through the main chamber, and back up the stairs. It was dark outside, and Chagua offered to light her a small fire and set up a tent in the shelter of the ruins. But she didn't want him to lose time on his work getting the underground chambers ready, and declined. She was quickly entertaining second thoughts as the night's chill continued to settle into the valley.

She wandered around the stable and the base of the tower, looking up to see warm light spilling out from several of the windows high overhead. She wasn't entirely happy about Tsegan keeping the tower to himself, warm and snug while they were freezing in the dark below, but it wasn't as if the old man seemed to care too much about what she thought. She contemplated going up into the tower to confront him, but a quick look around the stables where he had disappeared when they first arrived showed no sign of any doorway. And for some reason, she didn't want Chagua to find her looking.

She walked outside, around the tower and up the back side of the little hill to where the main keep had once stood. She wandered through rooms whose tumble-down walls barely reached her waist; in the midst of the wreckage she found the kitchen, with ovens recently repaired, nearly hidden beneath sprawling undergrowth and a pile of leaves, pine needles, and other detritus.

Other than the islander's recent work, there was no sign that anyone but else had been here in centuries.

And yet she still felt some presence in the valley around her, as if someone, or some thing, was watching her from the shadows. Visions of the malformed skull rose in her mind again, and the looming presence seemed to grow heavier. She pulled her cloak tightly around her shoulders and went back down the hill, around the tower and into the courtyard.

Shivering, mostly from the cold, she retreated back to the main room and settled down beneath as many blankets and furs as she could find.

It was not much longer before the islander, his own hands shaking visibly, finished the chimney, placing the last stones, and settled back to light their first fire. Moments later, they were both huddled in front of it, hands stretched out to the heat, as the room warmed perceptibly around them. They both shared a smile, and as Chagua set out to prepare them a quick dinner, she stretched, watching him, and admitted to herself that, as strange as this entire adventure was, she was excited to be here, to see what might happen next.

Chapter 8

Tyr rode with his hands crossed over the reins at the crest of his saddle, his mind wandering as it usually did toward the end of a day on the trail. His wounded arm still troubled him, sending shocks of pain down his arm and around his chest if he moved the wrong way. It hurt almost as much as the confirmation that Eirik had been drinking throughout this ridiculous journey.

Their travels had taken far longer than they should have, not least because of the round-about route they had taken to avoid Connat. His master had refused to go anywhere near the capital, and so they had moved through the smaller towns along the foothills, where the roads were not nearly as well-maintained as the long meadow of the greenway.

The map the old man had given them had been very clear, and he knew they had added at least a week, if not more, to the length of their journey. It was just one of the many reasons he was looking forward to reaching their destination. His winters were usually peaceful. There was only so much trouble Eirik could get into, fumbling around a small border town while they were snowed in for a few months. Nurse-maiding him through the most arduous trek they had taken in years was growing old. And ever since they had fought with the brigands, things had only gotten worse.

He hoped that was all coming to an end soon.

The map said they were on the last leg of the journey. Wherever they were going, whatever this mysterious destination might be, they should reach it today. Normally, they would have already stopped to make camp for the night. The darkness fell quickly up in the mountains, with the horizon hemmed in on all sides by the mighty, ice-wreathed peaks. But Tyr would not let Eirik slide from his horse. Not with their final goal so close.

The warrior had finished the bottle of spirits he had loudly declared would be the only one he imbibed that day, and he had grown surly as it became obvious that the boy wasn't going to let him stop for camp. Eirik's newly established pattern was to open a new bottle as soon as he was convinced camp was properly established for the night. And the more frustrated and annoyed he was, the less rigid his definition of established became.

But now, being driven down this treacherous path in the fading twilight, with his new bottle seemingly forever out of his reach, Eirik was almost ready to chew on his reins from frustration.

The trail itself was something of a mystery. The chain of small tracks and game trails they had been following since leaving the greenway had joined this truly remarkable road a few days ago. It appeared from any distance to be a typical pitted, rutted, uneven mess. But once on it, they had found it to be extremely well-maintained and easy to follow.

The map indicated that their destination should be coming up any moment now, and each time they turned a corner or crested a rise, he found his curiosity building. It was almost enough to offset Eirik's low, monotonous complaints.

The trail rose up before them and disappeared over yet another lip. It did this every few hundred paces, it seemed, and it was getting hard to maintain his enthusiasm. But this time, as he looked up toward the rise, he saw something he had not seen before. A gentle wisp of smoke, only half seen against the burning, sunset sky, curled overhead before fading quickly into the clouds above.

The wisp was gone at once, but there was no doubt in his mind of what he had seen.

He turned quickly to his master to see if Eirik had seen it as well, but then turned back forward with an annoyed curl to his lips. Eirik wouldn't have noticed if the entire valley before them was on fire.

He felt the expectation and curiosity rise once again, stronger than before. He found himself hoping he would not be disappointed yet again; that the smoke was, in fact, smoke from someone's warm, evening fire and not just a wick of mist or low cloud, or a figment of his over-worked imagination.

As they reached the top of the rise, looking down into the valley below, all of his hopes were rewarded.

In the middle of the valley sat a squat little hill, and crouched on one flank of the hill, as if thrusting up out of a fairy story, was a teetering old tower. It was a piece of ancient history, a small fortress built in the distant past, when every action of his ancestors had been made with the terrible Utan in mind. Like most strongholds of its kind up in the mountains, it had then been abandoned centuries ago. And now it was at the center of the mystery that had consumed his life.

It had never been a large keep. The outlines of the main holdfast could still be seen scattered along the crown of the hill. The single tower might have been the central building, or it might have been a strongpoint at one corner. It was hard to tell with the utter devastation of the place. Wrapped around the base of the hill he could see foundation stones peeking out of the tumbled wreckage cascading down from above, as well as fresh stonework and timber construction that looked like it was probably a stable or some other practical work area.

As he continued to stare, Tyr saw that the top of the tower also bore the marks of recent work, both the wide crown and the shingled roof. Someone had taken a great deal of time and effort to make the tower habitable, at any rate.

There were several windows along the length of the tower facing them, and two of them, near the top, were glowing warmly. It reminded Tyr of just how cold he was, and he glanced quickly to the side. Eirik was staring as well, but his look was more one of dismay than enchantment.

Trying to see the place through his master's eyes, Tyr's smile faded. The ruin was a wonderful piece of the romantic past, but it would not be a very comfortable place to spend the winter.

He nudged Vordr down into the valley, casting a quick look over his shoulder to make sure his master was following. Eirik's face was less than enthusiastic, but he kept moving.

As they approached the structure, Tyr saw why the smoke he had seen in the sky was so elusive. There appeared to be something attached to the tower's chimney that scattered the smoke as it rose, making it much harder to see from any distance. In addition, there seemed to be several small chimneys hidden among the wreckage, with hints of wispy smoke coming up from below. So, although it looked like a total wreck, clearly there were fires beneath the hill. Maybe the place wouldn't be so uncomfortable after all.

As they came to the bottom of the slope, approaching from the side with the stable-like structure, a figure completely wrapped in leather, wool, and fur came out, moving stiffly due to the layers of bulky clothing. It held a long rake in one mittened hand and rested on it as they drew near.

The stranger's face was wreathed in the fur trim of a heavy hood, features hidden in shadow. There was no sense of threat from the figure, although it did look large. Tyr found himself wondering how much of that bulk was due to the layers of winter clothing and how much of it belonged to the man beneath.

They approached cautiously, although this was undoubtedly where the map had led them. There was no particular reason to trust the old man any further than necessary, and his master had lived the life of a fugitive for more years than he, himself, had been alive. Tyr pushed his own hood away from his head with a consciously friendly smile and scanned the courtyard area around the base of the hill as casually as possible.

Eirik was less interested in making a good first impression, apparently, as he loosened his maekre blade in its saddle sheath, pale grey eyes never wavering from the mysterious figure in the courtyard. The long, cold journey, the lack of spirits, and the hour of the day all conspired against the old warrior in a situation like this. Diplomacy was not one of his strengths at the best of times. Given all of his recent troubles, things could go sour quickly. "Greetings!" Tyr hopped off Vordr's back, coincidentally coming down between Eirik and the figure with the rake.

The figure did not move, the hooded head only shifting slightly to follow his movements, then rising once again to stare invisibly at the big mounted warrior.

"We've been on the cold road for a long time, friend." He pulled off one glove and extended his hand in a gesture of peace and friendship. In the fyrdar kingdoms, they might clasp wrists as warriors; in Kun Makha they would clasp hands. Both gestures, however, began the same.

The stranger made no move to take the hand. In fact, there was no acknowledgment of Tyr's approach at all. The figure had clearly decided that, if there was a threat here, it was Eirik.

Tyr was at a loss as to how he might calm the situation, but before he could have taken any action in either case, another figure came rushing out of the stable.

The newcomer was slight compared to the first. Still, bundled up in furs and wool, it was difficult to tell much more about them than the difference in stature.

The newly-arrived figure reached out and slid its own hood down. Even at a distance of several paces, Tyr felt his heart skip a beat.

Dark hair, with a slight burnished quality, probably from the fading lights of the distance sunset, fell down around a long, slender neck. The hair wreathed quite easily the most beautiful face he had ever seen, with strong features softened just a little by the roundness of youth. Despite the long, straight dark hair, her eyes were a flashing, bright blue that mesmerized him despite the fading light.

The girl's eyes were alight with excitement, her breath coming in quick clouds that faded around her. She stared at him for a moment, her brows coming down in a silent question, then rose to look at Eirik in his dark armor, Hestir restless beneath him, enormous sword half out of its saddle sheath as if he was expecting trouble.

"No!" Tyr jumped between his master and the girl, one hand thrust toward each of them, wincing with the pain in his shoulder. "This can't be right! We're all friends here, right? Keep the sword where it is!"

But within the warrior's hood, Tyr could see that his master was beyond reason. He backed Hestir a few paces and drew the sword. His face twisted, his sense failing him, the real world lost in the haze of abuse and delusion his sodden mind had woven around himself.

"Eirik, no!" Tyr whipped around to face his master, both hands splayed toward him as if he could push the man and the massive charger back by force of will. "Stop!"

But Eirik was lost. Whether it was the spirits from earlier in the day, their lack now, exhaustion from the travel and the cold, or if the older man had just had enough, he wasn't going to be listening to anyone else's reason now.

Tyr pulled his small belt axe from its holder, casting anxious glances back to the two strangers and then to his master. There was almost no way he could protect these two from the old saemgard if his broken mind was committed to violence.

But he was damned if he was going to back down, even against such ridiculous odds, in front of those intense blue eyes.

Something cracked behind Tyr and he turned again, trying to keep a watch on Eirik, only to see the big, hooded figure had stepped on the head of his rake, snapping off the handle. It left a long length of wooden pole, shattered at one end, and he wandered what good that was going to be against a seasoned tourney fighter with a massive maekre blade.

Maybe the stranger didn't recognize the signs, or the blade, but there was no way this was going to end well.

"Wait!" he shouted again, waving his axe between the two would-be combatants. "You can't do this!"

But it was too late.

With a savage snarl, Eirik plunged his heels into Hestir's flanks. The big horse, startled by the sudden pain, screamed and reared up, its fore hooves clawing at the air. The animal came down churning the frozen, muddy earth and was racing toward the bundled figure in the blink of an eye.

Tyr's neck snapped between his master and the stranger. Once the horse got enough momentum behind him, there would be no stopping the charge.

The stranger did not seem troubled at all, merely standing its ground, the length of wood held easily in one hand.

Tyr took one last glance at his master, judged distances and angles, and rushed toward the dark-haired girl, whose eyes were wide at the sudden violent turn. She was standing as still as a statue, maybe not even realizing what was happening.

When it happened, it was all so fast that Tyr would have been hard-pressed to describe the event even moments later.

He reached the girl, both hands trying to grab her and pull her to safety as the echoing thunder of Eirik's approach shook the air. The look on the girl's face changed without warning from confusion to annoyance and with a great deal of natural agility she deflected both of his hands, sending him flailing and off balance, into the mouth of the stable and into a pile of straw.

As he flew past the girl, he watched her calmly sidestep the charging horse, not even sparing it a glance as she shouted something to the bundled figure that sounded suspiciously like "No!"

Why would she be telling the hapless stable worker no?

From his new vantage point in the hay, the three remaining players to the little drama all looked much, much taller. The girl was clearly out of the way, still shouting at the standing figure that made no attempt at all to evade the charging warrior.

Tyr didn't know if it was the vantage point, or the fact that he now had the time to watch his master's approach, but the man was definitely not sitting his horse well.

Eirik's eyes were wild, his face twisted in a mindless snarl. Over his head, the maekre blade flashed dully in the dying light. There was little anyone could do at this point to save the poor stranger with his pathetic length of wood.

And then there was a nearly deafening crack. Splinters were flying through the air all across the courtyard. Eirik was flying as well, but with considerably less grace.

The maekre blade spun out of his hands to fall into the dirt with a heavy thud as the warrior himself followed it, tumbling with a series of sad grunts that seemed to echo off the stone walls above. Hestir, relieved of the feverish goading of its big rider, skittered sideways to get away from the strangers and pulled in a tight circle, looking wildly down at Eirik in the mud.

Tyr knew the horse had seen that sight more than once in recent years and wondered if the animal was as tired of it as he was.

But Eirik was not done yet. With another pained grunt, he lurched to his feet, pulling an axe from his belt and glaring around the courtyard, looking for the figure who had knocked him so unceremoniously from his saddle.

The figure hadn't moved. The rake handle had been reduced to two short lengths of wood, three ends shattered and jagged with wooden teeth, one smooth and polished from long use. The hood was still in place, hiding the features within.

Eirik sounded like an enraged wolf as he rushed forward, heedless of the lessons of his last charge. His heavy axe rose into the darkening sky as he ran, and this time it appeared as if pain and anger had burned away whatever dulling effects had plagued his initial attack.

It didn't matter.

The two rods blurred as the bundled figure seemed to duck. The wood crossed, catching the axe handle between them, and then flashed again. The axe spun through the air and landed nearly on top of the mud-streaked maekre blade. The man then planted a foot on the big warrior's chest, moving too fast to follow, and gave a gentle shove that sent Eirik tumbling back onto his ass.

Tyr's eyes were wide as he silently wondered if the figure had intended for the weapons to end up so close together. It hardly seemed credible, but then, a person with a rake had just dismounted and disarmed a man who had once been one of the greatest warriors in the kingdom.

Those days might be lost in the past, but he was still far from finished, and he rose again, teeth bared. A small throwing axe appeared in his big hand and flashed through the air only to be deflected away with one casual swipe of a rod.

The figure in the courtyard seemed to be staring with utter contempt from the shadows of its hood. There was no tension in the stance, no concern; there was only one master of this situation, and it was not Eirik Hastiin.

But Eirik was either unaware of that, or he had been pushed past all reason. Unarmed, he surged toward the figure. This time he caught his opponent off guard. Wrapping his massive arms around the figure's chest, he lifted it bodily into the air and then brought it down onto the frozen mud of the courtyard with a monstrous roar. As they flew through the air, the stranger's hood slid away revealing long dark coils of hair wreathing a calm, dark-skinned face.

The entire time it was being lifted and dashed down, the figure was repeatedly bringing the rods down on Eirik's head.

When the two bodies hit the ground in a silent pile, the old warrior was insensate, eyes cloudy and staring, and the bundled up figure of his foe rose unsteadily to his feet. The man's skin was darker than any shade seen in Kun Makha, black eyes flashing with annoyance. The hair was the final clue Tyr needed to identify the man as one of the mysterious northerners from the distant island kingdoms, where it was said winter never touched, and summer reigned year-round.

But the islanders were said to be scholars and merchants, and this man had just devastated Eirik without any seeming effort.

Tyr had forgotten about the girl, and jerked his head around at her soft gasp. She ran, but not to the islander. Instead, she rushed to Eirik's fallen form and dropped to her knees in the hard mud beside him. She checked his eyes and listened to his breath, then settled back, glaring at the islander.

"I told you no. You could see the man wasn't in his right mind." She stood, looking around. "Get the little barrow you made for the feed and get him in out of the weather." She looked around to Tyr, and he scrambled to his feet, desperate to rise from his undignified state.

"Help get him inside. I think he'll be fine." She looked back down at Eirik. Tyr was confused by the look of peaceful repose on his master's face, regardless of the small trickle of blood staining one cheek.

The islander glared at the girl, then down at the sleeping warrior, then disappeared into the stable with a wordless grunt.

"I'm sorry about this." The girl moved to stand beside Tyr, looking down at Eirik's still form. "He didn't have to do that."

Feelings of loyalty for his master warred within Tyr's chest with a sudden, inexplicable desire to be seen as separate from him.

"He's been crazed on spirits for days." He shook his head.

The smile she gave him warmed him despite the evening's cold. "I could tell."

"How?" Eirik had a lot of practice hiding his drunken state. Most people who didn't know him could never tell when he was in his cups.

The girl shrugged. "Practice?"

Before he could ask her to explain that, the big islander came out rolling a wheeled barrow. He dropped it unceremoniously beside Eirik's body and glared over at the girl. "I'm not going to lift him."

The accent caught Tyr by surprise. It was smooth, rising and falling like a soft song. But there was no doubting the anger and annoyance in it.

The girl looked down at the big warrior with a slightly worried expression. "Well, I'm not going to be able to lift him." She looked back at Tyr with one eyebrow raised. "He's your friend, after all."

Tyr gave Eirik's slumbering face his own glare. He'd had to pick up his master more than once in the past, of course, but it was never something he was eager to do again.

"Oh, excellent! You've arrived!"

The new voice, somehow familiar and strange at the same time, brought Tyr out of his sour contemplation, and he turned to see a small figure move out from the stables.

The man who had called himself Tsegan Aqisiaq was standing there in long fur robes, his hands folded into the wide, deep sleeves, that half-familiar smile on his creased old face. When the old man's eyes found Eirik, prostrate in the frozen mud, however, the smile gave way to a slight, sad frown.

"Oh, no. No, no, no. This will never do." He cast an annoyed look at the dark-skinned islander. Beside Eirik, the girl rose. "Was this entirely necessary? It's not going to make your work any easier, you know."

That seemed to catch the girl by surprise, and Tyr had to admit to a certain amount of curiosity as well. They had little idea of what they were doing here, but clearly the old man intended the islander to have some role in it.

Tyr found himself hoping that the girl had something to do with it as well.

The islander grunted. "He needed to be calmed down." He gestured with one mittened hand. "I calmed him down."

Tsegan made a tsking sound and kneeled down beside the big warrior. "No, this is not an auspicious start to our endeavors at all, at all."

The old man reached out to put one hand on Eirik's forehead, the other on his chest. Tsegan tilted his head up as if he was looking at the sky, but his eyes were closed.

"Well, no permanent damage. That's good."

"I'm not an amateur." The islander seemed perturbed at the comment.

That appeared to amuse the old man, who barked a short laugh, shot a quick look over his shoulder, and smiled. "An interesting argument, considering the current state of your pupil."

Tyr felt his eyebrows draw down. Pupil? Could he have heard that right? What would Eirik, a former champion of the kingdom and a once-famous circuit fighter, have to learn from some strange islander?

Then he looked down at his master again and shook his head. More than he would have thought, obviously.

"Now, let's see. Nothing a little sojourn in warmer climes can't quickly take care of, yes?" The hands were back in place, and this time the old man's head fell to his chest as he muttered something under his breath.

Tyr felt the air in the little valley grow warm and was immediately reminded of that night in their tourney tent, when this old man had apparently burned away Eirik's mead-fueled, death-like slumber with the wave of a hand.

This time, it almost felt as if something out there in the looming shadows was responding; something hostile to them, or to the old man, or to his work. But he shook that off and looked down into his master's face, half-expecting what would happen next.

With a grunting cough, Eirik surged upright, sitting in the mud, wildly searching all around.

The old man jumped back with a laugh. "Whoa, big man! Easy!"

Eirik lurched to his feet, swaying slightly, and peered around the courtyard with wide, owlish, red-tinged eyes. When those eyes fell on the islander, they widened even further, and he took one stumbling step toward the man.

The man did not move.

"Now, now, none of that." Tsegan stepped up to put an arm around Eirik's shoulder, and Tyr was surprised to see the big man flinch slightly, then let the arm remain.

"You need food, no doubt, eh? And warmth? Maybe something warm to drink, as well?" Tsegan was making a point of speaking to both Eirik and Tyr, which Tyr appreciated.

"And after you are settled, I know, you would like to know what this is all about, I think. Yes?" The old man gestured toward the stable. "Chagua will take care of your horses, young Maiara will see that you have some warm food and drink, and I will join you presently. You are my honored guests, of course, and we have much to discuss.

"And so, please, welcome to Alden's Tor, the high keep, and, I hope, the beginning of a new age for the kingdoms of both the fyrdar and the oyathey."

Chapter 9

Eirik's hands were wrapped around a mug so warm it was almost painful to hold. But the heat leaching into his frozen flesh was so welcome he would not have let it go if it had burst into flames. The tea inside was weak, but he wasn't drinking it for the taste. Only spirits would have been more welcome. He was sitting in a rough-shaped chair wedged into a dark corner, one of several scattered across this side of the dimly-lit underground room beneath the stables. A table dominated the center of the area, but he had avoided it, uncomfortable with any impression of camaraderie with these strangers.

The room was clean, although it had obviously taken a lot of work to get there. The massive stones of the foundations surrounding them were ancient, with great cracks probably from when the keep above had collapsed. New mortar had been spread into the largest fissures. He saw bookshelves along the opposite wall and dismissed them without much interest.

In the far wall, by the bookshelves, a door led into a passageway entirely lost in shadow. His head still ached, and he felt something in the cool darkness beckoning him.

He watched as the girl, Maiara, prepared food. She was a pretty thing, with the most amazing, crystalline eyes. She moved with quick proficiency, obviously familiar with the process.

The damned islander came down and Eirik felt his face tighten. He could not remember much from their clash above, but he felt certain the dark-skinned stranger had used some sort of foreign trick on him. The man nodded to the girl as he took a mug, dropping several coats and a heavy cloak over another chair, and sat down gracefully without a sound, as far from Eirik as he could get.

That suited him just fine. The big man looked over at the bookshelves as if reassuring himself that no one had stolen any of the volumes, then settled in to drink his tea; his dark, flat gaze focused on the far wall, taking no notice of Eirik or Tyr.

For his part, Tyr was staring at the girl as she went about preparing the food. Eirik was sure his squire thought he was being subtle, but the big warrior had seen the girl catch him more than once. It might have brought a smile to his face, if face and pride weren't both still stinging. He settled back against the cold stone of the wall, hunching into the small seat, and did his best to ignore the islander, sinking deeper into his own brooding silence.

"Everyone comfortable?" The old man, Tsegan, bounced down the steps from the stable, clapping his hands together, a big smile on his face. "Are we settling in?" He saw the girl preparing food and frowned. "My dear, I believe you should join us. This will impact all of us, and every one of you deserves to know why we are here, and what we will be doing next. But you most of all."

The girl, Maiara, looked over to the old man with a silent question, then shrugged, wiped her hands on a rag she had kept nearby, and came over to the table with her own mug of tea. Tyr moved quickly to sit beside her, giving her his warmest smile as he settled in, doing his best to look relaxed. The lad probably had very little experience with women. One of the many injustices he had done his squire over the years, he imagined.

"Eirik, if you would give me a chance to explain where things stand?" Tsegan gestured him to an empty seat at the table. There was a moment during which Eirik himself did not know if he would join them, stay still, or storm out to find his horse. With an ungracious grunt, though, he rose, nodded, and moved to the table without throwing a glance at the big islander across the room.

"You've got one chance, old man. Your money's gone, and my patience quickly follows. If I'm not satisfied with your tale-spinning, we'll be heading north again without waiting for dawn."

He tried to ignore the desperate look Tyr gave him as he issued his threat. Eirik knew why and felt nearly the same. A warm meal, a roof over their heads, and a fire for the night had already settled into his mind as well.

"I understand, Eirik Hastiin. I believe you will find my tale worthy of your time, and my goals worthy of your attention."

People didn't often use Eirik's family name. None of the men and women on the circuit knew it; he had been trying to avoid the attention of King Einar's Shadow agents for years. At its sound, his grey eyes narrowed, and his hands, resting lightly on the table, clenched into fists. But he would not give the old man the satisfaction, and so said nothing. After a moment, Tsegan continued.

"My tale begins with an ancient set of writings called the Burdren Saga." Nothing but blank looks all around, and Tsegan nodded. "It is an obscure prophecy, little heeded by either the scholars of Kun Makha or the loremasters of the fyrdar kingdoms." He sighed, and Eirik thought the little man looked smaller than usual. "Even when such things were taken seriously, the Burdren Saga was not something familiar to any but the most devoted students of the ancient tales."

The little hands rapped on the table in a rhythm Eirik found vaguely disquieting. Glancing at the others from beneath his lowered brows, he saw that Tyr's open face was focused on the old man, eager to hear more. Maiara looked like she was trying to project interest with all her being. In the shadows by the wall, the islander was the only person in the room who was not even trying to pretend to pay attention, staring into his mug as if offended by the contents.

It was the first thing Eirik thought he might be able to agree with the big man on.

When Tsegan stood, he gathered up all their attention once again, and he looked down at each of them with a dark intensity Eirik didn't like at all.

"There is a great evil bearing down upon all the kingdoms of the fyrdar; an ancient evil that threatens to smash them all into oblivion. When they fall, and they will fall, Kun Makha will fall soon after. One of the great, hard-earned truths of life, forgotten now in this time of strife and bloodshed, is how intertwined the peoples of the fyrdar and the oyathey were at the height of their glory and power. When both peoples were one, there was not a force in the world that could have threatened them."

He sighed, his shoulders falling. "But mankind forgets. It is the central certainty of our condition. Given enough time, we can forget even the most important, powerful realities. And if there were a force out there, a force unknown and, until now, unknowable, that had sat waiting for the perfect time to strike, would now not be that time? Now, when the empire and the kingdoms are at their lowest ebb?"

Eirik knew a little of history. He could even accept that oyathey and fyrdar had been stronger when united. But this threat the old man seemed to be hinting at felt contrived to him. What was there, that could threaten both them in such a way? Was he hinting that the Utan, the ancient bogeymen of fyrdar myth and legend, were returning?

He knew Tyr, raised on a farm and then on the tourney circuit, knew next to nothing about history. The lad found little compelling in those old tales beyond the grand stories of war and glory that had led him to track Eirik down in the first place. He was shocked to realize that he didn't even know if Tyr could read. He promised himself that, if the boy could not, he would see that fixed at the first opportunity.

He almost smiled, remembering a young Einar making almost that same promise all those years ago, upon learning that Eirik couldn't read. The old king had been furious at the thought of an orphan, even a landed thane's orphan, joining his son at their studies. But Einar had been insistent, and Eirik had been taught to read, among all the other subjects, with the son of his king.

He almost smiled, but the weight of the intervening years, with their burden of fear and betrayal, was too much. He almost threw his flavorless cup against a wall.

He shook himself, forcing himself to pay attention once more.

The girl looked lost, as if she knew she should be concerned, but she, too, had no framework for understanding the threat the old man spoke of. She probably knew as little about the actual history of the kingdoms as Tyr. Eirik nodded, eager to have the old man complete his tale so they could all move on with their lives.

Tsegan misunderstood the gesture for something more agreeable and dipped his head in thanks. "This world is filled with foes we can hardly imagine. One such force chased the fyrdar from their ancestral homes centuries ago, driving them across the seas and into the lands of Kun Makha. Think about that for a moment. An enemy so great that all the fyrdar peoples fled, making a treacherous journey that many did not survive, to seek asylum on a distant shore."

"That's but one tale, old man." Eirik's scowl had deepened. "No one knows why they came to Kun Makha, nor that everyone did. Only children believe in the Utan." Eirik, for one, had always found it hard to swallow, that the entire fyrdar nation had fled this mysterious, terrible foe. Surely some had stayed behind.

The old man nodded, ceding the point. "The truth is obscured, that is true. As obscured as the Burdren Saga, to be honest." His lips twitched into a slight smile before settling back into their somber lines, and Eirik felt his old annoyance returning. Clearly the old man felt he had scored a point on Eirik, and it annoyed the warrior that he couldn't see if that was true or not. "Regardless of the ancient history, however, what cannot be denied is that a great danger even now descends upon the people of the Broken Kingdoms. It already moves in the shadows, darkening the hearts of kings and peasants alike. When it is strong enough to strike, no one will be able to stand against it."

At the mention of shadows and kings, Eirik felt an uncomfortable shift in his chest. He shot a glance at Tyr and then looked quickly away. Maiara spoke up, confusion still clouding her features. "I don't understand. What is coming? Who is going to attack?"

Tsegan sighed, sitting back in his char. "That, I do not know. The Burdren Saga does not speak of the danger directly. It speaks only of what must be done to stop it."

Eirik's eyes narrowed. "Let me guess. You need me to destroy it?" He snorted, pushing himself away from the table. "You've read too many children's stories, old man. The age of quests and heroes is long past. We are all just fallen men, now. None of us the equal of those who came before."

Tsegan reached out, his voice deepening, and Eirik stopped in the middle of turning to his furs with every intention of leaving. "You are correct. None of us are the equals of those who came before. But you are wrong when you think the Saga speaks of you as the hero that will stop the terror rising against us." The old man turned and pointed at Maiara. "Maiara is the only hope Astrigir and her sister kingdoms has now, Saemgard. Only she will be able to see that the kingdom is prepared." He turned back to Eirik, his smile gentle. "It falls to you to keep her alive."

Eirik froze in the middle of a contemptuous laugh. He glared at the old man, then at the girl. "She's your savior?"

"No." Maiara looked terrified and confused at the same time. "No, that can't be. I'm only—" Her voice choked off. Tyr looked as if he wanted to reach out and comfort her, but he stayed frozen.

Tsegan turned toward the girl and nodded, his expression kind and regretful. "Yes, my dear. I am sorry, but this burden will fall to you. There can be no doubting the Saga."

Eirik laughed, shaking his head. "Her? How terrifying must this ancient enemy be, that only a servant girl can save us all?"

For the first time, Eiric saw anger on Tsegan's face, and his laughter stopped as he felt his face heat up. It wasn't a sight he wanted to experience a second time. "You are the guardian, Eirik Hastiin. Son of a thane, you were born into your new life on a red day of terror and defeat, outcast and alone, only to rise again when the land needed you most. You were saemgard, yet your life at court was ended by the battle of Merrik Ford. You have wandered, lost and empty, ever since. But you will rise up now, my friend, to answer the call of history, and stand beside the princess as she unites the kingdom beneath her rule."

Eirik felt a cascade of emotions rush through him. The old man's words conjured up every painful moment from that time in his life where his greatest pride had turned into a terrible, burning shame. But even as he feared he might drown in the rush of memories and emotions, his mind latched onto one word that had swept past him, and confusion provided a brace against the tide. "Princess?"

"Princess?" The girl said the word in the same instant, in almost exactly the same tone.

Tsegan nodded, reaching across the table to take her hands. "This is a terrible burden for you to take up, my dear, I know. But there can be no denying the Burdren Saga, nor the signs. I have known you since your birth, I have watched over you your entire life. There can be no doubt that you are the hope of which the Saga speaks. You are the trueborn daughter of Einar Jalen of Astrigir."

That was too much, and Eirik shook his head violently. "No. I'm sorry, but no. Your tale unravels there, old man. Einar would never have risked the succession. Besides, I would have known. He would have told me."

Again, Tsegan's eyes became sorrowful. "My son, there was so much Einar did not share with you. Would such a fast friend have hunted you so tirelessly after a tragic loss you could not have prevented, no matter how strong you were?" That struck home again, to the core injustice of his life. It silenced Eirik's denials, and sent him back into his seat without a sound. "Einar fell in love with a young visitor at court before you were sworn into the saemgard. They were joined in secret by an envoy from Kun Makha, one of the new sun priests the old emperor had been sending out; probably to sow discord within Astrigir. For many years they pursued a secret life, beyond the sight of thanes or saemgard."

Eirik felt his face twist painfully. Any thought of Einar, the boy who had been his friend, the friend who had become his king, the king who had become his most dedicated foe, was enough to churn up terrible, burning emotions. Most of the brawls he had fought in his life had resulted from some comment or perceived slight involving the king of Astrigir in one way or another.

"The young lady came to be with child, but Einar knew he would never be able to claim the child as his own. Einar had been trained at an early age that he would one day have to marry for the good of the realm, setting aside his oyathey lover. Einar had every expectation that Astrigir would rise up to rule the fyrdar realms. One day, he would need to claim a fyrdar bride to secure that rule." He was speaking to both Eirik and Maiara, the two of them somehow linked together through the years by this strange, incredible tale. And something within the story rang true to Eirik. Einar's ambition, even when they had been younger, had been fierce. None of this was beyond him.

"I offered to take the girl away, to see that she would be cared for, far from Connat, where her very existence could tumble the kingdom into chaos and cost Einar the throne of all fyrdar."

That was, again, too much, and Eirik shook it off with a waved hand. Hearing of the man who had been the best friend of his youth spoken of in such a cavalier way could not stand. "And who were you, that Einar would heed you, or give you his firstborn child?"

Tsegan looked solemn, staring resolutely into Eirik's blue gaze. "I have told you, Eirik Hastiin, I am Tsegan Aqisiaq, and there was a time when kings heeded my every word."

That seemed to stop them all in their tracks. The tale was fantastical enough on its own, but now that the old man had seemingly taken up the mantle of the ancient magician in earnest, it all seemed to fall apart.

He sighed again. "Would you all deny the proof of your own eyes? Each of you has seen my powers now. You know I am capable of things that should not be possible." Eirik reflected for a moment that he didn't really know what the old man's powers were. He had Tyr's word that it was the old man who had dragged him out of his mead haze all those weeks ago, and again his squire told him it was the little man who had called him back from the brink of unconsciousness brought on by the islander and his damned sticks.

But magic? Eirik had seen nothing.

But what if it could all be true? What if Tsegan Aqisiaq, legendary sorcerer from the old tales, the great man who the sagas said had fought so long and hard to keep the oyathey and fyrdar united, had not died when he had disappeared from history? What if he lived on somehow, preserved through his magic, perhaps, to return when he was most needed?

"Wait," the girl's voice had hardened, and Eirik looked at her closely. Her features were fine, aristocratic without being cold. She was truly a beautiful girl, he would have to give his squire full marks for taste. And those eyes

... the layered, crystalline texture of their bright, shining blue ...

He shook himself, forcing himself to look away and listen to her words.

"You're saying that the king is my father? That this strange oyathey woman is my mother?"

The old man nodded, his face sad, and Eirik felt a moment of profound foolishness. He was not the only one being dealt a grievous blow in this story, he realized.

"My father." Those eyes grew distant; countless unnamed emotions flickered over her face. She looked back to the old man. "My father?"

The wizened head nodded again. "Yes, my dear. But not the man he could have been. We do not deal now with the wishful fantasies of a young girl, but with the distasteful realities of a world turned dark and bloody. Einar Jalen is not a man to claim as father with pride. He left his better nature behind long ago."

She nodded as if trying to puzzle something out. "But there was a time when he would listen to you. When he allowed you to take his only child from him."

"Yes."

"Because you are Tsegan Aqisiaq, and there was a time when you could command the ears of kings."

The old man shrugged. "Command is a strong word, but I was held in some esteem, yes."

She shook her head as if trying to clear it of one thought, as her gaze focused sharply on that old face. "If you're him, then what happened? If you're telling us you're really Tsegan Aqisiaq, and that magic is real ... what happened to the others? What happened to magic?"

Eirik watched the old man closely as he seemed to fold in on himself, arms coming up to cradle his chest as if a terrible pain were wracking his body. The warrior could see no sign of dishonesty or evasion in that stance, or in the old man's deep, dark eyes. "I do not know." The voice was like a whisper. "It was so long ago. Perhaps the spirits and the gods were not happy with how we used our gifts. Perhaps it was just time for such things to fade away and leave the earth?"

When he looked up, meeting each of their gazes, holding them for a moment before moving on, the impact, the sense of loss, was almost physical. "Each of the others, one by one, felt a drawing away, a sudden need to take themselves apart from the rest. They disappeared into the forests, up into the mountains, some would occasionally return for a brief time, but they would soon go off again ... I was so busy trying to keep the fyrdar from breaking away, to keep Kun Makha as one, that I hardly even noticed until I was all that remained." His head fell, and Eirik heard him say one word, softly, as if to himself. "Alone."

As the old man lapsed into silence, Eirik felt awkward and uncomfortable. He looked to Tyr first, then to the girl. Each of them was looking to him, pleading silently. He tried to keep the sneer off his face. He detested weakness in every form and wanted nothing more than to be done with this would-be wizard and his ridiculous schemes and fairy stories. Magic was nothing but a childish fancy, and the man's blathering talk cast doubt on all the rest of his tale as well. And Tsegan Aqisiaq, if he was even real, would have died well over a hundred years ago. There was no way this man was him.

But what if all the rest of it was real? For more years than he cared to count, his life had been nothing but a vague, drifting hell. From the moment the cold waters of the Merrick had closed over his head, he had wandered the land as a shifting, empty phantom; his life had meant nothing. What if there were things he didn't know? What if there was a way for him to seek redemption? To clasp the prize young King Einar had cared about more than any others? What if there was truly a way to turn time back to that golden moment, before Einar had lost his grand sense of justice and righteousness, and settled into being nothing more than yet another petty tyrant?

What if he could give that young child-king of his memory his fondest wish? Might that not destroy the despot he had become; recall him to his better self?

Perhaps he could realize his potential once more; turn time back to recapture the strength and purpose of his youth. Maybe they could raise Maiara to the throne, and then bring Vestan and Subraea under her rule. A united fyrdar kingdom would then treat with Kun Makha as an equal.

A small, harsh voice in his mind reminded him that it was the fyrdar who had chosen to break away from Kun Makha so long ago. The empire hadn't even tried to stop them.

He shook the voice away. He knew nothing of the wants and needs of empires, or the existence of some terrible enemy out of the darkness come to destroy them all. He remembered a young warrior whose dream had been to unite the Fyrdar kingdoms for his king. He remembered that boy well, and that boy's dreams.

"How do you know it's me?" Maiara, apparently, did not share the growing sense of hope rising in his own chest. Her voice was anguished, her pretty face twisted with something that might have been fear, but looked more akin to anger. "How do you know he's my father?"

The old man had been watching Eirik, as if staring into his mind. But when he turned back to the girl, the hard face softened, and once again the eyes were filled with empathy. "My dear, I was there when you were born. I carried you to the House of the Fallen Oak myself. I placed you in Turid Sayen's arms nearly twenty years ago."

"The safe place, away from court? Away from my father?" Her full lips were twisted in building anger. But the old man cut that short with a shake of his head.

"Maiara, your father abandoned you. He would have left you to die. My first task was to save you from him, and only then to bring you to a safe place. A place close enough that you would still feel as one with the people of Astrigir. A place where you could learn the management of a household, which is more important for a ruler than you might imagine. A place where you would be taught to read; not a common skill among the workers and the thralls of the fyrdar. And a place where you would be ready and able to leave when the time came, for you to take the next step on your destiny."

Tears shone in her eyes, unfallen. "A place like this ruin?"

He nodded again. "Yes, Princess. This ruin. Alden's Tor. The high seat of ancient kings. I have prepared for this moment for more years than you can know." He gestured to the bookshelves. "I have accumulated the best collection of works on leadership, civics, philosophy, and law. Every subject with which a true ruler must be knowledgeable. You learned to read, but now you must use that skill to learn so much more. You must learn how a man or woman thinks. You must know proper management, judgment, even military tactics and strategy. You have a keen mind, I know. When the winter is done, you will have only just begun to learn everything you must. Your entire life will revolve around learning and putting that knowledge to work for your people."

Eirik was impressed. He wasn't sure about any prophetic sagas, and he hadn't seen any magic himself, but it did appear that the old man had planned carefully to put all of this together.

"Where have you been for the last hundred years?" Eirik was surprised to hear Tyr speak. His mind had been so entangled with thoughts about his own past, and the girl's future, he had nearly forgotten about the boy.

"The old stories say Tsegan Aqisiaq disappeared soon after the Broken Kingdoms fell away from Kun Makha, over a hundred years ago, and he was an old man then." Tyr seemed more interested than angry, but Eirik couldn't remember the last time the boy was this intense over something other than his own drinking habits. "If you returned twenty years ago, why is it no one has heard of it?"

The old man nodded, giving the boy a smile that Eirik thought had more of an edge to it than it had earlier. "Very good, my boy. Excellent questions. It's simple, really. I have always known a great danger was looming in the future. I knew that I could best fight that power from the shadows, and so allowed my star to fade from the tales of the oyathey and the fyrdar. From time to time, I have made myself known to the rulers of one kingdom or another, or indeed in the empire itself, to help guide my charges in the best path forward. For the most part, I have spent the intervening years watching for the enemy, watching over the seas, and far to the north where empires stand of which even the sages of Kun Makha are unaware. For many years I have turned to the more obscure chronicles, believing that within one of them, the truth of all our tomorrows must rest." He shrugged, seeming to relax again. "And so it was that I found the Burdren Saga. At first, it was only one of many I had tried to unravel, but as events began to quicken, I realized that the truth of what I sought all along was to be found there, and nowhere else."

"And it talks about me, the protector, and about her, the princess?" Eirik found himself wanting to believe. Not because of the magic, or the fairy tale aspect of the thing, but because of what it had to offer him, after a lifetime wasted for another man's small-mindedness.

Tsegan nodded. "It does."

Eirik tipped his chin in Tyr's direction. "And he's here to help me?"

The old man smiled his colder smile and shook his head. "Young master Wayra is here because when I found you, you were incapable of finding here on your own. You see, you have your own tasks to see to this winter, Saemgard, if you are to be prepared for the spring."

Eirik felt his face tighten at that. He found himself disliking the old man's tone even more.

"Such as what?"

The smile on the old man's face widened. "You were the greatest warrior in Astrigir, Eirik Hastiin. To guard princess Maiara, you must be so again. You have a long road ahead of you, to undo the damage you have done to yourself through the years."

Training. He could handle training. And it was true, he was out of practice. He had allowed himself to go soft on the tourney circuit, where true challenges were few and far between. And if he was going to be entirely honest with himself, the drink probably hadn't helped.

"I can do that." He nodded, sitting up straighter. "Tyr and I will—"

"No."

That brought Eirik up short.

"No?"

"No, the task does not fall to you and Tyr." Tsegan turned to the back wall and gestured toward the islander, sitting in the shadows, staring at Eirik with flat eyes. "Chagua Emeru is one of the fabled Swords of the northern islands. His entire life has been dedicated to the study of mortal combat. He will retrain your body, your mind, and your soul to the tasks that lie ahead."

All the old rage surged up within his chest and Eirik rose to his full height. The others jumped away from the table, obviously afraid that the earlier fighting from the courtyard above was about to break out once again down here.

Only the islander, his dark skin gleaming in the shadows, did not move.

"Over my dead body would a filthy scholar from the islands teach me anything about combat!"

The teeth in the shadows gleamed in the dark face, and for the first time in his life, Eirik heard the lilting tones of the northern islands.

"If that is the only way to teach you, so be it."

Chapter 10

Tyr fed Vordr another of the dried apples from the stable, glancing around with a twinge of guilt. There weren't many apples left, and he didn't know who they belonged to. But he figured, if he was going to be miserable, and Eirik was going to be miserable, then at least the horses could be happy for a little while longer.

He had tried giving Hestir an apple as well, but the charger showed no interest. Maybe the horse was somehow picking up on Eirik's mood.

Tyr shrugged, happy to be away from the tensions in the common room.

The night had not improved after the confrontation between his master and the islander in the basement chamber. Eirik had muttered darkly, shaking his big shaggy head, and plodded off down the dark hall, his saddlebags slung over one shoulder. Tyr knew there was only one reason the big man would bring his luggage with him, and had tried to follow, hoping to keep the drinking to a reasonable level. He had failed, as he so often did on that score. He had fallen asleep at last in a cold corner, his master's muttered curses burning in his ears. He had left the common room for nothing.

He hadn't wanted to. He was fascinated by the girl, princess ... Maiara ... He was flustered even thinking about it, wondering how he was supposed to address her. He knew she had caught him staring more than once. He was no blushing virgin; he had met plenty of girls on the tourney circuit, and more than a few of them had fancied the squire of the mysterious Ruun Warrior. But something about this girl was different.

If what the old man had said was true, she was a princess, maybe, which made her very different indeed.

And what about the old man? A wizard? Tyr didn't much care for fairy stories and didn't know much about ancient history either. So whatever Tsegan Aqisiaq might or might not have been, at the moment, as far as Tyr was concerned, he was the crazy old man who had introduced him to the most beautiful girl he had ever met, and then placed her forever beyond his reach. Or, if not forever, at least until the world came back to its senses.

He gave Vordr's nose one more pat and then turned away, glancing into the shadowy recess that led down to their common room. He didn't want to face any of them again just yet. He knew the entrance to the tower must be hidden in the darkness beyond the stalls somewhere, but he had little interest in seeing the old man either, never mind trespassing to do it.

Pulling his gloves on against the bitter cold, he stepped into the bright morning sun and squinted up at the sky. There were low, dark clouds sweeping up over the glittering white peaks to the west, and he knew, despite the sunshine, that they would be wading through snow before long. There were shovels with the other supplies, he had seen, and he had a sour feeling he knew who would be the one clearing the snow when it came.

He tried not to let that bother him as he took in his surroundings, trying to ignore all of the nagging problems that had arisen since they crested the high ridge the day before. The walls of the valley were lined with tall pines, many of them still bearing snow from the last storm. The courtyard was swept clear, a rutted brown mess that crunched beneath his feet.

He had seen no animals, but tracks beneath the trees hinted that hunting for fresh meat might not be a total waste of time. It would also get him away from the ancient ruined keep before he screamed.

Tyr pulled his hood down and lifted his face to the sun. It was dim and cold, but pleasant despite the nip of winter, and much nicer than the ominous darkness beneath the clouds sweeping their way.

Tyr's expression tightened. A flash of movement beneath the trees caught his eye. It had been something large; he was sure of it. But the shape had been obscured by the other trees, and he had no idea what it could have been. A deer? Some other animal, coming to check on the encroaching men in their tumbled down lair?

The quiet was shattered by an animalistic howl echoing up from the common room. Tyr spun, hand on axe, and half-expected to see Eirik, or the islander, come barreling up and into the cold morning air. Instead, the howl resolved itself into a growling string of unintelligible sounds that nevertheless carried with them the unmistakable echoes of a terrible, boiling fury.

And they were clearly not coming from the islander.

Tyr ran for the stairs, taking them two at a time as he plunged into the common room. Several chairs were tumbled over, the table had been knocked askew, and the two big men were squaring off in the middle of the room, glaring at each other.

He bowed his head, shaking it in sad, embarrassed disbelief. Eirik was swaying as he faced the islander. His eyes were red-rimmed and bleary, with that vague, distant look he often got when a night of comatose slumber had not been enough to burn away the spirits.

His master must have really put a dent in his supply last night.

And here was the end result: Eirik's habit after a night of heavy drinking was usually to dive right back into the bottle the next morning. There was some sort of logic to that, he knew. Hells, watching that pattern play out over and over was his most common winter activity.

But instead of staying in their room with his little bottles, he was here, shouting at the big islander.

"Your words mean nothing to me, you bastard!" His shoulders heaved. "Where are they?"

Tyr pulled up at the bottom of the steps. Eirik was on the far side of the table, glaring at the dark-skinned stranger. Maiara stood in the doorway leading back to their rooms, a book clutched in one hand.

He couldn't see the islander's face, but judging from Eirik's reaction, it could not have been kind.

"I'll knock those white teeth down your throat, fool, if you don't answer me right now!"

The old man might have been able to stop this, but he was nowhere to be found. Tyr wasn't about to let Eirik get them kicked out into the coming storm through some sick combination of drink and pride. He rushed around the islander, placing himself between the two, one hand, palm out, toward each of them, and turned to his master.

"What's missing?" His eyes pled for calm, but he could see, now that he was close, the countless red roads of broken veins in Eirik's own eyes. His master really had done himself proud last night.

Eirik's big, shaking gaze lost focus for a moment, narrowed in on Tyr's hand, and then lifted up to his face, all as the big man continued to sway as if they were standing in the hold of a pitching ship.

"'S'gone, boy. 'S'all gone!" a flash of despair swept over his face, then the rage returned, and he jabbed a harsh finger over Tyr's shoulder at the islander. "An' I'd give you even coinage that black wolf took it!"

Tyr edged his way forward, doing everything in his power to keep his voice low and calm. "Master, please. Be rational. What is missing?"

The effort of both recalling his grievance and maintaining his anger appeared to be too much for Eirik, and his furiously knurled brow smoothed a bit as he focused once again on his squire.

"The spirits." The big man's voice was soft, like that of a lost child, and Tyr could almost pity him; almost. "The spirits are all gone."

"They are all gone." The lilting words of the islander cut through the cloud of wretchedness that had descended upon the big warrior, burning through the fog and igniting the smoldering fire of his anger all over again.

"Wolf!" As braced as he was, Tyr was not prepared for the full-on charge of the enraged warrior. He found himself sailing sideways, crashing into one of the overturned chairs and landing heavily on his hands and knees, his wound throbbing. He watched helplessly as his master knocked the table aside to get to grips with the islander.

Eirik staggered ahead, hands grasping before him, face purple with anger. The islander watched him come, dark eyes impassive. When the big warrior reached the dark-skinned man, the islander merely stepped aside and with a jerk of one heavily muscled arm, brought a fist down on the top of the drunken man's head.

Eirik stopped in his headlong rush as his neck shortened under the blow. Slowly, he rose back up to his full height, swaying gently like a tall tree caught in a stiff breeze, and then his legs gave out beneath him and he crumbled into a heap with a soft sigh.

Tyr got up and scrambled to his master's side, although the islander had not moved. Eirik's eyes were wide, flickering all around, and Tyr took a moment to give thanks to any spirits or gods who might be focused on this tiny, lost valley and his miserable, wandering master.

The blow to the head seemed to have taken the steam out of Eirik's anger. He sat, his shoulders slumped, and stared down at his big hands, lying palms up in his lap. For a moment, Tyr was afraid the big man was going to start crying, but instead, he just sighed, looked up at the squire with an expression that seemed more hopeless than sad, and craned his neck to look up at the looming figure of the islander.

"It is all gone, brother." The dark man above them was not mocking; the tone, as best could be construed through the musical accent, might even have been kind. But there was no room for compromise in it.

"Not my brother." Eirik muttered, his head falling back to his chest.

"Are you alright?" Maiara's soft voice brought Tyr jerking upright, and he began to answer before realizing that she wasn't talking to him. Why would she be talking to him? He worked his arm around, kneading around the wound, trying not to let the bitterness show.

Eirik looked up owlishly as the girl kneeled down on his other side. "You didn't have to hit him that hard!" She berated the islander, who looked down with a quizzical expression before shaking his head, sending the long coils of hair swaying like living snakes, and turning away.

For a moment, Tyr wondered what he would have to do to get the big man to knock him insensible, if that is what it took to catch the girl's attention.

"A little harmless fun, I trust?"

Tyr looked back at the stairs and watched the old man sweep into the room, his wide, open smile in place as usual. The dark eyes took in the disarranged furniture and the big warrior sitting disconsolately on the floor, and the smile faded just a bit. He shook his head.

"Master Hastiin, we must end this ceaseless bickering." The little man crossed to the warrior and eased himself to one knee.

"We are running out of time. Beyond these glacial peaks, the world continues to move apace. Enemies circle, preparing to strike, and only if the princess is established on the throne in time will we have a prayer of surviving. She will never reach Connat if you are not by her side."

Something about that bothered Tyr, and he cast a quick glance at the girl, but she was watching the old man, her face a mask that told him nothing.

"We must each do our part, or all will be lost."

The man stood, hands on hips, and glared down at the warrior. Tyr and Maiara quickly rose as well.

"Your part, I assure you, is not to drink yourself insensible each night. You must be your best self, we must all be our best selves, or we will fail."

Eirik glared up, then pushed himself to his knees, wavered slightly, and then rose unsteadily to his feet. Tyr wasn't sure, but his master looked almost embarrassed.

But the old man wasn't finished.

"You are in Chagua's hands, now. If, between you, you cannot rediscover your former glory, you will be worse than useless."

"And the first step on that journey is to ween you off this poison." The islander, Chagua, held a small dark bottle in his hand as if it contained something vile. With a casual flip of his hand, he tossed it into a corner where it tinkled into a pile of similar flasks.

Despite the tension of the moment, Tyr raised an eyebrow, impressed despite himself, at how many of the little containers Eirik had managed to secret amongst their baggage. There was obviously enough there for the man to have hibernated through most of the winter if he wished.

His eyes narrowed. Either the supplies had cost a lot less than Eirik had said, or the big warrior had been holding out on him, keeping a hidden stash of coinage secret from his squire. That shouldn't have surprised him, either, but it did.

Eirik stared owlishly at the pile of dark bottles, and Tyr braced himself for another outburst. Instead, the big warrior merely shrugged his shoulders in defeat, leaned down tentatively to pick up one of the chairs, and sat down.

The old man watched him and then nodded in satisfaction. "Good. Excellent." He clapped one hand against the cover of a dusty old book he had pulled out of his ever-present satchel. "Now, perhaps, we can make some progress."

The islander moved forward at some silent command and righted the table, sliding another chair into place behind the old man. He then gestured to two others for Maiara and Tyr while righting the last for himself.

The old man placed the book gently on the table and tapped it with the fingertips of one hand. "I know there is still some doubt in your minds. I knew all along there would be. The sorts of people needed in this dark hour would not be so easily swayed by a few glib words and fancy tricks. I have here one of the last remaining books containing the Burdren Saga. Any of you may read it, if you wish."

The book was clearly ancient, the cover a faded red cloth, its gilt wording worn into illegibility. The old man opened the book as if it was a holy relic, easing the pages over, one tattered leaf at a time. "I have had this book for a very, very long time." The creases of the old face fell into the lines of a sad, distant smile. "I inscribed it myself, in fact, in distant, happier days."

Eirik was staring at the book, and Tyr was forcibly reminded that the warrior had once been an elite nobleman. Eirik would have received the best education to be had. He would be no stranger to books, nor would the written word intimidate him the way it sometimes did Tyr. But he seemed to have no interest in taking up the book, merely staring at it from the depths of his misery.

The old man reached the passage he was searching for and rested his hands in his lap, leaning over the tight, flowing script. "It speaks of one who will rise from obscurity and exile to return her people to greatness." He looked up at Maiara with a smile. "The pronoun is vague, so for a long time I did not realize we would be sharing our temporary exile with a young princess."

She blushed, looking away, and Tyr thought he saw more embarrassment in the reaction than pleasure. That was interesting. Clearly she was still uncomfortable with the revelation. At heart, she was still a common girl, and for some reason, that loosened the tightness in his chest just a little.

"It speaks of a great injustice that must be put right, and of she who will redeem us all." He turned toward Eirik, the smile not wavering despite the warrior's skeptical gaze. "And it speaks of the guardian, an exile, lost to his people, born on a red day, who will rise again to fulfill his destiny."

Eirik nodded slowly, the vague cloud still hovering over his gaze. "I think you said all this last night." He jerked a surly thumb at the girl. "She's just got to learn everything there is to know about rulership before the spring thaw. Sounds like a treat. Just tell me what I need to do so I can finish this, get her to where she needs to be, and be rid of you all."

Chagua's head lowered to hide the flash of a smile beneath a fall of coiled hair, the old man made no attempt to hide his own grin.

"Your task is, admittedly, the hardest, my son. You must find your best self, remember why it was you first picked up the maekre blade, and stand firm as the entire society you once loved, that you once pledged your life to defend, turns on you." The smile was gone, the voice firm. The old man's look grew dark as he looked at each of them in turn. "Rest assured, my friends, we will be forced to fight our own people before we can concern ourselves with the great enemy that threatens us all."

That hadn't occurred to Tyr, and he sat back in his chair, stunned. It made sense, of course. King Eniar wasn't about to step aside so some peasant girl with questionable parentage could take his place. In fact, and now Tyr glanced at his master with unease, Maiara's claim, even it if was real, and even if they could prove it, would not be valid until the king was deposed or dead. The king who, he knew, had once been a young Eirik Hastiin's best and only friend.

Eirik was nodding. "Alright. So, I have to train, the big man from up north here will be training me, apparently, and I assume the lad will help us, while the girl becomes queen material. What will you be doing, old man?"

The smile returned, and Tyr found himself a little unnerved. Every time Eirik insulted the little old man, he only responded with a smile. He had no fear at all of the big warrior. Did Tsegan put that much faith in his island warrior? Or did he believe his supposed magic could save him?

"Chagua is more than just a 'big man from up north.' He is one of the sworn Swords of the islands. Do you know about the Swords, Eirik Hastiin?" Eirik shrugged. "He knows how to fight, I'll grant you that. What the dreamers from the islands call themselves is hardly a concern of mine. I'm more curious as to what you will be doing."

The man nodded again. "Very well, I will explain my part in this as well." He closed the book with great care and set it aside. "I will be traveling around the kingdom laying the groundwork for the princess' revelation. She will not be able to take her rightful place without help. I will ensure that we have that help when it is needed."

"What kind of help?" Maiara straightened in her chair.

Tsegan's smile slipped as he reached out to touch her hand. "My dear, we are speaking of nothing short of a full uprising; a rebellion. While you are all safe here, preparing for spring, I will be preparing the kingdom for your arrival. When you descend from the mountains, there will be a rebellion waiting for you."

She stared at him. "You're going to raise a rebellion before spring?"

The old man's smile returned, but it was different this time; harder. "These are dark times for Astrigir, my dear. The people groan beneath the weight of appalling taxes to fund Einar's eternal wars. They feel he has turned his back on them and their culture, giving more credence to visiting wise men of Kun Makha than the lorekeepers of the Broken Kingdoms. Even without the Burdren prophecy, the kingdom is ripe for revolution."

She sat back, and Tyr wished he could read her face. He thought he saw disquiet there, or distrust, but he couldn't be sure.

"You are going to raise an army?" Eirik's voice dripped contempt despite a vague slur to the words, either from the drink or the recent blow to his head. "Who are you, to raise any sort of army?"

The old man gave him a flat stare and then sighed. "I have walked this earth for a very long time. I have forgotten more on a host of topics than you will ever know. Please, trust me when I tell you that, when the time comes, we will have the force we need."

The warrior rose to the challenge in the old man's voice, a matching defiance in his pale eyes. "So, we'll swamp Einar with a wave of peasants, will we? You may have walked around the place for a long time, old man, but I once led the charge of the most formidable force the fyrdar kingdoms have ever known. I'll be the judge of this army of yours, when and if they materialize."

The twinkle was back in the old man's eye, and Tyr couldn't shake the feeling that his master had just walked headlong into a trap. "You did, indeed, ride at the head of a formidable force. And how did that end for you? Perhaps you should trust to me, and we will see what we shall see?"

Tyr winced as he watched the blow fall. Eirik looked as if he had been struck, his eyes flaring, but then he settled back with an ominous creak from the old chair. "Very well. So we shall lead a wave of peasants into the streets of Connat, right to the gates of the Bhorg itself. I assume they will provide their own weapons? Or should we be sure to bring along the rakes and shovels from the stable?"

Tyr saw the warm look in the old man's expression cool. "Eirik Hastiin, I grow tired of these spirit-soaked words. But I will indulge this last, and perhaps you will find the lesson salutary. On the Merrik Ford you led the charge, waving your great sword over your head with wild abandon. The maekre blade, a wonder of the weaponsmith's art, did no great service under that red sky, I think? Perhaps you will find that it is not so much a warrior's fearsome reputation nor the quality of his weapons that win a day, but rather the strength of his resolve and the strategy with which he and his fellows are employed?"

Eirik slouched down, his little remaining energy fading fast. Tyr could tell his master was finished with the verbal sparring, but that stubborn streak, as wide as the greenway, would not allow him to retire from the field without one last swing. "Why spring? What does your little book have to say about the coming spring?"

Tsegan looked back down at the book and nodded vaguely. "An excellent question, actually. I am afraid I lack an excellent answer for you. The saga does not mention anything so specific as times or places. But I know that the king's taxmen will be moving out in early spring to take their first claims from the people before they can get a crop into the ground. This will enrage most of the farmers and the merchants." He turned toward Eirik as if consulting a professional. "Spring and summer are campaigning season, and if things last longer than we wish, we will want as much time as possible to establish our victory."

Tyr's master nodded vaguely. It didn't seem to have convinced Maiara at all, but Tyr knew enough about warfare from listening around the night fires in countless tourney camps to know that the old man was right about the seasons.

Eirik cleared his throat. "Very well. And I am not to have my spirits." He spoke the words in a flat, empty voice, his gaze flicking to the pile of bottles on the floor, and then up to the islander's face.

"No. Drink is your master. Until you become your own man, there will be none for you." The islander's accent almost made that sound like a compliment, but the meaning of the words was not lost on any of them.

Eirik nodded again. "We may as well start now. There is less of winter than we might think, locked up here in the mountains, and far less than we will probably need." He pushed himself away from the table. "I will just need a cup of wine—"

"There is no wine." The words were short and clipped, as the big islander rose to his feet on the opposite side of the table.

"No wine before we begin?" Eirik's voice was resigned. "Very well. Then—"

"There is no wine at all. We have nothing for you to drink but water." Chagua stood calmly, his voice low.

"What?!" The rage began to surface again, the color fading from Eirik's cheeks, his hands balling into fists that rose as of their own accord before him. "How d—"

Chagua snapped a short punch across the table into Eirik's nose, his expression never changing.

Eirik stumbled backward, eyes crossing as if trying desperately to look at his own nose, and fell heavily into his chair, which then toppled over backward, spilling him onto the floor.

Tyr sighed, lowering his head into his hands.

It was going to be a long winter.

Chapter 11

Geir stared at the game board, lost in thought. He had played so many games of king's table in the warm, musty confines of the trading post that he thought he could almost recognize every one of the pieces, defenders and attackers, with his eyes closed.

He had forced Vidhar to play so many games the poor bandit had finally found the courage to say no. It was annoying, but Geir understood the sentiment, and had finally decided to let the man live. There were others he could bully into sitting at the table.

The insight he had gained from those early games had not returned. In his current assignment, those theories were of limited value. He could wait here in this tumbled-down old hovel for a year, and if his quarry had been smart during their preparations, there would be no sign of them throughout the dark winter months.

Not a single report had come to Bjornstad in weeks. Which was not to say there wasn't plenty for the mountain folk to discuss. The remains of the missing brigands had been found; four men and a woman, their wounds apparently terrible, according to the stories. He had spent some of his dwindling supply of coins treating too many of the denizens of this dark, smoky hell to the horse piss they passed over the bar, and they had proven only too eager to talk. Winters were long this high up, and any tale of mystery or violence was bandied back and forth for months until every last scrap of entertainment and diversion had been wrung from it.

He gathered the five missing brigands had been seasoned. Not the kind of folks who might be expected to bumble their way to gruesome deaths at the hands of a girl, an old man, and their driver. It wasn't uncommon for brigands to run afoul of mountain folk, but that usually resulted in deaths on both sides, and stories running back and forth between the settlements as cries for vengeance mounted.

Here, though, five hardened raiders were dead, and not a sign that they had so much as wounded their killers. And the injuries were said to have been horrific, even to the mountain folk. One was said to have been cut in two, the body hurled across the clearing to spill blood and offal over the snow.

It was that last that had caught his attention. There were few weapons that could even come close to cutting a man in half. Most axe blades lacked the span of blade for the job, and most swords lacked the weight and strength.

There was one blade almost famous for such injuries, of course, but vanishingly few had wielded a maekre blade in many years. They had fallen out of favor soon after the damned battle at the ford. The giant, heavy blades were now seen as a symbol of the failure and cost of that last, miserable battle.

A battle that had ended one phase of Geir's life as well. He remembered coming upon that clearing after the saemgard charge had been broken, the battle already lost. He remembered the moans of the wounded, the screams of the dying horses.

He would never forget those screams.

Of course, the big, flashy tourney circuit swords were similar to maekre blades. If sharpened, they could well cut a man in half. But those minstrel warriors fought with dulled blades, to ensure they couldn't really hurt each other.

Whoever had attacked those brigands had not concerned themselves with such things.

So who had snapped those necks? The little girl? Who had cut a warrior in half, the old man? The driver?

No. There were other players moving about the mountains, here to make his work just that much more difficult. He had a sense for these things, and it was telling him that he wasn't the only man of violence wandering the mountain trails this season.

And that other man was wielding a maekre blade.

He looked again down at the board and cursed. The game was mute on the subject of bloodthirsty killers, just as it was on little girls and their companions. No matter how often he played, he could make no more sense of the work he was to do here than before.

He looked up and gestured for one of his hired bladesmen to approach. Tore was worse even than Vidhar, knowing less of strategy than even the thrall behind the bar. But sadly, he was better than most of the others and had a strange store of guile when it came to defending his king that Geir had found almost challenging, if he allowed himself to become preoccupied while playing.

Tore nodded silently and pulled the board toward himself, setting up the pieces without a word. Geir watched for a moment then looked back out over the room. The mountain folk were quiet today. That could last for days, or it could end in an instant. There was little to relieve the boredom here, which was why most of those with work to do out on the trails went out. Well, that and because it was how they made a living. He often envied them in moments like this, when his own responsibilities forced him to stay in the cramped confines of the lodge for weeks on end.

The constant circulation of mountain folk meant that most didn't stay for more than a few days, and new members of their little society came in to replace them. It was unusual for anyone to stay for any length of time; even the hired blades were seldom left idle for long. But this time around, he had been forced to stay still for so long, trappers and hunters who had been here when he arrived were finishing their rounds and returning to find him and his band of killers still in residence.

Their suspicions were building, and he didn't care to have that kind of conversation with anyone, never mind bandits or mountain folk already jumpy from the mysterious deaths earlier in the season. So far, his reputation and the sheer number of brutes he had retained were enough to keep their curiosity at bay. That couldn't last forever.

He needed Lord Drostin to send him word. How long was he to wait for the damned girl to surface? Spring?

"My lord?" Tore's harsh voice was meek, and that was good. Often in a place like Bjornstad, boredom would erupt into violence without warning, as nerves were frazzled and violent minds left to their own devices. He almost thought he would welcome such a distraction, except that it would probably make his real work, when it came, only harder.

He looked down at the board. Tore had turned it to present him with the attacker's position, as was his usual habit when playing. But Geir shook his head. "No, this time I think we'll see what you've learned on the other side of the board." He spun the board in place, giving the other man the attacker's edge.

Again, he tried to ease his focus on the board as Tore made his opening move. This time, Geir tried to be mindful of giving too much of his intentions away with his early moves. Rather than take the time to prepare a well-defended corridor through which his king might retreat, one which would require him to move considerable forces to either kill or block attackers along the route, he kept his moves inconsistent. He calculated the number of pieces he would need to win free, and then in his mind wrote every other defender off. They were expendable; distractions to keep Tore guessing, hunting for his true strength while hiding his intended route of escape.

As he spun his strategy out, he watched Tore deploying his pieces, scattering his strength across all four edges. Eventually, there was a hole, and Geir's pieces were placed to take advantage of that hole. The game was over in an instant, but the man merely shrugged. He had never even come close to winning, and expected no other outcome.

Geir did not react to his win in any way. There was no sense of accomplishment, besting such an adversary. Neither was there much enlightenment, beyond his earlier discoveries. By watching an enemy in preparation for attack, you could see the ebb and flow of his intentions and move accordingly. By watching an enemy's defense, you could discern where his true concerns lay, and have your forces in place to pounce when the time was ripe.

But without a more gifted opponent, he couldn't help but feel the true mysteries the board promised to reveal were beyond him.

The frustration was enough to drive a man to violence.

"Yes!" A voice growled behind him. "I said you were stupid and ugly! Shall I add deaf to the list as well?"

It was a familiar tone, although the words were more artistic than usual. The boredom and fear had worked themselves up to a fever pitch, and the tension was about to be relieved through the time-honored tradition of senseless violence once again.

Geir would usually ignore such things unless his own hirelings were involved. He dared not make a habit of killing the patrons here, lest the landlord decide it was better for business that he leave ... or just disappear in the dark of a cold, silent night.

But he had been freezing in this mountainous hell for weeks, with no sign of an end to his banishment in sight. And the one intellectual distraction he had, the tantalizing truths promised him by those early games of king's table, had evaded his every attempt to follow them since.

He could not remember his frustration ever being greater.

He turned in his chair and glared at the table that was threatening to erupt. The speaker was standing tall over an overturned chair, arms on hips, big beard flowing over a bigger belly. Judging from the rising color in the cheeks of the woman he was glaring at, the target of his words was clear as well.

Geir wasn't sure if she was stupid or not, but the big fat man had certainly struck a true mark with his characterization of her appearance.

"I won't take words like that from a cowardly soft-stick like you, Erland!" The ugly woman rose like some monster from the depths of the sea, a mean-looking dagger glittering in her hand. "Don't think you'd be missed if I decided to cut the cost of your words from your hide, you bastard. You've no value here and you know it!"

The man, Erland, only laughed. "And your only value lies in the strength of your soft arm, Ylva, for it's sure no one would use you otherwise, even in the deepest, coldest night!"

The ugly woman gave a shriek that would have done a wounded troll justice and leapt over the table, knife high. She landed in front of the fat man and they began to wrestle, the blade tracing a shaky arc back and forth over their heads.

Geir looked around. These things usually went one of two ways: the two original combatants would end their dispute alone, or a general melee would erupt, drawing more and more patrons into the fracas until the entire establishment was merrily trying to kill each other with whatever weapons were handy, much like the clash earlier in the season. Such all-out brawls were usually rare, only occurring once or twice a winter, and they usually resulted in surprisingly few casualties, but they could definitely keep the blood warm and the light twinkling in your eyes when they happened.

Erland the fat rocked back, losing his balance in the face of Ylva the ugly's onslaught, and the two of them tumbled over backward, knocking down a man who had been sitting at the next table, back straight and head resolutely bowed over his own cup. But when the man's body was smashed down into the cup, sending a flood of thin beer washing over the table and into the laps of his companions, the afternoon's fate had been sealed.

The entire table rose as one, moving around to stomp the fallen Erland and Ylva into the disgusting floor. Their route was soon blocked by the others who had shared the two opponents' table, and just like that, it was begun. Fists were flying, daggers were out, and the dull quiet was shattered by screams, shouts, and manic laughter.

Geir's mercenaries did not join in the fray, watching their employer. They had no interest in endangering their easy positions for a quick jolt of energy on a lazy afternoon.

Geir watched them and then shrugged. There was really no reason to let the locals have all the fun. As one man, reeling from a massive blow to the temple, staggered into him, the king's shadow suppressed a smile, there was a form to such things, after all, and shouted, "Back off, you bastard, I'm drinking here!" And gave the man a solid crack to the back of the head. The man sank down to the floor with a slow, strange grace, and Geir looked around for his next target.

His pet bandits formed up around him, taking their punches and kicks where they could while making sure no one got too near the boss with a blade.

Scuffles like this were all in good fun, but there was no need to risk their winter's pay.

*****

Geir awoke to the pounding of a thin door and forced himself to release the knife handle he had grabbed before he had even remembered where he was. He was still sore from the evening's festivities, so he moved with a little more care than usual.

The rooms of the Bjornstad trading post were small, and they held little in the way of comfort. They were more partitioned berths in the attic than real rooms; each separated from the others with thin, rough-cut pine. The beds were small and shaky, the bedding flat and often infested with countless additional, freeloading guests.

There was a small table beside the narrow bed, and he reached out, with just a slight wince, to turn up the lamp he kept banked there while he slept. As the warm glow rose, he grabbed an axe from the pile of gear in the corner and eased himself toward the door.

"What?" He barked the word, lamp in one hand and axe in the other, as sounds rose all around him; men and women in the surrounding cubicles awakened by the noise.

"Muata?" The voice was high, probably one of the younger thralls the landlord kept to run drinks, clean, and entertain the more wealthy clients on cold nights. It sounded like a girl, but it could just as easily have been a young boy.

"What?" He snarled. He wasn't going to be opening the door in a place like this until he knew more about what was happening on the other side; especially after an all-out brawl. Of course, the walls were flimsy enough, any determined warrior with a decent axe and a steady arm could have made their own entry in a matter of moments. But that, at least, would give Geir some warning.

"There's a messenger for you, sir." The voice was timid, which could mean they were nervous about waking up a man with his reputation, or they were nervous because someone with a reputation as fearsome, or worse, was holding a knife to their throat.

"What is it?" He reached back and put the lantern on the table, taking the cast-iron door latch in his off hand.

"They won't say, sir. They'll only talk to you." The voice was wary and frightened at the same time. Down on the plains, it would have called him a lord three or four times, he was certain. But up here in the mountains, honorifics were a little harder to come by, and a lot harder to get out of the folks who made their home here; even a young bed warmer.

He grunted, then pulled the door quickly open, whipping out into the passageway, squinting against the flaring candle in the hand of the young ... girl, he thought ... standing alone there.

He looked back and forth along the narrow passageway and nodded. "I'll be right down."

"Thank you, sir." She nodded and turned away.

"Wait! Leave the candle." He held out his empty hand, and after a moment's hesitation, she gave it to him.

He had no desire to bring his little bullseye lantern down with him. A piece of gear like that cost a small fortune, and he'd rather not announce to the entire post how well-equipped he was.

He rushed into trousers and a loose shirt, slipping his boots on despite their cold. The landlord banked the fires in the common room at night, and the temperature, even in the attic, soon plunged to uncomfortable levels.

By the time he came down the rickety stairs, the landlord was behind the long pine bar, preparing two steaming mugs and looking morosely at a lone traveler seated at a table near the fire, poking the embers back into life with a long metal rod. Even enveloped in a dark cloak and from behind, he recognized the figure.

"Eydris." He had expected Drostin to give him more time at his task before the man began to hound him from afar.

Eydris was another of the king's shadow agents; a tall, whip-thin woman whose close-cropped blonde hair revealed her fyrdar heritage despite the piercing black gaze and regal face of an oyathey.

The woman turned, her thin lips curled in a vague smile, as he said her name.

"Geir." She nodded, putting down the rod and standing. "Thank the gods I've found you."

That didn't sound like Eydris. She seldom let anything unnerve her, even the unusual situations that often claimed the attention of a shadow of the king.

"What's wrong?" He looked around the room, but they were alone. Whatever had caused Drostin to send Eydris, it had not been bad enough for him to send more fighters with her.

"What's wrong?" She laughed and gestured around them with both arms, her cloak flaring dramatically. "What else could be wrong? Thank the gods you were here, and I didn't have to track you all the way up to Gnaefa." She dropped back down into her seat and nodded to the landlord as he placed the two mugs before her. "I'm not sure I would have been able to face wandering the mountains all winter looking for you."

He made a bitter face as he walked up to the woman. "Welcome to my world."

She laughed again, her dark eyes sparkling, and grabbed a mug. "Exactly! Your world! The last place I want to spend any time at all!"

He grunted, silently sharing the sentiment. Eydris spent most of her time in the cities, often traveling to the other fyrdar kingdoms. They had worked together several times on the plains of Astrigir, and he liked her as well as he liked any of the other shadow agents he had met over the years. She was steady in a fight, had a good head on her shoulders, and didn't take dirt from anyone.

In fact, she was much too effective to be sent into the mountains as a messenger.

"You're not just here with his lordship's latest whim, I think."

She smiled and eased back, holding the warm mug to her chest. "You're good, Geir. You were always good. No. Lord Drostin wishes me to stay on and assist. Apparently, things are getting grim. He told me you would provide the details when I caught up with you." She looked out of the corner of one eye with a grin. "Details?"

He sat down but made no move toward the mug. "How about you give me the message first, and then maybe we can discuss the mission?"

She laughed. Eydris always laughed, no matter how dark things got. It was almost as if she felt the rest of the world had been placed there for her amusement, and anything that got accomplished in the process was secondary.

"Alright. It's your job, we'll do it your way." She produced a tight roll of parchment and moved to hand it over, jerking it away from his fingers just as they were about to close.

"You promise you'll tell me what you're up to?" Again, with that annoying smile.

He nodded. "If you're going to help me, there's no reason to keep anything from you." He sat and shook his head. "Although, unless this is some magical scroll, I'm not sure what the old man might have to say that will make this assignment any more palatable, or any closer to completion, with or without you."

He took the paper from her and broke the small black seal without looking at it. He'd seen the single, haunting eye transfixed with a dagger a thousand times before. It never changed.

He read the terse words quickly, his head rearing back in wonder, and then read them again.

He must have grunted in surprise, as Eydris leaned forward, reaching for the paper. "What? Something interesting? Is it a magical scroll?"

"No, but it might be something nearly as good. It would appear our patron has been working his mysterious ways again."

He let her have the scroll as he sat back in the rickety chair, lost in thought.

She finished reading and looked up with annoyed confusion. "So we just have to wait for this boy to stumble along in the middle of winter and follow him?" She arched an eyebrow at him, clearly mistrusting the message.

Geir shrugged. "That's what it says. We stay here, keeping an eye out on the greenway, and eventually this hapless target will come along and lead us right to our quarry." He lapsed back into silence, his mind churning.

"You're remembering something." The accusing tone was playful, but he had learned long ago not to ignore it.

"Hmm? Oh, it's nothing. I was wondering what the lad had under his shirt, that he was so eager for me not to see. To think that it might have been a map, that I was that close all along..."

That seemed to take her aback. "You know the boy? Can't we just go grab him and make him tell us what we need to know?"

He shook his head. "I don't know him. I've met him. A stable boy at a third-rank hostel in the foothills. And he knows I've met him." He pointed to the paper. "If Drostin wanted us to grab the lad, he'd have told us to. For some reason, he wants us to follow, instead."

He leaned back and glanced at the king's table board sitting nearby.

Eydris looked around. "What are you so lost about? Are you still playing that game? I told you, that'll make your eyes go bad."

He gave her a smile, but there was no real humor in it. "So you have."

But he was thinking about his first revelations, weeks ago, when he had been playing with Vidhar. Eventually, your opponent will show where to move.

Somewhere out there in the frozen mountains was a little girl he had been ordered to find. Their meeting had been foreordained by forces far beyond their control, but he would do his duty, as he had always done in the past. For king and kingdom, the girl would die.

And now he would be able to find her. He would find her, and then he would return to Connat and be done with these spirit-damned mountains for the rest of the winter.

His gaze flicked back up to Eydris, who was staring at him like something strange she had pulled out of a pond. "Are you ready to tell me what's going on yet?"

He smiled again, and nodded. "Sure. How good are you against a maekre blade?"

Chapter 12

A great crash echoed down the valley, and Tyr cringed.

Eirik staggered to his feet, coughing blood as the islander sauntered easily away, a massive wooden club over one shoulder.

"You are slow, Saemgard." The man's accent was easier to understand after more than a week, and the contempt dripping from every lyrical word was like salt in the fyrdar warrior's wounds.

Tyr shook his head. He remembered Eirik when the man had been the terror of the tourney circuit. He remembered when mere rumor of the Ruun had doubled purses and made strong men pale.

But did he truly remember? As he watched his master beaten into the frozen mud time and time again, he had begun to wonder how trustworthy those memories were. Had he been so eager, for so long, for Eirik to amount to something, that he had justified those wishes by inflating his own memories of the man's abilities?

The more he watched Chagua spar, the less faith he had in his own recollection.

The islander paced circles around his slow, burly master. Eirik had yet to land a single blow, while Tyr had stopped keeping count of the times his master had been knocked into the mud.

To make matters even worse, Chagua wasn't using a sword, or even an axe. The islander had said, often and loudly, that he would use a true weapon when Eirik was worthy of being hit with one. So far, he said, there was little sign he would ever need anything more formal than a tree branch.

For the first few days, Tyr believed him. Eirik had been plagued with uncontrollable tremors that wracked his body, leaving him nearly defenseless before the quick, nimble islander. That had not stopped Chagua from demanding hours of sparring each day, it had only meant that it wasn't even sporting, as he sent the big tourney knight tumbling into the mud time and time again.

But as time went on, and with each day further from the drink, the shakes had subsided. It had been almost a week, now, and the lingering signs of Eirik's struggles with the spirits were nearly faded. And yet, still, no matter what weapon he was given, he could not touch the islander, who seemed capable of rapping him in any part of the body he wished, at any time.

It was almost enough to convince Tyr that his faith in Eirik had been nothing but the errant fancy of a little boy; beliefs he should have left behind long ago, with pixies, horned serpents, and trolls.

"Again, then, islander. There will come a time when you come within blade's reach, and then we'll see who's laughing." Eirik wiped sweat from his eyes, hair plastered to his forehead, and assumed a ready stance once again. He was not using the enormous maekre blade, but rather the long oak handle of a fighting axe weighted with a dull stone head.

Chagua had invited the big man to use his 'butcher's blade' if he wanted to, but that had only enraged Eirik more.

The problem, Tyr knew from watching more combat than he ever had before, was that the islander was not only faster than his master, but it appeared as if Eirik's muscles were betraying him, refusing to lift the stone axe fast enough to take advantage of any opening he might find.

In fact, Tyr had watched them fight so many times now, he felt like he could step in, pick up the damned axe, and have at least an even chance of striking the islander a glancing blow himself.

He looked away as the stout wooden cudgel wove around the flailing axe to give Eirik a slight blow to the back of the head that knocked him off balance and sent him, once again, crashing to the ground.

One can only watch one's childhood hero bested so often before one felt the overwhelming need to go for a long, quiet walk.

*****

Beyond the sheltered valley, a terrible storm was raging. Their small keep was snow-free, but the temperature was frigid, and Tyr was bundled up in several furs and two cloaks as he sat, perched atop the ruined keep on the hill, to watch Eirik and Chagua spar once again.

Every day the islander put his master through this ritual of pain and humiliation, and every day Tyr dutifully went out and watched. Between the shielding walls of the valley and the hot springs behind their hill, there was far less snow to clear than he had first feared. He made sure they had plenty of wood for their fires, made what repairs he could to gear and weapons, and did whatever work the others could think to assign him. But aside from all of that, he never missed a match between the two warriors.

Maiara ... or princess, as Tsegan forced him to call her whenever the old man was around, spent most of her days in the common room with one book or another. She seemed perfectly happy, and claimed to be learning a great deal. But she didn't seem to be acting any smarter, nor did she seem to be radiating any queen-like properties she hadn't possessed before.

All in all, between watching Eirik be destroyed in bout after bout, and watching Maiara apparently coming ever-closer to being a queen without changing at all, he found his faith in anything he had ever thought or known shaken daily.

"If you insist upon fighting with such a heavy weapon, you need to keep your distance until you are ready to strike." Chagua was instructing Eirik before they clashed again.

Today, the islander was using a slender length of wood that he had carved into a slight curve. Maiara had told Tyr it reminded her of a sword the man kept in his quarters, but he had never heard of any sword so slight or light before.

Eirik was still using the stone axe. He had said he would not take up another weapon until he struck Chagua with it at least once. Chagua had laughed at that, and told him he was welcome to whatever he cared to use.

Tyr watched as they squared off against each other once again, this time Eirik started farther back and tried to maintain his distance as he swung the axe back and forth, sustaining his momentum while not announcing his intended target.

Then Chagua danced in, light on his feet, ran under the swinging axe, spun around behind the bearded warrior, and rapped him lightly on the back of the head.

This time, Eirik managed to keep his balance but staggered forward several steps as he did so.

"Distance, Saemgard." Chagua spun his blade in lazy, intricate arcs, his bright smile flashing in his dark face.

Whenever the islander called Eirik 'Saemgard', Tyr could tell it drove his master to distraction. He had figured, early on in the process, that this was exactly the effect Chagua was going for.

Eirik's face was flat, his grey eyes blazing, when he turned back to face the islander again. Tyr was glad. He would rather not have to see his master's face when this part of the day came. Clearly, Chagua had tired of his games and decided it was time to put Eirik through his paces and then crush him, thus exhausting him into silence for the night. It was far preferable, to all involved, than having to listen to the warrior mumble, curse, and complain of his bruises and fatigue until they all were driven to their sleeping furs out of sheer exhaustion.

This time, as Eirik approached, trying his best to keep his distance while at the same time prepare for an attack, Chagua allowed him to stay away, his wooden sword weaving a mesmerizing pattern back and forth, from hand to another, around his head, and then back like a juggler from a minstrel show.

It was clear that Eirik was not mesmerized, but rather moved with a heavy determination, the stone axe moving back and forth, waiting for the ideal time to strike. They circled each other, feinting and drawing their weapons close. They exchanged several short jabbing attacks, neither coming close to the other, and Tyr felt hope rising in his heart. Eirik was not being brash, not allowing Chagua's mocking tone to draw him into an unwise attack. Instead, he was testing the man's defenses, measuring his resolve with each short attack, looking for an opening where he would be able to drive the axe into the islander and silence the taunts, at least for a day.

Then he thought he saw it. The axe came sweeping up, hovering over his master's head; massive muscles knotted, pulling the axe down and through the islander.

Except Chagua wasn't there. The axe whistled harmlessly through the air, and the islander reached out with the tip of his sword and gave the axe handle a gentle tap, redirecting its force and momentum. Rather than slamming into the ground, the axe continued flying through the air. Eirik had been braced for the bone-rattling impact with the ground, but he was not ready for the sudden, forceful pull of the weapon as it continued on its flight.

The axe pulled the warrior off balance, he staggered, arms outstretched, and Chagua brought the blade of his wooden sword down on Eirik's wrists with a vicious crack.

The warrior screamed, the axe fell to the ground, and Chagua jabbed the pummel of his weapon into Eirik's gut.

The air rushed from his master's lungs in a pained grunt, the man fell to his knees, and Tyr hopped down from his perch and moved toward the stables.

The aftermath of these bouts was not something he needed to see again.

*****

"It is not a sword. It is a huge, clumsy axe with a four foot head." Chagua's contempt for the maekre blade had been obvious from the beginning of their training. Until now, it had been confined to the common room. But yesterday, against all sane predictions, Eirik had managed to graze his opponent's leg with the stone axe head. With a haughty air Tyr didn't think he'd entirely earned, he had announced that he would be moving on to train with his own blade from now on.

Tyr had been horrified at the pronouncement. He had seen the kind of damage dulled tourney swords could do, and he knew that Eirik had taken to keeping his own blade razor sharp. The fact that his master had replaced the leather guard over the sharpened blade did not improve matters much. He vaguely remembered what had happened to the bandits who had attacked them in the mountain clearing. He was coming to like Chagua and didn't want to see the quiet islander cut in half.

But Chagua had shown no concern at all. After making a few comments about being unsure if the axe had actually struck him, he had shrugged and told Eirik he was welcome to use whatever weapon he wished.

Then he had taken his evening's habit of ridiculing the maekre blade out into the courtyard for their practice sessions. Eirik found it almost as maddening as when the islander called him 'Saemgard', and so Chagua did it twice as often.

Tyr sighed, perched once more amidst the tumbled stones of the keep's upper stories, and looked up into the swirling clouds. The world outside their little valley had been hit with another massive blizzard, but the cold winter sun was out again, and the distant peaks all around them sparkled with new snow.

He had seen no further signs of whatever creature he had glimpsed on that first day, although the sense of being watched, of something crouching out in the forest, peering at them all, had only grown as the winter came on. During his long hikes and winter hunts, he often felt as if he was being followed.

He heard a soft grunt behind him and turned quickly, his mind unquiet with such thoughts, but it was only Maiara clambering down the ruins toward him.

Tyr felt unreasoning panic rising up inside his chest and schooled his face to what he hoped was a pleasant, welcoming neutrality.

All the while, of course, reciting a now-familiar litany in his head.

-She's not a princess, she's not a queen, she's just a girl. She's not a princess, she's not a queen, she's just a girl-

Unfortunately, it usually didn't help. He had been miserably tongue-tied around her even when she was just a girl, before she was a princess, or going to be a queen.

"I can't stand being cooped up in that little room any longer." She made the announcement as if she needed to justify her presence on the wall, and he thought that maybe, just maybe, he wasn't the only one who was nervous.

"No reason you should be, but I'm not sure watching Eirik get knocked up and down the courtyard is going to be much more interesting." He kept his tone light, fixing his gaze on the pair below, trying to seem as natural as he could.

"He does seem to get hurt a lot." Maiara's tone was kind, but also a little hesitant. "I've tried to stay away so he wouldn't be distracted."

A strange little flare burst in Tyr's chest and he stiffened. "Why should he be distracted?"

"Well, he's supposed to be my protector," she reasoned. "I thought, if he's getting beaten every day in practice, he might not like me to see..."

The flare died, and Tyr decided, once again, he needed to stop examining her every word. "Well, I think he's already distracted enough, getting beaten. It's not something he's accustomed to." Honesty compelled him to complete that thought. "Well, at least not until recently."

"He used to be better?" He was sure she didn't mean anything by the question, but the honest tone of it had teeth all its own.

"Well, he used to be the best, like Tsegan said. He was the youngest warrior ever to be sworn into the saemgard." He tried to sound proud as he said the words, but those triumphs seemed to be a long time ago, with a lot of pain and failure between then and now. "Even after, when he joined the tourney circuit as a ruun, he was almost unstoppable. He was undefeated for more seasons than any champion before him."

"Was that when you came to serve him?" Again, he was certain it was an honest, innocent question. But it was also one of the most painful anyone had ever asked, for all that.

"Well, no ... By the time I became his squire, things had already started to ... change."

She turned from the sparring men below. "What changed?"

Tyr shrugged. He didn't really know, so telling the story was hard. "I'm not sure. He got tired. He got old." He looked down at his hands, his voice falling. "I think he always wished for something to happen that never did."

She turned in place, pivoting toward him. "What?"

This felt too much like betrayal. He had never spoken of these things with Eirik, wasn't even sure his suspicions bore any resemblance to reality. But maybe because he had never spoken about it, the words just tumbled out.

"I think he wanted the king to forgive him. Even as we fled from camp to camp, running from agents, or men Eirik said were agents, I think he always hoped he was wrong, somehow, or that the king would send a messenger instead of an assassin."

Her eyes widened. "The king wants to assassinate him?" She looked back down at Eirik, her brows furrowed. "Why?"

Tyr frowned and shrugged. "I'm not sure."

She looked back to him. "You've seen these assassins? Did you have to fight any of them?"

Tyr shook his head, uncomfortable. There were some parts of the past few years he didn't completely understand. "No. He would see them, or sense them, and we would run. I've never seen them, except from far off." He looked away. He had never admitted this out loud before. "To be honest, I'm not sure there even is such a thing as a King's Shadow."

She looked like she would speak again, then turned back to watch the sparring. He felt his shoulders sag with relief. He didn't have any more answers, so it was best she not continue to ask any questions.

He looked down at the book in her hands and noticed that it was the same book Tsegan showed them that morning over a week ago; their first morning in Alden's Tor.

"Is that the old saga?"

Maiara looked down at the book as if it was a puzzle box that refused to open. "Yes. And I've been reading it for most of the day, taking a break from all the treatises on leadership, politics, philosophy and all that." She sighed. "I never thought I'd wish I was back to only having the old almanac and the fairy stories." She looked at him with a weak smile. "At least now I know why they bothered to teach me to read."

That touched on another sore spot he hadn't expected. Knowing that Maiara was such a reader, suddenly he found his weakness in that area to be particularly embarrassing. He shook his head and smiled back. "Those were the two books at the inn? That's all you had to read?"

She nodded, glancing back down to where Chagua was dancing circles around his master. "Yeah. Well, those and the ledgers for the guesthouse. For the past few years, it's been mostly those." She almost seemed embarrassed. "I pretty much had the other two memorized a long time ago."

Which was even more impressive and intimidating. "You memorized an almanac? What did it say?"

She shrugged. "Mostly things about weather, and planting crops, the phases of the moon a decade ago, things like that."

That hardly seemed worth memorizing, but he didn't want the conversation to lapse into silence; she might go back inside. "Did you learn anything interesting?"

She looked sideways at him, and then gestured up to the distant, ice-shrouded crests surrounding them. "The glaciers all along the White Mountains have been getting smaller each year for over twenty years. The almanac said that meant there would be more farmable land exposed. It said that would eventually lead to an increase in population, either from migrations or from general expansion of the population already in the mountains." Tyr shook his head. "Well, that's wrong. We didn't see any farms on our way up, or big crowds of workers making their way toward the peaks. And besides, how would you farm on the side of a mountain, even without a big glacier in the way?" He waved his hand toward one particularly high mountain. "And I haven't noticed the ice going away. It's only gotten bigger since we showed up."

She smiled, and he felt that little knot of nerves in his chest tighten. "Well, the almanac said it would take a long time. It also had several entries on ways you could make a farm work on the slopes of a mountain. There was even one article about other benefits the same technique could bring to the farmers. It was a Kun Makha almanac, so, you know, it had some strange ideas."

He shook his head. That figured. Anything from Kun Makha was going to be full of oddities he couldn't be expected to understand. Most of those oyathey from the warmer northern regions were just plain crazy.

As he thought about the strangeness of the oyathey, he realized that the dreaded silence had descended upon their conversation. He tried to remain casual as he cast around for some way to keep her interested and engaged. He took one hand off the stone beneath himself and gestured to the book. "Finding anything interesting in there?" A flickering spark rose up in him before he could suppress it. "Anything in there about me?"

She laughed. "No, but don't be offended. There really isn't anything in here about me either, or about," she gestured down to the courtyard, "your master."

That didn't make any sense. "But I thought that book was the whole reason we were here? I mean, the old man did say we were going to fulfill some great prophecy. What does that mean if we're not in there? Was he lying?"

She sighed, glancing down at the book in her lap. "I don't think so ... I don't know. It's not like I could ask him, he's gone so often."

The old man had been gone for almost a week this time, heading down out of the mountains, he said, to prepare the way for the princess to emerge from the shadows; whatever that meant.

"It's all very vague. Doesn't mention anyone by name, of course. I'm gathering that this type of saga seldom does. But it does refer to a guardian riding out of the shadows after fate has laid him low, to usher in a new age of hope ... and about a birth, and a red day ... You see? It doesn't make much sense. But I think that part is talking about him." She gestured down to where Eirik was on his back, roaring in frustration while Chagua paced around him, making some sort of commentary.

Tyr's brow furrowed. "'Fate laid him low'?"

Maiara looked sheepishly at him from behind the fall of black hair. "Wasn't he defeated at some great battle, somewhere?"

It was Tyr's turn to sigh. "Yeah. The Battle of Merrik Ford. King Einar thought he could unite the fyrdar kingdoms under his rule and treat with the oyathey of Kun Makha as equals ... didn't end so well."

She nodded, a small line of annoyance appearing between her eyes. "I've read about the Battle of Merrick Ford." She shrugged, looking back down to watch as Eirik was helped back up to his feet. "But before then, he was supposed to be a great warrior, right?"

Loyalty surged up in Tyr's breast and grasped control of his mouth. "Yes! He was a great warrior! He was the best!" Down in the yard, the great warrior was again spun about by the dexterous islander and ended up landing in the frozen mud on his face. "That was a long time ago."

Maiara reached out and touched Tyr's shoulder, and he felt a flare of heat go straight around his chest. "Chagua's really something special. I'm sure he can bring your master back."

He had wanted to keep her here, so that they could continue to talk, and he would have an excuse to look at her eyes ... but he'd rather not continue this conversation. He searched for something else they could discuss.

"Is there anything in any of those books about magic?"

Why had he asked that? He didn't want her to think of him as some gullible infant! He stuttered, trying to mitigate the damage. "I mean, if the old man fancies himself a great wizard from a hundred years ago, his library should have some books on magic, shouldn't they?"

Maiara frowned. "Not really. And he would be considerably older than a hundred, if he is who he says he is. There are some mentions of Tsegan Aqisiaq in the older histories, of course. I even found one or two mentions of something that might be magic as he tried to keep the fyrdar from seceding from the empire." Her voice grew soft and she shifted her focus to some distant point. "And there's something about the descriptions of his powers ..."

"What did he do that you saw?" This was an honest area of curiosity for Tyr; no need for him to feign interest.

Her brows lowered as she tried to remember. "In the House of the Fallen Oak, he seemed to make the fire flare up, and the common room was suddenly filled with an over-powering heat, and all the patrons left."

Tyr didn't try to hide his disappointment. "That's all? He made it hot and everyone left? I've seen countless roadside tricksters make fire flare up at a gesture. They do it with powders. They can even make the fire flare with different colors. There's no magic in that!"

That seemed to annoy her. "Well, what have you seen him do? You seem eager to believe he is who he claims. Have you seen him do anything amazing?"

That brought Tyr up short. He didn't enjoy talking about his master's drinking, it felt like another betrayal. He shrugged. "Eirik was very ill, and the old man healed him like that." He tried to snap his fingers, but his gloves got in the way. "In a snap, anyway."

Maiara nodded, looking back down to where Eirik was on his back once more. "I've seen that kind of illness many times back at the Fallen Oak." She looked back to him with one arched eyebrow. "There are powders that cure that as well, I think."

They fell silent, each glaring, then turned away at the same time.

For several minutes the two warriors below took a breather, drank from a shared water skin, and then returned to circling the courtyard. Then she muttered, "I saw him do something else, as well."

He recognized a peace offering when he saw one, and grasped at it eagerly. "What?"

She shivered, pulling her cloak more tightly around her shoulders. "He ... killed something, I think. In the forest, on our way here."

Tyr felt himself ready to react again with disbelief but took greater control. He had killed on his way up into the mountains as well, and he was no magician. That had been the first time he had ever killed anyone. In fact, he wasn't completely sure he had killed anyone. The wound in his shoulder had cost him a lot of blood, and he had lost consciousness toward the end. When he awoke the next morning, wrapped tightly in his furs, the wound carefully bound up with clean linen, the bodies had all been gone.

He shook himself out of the violent reverie and kept his voice level. "He killed something? What?"

She shook her head. "I don't know. A bear, maybe? The skull is down in the common room, near the books. I'll show you later, if you want."

"That thing? He killed that thing? It doesn't look like any bear I've ever seen. It was a bear? How did he kill it?"

She started to speak, then stopped, glancing at him sheepishly, and shrugged. "I don't know what it was. It was dark. And I don't know how he killed it. Chagua had rushed into the woods to fight it, but it knocked him away, back out into the light. Then Tsegan went down and ... did something.

The shadows moved, there was a lot of noise and thrashing about, it got very hot and dry for a moment, then there was a scream. Chagua went back into the woods a little while later and brought the skull out. And that was it."

He stared at her, finding it hard to believe that what she was describing was magic. She hadn't actually seen anything, right? And the only person who had been close, who had produced the skull, was the old man's servant? He could see in her eyes that she was thinking the same things, and he realized that they were terribly close to ending this conversation.

"That sounds ... scary."

Honestly? That was the best he could do? Maybe it would be enough. But it wasn't. She nodded. "It was."

She rose gracefully to her feet. "It looks like they'll be finished soon." She gestured down to the courtyard, where, once again, Eirik was being helped back to his feet. "It will be time for dinner. It's my turn to cook, I think." And she was gone. Leaping nimbly from one tumbled stone to the next, she went up the piled ruin and disappeared over the top.

Tyr watched her go, sighed, cursed himself for an idiot, and then turned back just in time to see Chagua dump his master back into the mud.

It was going to be a long, long winter.

Chapter 13

Maiara closed the book with slow, gentle motions. She did this because she knew if she gave in to her impulses, she would have slammed it shut with enough violence to crack the table beneath.

Ever since that night in the common room, when she had first learned about her supposed father and the role Tsegan claimed fate held for her, she had found it difficult to contain her temper. She had never had such a hard time before. But then, before that moment, she had been an unremarkable orphan, with no parents, and nothing more in her future than the stewardship of a quiet guesthouse.

Now, she was supposed to think of herself as a princess, and beyond that, she was part of a plot to kill the man she had only recently been told was her father.

She believed, next to everything else that had been piled up on her shoulders of late, a certain amount of angry confusion was understandable.

She glared at the wall of books with disgust. Her grand winter of adventure into the mountains was not proving to be all that grand, or that adventurous. Instead, she found herself trapped in the close, humid confines of their little refuge, pouring over old books all day, every day. At night, Chagua and the old warrior were too tired to talk, and although she enjoyed Tyr's company, he had started to act strangely toward her. She thought she recognized the look from some of the less comfortable conversations with Kustaa back in Baedr. She was already neck deep in confusion and complication; she didn't need to court more.

And all of it in preparation to kill a king she was to believe was her father.

She still wasn't sure if she quite believed the old man's stories, but she had decided it would be best if she pretended she did – for now. She could always go back to the Fallen Oak in the springtime; the old man had promised. But for now, it would be best if she seemed to believe that she was a princess, focusing on the lessons he thought she needed to learn.

But she would be damned if she was going to enjoy it.

She understood many of the concepts contained in the books already. There was a certain tradeoff required between a ruler and his subjects ... or her subjects.

In order to rule over a people as diverse and independent as the fyrdar, one needed to offer something in return for their fealty. No one descended from the fierce raiders of the sagas would allow a weak man – person – to lead them. She understood that at the same time that she had to wonder what she might have to offer them.

The books spoke at length of duty, honor, and justice. Those few that dealt directly with the fyrdar were the newest in the collection, written and transcribed within the last hundred years, just after the fyrdar had shattered the ancient empire of Kun Makha. There seemed to be a great deal of time spent on discussing the great virtues of the fyrdar and their shining destiny. She had a definite sense that she was meant to come away from those books confident in the superiority of the fyrdar and contemptuous of the weak oyathey of Kun Makha.

The problem with that approach, with her in particular, was that she had not been raised with such a glowing regard for 'her' people, nor had her upbringing in the Fallen Oak imparted in her any sort of active disdain for the people of Kun Makha.

In fact, her long, shining dark hair and bright blue eyes marked her out quite clearly as a mixed-breed herself. So, if King Einar was her father, he must not have shared the depth of contempt for the oyathey that these books professed. She had grown up knowing that whoever her parents had been, her blood carried the heritage of both the empire and the kingdoms. And so each time she finished another narrow-minded tome on fyrdar rulership, she wanted to scream.

There were other books she had found more interesting. The histories were filled with intriguing stories of bravery and cowardice, sacrifice and greed. They seemed far less biased than the others. And yet, there were undeniably holes in them as well. The fyrdar had come to the empire of Kun Makha over five hundred years ago, she knew. But from where? And the oyathey had greeted them with open arms, even granting them lands within their own empire. For centuries the fyrdar and the oyathey had lived in peace, forging a single, powerful nation stronger than either culture would have been alone.

The breaking of the empire was something everyone took for granted, and in fact most of the histories seemed to have been written before the shattering. The rest took up the tale after the formation of the Broken Kingdoms.

Nothing she had found in the library spoke about why the fyrdar had decided to shatter the empire, first breaking away from the original Kun Makha to form a fyrdar realm, and then turning on each other. There was no hint of why her ancestors had turned away from their great partnership, plunging their lands into endless chaos and bloodshed.

In one book, Kun Makha was an unstoppable fusion of the nature-loving, thoughtful oyathey and the frenzied, passionate fyrdar. In the next, Kun

Makha was broken, most of the fyrdar consigned to the Broken Kingdoms, fighting petty wars amongst themselves for more than a century.

As she poured over the histories, the strange lapse in the narrative had become more and more troubling. She found herself with three or four books open on the table at a time, trying to trace the events that had brought them all to the current, sorry state.

There was nothing.

Either Tsegan had chosen the books very carefully, purposefully hiding that information from her, or no historian in the last hundred years had concerned themselves with the shattering of the greatest empire known to oyathey or fyrdar.

As the ward of a successful fyrdar landlord, she was sophisticated enough to have met many oyathey from Kun Makha, most of them traveling from the empire to Einar's Bhorg in Connat. She recognized the image of effete weakness and easily-offended sensibilities as a caricature; the oyathey she had met had seemed to reflect the same general patterns of good and bad found in the fyrdar she knew so well.

There was plenty of trade between the empire and the Broken Kingdoms. In fact, the empire of Kun Makha seemed to hold no ill feelings at all over the dissolution of their southern regions and the act of betrayal by those they had accepted as their own for so long.

Because that is how Maiara was coming to see the hidden events that had brought about the Broken Kingdoms. It was clearly a betrayal of the oyathey and the hospitality that had made firm friends of fearsome raiders ... for a time.

She knew that many individual oyathey viewed the fyrdar that way still; as barbaric cretins barely deserving of common courtesy. But from what she had seen, there was more than enough truth in that generalization to make it at the very least understandable.

And so now she was supposed to untangle this knot? Somehow Tsegan meant for her, the supposed daughter of the current king of Astrigir, to not only save her own kingdom from some mysterious enemy rising somewhere, unseen, in the world, but she was then supposed to unite the three fyrdar realms into one, and save the oyathey as well?

She pushed the latest book farther away. She had no interest in reading more today. In fact, she thought she might stop reading altogether until Tsegan returned to force the issue.

She knew the men were up in the courtyard. They were always up in the courtyard. Unless Chagua had pushed Eirik into running in the frozen, snow-locked forests beyond the valley. She wasn't sure why the islander was so intent on forcing these wretched runs on the big man, but she had seen their aftermath many times. Eirik returned exhausted, filthy, and sullen. It made for some of the most peaceful, quiet evenings the little foursome had experienced.

Maybe that was Chagua's true purpose.

She felt a little shock of guilt whenever she had one of these ungenerous thoughts. Eirik's tale was not much different than hers – in its recent chapters, anyway. He and Tyr had been pulled from their lives to come up into the mountains on the word of some strange old man and a dusty book, and Eirik had not even been promised a kingdom for his troubles!

Maiara often wondered, as she was drifting off to sleep, why Eirik had agreed to stay and subject himself to the islander's abuse. What did he have to gain, even if the little old man's story proved true? Would he spend the rest of his life protecting Maiara? Did that mean they would need to be together for the rest of her life? That hardly seemed like an ideal outcome for either of them.

She shook her head and rose to fetch her cloak from a row of hooks by the entrance. Maybe they would be practicing something amusing to watch. Or maybe Tyr would be up there, idle enough to have a conversation while his master was humiliated time after time in the yard.

It was a less-than-charitable thought, and once again she fought down the pang of guilt. If she expected the man to defend her against – gods and spirits knew what – then she should be nicer to him, both in the waking world and in the silence of her own mind.

She emerged from the stables and immediately, once again, was surprised to feel the temperature of the valley. Just a few hundred paces in every direction, winter reigned supreme. But here, this little area was almost, almost, warm. It was still chilly, and she was thankful for the cloak and gloves. But it was warmer than it should have been.

It reminded her, just a little, of the hot, dry dreams that still haunted her nights.

Chagua and her supposed champion were squaring off against each other, and she leaned up against the frame of the stable's opening to watch.

She was no warrior, and Baedr had been home to no great fighters, but she had seen her fair share of tourneys, and she thought she could judge the quality of a man's fighting prowess in general terms, at least. It was clear that Chagua was far superior to Eirik in nearly every respect. She admitted to herself, however, that it appeared that Eirik had been making great improvements in recent days. His color, beneath the bristly, grizzled yellow beard, was not nearly so crimson as it had been when they had first met the big man.

He had even taken to shaving the sides of his head again, leaving the broad strip down the center just long enough that it stood out from his big skull, waving with every movement. Tyr thought it meant he was taking more pride in his appearance, and although that sentiment made sense to her, she was a little doubtful as to how much pride the haircut might indicate.

As she watched, the big man was hoisting his dark, massive sword up in two hands. She thought once again how one-sided these bouts always appeared to be at the beginning. They were one sided, she knew, but not in the way the early moments might have made her think.

Chagua still wielded his carved wooden sword. It was a fairly good replica of the iron blade she had seen him tend to on the trail; the sword he had drawn against the beast in the woods. Why he was not using the real weapon when Eirik was swinging his own weighty monstrosity, she didn't know. But he never seemed to need it, so she was willing to admit he knew what he was doing.

She knew nothing of island culture, nor why the man seemed so fixated on the library down in the basement. She had flipped through the books on the first couple of days they were in the valley, before Eirik and Tyr had arrived, but she had found no mention of the northern islands, or, in fact, any culture other than Kun Makha and the Broken Kingdoms. So Chagua was a mystery to her, and she had always found it difficult to leave a mystery alone.

In fact, she had driven Kustaa to distraction more than once, tracking a missing animal or town rumor through Baedr.

Thoughts of the only friend from her childhood gave her pause, and she settled more heavily against the wooden frame, her earlier twinge of remorse giving way to a far heavier weight of guilt. She had thought less and less of Baedr, of the Fallen Oak, of Turid and Vali Sayen, and, worst of all, of Kustaa, since she had arrived in the little valley.

She remembered the night Tsegan had taken her away from everything she had ever known. She remembered how Kustaa had stood up for her, the only one willing to stand against the strange old man.

Her throat grew dry and her vision blurred as thoughts of that night ran through her mind again. She had always known Kustaa cared for her. How could she not? They had practically lived in the same house for years. And there had been those times, when she had seen that look pass behind his eyes more than once. But she had not realized the depth of his feelings until he had placed himself between her guardians, their strange guest, and her. Vali Sayen could destroy his hopes and dreams with a word, and yet Kustaa had stood his ground.

Until Tsegan had taken him aside, that was. What had the old man told him? How had he convinced the boy, in a matter of moments, to give up his hopeless objections and let her leave?

It was too much. If things fell out the way Tsegan said they would, she might never see him again. She needed to continue down this path, pretending to believe, before she drove herself insane with thoughts of the past. She wiped tears away and moved out into the courtyard. Eirik's massive sword was buried in the mud about twenty paces away. The big warrior stood in a fighter's crouch before Chagua, who held a shortened wooden sword, one end a splintered ruin.

Eirik charged, and even Maiara could tell he had abandoned all sense of tactical awareness in favor of blind, animal rage.

Chagua looked like a dancer as he leapt into the air, sailing over the running warrior, and rapped him on the back of the head as he flipped, landing in a crouch, watching as Eirik, arms wheeling wildly, crashed into a mumbling heap in the mud.

"You must fight with your brain as much as with your brawn. You knew this once, I know. You must learn it again." Chagua stood casually in the center of the courtyard, his arms at his side. "You will never be able to reacquire your full potential until you can master your own mind."

Eirik spat mud off to the side, glaring at the islander as he rose to shaky feet, his face red and sheened with sweat. His shouldered heaved as he worked to control his breathing.

"There are habits that saved your life once, warrior. You have forgotten them, and until you find them again, you will be useless to anyone, including the princess."

Eirik's gaze flicked to where Maiara stood, and a confused look crossed his face. She thought she saw anger there, but also guilt, embarrassment, and maybe even sadness. He spat again, then turned toward the trail leading out of the valley.

"Where are you going, Saemgard?" Chagua's voice was light, his hands resting easily on his hips.

Eirik glared back at him, Maiara seemingly forgotten. "You were going to send me on another amusing little run, I believe?"

The islander barked a quick laugh and nodded. "So I was! So I was, indeed. Yes, you may go. Take the route down to the small creek, if you would be so good. And then run in it until you reach the waterfall, then double back. That should be enough."

Eirik's glare lasted one more long, awkward second, then he was off. He was dressed only in leather pants and a thick padded shirt, his boots the heavy footgear Tyr had told her was worn during tourney bouts. They would not make running through frigid water any more enjoyable.

She watched as the warrior loped up the hillside and disappeared over the ridge, then she turned to Chagua, who was pulling the heavy sword out of the muck.

"Ah, princess. I didn't see you there." He was lying, she was certain. And he was the only person in their little exile who seemed comfortable calling her 'princess', but his small smile was genuine. The long, tight rolls of his hair hung down over his shoulders, dark against the light muslin of his shirt. She noticed he wasn't even breathing heavily, and no moisture glistened on his dark skin.

"Just watching." She moved out into the courtyard, trying to appear nonchalant. "You are not kind to him." She tilted her head up to indicate where the big warrior had just recently disappeared.

His dark eyes narrowed. "It would not be kind to allow him to take the field with insufficient skill to defend himself, never mind you."

She nodded with a smile, as if ceding a point. "Well, I think maybe you're a bit crueler than you need to be."

His smile faded. "That is, thankfully, my decision to make. The man is stubborn. You do not break an obstinate horse through kindness. That man must be equal to whatever task master Aqisiaq sets before him, and I do not mean to 'go easy' on him until I decide that he is prepared."

She nodded, tracing a random, meandering path around the courtyard. It amused her on some level that he pivoted to follow her. "Still, though, I think I should be able to defend myself, in case things with Eirik don't go well?"

Chagua's brows came down in confusion. "You have your tasks, princess, I have mine. Yours, I think, are far more difficult. Ruling a kingdom is no simple feat, and you have not been raised to it, as most who find themselves in your position usually are."

She shook her head. "Still, I think being able to defend myself, just in case, should be part of my preparation."

Chagua looked down at the broken sword stick in his hand. "You will have Eirik Hastiin. And there will be others, I am certain. Your protection will be the task of countless men and women with far more training than you will ever attain."

She shook her head. "Even so, those guardians will be human. Guards can be beaten, they can be bribed, they can betray their trust for a hundred different reasons." She smiled, trying on him a look that had worked on Kustaa, when she had had the nerve to try it. "Surely just a small amount of training with some simple weapon would be possible? It might make all the difference someday, if things went wrong."

A strange light flared in his eyes in response to that smile, and for a moment, she feared she had gravely misunderstood the situation. But then he grinned, bowed his shaking head, and she could have sworn he had chuckled just a little.

"Very well, princess. But we will stay well clear of live steel, I think. We will start with something basic. Something you might reasonably expect to find on hand, if things, as you say, get desperate?"

Chagua looked around and found what he was searching for. A rake, handle replaced after the day the islander had used it to beat Eirik senseless. With a short kick, the head was snapped off once again, and he was left holding a straight, smooth-sided staff.

"You're going to teach me how to fight with a stick?" She didn't try to hide her disappointment.

He nodded, looking down at the staff. "It's not a difficult weapon to grasp, and any mistakes you make will, most likely, not cause undo damage to your opponent or yourself."

There was a heavy thud behind her and she spun to see Tyr standing up from a crouch. He had obviously dropped from the ruins above. "I'll spar with her. I won't have much to do before he comes back, anyway."

Chagua's smile gleamed, and Maiara couldn't help but feel that there was some sense of relief behind the expression. She felt a stir of anger that she couldn't explain and grabbed the stick from the man's hands, putting some distance between them as she felt its balance, to hide the emotion on her face.

When she turned, Tyr had his own stick at the ready. But he was holding his in an easy, loose grip, across his body, and she realized he would have been trained on many different weapons as he travelled the kingdoms with Eirik.

"So, let us begin with the proper grip." Chagua moved to Tyr and took his stick to show her how to hold the staff, and the boy gave her a bright, brittle smile.

She smiled back with a shrug. Might as well have some fun, anyway. And who knew? Maybe, someday, it would prove useful.

She shifted her hands along the staff as Chagua showed her, settling uneasily into a crouch to mirror Tyr's.

To the accompaniment of Chagua's calm, musical voice, they began to pace back and forth over the mud, the sticks hitting with high, rhythmic clacks.

*****

The walls of the valley were lined with thick pines, an occasional hardwood reaching its bare branches up into the cloud-filled sky. She reached out and grabbed a young sapling, pulling herself up, setting one foot against the trunk to push herself higher.

Her hand still stung from the last rap Tyr had given it with his staff, but she felt like she had accomplished something. By the end of Chagua's lessons, she had been holding her own, and she had been surprised at how much she enjoyed it. The feeling of rising confidence had been a pleasant side effect.

By the time the islander ended the lesson, all three of them had been smiling and laughing. She had felt like she might just come to belong here for the first time since leaving the Fallen Oak.

It had been fun, and nice to get out of that stuffy basement after weeks of study. She wasn't sure if Tsegan would be satisfied with her progress on the bookshelves, but she didn't really care right now. When Chagua announced they were done for the day, the last thing she had wanted to do was go back into the basement.

So she had started to climb the slope behind the old fortress.

Both Chagua and Tyr had given her strange looks, and Tyr had offered to accompany her into the trees. All of them had spoken at one time or another about that feeling of being watched, of something sharing the valley with them that could not be described. No one had found any signs of anything beyond the usual game you would expect, but it was a favorite topic of conversation at night. She had waved them off, saying she wanted to be alone, and she had turned and moved off before they could say anything more.

She was now having second thoughts. She was glad to be out in the fresh air, and she had little concern that she would run into anything she couldn't handle; she still had the long pole Chagua had given her. But beside that, she was fairly certain that, despite those haunting feelings, if there was something to fear in the woods, one of them would have encountered it by now.

Still, though, things felt different up here, away from their decrepit wreck of Alden's Tor. It was as if a power crouched up here, separate and aloof, looking down upon their little encampment with disdain.

She was high up on the valley wall, staring down at Tsegan's dark tower, when a sound made her jump, nearly losing her grip on the sapling she was braced against. She almost went tumbling back down to the valley floor.

Someone had cleared their throat behind her.

At first she thought it must be Eirik, returning from his run along a different path. But as she turned, the rake handle across her body and a biting remark on her lips, she stopped, her mouth dropping open, her eyes widening in surprise.

A man crouched against a tall pine about four or five strides farther up the slope. Dressed in dirty, many-layered robes that might have been white in the distant past, he stared back at her with a black, serene gaze.

He was ancient, his face crisscrossed with deep lines. His hair may once have been black, but it was stark white now. By his face, he was an oyathey, and something about his features reminded her just a little bit of Tsegan. As the man scurried down toward her, he seemed to use all of his limbs, more like some forest creature than an old man, and any resemblance to Tsegan disappeared from her mind. This man was like nothing she had ever seen before.

Overhead, the wind picked up, rushing through the branches of the sleeping trees, a shiver she could not explain ran down her spine.

She brandished her staff, bracing herself against the thick bole of a birch tree, and tried to put a stern tone in her voice. "Who are you? What are you doing here?"

The man stopped little more than a pace away, resting easily against a tree, and regarded her with wide eyes, wrinkled face cocked to one side as if trying to puzzle something out.

"You are her?" The voice was dry and cracked. The eyes clouded, he shook his head, and spoke again. "You are she?" The voice was a little smoother this time, but still rough with age and disuse. The old man shook his head yet again, as if still not satisfied. "Who are you?"

That seemed to convey what he had intended, and he nodded with a toothless smile.

Maiara wasn't sure how to respond. As she tried to formulate a reply, she realized she wasn't sure how.

The old man swung around his tree to peer at her from the other side. "What are you doing here?"

For the first time, the true gravity of their intentions pressed down upon her. She was part of a conspiracy to kill a king. They were crouched up in this hidden valley to hide their intentions, to plan the overthrow of not just one kingdom, but three.

She probably shouldn't be talking to anyone. Especially strange old man she found wandering in the woods.

She looked back into the valley, but she was too far in now. She had lost sight of the tower. The little man swung back around again, switching sides of the trunk, his wrinkled, browless forehead rising high. "What are you expecting to see down there? The answers to my questions? You don't know who you are, or what you are doing here?"

She stammered, trying to come up with a response. For some reason she could not have explained, she felt like lying to the strange little man would be a bad idea.

"My name is Mai." She used the nickname only Kustaa had ever used and felt another jolt in her chest. But it wasn't a lie, not really, and it seemed to satisfy the man as he nodded slowly.

"Yes. Mai." He seemed to taste the word, making strange, sucking noises with his toothless mouth. "Mai. And what are you doing, Mai?"

She opened her mouth to try to reply to that question, but then shook her head. "No! Who are you, and what are you doing here!"

His smile was enormous, and as the wrinkles shifted around his ancient face, they threatened to swallow the man's entire head. "Very good! Very good! Don't let me push you around!" He nodded, his hands curling around themselves, and then looked slyly at her from the corner of his eye. "My name is Wapayekha now, but you can call me Wapa. And as for why I am here? I live here."

The name was certainly a mouthful, and obviously oyathey. What had he meant by 'now'?

"Well, Wapa, if you live here, why haven't we seen you before?" She knew the name had come out like the whine of a petulant child, but she was still trying to get her feet back under her in this conversation.

He didn't seem to be offended. "I live here." He gestured with one boney arm, loose sleeve flapping, seeming to indicate far more than the small valley. "Here is a big place. I haven't been here in a long time." He stabbed one stick-like finger at the earth beneath his feet.

She nodded, aware that she needed to get answers if she was going to reassure the others at all. "You live here alone?"

That seemed to amuse the man to no end, and his rough, disturbing cackles bounced through the trees, echoing back with odd reverberations.

"No one is alone in the mountains." He looked at her with an open, curious expression. "You are never alone, up in the mountains."

Maiara shook her head. What did that mean? Was he talking about the others? Had he been spying on them? She needed to get out of this and back down to warn Chagua and Tyr. Whoever this old man was, he could tell others where they were. If King Einar found them, Tsegan's plans would be over before they began. Maybe if she got him to go down with her, to where

Chagua could question him?

She tried her biggest smile. "Would you like some food, Wapa?"

The big eyes sparkled, and he smacked his lips together. "What kind?" A hint of suspicion kindled there. "Not meat?" He opened his mouth wide to show his pronounced lack of teeth and then closed it with a more wistful smile. "I'm not so good anymore with meats."

She shook her head, her mouth working faster than her head. "No, of course not. What about bread? Would you like some bread?"

The old ovens in the keep's kitchen had been working for a while now, since Chagua had repaired them. One of the most pleasant surprises of the winter had been fresh-baked bread several times a week.

At the mention of bread, the old man's eyes widened alarmingly. "It's been a long time since I've had bread!"

She nodded, gesturing downward. "Good! Then come with me, and we'll get you some!"

She took a step, placing her foot against a trunk further down the hill, but when she looked back, Wapa had not moved.

"Aren't you coming?"

He looked at her, and for once his face was not alight with mirth or mischief. They were flat and hard. "I won't be going down there."

That stopped her. "Why not? What's wrong?"

He clambered over the tree, moving to her side to cling to another, staring downward as if he could pierce the thick forest to the ruins below. "I'm not going down there." His voice was rigid.

Maiara stopped and turned to stare at him, frowning. "Why?"

The old man shook his head, wispy hair flying. "The weight of ages lies upon that place. The weight of destiny." He turned back to look at her, and his expression softened a little. "It lies upon you, as well."

She grew cold; colder than the winter winds howling through the trees above their heads would explain. Could the old man know about the saga, or Tsegan's interpretation? Were they already betrayed?

"I don't know what that means. What does that mean?"

His face took on a more sly look. "Maybe we speak some more ... after a little bread?"

She watched his face for a moment, but it remained stubbornly bland, and she sighed. She couldn't have said why, but the thought of not bringing bread back to the strange little man never even crossed her mind.

It took her a while to make her way down to the valley floor, sneak into the keep to steal a loaf of bread, and then climb back up. When she returned, as far as she could tell, Wapa had not moved at all.

He hooted with pleasure when she showed him the bread, grabbing it and ripping a piece off, shoving it into his mouth. He smacked at it for what seemed like an eternity, his eyes half-closed in ecstasy, until he swallowed, the apple of his throat rising and falling dramatically amidst the wrinkles scoring his neck.

He smacked his lips again and bent down to tear off another piece, but Maiara reached out and put one hand over the bread as gently as she could. "Before you eat some more, can we talk a bit?"

He looked at her suspiciously, then down at the bread, then back to her. He nodded, but it was slow and doubtful.

She tried another smile. "Good! Good. You said that the valley was weighted down with destiny. What did you mean?"

Wapa regarded her with another tilted glance, this time with a warm smile. "Ah, my girl. You are good, Mai. Everything is going to be alright." He looked around her, back down the slope. "Destiny cares nothing for the valley. It lies very heavily upon the stones of the keep, however."

He looked at her again. "The snow and the ice and the stone know that place, and they know you." His expression softened. "They place a heavy price, more than you can know, upon what you will ask of them."

He took one hand off the bread to pat her arm, then clasped the loaf once more to his bony chest. "But you'll be okay. It will all be okay."

The words seemed to hit her like heavy weights. There was a strange, passive strength to the odd little man. His dark, glittering eyes seemed almost to stare right through her as he absentmindedly brought a chunk of bread back up to his lips.

She needed to tell someone. She should have had Chagua sneak up after her; grab the old man while he was distracted by the bread.

But even as fear tightened her belly, something about him seemed to settle her nerves. How dangerous could he be; one ancient old hermit, lost in the wide mountains?

"You won't tell anyone about us?"

He smiled. "No need, Mai. No need to tell anyone. Everyone who needs to know, knows already." He winked at her as if the two of them shared some exciting secret.

She felt better about the old man, but something about his words sent a chill down her spine.

Chapter 14

His breath roared in his ears, but he did his best to ignore it. His lungs burned, his throat burned, his face burned. And yet cold cramped his body, making each step more difficult than the last. When he came to the river, the thrice damned little rill that had become the bane of his existence, he almost didn't jump in.

These punishing runs had come less and less often over the last several weeks, but still, they came. And Eirik was just about ready to abandon this entire foolish quest and slip away; find some little mountain village to hide in until winter broke and he could rejoin the circuit and his anonymous life.

But he remembered, each time this despair gripped him, that he didn't have any coinage left; they had spent their entire savings to reach this cursed place. This entire misadventure had been a last desperate throw of the dice. Even if he could make his way to one of the small settlements scattered across the mountains, he didn't have enough coin left to buy a bed and a bottle for a night, never mind provisions for the dark months that stretched ahead.

His weapon was back at the ruins as well, and he would never leave the maekre blade behind. This was not the weapon he had lost so many years ago; not the sword given to him by Einar himself. But he had gone through hells to acquire it, all the same; it was the only link to a nearly-forgotten past, and he would never let himself fall so low as to leave it behind.

At least, that was what he told himself, when he remembered the sword, after he thought about the coins and the bottles.

His breath caught in his throat as he threw himself into the river, feeling the bite of the freezing water as it leached through his pants and down into his boots.

But it wasn't the deathly cold that snapped at his breath. It was that errant thought, never far from his mind no matter how hard he tried. The image of those bottles he had stashed away among his things that the damned islander had emptied and destroyed.

The power that had dominated his life for years now, despite everything he tried.

Eirik was not proud of that life. He was vividly aware of what he had become. Ironically, it was one of the main reasons he continued to drink.

For years he had been able to convince himself the circuit was only a means to an end; a place to hide until the time was ripe for him to reveal himself and return to his rightful place, by his king's side. He had taken pride in building the reputation of the Ruun Warrior, the mysterious fighter who could take on any challenger, defeating even the greatest champions the circuit masters could find to throw against him.

But that life had stretched on and on. The years had rolled by, and the time to confront Einar had never come. Instead, the tourneys began to blend into one another, and the dark voice in his head had grown louder and louder. The voice that said he was a traitor, that he was a useless craven whose final duty was to die. The voice that convinced him that Einar, the man who had been his closest friend, wanted nothing more than to see him dead and make an end of the debacle that had only begun on the banks of the Merrick.

Even when Tyr had found him, unconscious beneath the rickety stand of seats, he had harbored illusions of his own self-worth. Tyr had come bearing the binding price of an apprentice, pleading with him to be taken on as a squire, despite the fact that the last true squires had died with their masters years ago, as the endless wars had ground down the old martial structures.

All Eirik had seen had been the mead, the ale, the spirits that could be had with the coins in the boy's hand. He had agreed to take him on, and then put a large dent in the fee by going on a week-long bender that had only ended when Tyr had stolen the money back. From that time on, the boy had taken control of their finances. He only gave Eirik enough, one day at a time, to resupply and prepare for the next tourney. Finding the coins and the opportunity for drink had provided a challenge, for a while, at least.

By then, Eirik's wins were few and far between. He was no longer the dreaded Ruun Warrior. He was the Ruun, the once great warrior now caught up in the chaos of his own destruction. The warriors of the circuit remembered his greatness; they respected the instincts that still posed a threat to any opponent that forgot who he once had been. But his own champion's days were lost. As lost as that misty morning, amidst the swirling crimson leaves of autumn, on the banks of Merrick Ford.

Another phase of his life was over, leaving him nothing but blurry moments between bottles, embarrassing showings at small-town tourneys, and a boy, now a man, who followed him faithfully, believing that one day he could rediscover the champion he once had been.

Had there been any way he could have said no to the old man when he had made his offer in the tattered tourney tent that had become their only home? With Tyr looking on, offered redemption, could he have turned away from that chance and crawled back into the bottle?

His new secret was that he didn't care if Tsegan was an all-powerful wizard or a foolish little old man. The true offer here wasn't to be honor guard to some little tavern waif pretending to be a princess, but to leave the bottle behind, to wrench every last drop of spirits from his blood, redeem himself in his own eyes and, just maybe, in the eyes of his squire.

Princess. As if that little girl could be Einar's daughter. It didn't matter what tales Tsegan spun, there was no hiding that Maiara was a mixed-breed, with the hair and features of the oyathey and the piercing eyes of a high-born fyrdar. Einar had never been attracted to oyathey women. They had shared enough tales of women with each other that he would have sworn by that. And there was no way his friend could have had a secret affair without him knowing about it.

No way at all.

So he knew the girl was no princess. But he also knew, especially now, that this was his one and only chance of rediscovering the man he used to be. He would not return to Connat, there would be no reconciliation with Einar. He had known that for years. But at least he could rejoin the circuit, make Tyr proud, and this time be wiser with his prize purses. There would be an end to this interminable existence, and he would find something else on the other side.

All he needed to do was shed the man he had become.

And all he needed to make that happen was to follow some damned islander's every whim and instruction, and not die in the process.

His feet plunged through the churning, icy waters. He could hear himself sobbing now and didn't look too closely to see if it was from exhaustion or wretched desperation.

Chagua Emeru: his sole salvation and his bitterest enemy.

The islander was a great warrior, he could admit that to himself. Never mind all the stories of the people of the northern islands being philosophers and worse. Clearly they had warriors amongst them as well, and Chagua had to have been among their best. He knew little of the northern islands and had never heard the title Sword before. He had little concept, beyond the obvious, of what that might mean.

Whatever it meant, Eirik knew he had found the man to break away those parts of himself that were holding him back, and to rebuild him with what remained.

His days and nights were steeped in anger and frustration. The anger was not directed toward Chagua, however, beyond a momentary flash of embarrassed rage from time to time. He was angry with himself for having fallen so far from the man he should have been, for knowing what he needed to do to redeem himself, and lacking the strength to do it.

As he tore up the stream; arms pumping; ice forming in his beard, his crest of hair, and his clothing from the flying water, he caught a flash of movement out of the corner of one eye.

Eirik drove his lead foot down into the water and stopped his run without warning, whipping around to find whoever had been watching him in his humiliation. If it was the girl, he swore—

But there was no one there. The forest was growing dark, the sun falling behind the towering wall of stone and ice to the west. The shadows were stark against the fallen snow, giving the forest a silver gilt appearance that he knew could toy with a man's eyes at the best of times. As he stood in the surging water, shaking uncontrollably as his body slowly froze, he could have sworn he had seen movement amidst a stand of pines.

He had the sudden, overwhelming impression that he was being watched. Something seemed to loom in those shadows, regarding him with what he felt certain was contempt. A powerful feeling of inconsequence, stronger than his normal low self-regard, swept over him.

He peered into the shadows, trying to pierce the gloom. But there was nothing there.

Eirik knew he was still susceptible to strange spirit visions even now, well over a month since his last drink. The movement among the trees, this sense of observation and judgment, must have been more of the same. He shook his head, peering one last time into the woods, and then dug his heel into the rocky riverbed and pushed himself off once more.

Could it have been Tyr, checking up on him? It certainly wasn't Ch-agua, he knew that. As soon as the islander gave him a task, the big dark-skinned man turned away from him as if he didn't exist. It might have been the girl. She had taken to wandering the woods more and more recently, as if she were a restless animal growing wary of her forced seclusion.

He didn't talk to any of them very much. In fact, he felt as if all of them were pulling away from him more and more. Could he blame them? He was exhausted each night, and always surly no matter the time of day. Disappointment in himself, anger, and frustration colored his every word, and his interpretation of every word the others said to him. He had locked himself in a cell of his own devising and shouldn't blame any of the others for not opening the door.

Pulling himself out of the river just above the waterfall and Eirik pushed himself back up into a loping run on the far side, using trees to pull himself up the rise toward their hidden valley.

Could it have been someone else? Someone searching for Tsegan, or even worse, for the girl? No. There hadn't been any sign of outsiders all winter, and they were all careful to follow the old man's directions for avoiding detection. Though he was the only one to leave the valley for any length of time, Tsegan was the director of all their paranoid precautions; there was no way he would lead anyone back to them.

It could have been Tsegan himself, he supposed. The old man had been gone for days again; he would often return without warning, spend two or three nights in his tower, and then disappear once more. He said the preparations for the spring emergence were going well, which made Eirik a little nervous. What if Tsegan really was planning on attacking King Einar? What if this plot was more than just the fanciful fever dreams of an old man with too much coin in his purse and a ruined keep lost in the mountains?

Well, he would cross that river when he came to it, he had decided weeks ago. It was possible Einar had become the man of his nightmares. There was no dismissing the shadows he knew were searching for him as mere phantoms of his sodden mind. The king was searching for him, and they had tried to kill him more than once.

But still, Tsegan would never manage to raise an army against Einar if the king was truly good and just, surely? He took some comfort from that thought, when things around him seemed too real. But he would keep his eyes open and watch for an opportunity. Perhaps, even if all of this was real, and the ridiculous tale of this prophetic saga proved true ... it had not mentioned the king's death. All Tsegan had said was that Maiara would rise to rule Astrigir.

Even if it was all true, there would have to be a chance to save Einar from himself. If this rebellion of the old man's did occur, he would save the king. They would have words. One way or another, he would find redemption.

*****

Eirik stared owlishly into the gloom. He was bundled up in several layers of fur and wool, one hand wrapped in a soft mitten that kept him nice and warm. It took a lot to get the chill out of his bones after a run like that. He would take dry clothing in a large, fur-wrapped bundle with him to the hot spring on the far side of the hill, and he would soak in the water until he thought he could feel the flesh starting to slough from his bones. No one followed him, maybe thinking he would rather be alone, or maybe embarrassed for him in his current state. He could never be sure which.

Upon returning to the common room, he would sit before the fire, close enough he could almost smell his blankets scorching, until he could stand it no longer. He would sip hot broth the entire time, warming inside as well as outside, and then, when he felt prickles of sweat standing out on his forehead, he knew he was warm enough.

Usually, at that point, he would lapse into silence in a corner and brood until he could justify taking to his little room. That night, his mind still wrapped up in all the thoughts that had dogged the steps of his run, he was too restless to sit; but he cared little for any conversation he might have with the others.

Chagua sat alone by the bookshelves, staring at them without touching them. It was something he did some nights and never cared to explain. It was a mystery, but it made the islander seem a little more human to Eirik, knowing that the man was not quite as composed as he often seemed.

Nevertheless, Eirik pulled on his heavy cloak and grabbed a pair of fur mittens.

There were things he needed to think about, and decisions he needed to make, before events caught him up once again and he was swept along with life, instead of choosing his own path.

He took four throwing axes from the stores in the back of the stable. Then, after looking around to make sure no one was there to notice, he snuck one of their last apples to Hestir, rubbing the horse's muzzle while he ate. Then, feeling guilty, he had gone back to sneak Vordr one as well.

He made his way out of the stable, around the hill, and up to Alden Tor's ruined ring. Several targets had been set up within the ring, rough burlap from stores they had already eaten or used stuff with twigs and winter grass from the slopes of the hill. They were ragged now, probably ready to be replaced with fresh sacks, but that wasn't why he'd made the climb.

Taking out the small axes he began methodically throwing them at the targets. First he threw all four with one hand then with the other. Then he alternated. He found several different variations, and soon he was dancing through the tumbled stones, working up a good honest sweat as he lobbed one axe after another toward the targets.

He couldn't help but notice he was hitting a lot more often than he had at the start of the winter.

Chagua was a great warrior, but, although he hated to admit it, the man was an effective weapons master as well. Eirik had not felt so good in years. He was failing at almost every task the islander set him, and most of those he set himself as well. But he knew those tasks were getting progressively more difficult, always keeping pace with his improvement, to keep them just out of his reach.

He had caught on to that a few weeks ago, when his constant inability to best the man in the courtyard had driven him to distraction. He had realized, in a flash, that Chagua was toying with him. The man was still using a wooden sword, which drove Eirik half mad. But the wood was now hardwood, and there was an edge carved into the blade. He seldom parried the great maekre blade with the wooden weapon, but he could dance around the older warrior whenever he chose, and so Eirik had taken to fighting at a greater distance, keeping his blade closer to make it easier to swing quickly in response to any opening he saw, or a misstep in his opponent's endless dance.

He had not caught Chagua yet, and the confidence that he never would made it easier to swing the heavy blade with his full force behind the blows. He knew he would be close one day. And when Chagua first drew his own live steel, Eirik would know that he had won a great victory, most likely without landing a blow.

He knew, even as he grumbled to the others, that he was learning new ways to use the maekre blade. No saemgard had ever held it quite the way he needed to in order to counter Chagua's lightning attacks or swift ripostes. There were slashes and cuts he had discovered, folding into his regular regimen, that no tourney crowd had ever seen.

He had realized recently, as he dressed after one of his habitual burning baths, that his body was quickly losing the softness of sloth and drink as well. For years, the maekre blade had seemed to grow heavier in his hands, but now it grew lighter with each passing day. Not light, of course; that massive slab of iron was never going to be light. But it was lighter than it was, and it moved faster now than it had ever moved before, even in his youngest days in the saemgard.

As Eirik went to collect the axes from the targets, he saw that one had flown straight through, caroming off the stones behind to land on the ragged rim of the toppled wall.

He stopped to pick up the errant axe and stood, surveying the valley below him. It was a good place, he decided; even if he was still dissatisfied with his own progress.

He caught a flash of movement in the darkness, at the head of the trail coming over the lip and into the valley. Narrowing his eyes, he thought he saw a lone figure, running raggedly down the slope. It was casting constant, anxious looks over its shoulder.

It wasn't Tsegan. Despite the obvious fear, this person moved with the speed of youth. The others were below. There was no way they could have run up to the ridge without him seeing them.

Then who was it?

Eirik tucked the throwing axes into his wide belt and moved quickly through the ring of rubble, down the back of the hill and around Tsegan's tower. He heard a voice over the rushing wind and the pounding of his own heart. It seemed to be calling out a single word over and over in a voice pitched high with pain, fear, or youth.

As he came running around the back of the stables and the courtyard came into sight, he brought himself up short, an axe in either hand.

It was a young man, hands on knees, desperately gasping in huge, desperate breaths. Dull blond hair hung down over his face. His clothing was filthy, hanging in disarray, and seemed to be far too large for his tall, gaunt frame.

He was still calling out the word between gasps, and now, closer, he could just make them out; a single word, repeated over and over.

"Mai ... Mai."

His voice was weak, growing weaker by the second, fading in and out as he turned, still bent nearly double, to cast a quick, frightened glance up the trail.

Could he mean Maiara? A shadow agent of the king would know her name, although this seemingly terrified youth hardly seemed to fit the image of a heartless killer with a royal warrant.

He moved toward the boy, ready to swing with either hand. If he seemed harmless, Eirik would crack him with the flat of an axe head, leaving plenty of time to discuss the situation with Tsegan's princess. If he proved more than he appeared, well, the sharp side of an axe would settle the situation even more quickly.

But as Eirik approached the boy, voices came echoing up from the basement beneath the stable. Maiara stumbled out, a green cloak half-wrapped around her shoulders. Tyr was behind her, not having bothered with his own cloak, but Eirik was proud to see that he had had the presence of mind to grab a long-handled axe from below, held loosely in his hands. Behind them, a cup of something warm steaming in his hands, Chagua came to stand in the shadows of the stable, regarding the newcomer with flat eyes. When the boy saw Maiara, he gasped. "Oh, thank the gods!" He staggered toward her and collapsed to his knees. "Mai ... Mai ..."

"Kustaa?" She moved toward the boy carefully, sidling up to him, one hand on her dagger.

It seemed as if they had all learned a certain level of paranoia thanks to the old man.

"Mai ... I can't believe ...." He was sobbing now, settling down into the mud, his breath coming in ragged gasps.

"Kustaa ... how did you get here? How did you find me?" She had closed the distance between them but was keeping herself at arm's length. Her own lessons with the islander were obviously paying off.

"Mai ... Mai ... I wanted to come sooner, but I couldn't. I couldn't get away!" Eirik stopped a few paces from the pair. He was plenty close to take the boy down with a thrown axe if it proved necessary but gave them the illusion of separation, for now. He saw Tyr sidle around to stand behind them on the other side and nodded his approval. Chagua, he noted out of the corner of his eye, hadn't moved.

Maiara settled down to one knee near the boy, leaning toward him with a worried expression. Her voice was calming, but there was steel within it. "Kustaa, how did you find me?"

The boy shook his head, clearly at the end of his energy. "The map. He gave me a map, before you left." One hand fumbled at a pocket, and Eirik was shocked to see that the boy wasn't wearing gloves. The fingers were splotchy, red and white, ominously dark at the tips.

Maiara took the slip of paper and unfolded it. It looked worn, with several short tears along the ragged fold lines. She opened it gently and scanned what she found there. She looked up at the boy again, and this time her voice matched the frigid night.

"Where did you get this, Kustaa? I need to know."

He looked at her again from beneath his fall of greasy hair. "The old man. He gave it to me. Told me I could come to you when I felt the need."

He had stopped sobbing, wiping at his nose with one torn sleeve, but now, as his fear slowly abated, he began to shake violently.

"You might want to get him inside where it's warm, and then interrogate him?" Chagua's even tones broke the scene in the courtyard. Without looking away from the boy's face, Maiara nodded.

"Come inside, Kustaa. We'll get you warmed up, and then we can talk." She looked about them. "Where's your gear?"

The boy shook his head. "I left it. This morning. I ... I knew I was close. Had to be close. But I ... saw someone. Someone was following me. I saw them." He cast a frightened glance over his shoulder into the dark stands of trees, then bowed his head, sobbing again. "They followed me."

Eirik thought immediately of the movement he thought he had seen during his run. A strange look crossed Maiara's face as well, but he dismissed it as just another aspect of a strange night.

"I'm sure you weren't followed." Maiara, apparently convinced she could trust the boy, sheathed her dagger and moved to put her arm around his shoulder and help him to stand. He was none too steady on his legs but managed a few steps toward the stable entrance.

"No, Mai." He was crying again, and Eirik felt the urge to knock him unconscious just to spare them all further drama. "He's after you. There's a man after you. Had your description. I didn't tell him anything, but I couldn't get away to warn you! I tried to get away to warn you, but I couldn't! Vali and Turid watched like a hawk after you left. They wouldn't let me leave!"

She patted him awkwardly on the back as they made their way toward the stable, Tyr and Eirik falling in behind them.

Eirik made a quick sweep of the ridgeline where the trail swept out of the valley and disappeared from view. There was no one there.

"No one is after me, Kustaa. It's alright. Everything is going to be fine." She was talking to him as if he were a child now, and Eirik could only hope that might calm him.

But it didn't. Without warning, the boy pulled away from her and made several halting steps, between Eirik and Tyr, back up the trail. "No!" He shouted, finding the energy within the depths of his obvious despair. "He's coming! I saw him. I talked to him. He's coming, and you have to—"

The arrow flew out of the night and caught the boy square in the chest with a solid sound heavy with finality. The impact knocked him onto his back. With wide, uncomprehending eyes, the boy stared up at the feathers as they gave a slight quiver with each fading heartbeat.

Eirik stared at the dying boy for several moments. Too long, he knew, but he couldn't gather his wits. As he watched, the light faded from the boy's eyes, his weak pawing at the arrow slowed, then stopped completely, his arms falling back into the frozen mud. The feathers of the shaft grew still.

Tyr took up his axe in a cross-chest guard position while Maiara screamed, tumbling toward the boy she had called Kustaa.

Behind them, Chagua was roaring orders. "Back into the keep! Now! Arm yourselves!"

Eirik looked back up the hill and saw dark figures moving through the trees. Another arrow flashed down but clattered harmless against the tumbled walls of Alden's Tor behind them.

The dead boy had been right. Someone had found them.

Chapter 15

Geir cursed under his breath as Tore's arrow caught the hapless boy in the chest. He knew something like that was going to happen as soon as the boy staggered toward their position. He cursed again. The lad couldn't have known they were approaching. His mercenaries weren't the greatest warriors that had ever drawn a blade, but they were skilled at sneaking up on people and taking them unawares. And yet now, because of Tore's panic, their approach had been revealed.

The boy was on his back, and Geir had seen enough arrow wounds to know they had killed him. It was too bad; as far as he could tell, he had done nothing to deserve to die here in the high, cold mountains so far from the little tavern that had been his home.

That would be another bill to lay at the girl's feet. When one fled the justice of the king, one was responsible for whatever havoc followed.

There were only four of them, and he had nearly twenty mountain fighters with him, many of whom were already moving down the sides of the valley to take the old fortress in the flanks. He liked his odds and spat a bit of bark he had been chewing off into the snow.

"Alright, let's go."

His fighters nodded and began to make their way down the slope, drawing weapons darkened with soot. Their faces were streaked the same way, giving each of them a demonic visage that blended easily into the dark forest.

He watched as the two axe-wielding warriors moved to where the girl had collapsed next to the dead boy. They began dragging her toward the wood and stone structure at the base of the canted tower. They ducked as another of Tore's arrows flew high, clattering into the tumbled stones at the base of the little hill.

Archers weren't very effective under these conditions, where fingers grew cold and stiff without gloves, or bulky and unwieldy with them. The strings didn't care much for the cold either, making them less accurate than in warmer climes. He hadn't cared too much that most of the fighters from Bjornstad had not been proficient with a bow. In fact, Tore's first shot had probably been more luck than skill.

But the arrows would serve to keep their quarry's heads down while the rest of his force approached. There was no need to leave any of them alive, as far as Drostin was concerned. And if the king's master of shadows didn't need any of them alive, then Geir was damned sure he wasn't going to endanger his fighters' lives, or his own, by taking half measures.

One of his men reached the courtyard outside what looked like a stable, a crude steel sword over his head as he screamed a strange, mountain-clan battle cry.

The big figure by the door, wrapped in shaggy furs and leathers, brought a raised hand down with a flash, and Geir's fighter was thrown backward as something struck him in the face. The man tumbled to a halt in the frozen mud.

The other mountain fighters drew up around the edges of the courtyard, casting dark looks back at their employer. He had told them they were after a girl with an old man and a drover. They had not expected obstacles such as expertly thrown axes. Their bravery, always questionable, was wavering.

"It was a lucky throw, damn you! We still outnumber them five to one! Go! Go!"

They hesitated a moment longer but then turned back toward the ruined keep of Alden's Tor, hefting their weapons as they plucked up their courage.

By the flickering torchlight around the entrance, he saw the foursome disappear below. A large man with long dark hair was the last to spin inside, watching Geir's warriors approach before disappearing from view.

Probably the drover, Geir thought. Eydris was moving through the trees off to his left with most of his remaining fighters, but he would very much enjoy finishing this before she was in position. Word would get back to Drostin, and that would only improve his stock with the master of shadows.

"There's only one real warrior among them, but let's not give them the chance to set any defenses, alright you bloody bastards?" He kept his voice low. He had seen such a comment elicit a terrified, desperate courage in cornered prey before.

"Uh, sir?" Vidhar gestured toward the ruins and Geir turned, a slow, burning anger for those who would not bow to the inevitable bubbling up in his chest.

The man with the black hair was back, wielding a long, shining sword that looked too thin to survive serious combat. The weapon's blade was curved, as well, which only served to further the impression of fragility. His face was dark; too dark for even a dark-skinned oyathey. An islander? He had no idea why one of those sophists would be so far south, but it wouldn't matter.

Behind the islander came the other two men he had seen, now wearing leathers and furs. Glints of metal reflected torchlight: armor. The smaller held two fighting axes in practiced hands, a look of cold determination on his young face.

The other man, a tall, brawny warrior, held a massive sword in a two-handed grip that promised disaster for anyone who came within its reach. At first, Geir thought it might have been one of the big, dull blades used by tourney warriors traveling the circuit of coward and failed warriors too old or frail to fight in real battles. But the shine of the light from the metal was wrong. And the glint along the blade, like diamonds by candlelight, was wrong as well.

It was a maekre blade, the weapon once used almost exclusively by the king's now defunct saemgard.

Visions of butchered mountain brigands filled his mind, and Geir wanted to shout to the heavens at the injustice of it all. He had prepared for almost any eventuality. Tracking down a little girl, an old man, and a cart driver, he had brought enough fighters to take down many times number of green targets, he was certain.

But the man stepping out of the torchlight and into the frozen night wielded a weapon so deadly only the greatest warriors of the kingdom had ever been granted the right to bear them.

The saemgard were long dead. He knew that with the same conviction he knew that it was night, or freezing. They had all died nearly two decades ago at the battle of the Merrick Ford. All except the one traitor who had somehow survived the slaughter of the most deadly warriors Astrigir had ever known.

There had been no sign of Eirik Hastiin for years. Geir should know, he had spent enough of his life trying to track the man down. It couldn't be him. Every lead had been a dead end. Besides, even if it was, rumor had it the man was a drunken sot, wasting away on the circuit, hiding behind black shields and a false name. He had probably drunk himself to death years ago. But that knowledge did not make the tall man wielding the maekre blade in the valley any less real. Whoever he was, he needed to be dealt with, and that would not be easy. A drunken memory had not savaged that party of bandits in the early days of winter.

"Get them!" He still outnumbered the little band by a foolish degree, and there was no way his people could be any more prepared. There should be no doubting the inevitable outcome, if he could only keep his warriors focused on the task at hand.

Geir pulled his own paired fighting axes from their sheaths on his back. Each curved handle slid smoothly into his hands, and he spun them into a blurring pattern without hesitation, running toward the enemy with a wordless growl. There was one way to ensure even the dregs he had brought with him would charge into battle. Watching their employer rush forward, taking with him any chance of their being paid if he died, did it almost every time.

Several of his fighters charged after him, including Ylva, the woman he had hired after the brawl in the Bjornstad tavern. He could hear their footsteps crunching through the frozen mud and smiled. So many seasoned warriors against a boy, a scholar, and one big oaf with an enormous sword ... he liked those odds well enough.

And if it came down to it, he knew that all he really needed to do was sneak past these three into the ruin, find the girl, and end her quickly. Drostin had no need for his hirelings to survive this battle. Hiring the next batch would be more difficult if word spread that he had led this crew to their deaths, but there would always be desperate men and women ready to fight for coin. It just might cost his master a little more in the future, was all.

An arrow flashed past him and snapped into the young warrior's shoulder. It shattered against some bit of armor beneath the furs but staggered him sideways, sending him sprawling to the ground, and suddenly his people faced only two.

That was when the islander, his strange, coiled hair flying wildly around his head, threw himself forward into a blurring roll that ended at the feet of one of the attackers. The man stood, his strange sword whistling up as the tip caught his man in the sternum, piercing his chest and continuing on through to emerge from his surprised face in a spray of blood and teeth.

The mercenary was limp in an instant, dead in mid-stride, and the islander tore his sword blade from the corpse, spinning like a whirlwind. Two more brigands tumbled away screaming, blood splashing into the night. The dark skinned man came down in a crouch to face off against the next foe, blade whirling before him like a glittering shield.

Geir growled. He hated surprises. He could sense his people wavering again, and this time he felt the first stirring of doubt in his own chest. He needed to do something dramatic before they fled. Suddenly, he found himself wishing that Eydris would arrive, or his fighters flanking in from the other side.

Geir moved against the man with the maekre blade, joined by three of his more brave hirelings. The weapon was terrifying in the right hands, but it was clumsy on the defense. His own dual-axe style had been formed, in part, during his time working for the king after the battle at the ford, when Drostin had tasked him with hunting down anyone wielding a maekre blade to see that the last stains of dishonor from that ill-conceived attack would be scrubbed from the realm.

The two axes whirred around him, and he smiled as he saw the other man's bright blue eyes widen in surprise, even as his own men took heart from his obvious prowess. Most dual-wielding styles called for small-hafted axes or swords, to avoid entangling the weapons. Geir knew of no other warrior who had perfected the skills necessary to fight with a long-handled axe in either hand.

Then the younger fighter was on him, driving him away from the bigger foe, and he found himself mounting a desperate defense as the boy's axes seemed to come flying out of the darkness at him from a thousand directions at once. He would block one attack with the shaft of an axe, and another was sailing in on him from the other direction before he could attack with his off-hand.

He snarled. No puppy was going to keep him from this fight. His eyes flared and he knocked the next attack aside with extra force, attacking into the gap that provided. The boy reeled one axe in to block the attack in time, but only by stepping back, creating a gap between them.

Casting a quick glance at the unexpected battle unfolding around them, he was surprised to see that his remaining fighters seemed to be keeping the other two enemies at bay. Movement off to his side resolved into Eydris with another group of fur-clad mountain men coming down out of the trees.

"Inside. The girl. Get her!" He saw the ice-blue eyes of his young opponent flare, and he smiled. Never give your enemy a glimpse into your mind. "She will die here tonight. You are surrounded, and nothing you can do will change her fate."

Geir's words were rewarded with a roar, and a flurry of attacks that might have pounded down a lesser foe. But Geir had spent a lifetime fighting the king's most powerful enemies, and this boy couldn't hold a candle to half of them.

He settled into a deadly rhythm that had worn down far more practiced opponents and smiled as he saw Eydris and her men moving to the entrance.

His head was jerked to the side as he heard a howl from the structure a moment later and a flash of green. One of his men was on the ground, stunned, being helped up by another, as Eydris and the rest of her men tore after the disappearing girl.

She must have hit one of his men with something and ran. She knew she was cornered, and she had come out to fight.

Geir grimaced. Who were these people? He had found no reason to believe this girl was anything more than an orphan raised by a peasant land-lord and his wife. He had certainly had no reason to believe she would be able to fend off a determined attack by trained killers.

His attention was then ripped from that bitter reflection as his opponent snuck a blow past his guard, grazing his left arm.

The boy was slowing, clearly exhausted, and that last attack had been fueled by a desperate need to take Geir's attention off the girl. His teeth ground tight in a fierce grin as he moved to oblige the young warrior, and he sent a flurry of attacks sweeping in from either side, forcing him back step by step.

The islander had killed two more men, an arm and a head dancing off in separate directions from their falling bodies, and was turning to run after Eydris when her two companions ran back into the fight, launching a double attack at his broad back. The islander spun as if he had sensed their approach, and his sword flashed again, parrying blow after blow as his own attacks seemed to slither through the mercenaries' defenses like silver snakes, biting with every thrust.

The big man with the maekre blade, four mountain fighters ranged about him, began to take long, sweeping attacks that kept the warriors dancing just out of reach. As the heavy sword passed each man, he would come rushing back against the towering warrior like an incoming tide, but the man was devilishly fast despite the weight of the weapon, and the mountain men would be forced to retreat with nothing to show for their bravery. They seemed to have reached a standoff until help from one side or the other could arrive.

The boy was driving Geir to distraction, and he decided to finish this little bout so he could direct the rest of the battle. His arms were a blur as he threw attack after attack into the boy's face. The blue eyes grew wide and round, sweat standing out on the smooth forehead despite the winter's cold, and in a flash, they both knew it was over.

Geir gave the boy a sad, grudging nod. It wasn't his fault the gods had put him in the shadow's path.

Unfortunately, the blow that sailed through the boy's defenses was ill-timed, and caught him only a glancing blow off the top of his head with the flat of a blade. The eyes widened even further, then rolled up into his head as his body fell limply to the ground, a sheen of blood running down over his face. The two axes tumbled into the frozen muck beside him.

Geir didn't have time to finish the boy off, not with the rest of his band so sorely pressed. So he moved to take on the maekre blade's bearer, allowing an eager smile to sweep across his face.

The smile faltered as his fighters parted, giving him his first clear look at the big man in the fur and leather.

It was Eirik Hastiin.

There could be no doubt in Geir's mind. The only survivor of the battle of Merrick Ford was standing before him, defiling the Astrigir mountain air with his every breath. And to make matters even worse, he had the absolute gall to wield a maekre blade.

Geir growled low in his throat. This man was the essence of everything that had driven him to a lifetime of dark service to his king. Eirik Hastiin's cowardice on the day of that battle was legendary, as were the whispered stories that it was Hastiin's betrayal that had let king Iver of Vestan know where the saemgard would be that day.

The girl in the green cloak disappeared from his mind. There was nothing in that valley but the huge dark sword and the flashing, icy grey eyes behind it. Killing Eirik Hastiin would close the worst chapter in his king's reign.

He descended upon the fallen saemgard with a howl of rage. The two axes flashed in the torch light.

Geir was rewarded with a look of sudden fear in Hastiin's eyes, but then they narrowed, and he turned toward one of Geir's other fighters. It was

Ylva, the ugly mountain woman.

Maekre blades were never designed to thrust. They were wide and thick, with a massive cutting edge on one side and the rest meant to provide enough weight and power to batter through almost anything that might stand in its way.

But there was nothing stopping them from being used to thrust, if the wielder was strong enough and skilled enough. Hastiin was obviously both.

Geir could only watch as the heavy blade spiraled in beneath Ylva's desperate parry and caught her in the belly, sliding right through wool and leather. The wound was terrible, the width of the blade cutting right through her innards and bringing forth a fountain of blood that splashed into the frozen mud at her feet.

The woman's eyes widened, and Geir, running across the courtyard, thought she looked at him as the light faded from her eyes. Hastiin lowered the blade, letting the limp body slide off into a heap before him, then he looked between the last standing mercenary and the charging shadow.

The man smiled.

Geir would have sworn that less than ten strides had separated him from the boy he had bested and the traitor saemgard, but it felt as if it took him an eternity to reach the man.

And in that eternity, two more of his people died.

With Ylva's blood still glistening from his sword, Hastiin spun in place, his eyes fixed on Geir's, and brought the maekre blade roaring in a flat trajectory that took it beneath the last man's raised guard and into his side, just above the hip.

It was one of the horrible wounds the weapon had been famous for and sent the brigand tumbling across the ground. There was no way to know if the blow itself had cut the man cleanly in half or if the force of the landing and subsequent roll had torn the two parts asunder, but by the time the body had stopped, there was no denying that it was in two pieces, each laying in a spreading pool of blood that glittered black in the torchlight.

Geir came to a stop, looking between the butchered man and the traitor. Hastiin's smile was a red gash nestled within his tangled beard, and the agent thought he would lose his mind to that bloodless expression.

Then Hastiin's grey eyes flicked to the ground behind Geir, and widened in horror.

There was no warning. There was no sign that the storm was about to break. One moment Hastiin was standing there, staring into the distance, and then the maekre blade was crashing through the air toward him.

He knew that his axes would be no match for the obscene weapon if he tried to parry, so he was forced to dance away from the blow, bringing one of his axes down on the flat of the blade in an attempt to knock the traitor off balance.

Hastiin pulled the big sword in, circling around, keeping a good distance from Geir, denying him the chance to launch a quick attack. Behind the big renegade, the islander had killed three more of his men and was spinning around to join his friend.

Geir knew he couldn't fight both the traitor saemgard and the mysterious islander at the same time. He cast his eyes around the courtyard, hoping to see Eydris returning from her hunt.

Instead, he watched as the girl in the green cloak, holding a long pole in one hand, ran back into the torchlight.

The islander watched the girl approach, then fell back to stand before her as she stopped within the low entrance to the building, gasping for breath.

Eydris emerged from the darkness, blood staining one side of her mouth and fury burning in her eyes. Three more of his men were behind her, an answering rage in their own expressions.

Eydris and the mercenaries should be able to hold off the islander and the girl long enough for him to take care of the saemgard. He turned his eyes back to the big warrior and gave him a smile of his own.

Twin axes flashed, a howl of arrhythmic attacks stuttering against the heavy steel of the maekre blade. Hastiin was forced back, step by grudging step. His eyes grew wide as he realized he lacked the space or the time to make one of his wide, devastating swings. Hastiin tried for several quick jabs, but the blade was not suited to such attacks, and Geir had no problem avoiding the clumsy attempts.

Without warning, Geir brought both of his weapons straight for Hastiin's head at the same time. His chest burned with the effort, but if the blow landed, there would be nothing left of the filthy betrayer but a headless corpse.

Hastiin brought his heavy blade up with more speed than Geir would have thought possible, blocking both of the blows before they reached him, but that was fine with the agent. The attack had never been intended to land anyway.

Geir brought one booted foot up and planted it in Hastiin's chest as the big sword rose to protect his head. With a vicious grunt, he pushed the big man away, sending him sailing up into the air. He landed poorly, one hand releasing the maekre blade to try to catch himself as he fell. The big man tumbled to the ground, barely managing to keep hold of the sword.

Geir made no attempt to hide the feral grin that twisted across his face. He strode forward, whirling first one axe in a great circle, then the other, as Hastiin scrambled backward, trying to find enough space to rise.

For a moment it felt as if the air in the valley had frozen solid, as if a moment in time was stretching painfully into eternity, never to be fulfilled. Geir saw off to one side that the boy had risen to a crouch, legs stretching behind him; half his face a mask of blood, his eyes wide and white.

Before him, something had caught Hastiin's attention as well, behind him and over his shoulder.

The time would have been perfect for Geir to plant an axe in the big man's chest and end this for good, but tortured time was frozen for him as well.

In fact, it was as if the entire valley was frozen in a tableau of battle, focused on the green-cloaked girl, the islander crouched before her, his sword held in a ready position as Eydris stood before him, one of her men already dead beside her.

The only thing that moved in the entire valley was the arrow, rough-fletched and spinning, that made its slow, inevitable way through the gelid air, seeming almost to leave a trail of tortured wind in its wake.

The arrow spiraled through the air heading straight for the green-cloaked girl. There was nothing that could hinder its flight. The path between missile and target was empty save for the solid-seeming air, and Geir would have smiled if he had been able to move at all.

Off to the side, the boy on the ground opened his mouth to scream, reaching one hand toward the girl in nightmare slowness.

Before Geir, Hastiin twisted around on the ground, hand reaching hopelessly out with an equal lack of speed.

Wedged into the corner, where the new construction of the low shack met the tumbled stones rubble, the girl shied away, both of her hands rising as if to shield herself from the arrow.

And then the air released them all.

The boy's scream echoed off the stone.

Hastiin's roar enveloped the scream and drowned it in his own horror.

The girl made no sound at all.

Then a bright blue flash of sourceless light lit the valley.

The arrow disintegrated less than a pace from the girl's heart, flecks of white scattering harmlessly in a spray that covered her in glittering powder.

Silence returned to the valley as they all stared. Geir's eyes had been fixed on the girl. He knew what he had seen. Nothing could have stopped that arrow in its flight.

And yet it had been stopped. No, it had been destroyed.

Nothing could have done that, and yet he knew what he had seen. He looked down at Hastiin, then over at the boy. Which of them had done this? What weapon had they used that could strike an arrow out of midair?

He brought both of his axes high. It didn't matter. He was going to end this bastard traitor, then he was going to kill the rest of them, and then, after she had seen each of her protectors brought low, he was going to kill the girl, whoever she was. And then he would be free to leave the damned mountains.

The axes were falling. Hastiin turned onto his back again, eyes widening to watch the blades descend.

Geir was thrown backward, dust and grit flaring into his face, as if a hot, dry wind had blown him onto his back. But the wind didn't stop there. It tumbled him over and over and over again out of the courtyard and into the shadows of the forest beyond.

"Begone, vermin!"

Geir could barely make sense of the words as they bounced up and down the valley. He was nearly blinded, his ears ringing with the howling demon wind, his eyes blinded by flying grit.

He forced himself back up to his hands and knees. He had lost his axes. He dragged a long dagger from its sheath out of habit. He rubbed one forearm across his eyes trying to clear them, but his vision remained blurred and leaden.

He saw three figures running toward him, while a billowing shape rose up behind.

Geir forced himself back to his feet, squinting, dragging his forearm again over his eyes and shaking his head with frustration.

It was Eydris with two of his remaining men. He could just make them out through the blur of desperate tears. They pounded toward him, their faces desperate and wild. The billowing shape resolved itself into a churning cloud of sand that crashed down upon them. As he watched furs, leathers, and then bloody flesh was stripped from the two men as they ran. They screamed in agony. Eydris was caught up in the cloud, her own clothing rent and torn, but whatever force had created the roiling stormfront must have exhausted itself on the two men, and she was tossed out of the heavy, burning cloud, rolling to a stop at Geir's feet. He stared down at her. Her skin was red and burned, dry and cracking. He caught her beneath the arms and dragged her, screaming, into the shadows, watching the hellish cloud dissipate, swirling up into the sky as if it had never been.

Except for the dry, cracked bones scattered across the courtyard.

Geir heard a desperate, horrified choking behind him, and turned to watch Tore stand from his shooter's blind, eyes wide and devoid of thought. The man cast his bow aside as if it had become a serpent, then turned to run up the path and out of the valley of horrors.

Geir didn't know what he was expecting to happen next. He crouched beside Eydris's whimpering form, trying to make soft, reassuring sounds in her ear as he peered deeper into the valley.

A form stood atop the ruins. Dressed in dark robes, the stature was hard to gauge as it stood alone amid the stones, but Geir had the impression it was not large. The features were obscured within the shadows of a deep hood, and it raised its hands over its head, the voice that had tumbled through the valley again ringing out.

"There is no escape!"

From the figure's upraised hands a sense of motion gathered, spinning into being. It became a dun-colored worm that writhed across the sky with incredible speed.

The shape swept the yard clear of his remaining men, their screams bouncing off the mountains all around. But this killer wind's power was not spent so quickly. A spiraling tendril of darkness lashed out over Geir's head and struck Tore in the back. The man's still-running body was spun up into the sky, disintegrating, to fall among the trees further up the slope.

An ominous silence fell once more upon the valley. Geir watched, not knowing what he was seeing, as first the boy, and then the traitor saemgard rose. They looked dazed themselves, which was little comfort to the agent as he crouched in the darkness with his wounded companion.

The islander and the girl joined the two warriors and they approached the still body of the boy from the Baedre tavern. It felt like that arrow had soared through the valley hours ago, although Geir knew it had been mere moments.

A heart-wrenching sob brought him upright, and Geir watched as the girl fell to her knees beside the body.

The figure from the hilltop came around the tower, hood still over its head, and seemed to gather the four up, ushering them toward the torchlit doorway. The islander and the younger warrior knelt to pick up the dead boy, carrying him toward the ruin.

Hastiin stood, staring back out at the forest; at Geir's own position. The figure in the robe, short indeed next to the renegade, came up beside him and said something. The big man nodded, looking out once more, and then turned to follow the others.

The hollow darkness of the hood then turned, and Geir knew the creature, whatever it was, was staring right at him. It had just killed his last men without a thought. He paused. That deadly wind had killed more than that, if Eydris's wounds were as grave as they seemed.

There was nothing stopping it from killing him as well.

But after a terrifying moment that seemed to stretch into eternity, the hooded figure turned and entered the shanty building. Behind it, the torches flickered once and went out.

Geir was never sure how long he crouched there, stroking Eydris's brittle hair, murmuring to her until her panicked, pain-filled sobs subsided into low, hopeless moans. But no one emerged from the wreckage of the old fyrdar fortress, and eventually he picked Eydris up, as careful as he could be about her wounds and her tormented skin, and made his slow, careful way back up the side of the canyon, avoiding the road, toward their encampment in the next valley. There were supplies enough there to see them to Bjornstad, and he could hope for enough time, and maybe a healer there, to make sure Eydris was healthy enough to return to Connat.

He had no idea what had just happened, but as far as he was concerned, Drostin had a lot to answer for.

And he, Geir Muata, would never enter the mountains again.

Chapter 16

She had brought an extra blanket with her, but she was still shivering.

Maiara knew, on some level, that the chill had nothing to do with the freeze that had settled upon their sheltered little valley the day after the attack, or even the wretched anguish of her destination. It had been four days since the battle. The site had been completed two days ago, the weather had shown no signs of letting up, and neither had the depths of her misery.

For days now, she jumped at every little sound. She found it nearly impossible to focus on anything, whether it be cooking, practicing with her staff, or reading. She shied away from any of the others whenever they came too close. She hadn't been able to sleep since that night.

Whenever she closed her eyes, she knew that Kustaa's face would be waiting there, wide-eyed, bloody, and resentful.

After the battle, a terrible chill had settled into her bones. She had been utterly exhausted; sleeping for almost an entire day before she had awakened to the new nightmare her life had become.

Her sheltered life in Baedr had never prepared her for anything like this. She had seen a few bad tavern brawls, of course. They were inevitable even in an establishment as respectable and well-governed as the House of the Fallen Oak.

She had even seen a person die once. Although the passing of old man Keld, who had fallen leaving the common room one night and never risen again, had been nothing like the bloody murder she had seen in the courtyard.

Nothing from her sleepy little town could have prepared her for the carnage and imminent peril of that terrible night.

Her mind insisted on reviewing bits and pieces over and over again, and nothing she had learned about discipline would stop it.

She saw Kustaa fall. She saw Eirik, Chagua, and even Tyr kill in her defense, the bodies of their attackers ripped open, spilling their insides all over the cold ground. She saw the faces of the men and woman who had come for her as she ran from their little sanctuary, fleeing into the darkness after striking the one man to get past him. Their ragged furs and leathers had been shabby and ill-kept, more like peasants or thralls than deadly warriors.

But to Kustaa, anyway, they had been deadly enough. And she had never doubted the danger they had posed to her.

She still wasn't entirely sure why she had left the underground warren. She tried to convince herself, after the fact, that it made sense. If they came in looking for treasure or further victims, she would have been trapped and alone. But the entire night was such a blur, she wasn't sure those thoughts had ever truly crossed her mind. All she could remember was a sense of blind panic.

She had fled up the stairs to find the men coming toward her, swung her staff without even really thinking about it, and dodged past as one of the men fell, grabbing himself, screaming with a haunting, high-pitched shriek. One vibrant memory was the shock that had run down her staff as it impacted with the man's flesh. Her palms still crawled whenever she thought of that.

Pulling the furs and blankets closer about her as she rounded the hill, she wove through the somehow subdued springs, and came face to face with the barrow on the far side. Chagua said he had discovered it while he was making the repairs to the old kitchens, before any of them had met. It was so overgrown and misshapen; you could only tell it was a barrow if you knew what you were looking for. She had probably hiked right over it half a hundred times and never known what it was. But there was a low stone doorway facing away from the keep's hill, hidden behind bushes and hundreds of years of leaves and needles.

The day after the fighting, they had decided to open it up and place Kustaa among the forgotten heroes of the past. The ground was too frozen for a burial, and with an unknown and unknowable enemy stalking them through the mountains, they had not wanted to risk the thick smoke of a pyre. They had asked her for her opinion, of course, but she had been all but useless, unable to give any sort of constructive recommendations or consent.

And so now her closest and oldest friend lay in a cold, ancient tomb, only the bones of forgotten raiders for company. A cruel voice in her head, one that had been gaining volume for days, whispered that Kustaa had not been her closest and oldest friend; the sadly dedicated young man from Baedr had been her only friend. And now she was alone.

She had put off visiting the barrow until now because she was terrified to think of how she might react when confronted with the cold, undeniable reality of the ancient stone door. She had snuck out through the courtyard, although there had been no need. It was almost always empty at this time of night. The three men seemed not to have been bothered by the fighting and the death, even cheerfully reminiscing about this blow or that parry. There was a sense of camaraderie among them now that hadn't been there before; a sense of coming together through a shared ordeal. There was also a fierce pride to their talk; they had survived a terrible battle against overwhelming odds nearly unscathed.

They were all concerned with who their attackers might have been, and how they had found the valley in the first place. There seemed to be no doubt, of course, that the warriors had come at the behest of King Einar. Somehow, the king's shadow agents had found them despite all of their precautions. It was only a matter of time before Einar sent even greater forces after them.

But those concerns were secondary to the visceral understanding that they were alive while those who had attacked them were not. She could understand what drove their loud, animated conversations now. But she couldn't share in it.

They hadn't known Kustaa. They had no idea what his death meant to her.

They tried to be understanding; especially Tyr. But nothing they said or did had any impact on the icy lump in her stomach. It had all happened just as she remembered. It had not been a nightmare. She had seen men and women die in droves, and one of them had been her only friend.

And the worst part about of it all was that none of those details weighed nearly as heavily on her thoughts as the moment that arrow had flashed toward her and what had happened after.

She made her way through the low scrub at the back of the hill. The men had tramped a path through the undergrowth making the barrow ready and then carrying Kustaa to his final resting place. But she couldn't find the path in the dark and didn't much care. Her heavy boots and layers of cloaks and blankets were proof against any danger the brambles or thorns might pose. And to be honest, forging her own path was forcing her to go more slowly, and she was not eager to reach her destination.

Her mind, as it always did now, drifted back to that night. She remembered the clattering of arrows around her when she first fled the stables. She had made it to the false safety of the shadows behind the hill only to find more attackers coming for her out of the trees. She remembered the shock of realization as she saw a woman pull up before her, a look of grim triumph in her eyes. Maiara, again without conscious thought, spun her thin stick around, surprising the hardened woman and catching her a glancing blow to the face. While the woman's eyes widened, her cruel smile shifting into an enraged snarl, Maiara had panicked again, turning in a blind panic and running directly back into the battle; directly back into the hidden archer's line of fire. That last moment was etched into her mind like an epitaph carved in stone. She would never forget it.

Time had slowed as she skidded to a stop. Chagua had been nearby, threatening anyone who approached. Then there was a quick flash of movement in the distance. She saw a small, shining object floating slowly toward her with the strange menace of a nightmare. She had known it was coming straight for her without even really knowing what it was. It was going to strike her in the chest and there was nothing she could do about it.

She remembered raising her hand as if to ward off a fly. She remembered Tyr, at the edge of her vision, raising his hand toward her. And Eirik, on the ground and at the mercy of the big, fork-bearded warrior in black, twisting around in the mud, reaching out as if he could catch the missile as it past. None of them had stopped it, of course. How could they? There was no way anyone could stop the arrow from piercing her heart and ending her story in the frozen courtyard of a ruined keep leagues from the only home she had ever known.

Then there had been a burst of light, so quick it was gone before she was sure it had ever been. It filled the valley like lightning. It had felt like the mountains themselves had reached down into the sheltered little dell. Something wrenched inside her, and the arrow had shattered into a million pieces of what had seemed like snow or ice, scattering harmlessly across her as she gasped what she had assumed would be her last breath.

Time was frozen for one more moment as everyone stared at her snow-spattered chest, then the battle had crashed back into being as if nothing had happened. Only for a moment, though. Oh, yes, she shivered at the memory. The mundane clash of steel on steel, flesh, blood, and the exertion of mortal men had lasted only a moment more; and then the nightmare had surged forward.

She had been barely aware of Eirik's position, still on his back, as the big man in black reared up over him, both axes high, driving them down toward the big man's head.

But then the air had dried, the wind had stirred, leached of the cold and moisture of the winter mountains, and a coil of churning sand had lashed out through the air, striking the axes like a hammer blow, knocking them away into a stand of trees, smashing their wielder into a wild, tumbling sprawl after them.

When Tsegan had appeared atop the hill where she had spent so many hours watching the warriors spar, she had already been lost to the shock of the moment. The vision of the arrow piercing her flesh was still too real; the moment the arrow had vanished still held her frozen.

The old man had shouted something, and a wave of arid wind and sand, so alien to their high fastness, had tumbled into the courtyard. It had struck only the enemy, weaving among her friends, leaving them untouched by its passing.

But what it did to the attackers...

Clothing and flesh was stripped from bones still writhing in agony. Faces pale with horror and pain were scoured away leaving only skulls, jaws agape even as they tumbled to the frozen ground. The screams of the dying had been enveloped by the roaring of that hellish wind as it crashed through the valley.

When silence once more fell, there were only dry, brittle bones and her three companions, glaring about. She couldn't be sure, but she thought there had been no survivors. It was only later, when they were trying to piece together everything that happened, that Tyr had sworn he saw one of their attackers blasted into the forest. When they went to look, there had been a faint blood trail that faded before it even left the valley. Someone had escaped.

Eirik swore the man in black had not been killed by the blow that had disarmed him, and so, as far as they could tell, at least two survivors had escaped Tsegan's fury.

The archer definitely had not. Tyr had found the man's body, torn and bloody, nearly a hundred paces up the trail.

Tsegan had been silent in the aftermath of the battle, clearly exhausted by his efforts. He directed them to gather the bones, weapons, and other signs of their mysterious enemies and had them brought to the storage area in the back of the stable where they had later disappeared. Maiara assumed he had taken them up into the tower, although she refused to think about why he might have wanted them. Those bodies that had died a more mundane death had been dragged off into the woods and dealt with by Chagua and Eirik.

The little white-haired man had been furious as they all huddled in the common room that night, despite his obvious fatigue. He was undoubtedly annoyed with the four of them, and Maiara in particular, for rushing out into the fight; but most of his ire seemed to be reserved for himself, or perhaps fate.

He muttered to himself all night about timetables and schedules, told them all he needed them to work harder, and then he had staggered off to the tower. He had stayed up there for two days and then left without a word.

Maiara could only tell when he was gone by the deep blackness of the dark and empty windows of his tower. While he was with them, there was always at least one light glimmering up there in the shadows.

Remembering those empty windows brought her back to herself as her feet, following the lay of the land without her conscious control, had brought her to the back of the small burial mound. The door was just as they had described it; a rough-carved frame with courses of well-set stones within. They had needed to use heavy iron crows to open it up. At least Kustaa's bones would be safe, she thought, as she settled to her knees in the frozen grass before the doorway.

Tears traced icy pathways down her cheeks as she stared at the mute wall. Desperate for anything to take her mind off this reality, she noted the bright white scratches in the age-darkened granite where the iron crows had chipped the stone. There had been a great deal of moss, brown with winter, spread across the wall when they found it. Most of the spongy growth had been scraped away during their work, but patches still remained, here or there, and she found herself wondering if it would heal in the spring, or if it was truly dead.

Dead like Kustaa, wrapped up in his dirty old cloak inside the cold, barren hill.

She bowed her head, trying to force her mind into the proper frame of reference for guilt and mourning. Kustaa would never have been in this valley if it wasn't for her. His death was very much on her hands. But instead, she was buffeted with image after image of the battle, always culminating in that moment when the arrow that should have killed her disappeared into nothingness.

Was it magic? And if so, how? Who had done it? Every time she had seen Tsegan use whatever power he had, it had been different; dry and devoid of life, the rustling sand and empty howling of a wind that felt like it had come from far, far away.

But the pulse that had shattered the arrow had been soft and gentle. It had felt natural, as if the surrounding mountains had reached down to save her.

When she had confronted him with the event, she would have sworn he hadn't known what she was talking about. Admittedly, she had been distracted when he had made his presence known. Had he been there all along? Or had he arrived after the arrow's fateful flight? She had explained the situation, and his old face had smoothed over into his old smile. He had nodded, reassured her that, of course he had destroyed the arrow. He had too much time and faith invested in her, he had said with a smile.

But she wasn't entirely convinced, somehow.

Why had she felt that wrench in her chest as it happened? Common sense told her that it had merely been a flinch as she anticipated the arrow piercing her heart. She couldn't imagine what else it might have been, although perhaps it had been a thoughtless flinch from the flash of blue light?

She shook her head and wiped at the tears, ashamed that there weren't more. She knew there should be more. She should be sobbing here, collapsed like a helpless maiden from the old sagas. But, although she was ashamed to admit it, there was a great deal of anger mixed in with the sorrow and guilt. Kustaa would not be dead now if it wasn't for her, that was true. But he also wouldn't be dead now if he had left her alone instead of following her up into the mountains.

They had found the map he claimed Tsegan had given him crushed into the mud of the yard. The old man had admitted to giving it to the boy in the hopes that it would quiet him. He had told Kustaa that, if things ever became unbearable, he could follow the map and find her. But he had also instructed the Sayens to watch him closely and not let him leave.

It seemed like such a slim thread, given the danger of their situation, but she had let it lie at the time. Kustaa's death had been too recent, too raw, for her to worry about how he had come to be there.

That must have been what he was babbling about before ... right before the arrow had struck him in the chest. Something had driven him to seek her out; to sneak away from Vali and Turid. She smiled for a moment beneath her tears; she knew how difficult that could be, even when they weren't prepared.

But then a gut-wrenching sob clenched her in its fist and she doubled over, falling to the hard ground. The grief came crashing over her in waves, then, and all thoughts of the battle were gone for a little while as only his face, clean and happy and smiling, floated in her mind.

She came to herself curled around her pain, shivering uncontrollably in the cold of the deep night. Her tears had stopped sometime before, but it hurt to open her eyes as ice fused her lashes into a tangle.

She became aware of someone standing nearby and jumped to her feet, her hand snagging her staff as she rose without her even thinking about it.

She was about to berate whoever had followed her. She had told them all she wanted to be alone. But she stopped before the words were even formed.

The ancient little hermit, Wapa, stood nearby, bundled in furs. He held a ratty old cowl in both hands, wringing it as if trying to remove every last drop of moisture during a washing. His dark eyes were huge in the black of night, his white hair in a wild halo around his head. He looked very sad, and his big eyes were luminous as if he was barely holding back tears.

She tried to compose herself, pulling her cloaks and blankets into a more comfortable fall, looking at the staff with chagrin. It felt silly to brandish even such a weapon as this at the wretched old man.

"Hello." Her voice was harsh from the cold and the torture of her wracking sobs, but she cleared her throat and tried again. "Hello."

The old man nodded with a quick jerk of his chin, then tilted his head toward the barrow. "I am sorry."

The words were simple, but they felt as heavy as stone, and she felt her grief rising up in her throat again.

Fighting back tears, she shook her head, waving the words away. "Thank you, but it's not your fault." She turned to look at the tight courses of stone, and a hitch in her breath slowed her response. "It's my fault."

The old man turned her forcefully with a hand on either shoulder. She shied away from his unexpected strength.

"None of this is your fault, girl." The heat in his voice was strange, as was the anger in the ancient eyes. He bowed his head, releasing her. "None of this is your fault."

She stared at him, not sure how to respond to either his words or his angry tone.

The old man's eyes were unfocused, fixed, unseeing, on the old stone doorway. "Not your fault."

A strange feeling began to build in her gut, and Maiara felt her eyes narrowing. The little old man made for a ridiculous figure, when she thought about it, all bundled up in furs and tattered woolens. But there was also something about him that suggested there was more here than just a strange old hermit.

She remembered that same thought from the first time she had met him up near the edge of the valley. Now, in the darkness before her friend's cold tomb, she had it again.

There was something about him that seemed bigger than it should be.

She remembered again the feeling that the mountain itself had reached out and destroyed the arrow that would have killed her.

Could it have been—?

She almost laughed. Her life here was so strange, she could believe almost anything at this point. Tsegan might or might not be a figure out of the ancient sagas, and he definitely wielded powers she could not begin to understand. And that might mean that there could be others in the world with similar abilities. But that one of those could be crazy little Wapa?

She did laugh as the thought finished working its way through her mind. She could imagine the mountains saving her with mystical powers before she could imagine the little old hermit wielding arcane forces from ancient times.

Her laugh had a strange effect on him, and he turned back to her, his eyes narrowing. "Laughter is healthy at a time like this; it means you heal. But I sense that the object of your wit would not please me."

She straightened herself and tamped down the giggles that still threatened to rise up. "No, sorry, Wapa. I'm not laughing at you." She schooled her features to a more somber mask, made much easier as she saw once again the entrance to the tomb looming behind them. "Never mind."

The old man nodded, stretching his arms out as if he had just awakened from a nap. He nodded off to the side, where the bulk of the keep's small hill hunched in shadow. "It was a mighty battle."

The thought of him being her savior rose again, and she shook it away. "You saw?"

The wavy white hair swayed as the old man nodded. "I saw. I was here. We all were. Evil walked in this valley that night. The moon hid her face." His eyes grew dark.

Maiara took a moment to interpret the old man's words then nodded herself. "It was dark, with no moon."

"She hid her face." He insisted. "The moon cannot abide such evil."

She had not taken the time to wonder at the attackers' motives, but she didn't think it was much of a stretch to say they were evil.

She had often slipped away to seek out the old man over the last weeks. Sometimes she found him, sometimes she didn't. She always had bread or some other soft treat for him from their stores, and he was always appreciative. But their talk had been innocent and mundane; no more of those cryptic comments from their first encounter. Half the time she didn't understand his words, the other half he was like a restive child. He had never seemed nervous or frightened, however, until now.

She leaned against her staff, twisting it this way and that to force it into the frozen earth as she thought. "Wapa, did you see the whole battle?"

The distant look faded from his eyes and he shifted his gaze from side to side, then gave a jerky, one-sided nodded. "I saw everything."

"What happened, at the end?" Her fascination with Tsegan's claims of power had been building since that first night in the Fallen Oak, but she still hadn't been sure what she had seen, or if she even believed in magic. It was supposed to have been gone for so long, if it ever existed at all. But, then, what else could explain what had happened here?

He nodded again, a sly look in his eyes. "Yes. The end." Again, he looked around as if he was afraid someone would overhear. "Yes."

His mannerisms were annoying, but she was a little embarrassed when she lost control enough to actually stomp one booted foot. "What did you see?"

He jumped at the tone, looking offended. "What did I see? What did you see? What was there to see?"

Her grip on the staff tightened almost painfully. "Was it ..." She couldn't bring herself to say the word out loud. She felt as if she was about to ask if the fairies were real. But she knew what she had seen that night. All of the rest might have been possible with minstrel show trickery, but she had seen the wave of sand, had heard the roar of the wind. She had seen the bodies.

"Was it magic?" She stammered the words out before she could hesitate again.

He looked at her owlishly, all movement in his body frozen still.

And then he laughed. "Magic? What is magic? Was it hocus pocus? Did he wave his hand and make some coin dance and spin? Where was the crowd? Where were the cheers?" He made a spitting sound, and the wrinkles of his face shifted around into flat frown. "Magic."

That brought her up short. "Well, if it wasn't magic, what was it?"

Instead of answering her, he looked at her through suspicious eyes and repeated himself. "What is magic?"

She paused. What was she supposed to say? She waved her hand. "You know, doing something that shouldn't be possible. That normal people can't do. Making something happen with power, with..." She groped for words that wouldn't come. She felt like everyone knew what magic was, and the old man was just being purposefully ignorant. Her shoulders slumped as she failed to come up with any decent description that fit her thoughts. "You know, magic!"

Wapa shook his head. He put up one stick-like finger. "There is nothing that is impossible." Another finger rose into the air. "There are countless kinds of power." And another finger. "Normal is a box that traps the mind and chains the soul."

What the hells did that mean?

"I don't understand." Much of the frustration that had haunted her every step since that night in the Fallen Oak bubbled to the surface. "If that wasn't magic, what was it?"

As if someone had blown out a candle, the mischievous flare in the old man's eyes was gone. He shrugged; his face vaguely pleasant. "Why don't you ask him?"

The frustration rose again. Tsegan always refused to talk about what she thought of as magic. He had said, time and time again, that power should never be used to prove a point.

She punched the butt of the staff into the shallow hole she had worn into the frozen ground.

Almost as if he could read her mind, Wapa's eyes softened and he placed one hand on her shoulder. "There are countless kinds of power." He repeated the words carefully, slowly. "There is power in me," he tapped himself on the chest. "There is power in the trees," he tapped on the tree nearest him. "There is power in this hill," he gestured to the barrow. "There is power all around us. It has lived in the mountains for eons. Since before your people first arrived here."

Her people? She was clearly half oyathey and half fyrdar; everyone took that for granted. And the strange little old man was obviously oyathey. What did he mean by her people? But before she could stop him, he continued.

"There is much power in your friends," he nodded back down the valley. "And there is power in you." He tapped her on the chest, right where the arrow would have landed.

She straightened at those words and then sagged again. It was hopeless.

Wapa tilted his head to one side and regarded her with worry. "If you feel lost, why not ask him?"

She shook her head, looking down at the frost-covered mold at her feet. "He doesn't answer questions like that."

Wapa shrugged, looking back out into the forest. "So, aren't there things that can tell you?"

She looked over at him, her own head tilting now. "Things?"

Wapa nodded. "Things. Does he not have things that he carries with him? Might those things answer your questions?"

She backed away. "His things? Go up into his rooms? I can't do that!" That seemed to genuinely confuse the old man. "His things? His rooms?"

"You know what I mean. Yes, his things, his rooms!" She took a step away from the old man, but the seed had been planted.

"Things are. They are before you, they are now, they will be when you are gone." He shrugged. "Same with me. Same with your friends. Same with the old man."

Could it be possible that Wapa had no concept of private property? There were some who said the oyathey had once been like that, before the fyrdar came.

But Tsegan, despite being oyathey himself, definitely understood the fyrdar concept of private ownership, and endorsed it wholeheartedly. He had been quite adamant about any of them even looking for the hidden entrance to the tower, never mind going up into it while he was gone.

But still ... if there was anything that could answer her questions, it would be up there, wouldn't it?

"The things he keeps with him might tell me things?"

Wapa nodded, but his face had become vague again, and he was turning away. "Things tell you things. They always do."

She thought back to all the reading she had been doing. "Maybe he has books about magic up there..."

She was startled by the sound that burst from the old man's mouth, but when she turned to glare at him, she could tell, by the position of the countless lines on his face, that he was laughing.

"What?" She had been very sensitive lately, and even the hint of being laughed at was enough to set her off. "What did I say that was so funny?"

He cackled some more, shaking his head as if trying to deny something, but then collapsed again beneath the weight of his laughter.

When he had calmed down enough to answer, he tried to wave away her anger with one bony hand. "No, no, no. What you are looking for is not in books. You cannot contain what you are looking for in books."

He gave her a pitying glance, as if she were a child. "Still, things will tell you things, and you never know what they will say."

He turned away again and started to move out into the darkness.

"Wait! What does that even mean? And if there's no such thing as magic, how can it not be in books, but be somewhere else?" She was so confused now she couldn't even form a coherent question.

He turned back to her, smiling. "There are so many things beneath the sun and the moon, and so many words for each of these things. What you call red I may call blue. What you call hot I may call cold. And yet, you will know what you seek when you find it."

And with that, he was gone.

She shouted out to him, yelling, pleading, screaming. But he had disappeared as thoroughly as if he had never been.

Who in the names of all the gods and spirits could he be? And how could he even begin to know what she was looking for, or where she could find it?

She settled back against a tree, lowering herself to the ground beside the tomb. There must be things up in that tower that could explain this all. She understood about the saga, she thought. She understood her part in all of this, as much as was possible. But there was so much more happening here, between Tsegan's powers, and whatever had saved her life.

Something in that tower would tell her what she wanted to know. Or at least tell her where to look next. She owed it herself. She owed it to Kustaa. Snow began to sift through the trees overhead and she pulled her hood farther over her face. She stared at the stones of the barrow door, her mind thinking of her friend, and all of his hopes and dreams.

The tears came again, but this time they were softer, silent. And around her, the specks of snow drifted down, curling into nothingness as they hit the ground.

Chapter 17

Tyr watched the two older men spar, but his mind was focused elsewhere. It had been over a week since the attack, and he was as glad to be alive as anyone who had ever survived a battle. But as the heady energy of survival had faded over the days after the fighting, his mind had begun to plague him with questions he could not answer.

Who had attacked them? Why had they been attacked? How had they been found? It was a vicious circle that had his mind locked into a pattern he could not break, no matter how hard he tried. He had been training harder than ever before, he had tried to follow Maiara's example and taken long walks out into the surrounding wilderness. But that sense of being watched had quickly driven him back into the ruined keep. He wasn't sure how she managed to stay out there as long as she did.

He had even tried to pour through a few of the thinner books on the shelves in the common room. But he was not a strong reader, despite the practice, and no matter what he tried to do, his mind kept returning to those questions.

And never mind about the rest of that night. Never mind about the fairy story aspects that gave him a headache just to remember. The nature of the threat against them, the raggedly-dressed men and women who had sought their deaths with steel and bloody-mindedness, were enough for him to puzzle over for now. Leave it up to Tsegan, Eirik, and the others to worry about the rest.

But still ... that moment when he saw the arrow flying toward Maiara's heart still dragged him, screaming, from his sleep each night.

He remembered, with vivid clarity, the long, thin missile as it floated gracefully through the cold air. He remembered reaching out as if he could grab it, stop it somehow.

And then he remembered, as it had sailed passed, toward Maiara as she cowered before it, the flash, a pull in his chest as he gasped in expectation of horror, and then the arrow just ... disappeared.

How could that happen? What could have done that?

He might have half been able to convince himself it was just some natural event, that his eyes had deceived him, if it wasn't for the powerful forces Tsegan had then turned upon their attackers.

He had no fears of those memories. He didn't understand the powers the old man might command, but he knew a well-crafted weapon wielded by an expert when he saw it. That is what he had seen that night.

The old man had most likely been the one to dash that arrow into nothingness, as well, although none of them had seen him in that moment. When they asked him, Tsegan had shrugged with a vague smile. What else could it have been?

The attack had bothered their old patron. That was obvious, and it made Tyr even more nervous.

He was certain at least one of the attackers had survived. They had found the blood trail, and although it was hard to count up the dead when half of them had been reduced to intermingled piles of ancient-looking bones, he was almost certain they were two bodies short.

As for how they could have found the valley, both Chagua and Eirik seemed willing to accept that Maiara's friend had been followed during his ill-conceived trek up into the mountains to follow her.

And who had that been? What kind of friends had they been?

He refused to think along those lines or to pine after the girl. She was too busy with her constant studies anyway. They got to talk when she came up for staff practice and sometimes over meals. He had convinced himself that was more than enough.

But then he would think about the dead boy buried in the hill, and he would wonder, all over again, who he had been to Maiara.

Thoughts about her, as they often did, made watching the sparring below intolerable. He pushed himself up, tapped the snow off his gloves, and clambered down to the courtyard, keeping well clear of the fighting, to find his own staff near the front of the stables.

The horses whickered at his approach. He wasn't sure about the others, but he tried to spend a little time with the animals each day. He thought the dried apples in their stores were disappearing faster than his own raids would explain, but he couldn't be certain.

Either way, he had no intention of stopping his daily visits.

When he went to grab his staff, he saw that Maiara's was still there. That was a disappointment he hadn't expected until it hit. Often he would find her practicing her forms alone behind the hill, in the gentle saddle between the ruin of Alden's Tor and the barrow. If he happened upon her while she practiced, they would often take to sparring, or going through drill together, and several times that had resulted in an entire afternoon's pleasant diversion as they talked and laughed their way through practice.

But her staff was here, which meant she was probably downstairs with her nose buried in a book.

He decided to abandon the excuses and go find her. Leaving the staves where they were, he headed down into the common room, trying to come up with some question he could ask that would start a conversation without appearing overbearing or foolish.

He had wasted his time. She was nowhere to be found. The fire was banked; the room cooler than he was used to, but they often did that when their store of firewood was running low and no one wanted to run out and find more.

Maybe that was where Maiara had gone. But before he went haring off into the woods, he decided to make a good search of their living quarters first. He wouldn't want to waste his time trudging through the frozen forests if she was down here, just a few steps away.

He went into the living area, ignoring the faint tingle he felt as he approached the girl's room. He looked into each chamber as he passed, trying to make enough noise that he wouldn't catch the girl unaware while at the same time not seeming to be a complete clod, either.

He almost felt light headed, as if he had had one too many cups of mead, as he reached out for the curtain across Maiara's chamber. But when he pulled it aside, the room was empty.

Tyr looked back toward the common room, then stepped into the little cell. It was neat, as he would have expected. Much neater than his own, to be honest. The bedding was folded neatly in the corner, and her clothing was organized along one wall in neat stacks.

She had taken one of the small stools from the common room and put it beside her bedding. There were several books arranged upon it, as well as a small candlestick, its candle burned nearly down to the pewter cup.

He stared at the bedding for a moment more than was probably necessary, then quickly backed out. He moved through the common room and took the stairs two at a time. Only when he was back among the horses, the grunts and clashes of sparring echoing in the distance, did he slow his pace to an almost comical stroll.

As foolish as he had seen Eirik act over the years, there were occasionally moments when he felt that the real fool was undoubtedly him.

If she wasn't in any of their living areas, and she wasn't watching the sparring, or off practicing on her own, that meant she was almost definitely off in the woods somewhere, which meant his chances of finding her were slim.

He would rather not spend another afternoon letting his fears run circles around his peace of mind, however, and so he grabbed one of the cloth wraps they used to carry wood, tucked a hatchet into his belt, and moved out. The warriors didn't even look at him as he passed, which was just as well. He knew that the grin he had forced onto his face was probably fairly gruesome, and he didn't relish the idea of having to explain his current state of mind to either of the older men.

He made his way into the woods by a meandering route; eyes open for any fallen branches as he let his mind wander down familiar paths. They had been in the mountains for more than two months, and most of the easily collected wood was long gone. He looked nonetheless, since gathering firewood wasn't really why he had come out, after all.

Occasionally he would find a fallen branch, or a dead sapling they had somehow missed, and he made sure he was as noisy as possible, chopping the pieces into manageable lengths and then putting them into the wrap to sling over his shoulder. He figured that if Maiara were anywhere nearby, she would hear, and she would find him. He didn't spend much time thinking about what might happen if she heard him and didn't want to talk.

Soon that old feeling of being watched returned. It was like a heavy weight hanging over his head, and he found himself looking up often, only to find the high white clouds of winter scudding by in the deepening gloom. No one, or nothing, was watching him that he could find.

Still, though, he couldn't shake the sense he wasn't alone.

The wrap was full sooner than he would have liked, although he was a little surprised, looking up, to see that evening was fast approaching. The forest around him had darkened into gloom without his noticing.

With a sigh he turned and began to make his way back down the valley, wondering where Maiara was hiding. He had taken a spiraling path up the valley and was fairly sure he had covered most of the territory sheltered by its high rim. At least, he knew that he had roamed widely enough that his chopping would have been heard everywhere.

There had been no sign of the girl.

He emerged from the woods, breath steaming in great gusts as the weight of the wood made itself felt. The men were no longer sparring, probably having retreated from the stretching shadows of evening back into the common room. He cast his eyes up and over the hill and its ancient fortress, the tower with its shining window light, and the stable where the horses were neighing for their dinner.

And he stopped.

Tsegan had been gone for almost a week. The windows of the tower had been dark for all that time.

But one of them now glowed softly.

Tyr stared up into the gloomy night, the moon a silver smudge behind a layer of high clouds. The tower, silhouetted against the soft light, looked dark and sinister, its lean far more noticeable than during the day. From where he stood, the straps of the wood carrier digging into his shoulder, it looked as if the whole thing was about to tumble down into the stable.

But the strangest thing about the sight was that light. No one should be up in the tower. Unless Tsegan had returned, and he felt sure the old man hadn't, there shouldn't be any light coming from that top chamber. Tsegan had been gone for days, and for weeks and weeks over the course of the winter, and the tower had been dark whenever he was away. But now, this light seemed more ominous than the dark tower alone had ever been.

Tyr picked up his pace, grunting with the pain of the strap through leather and fur. Outside the stable, he dumped the wood unceremoniously into a scattered heap and ran back down the stairs, asking the question before he had even reached the bottom to see if anyone was there.

"Is Tsegan back?" He stopped, looking between his master, collapsed in one of the chairs with a cup of water held to his forehead, and Chagua, who was preparing dinner by the hearth.

Both men looked up at his voice, Chagua's dark eyes searching him up and down and then frowning.

"You didn't get any wood?" Sometimes, when he was annoyed, the singsong accent of the islander was a jarring contrast to the emotions clearly displayed on his face.

"It's upstairs. Is the old man in the tower?" He was trying not to breathe hard, but that light, coupled with his shuffling run down the last slopes of the valley with the load of wood, was conspiring against the effort.

"We haven't seen him." Eirik had lowered the cup, his eyes narrowed with suspicion. "Why?"

Tyr cursed his heavy breathing and leaned against the doorway, doing his best to act casual. "No reason. I thought I saw smoke, is all. I had a question for him, if he was back."

That was hardly a good excuse; even if the old man had returned, and even if Tyr had a question for him, there would have been nothing he could do. Tsegan had made it clear early on that he would not have anyone approaching his tower, no matter the reason. When he was needed, he would arrive, and that was an end to it.

But the two men were either not listening or had other things on their minds. They merely shrugged and went back to what they were doing.

"Bring down some of the wood, or dinner will be cold." Chagua threw the words over his shoulder, not bothering to look back.

"Yeah." Tyr looked from the islander's broad back to his master face, once again hidden behind the raised cup. "Yeah, I'll be right down with that."

He took the stairs two at a time again, heedless of his breath. If Tsegan had not returned, and Maiara was missing, but there was a light on in the tower ...

The girl had been acting strangely since the battle. But surely she wouldn't—

He ran to the back of the stable, through the storage area. There was a lot more room back here, which was a silent worry totally separate from all the others. Did they have enough food to last them the winter? Eirik claimed there were settlements and trading posts scattered throughout the mountains; they wouldn't starve if they ran out of something. But given their situation, Tyr was fairly certain the old man would frown upon their leaving the valley for flour or dried apples.

There was no obvious entrance to the tower anywhere along its base. There was nothing but the blank surface of closely-laid stone, covered with stretches of winter browned lichen. Maiara and Tyr had often talked about where the entrance might be, and why the old man was so mysterious about it. There was really only one place, unless the warren of unused underground chambers where they all lived somehow connected to a tower basement somewhere below. The tower butted up against the stable, and although neither of them had felt the need at the time, they were both fairly certain it would have to be somewhere beyond the supplies.

The back wall of the space was in deep shadow, and he had to go back and get one of the lamps hanging by the entrance, lighting it with a straw he ignited from one of the torches. The light was glaring, throwing confusing shadows across the walls, but as he felt his way further and further back, he realized that one of the shadows was actually a passage, irregularly shaped, bearing no resemblance at all to a doorway.

In the normal course of their lives in the valley, unless one brought a lantern or torch all the way back, the crack looked like a natural roughness in the stone.

He stood with the lantern, staring at the passage. If he was wrong; if Tsegan was back and had just gone straight up to the top chamber; if Maiara was out on one of her longer walks...

Before he could talk himself out of it, Tyr pushed on, forcing himself to walk tall as he passed beneath the low overhang of the entrance and into the winding passageway beyond.

He walked on for several paces, expecting to reach the tower around every bend, but the narrow corridor just continued to wend its way deeper into the hill. He was getting nervous that he had somehow missed a turn or a doorway when the passage ended in a stretch of smooth stonework that matched the outside walls of the tower.

A new door had been placed within the frame, with cast-iron hardware and a heavy-looking lock.

He panicked. How was he supposed to get through this? And if he was right, how had she gotten through it?

But as he waited, reaching out to brush the fresh wood, it creaked open. The lock was not secured; nothing held the door shut at all.

The door drifted open on silent, well-oiled hinges, only darkness beyond. Tyr stood, wavering, for a long time before once again forcing himself to continue, pushing the door fully open and then, turning, easing it almost shut again behind him.

The lantern revealed a small chamber with hooks freshly sunk into the walls, a table against one wall, and some shelves. There wasn't anything on the table or the shelves beyond a thin layer of dust. On the far wall, a circular stair was set into the outer wall itself, rising up to the heavy-beamed ceiling overhead and disappearing into a hatchway.

Casting one last quick glance around, Tyr moved to the stairs, trying to make as little noise as possible, and eased his way up. As he peeked through the hatchway, his lantern held high, he found himself in another wide chamber that seemed to take up the entire tower, judging from the rounded walls. This chamber was empty as well, although a series of old, warped high tables and tall chairs scattered around made it look almost like a tavern. Again, on the opposite wall, he saw another set of stairs leading up.

The next two levels of the tower were the same, differing only in the types of furniture scattered about. The third level had only three or four loosely-constructed racks, not unlike the weapon racks the tourney warriors used to store their equipment when they weren't fighting. These were empty, and the dust here was thick except for the pathway connecting the top of the stair with the base of the next set, across the room.

The fourth level contained more tables, but this time there was very little dust. Most of the tables were empty, although, as he moved toward the far staircase, he thought he saw some small, low objects scattered across the farthest. What he didn't see was an enraged old man or a guilt-ridden girl, so he continued on his way.

Things changed, and became much more nerve-wracking, on the fifth level. There was fresh wood work, creating a long hall leading from the head of his stair to the foot of the next. Along the hall, to either side, were doors, all closed and dark. Three to the left and two on the right, they were plain, with wrought iron hardware matching the door in the cavern below. The floor was as silent as a grave.

Tyr crept along the hall, feeling now, more than ever, that he was trespassing on someone's private domain. He reached the first door, on his left, and put his hand on the latch. The door was locked but made a loud clicking sound when he lifted the handle that almost caused his heart to jump out of his throat. He eased the latch back down again and wiped sweat from his brow. He wished he had removed some of his winter clothing before heading up, but he'd lacked the presence of mind. He thought for a moment of at least dropping his heavy cloak here in the hall, but what if he had to leave in a hurry?

Instead, he wiped the sweat out of his eyes and eased his way over to the next door. Each door was locked, and each one sounded louder than the last to his nerve-strained ears.

Finally, at the end of the hall, he stood at the foot of the next stairway, looking up into the darkness.

Except that this time, it wasn't exactly dark.

There was a soft, dim light flickering somewhere in the level above him, and he was gripped by a chill that was only made worse by the oily feeling of sweat all over his body.

He had not been discovered yet. He had seen no secrets, broken no locks. He could head back down now, busy himself with the wood and dinner, and forget, with a nearly-clear conscience, that he had ever gone into the tower in the first place.

Except that the tower had a strange feeling of emptiness to it that seemed to urge him on. He didn't know why, but with each vacant level, with each dark room and locked door, his conviction that Tsegan was away grew firmer, and the feeling that he would find Maiara with the light above grew stronger.

With one last glance down the hallway and one last swipe of his forearm over his brow, he made his slow, careful way up the stairs to the next level.

It was empty.

He took in the entire chamber with his eyes, trying to move his head as little as possible, holding his lantern beneath the lip of the opening. The source of the meager light he had seen was not here, but filtered through another opening to the level above. This chamber was a workshop of some kind, with long low tables cluttered with all sorts of shapes he could not identify from his current vantage. There were windows as well, opening out into the cold winter night. The frigid breeze felt like a godsend as it swept over his face.

Tyr reached down without looking and turned the little handle on the side of his lantern, withdrawing the wick until it dimmed, flickered, and went out. From here, he would go by the light he found and not give himself away with the blazing lantern light.

There was a loud bang from the next floor up and a muffled curse. Tyr jumped, nearly bashing his shoulder against the trap frame, and then leapt forward. He left the lantern behind, at the edge of the trap in case he had to grab it on the way out, and pulled the small hatchet from his belt, although he could not have said what good he thought it might do.

He rushed through the chamber, past the tables without looking at the objects they held, and up the stairs without trying to be quiet. He charged up the ascent, brandishing the small axe, and swept the room above with wild eyes.

He stopped, his shoulders sagging as all the tension ran out of his body.

The room was comfortable, with widely spaced windows and a small hearth along the circular wall. It was larger than the chambers below, and he realized he must be at the swollen top of the tower. There were no more stone stairs, but an ugly, serviceable ladder led up to a closed hatch in the high ceiling.

Standing before a comfortable-looking chair at a long, polished table was Maiara. There was a book lying on the floor against the far wall, with several other books scattered across the table. A candelabrum stood at one end, near a window that appeared to be heavily glazed with thick glass. She was on her feet, her crystalline blue eyes wide.

He looked around, trying to find what might have caused her to shout, but aside from the tall girl, now glaring at him, the chamber was empty. There were two long couches near the hearth, as well as a low bookshelf against one wall. He was surprised to see how few books were on the shelves, even taking into account those Maiara had obviously taken with her to the table.

"What in the name of all the hells are you doing?" She screamed the words at him, color flooding back into her face as her eyes began to glow like lightning with a rage fueled by the fright he had just given her. "What are you thinking?"

Tyr straightened, looking around again, trying to grasp some excuse that might not seem contrived. It was hopeless, and he decided not to try. With a shrug, he said, "I saw the light, and knew Tsegan was away. I was afraid someone had broken in."

Her eyes narrowed. "You were afraid someone had broken in?"

He nodded. "I was. I was afraid you had broken in. You're not supposed to be up here, Maiara. If he finds out, what will he think?"

She laughed at him, falling back into the seat. "I'm not supposed to be up here?" The anger was still there, but now it was mixed with a strange bitterness. "What about you? Where are you supposed to be in all of this?"

That set him back. He was not prepared to defend his position in their little cabal at the moment, with the energy of his nervous climb and the last fearful moments still crashing through his veins. "Neither of us is supposed to be here. How did you get in, anyway? Did Tsegan leave the door unlocked?"

She laughed again, and again there was little amusement in the sound. "You don't live in a guest house for long without learning how to pick a lock, Tyr. It's almost an essential skill."

His jaw fell open. "You picked the lock? You broke in? You really broke in?"

He hadn't thought that was even a possibility, assuming the door had been left open somehow. But that didn't seem to be the case. Maiara was here because she willfully disobeyed the man who had brought them all together. The man who controlled their every moment while they were here in his little sanctuary in the mountains. The man who had killed a band of attackers just a few days ago, seemingly with a wave of his hand.

She had the good grace to look sheepish at his question, though, and her shoulders sagged as the heat flickered and dimmed in her eyes. "I wanted to know. I needed to know." Her voice was soft without the anger behind it, and he wanted to put an arm around her, to comfort her, but he knew that wouldn't have the desired effect at all.

Even thinking about it, he remembered the hatchet still in his hand. With a quick look back at the girl, he slid it into his belt, and then moved through the room, noting the small pile of wood by the cold hearth, and several strange objects strewn about the room that he couldn't make any sense of.

As he approached, he looked at the books scattered before Maiara and was not overly surprised he couldn't read the words inscribed on their covers. He was surprised, however, as he sat down across from her, pulling one toward him, that he couldn't even recognize the writing. He looked up at the girl, one eyebrow cocked in question.

She shrugged. "They're supposedly books about magic." She seemed so annoyed she wanted to spit. "They're useless. Worse than useless, they're a joke."

That cleared nothing up for Tyr as he leaned forward in his chair. "What do you mean, they're a joke?" He waved one hand behind them, gesturing vaguely toward the window. "Some joke, to strip the flesh from nearly a dozen men."

Maiara shook her head. "What he did was not a joke. What these books say about how he did it is the joke." She spun one around and pushed it toward him. He recognized the writing this time and could pick out a few of the smaller words. But most of the pages she showed him were covered in diagrams and strange looking symbols that he had never seen before.

She leaned toward him, and the anger was back. "Do you see these? This book claims that all the magic in the world comes from beings from another place, another time, another ... I don't know!" She threw up here hands in aggravation. "It says you control these creatures by summoning them into these diagrams written on the floor. It's a long process that takes days and days but should give the person who can control them nearly unlimited power."

He nodded. He had heard tales like that before. "Alright. So?"

She growled and reached for another book. "I've been all through this whole tower. There isn't a single room prepared as that book suggests. No diagrams, none of the materials it says you would need. Nothing at all to suggest Tsegan has ever done something like that here."

"Maybe he didn't?" As far as Tyr was concerned, you could call it what you wanted, but he had seen the power the old man wielded, and he knew it was real. "Maybe he did all of that somewhere else?"

She shook her head and pushed another book toward him. "This one claims that all magic comes from the stars. If you align yourself just right, and with the proper materials, you can harness their power for your own designs."

That one sounded familiar too. As a child, he had often wondered how much power one might be able to siphon off the tiny little lights in the sky, but then, the wizards in the old stories could do quite a lot, so what did he know?

"Well, maybe—"

She pushed another book toward him. "This one claims that the spirits fuel a sorcerer's magical power."

He opened his mouth to speak, but she was shoving another tome his way.

"This one says it has to do with lines of power in the earth."

He had caught the rhythm of the discussion now so didn't try to break in, instead just sitting back and waiting to hear where she was going.

"This one says it's gods. This one says it's animal sacrifice. This one says human sacrifice!"

She had run out of books, but her head swept back and forth as if looking for more, and she was breathing heavily as anger roiled behind her eyes.

"I think I understand." He tapped the scattered pile of books before him. "They all say something different?"

She nodded. "None of them agree on anything! And none of them talk about anything like what we saw in the courtyard that day, or any of the other stories any of us have told since we all came here!"

And then it came to him. "Is this about the arrow?"

She stopped, staring at him with those intense, crystalline blue eyes, and the anger faded slightly. "Well, that's only part of it ..."

He nodded. "Only part of it, and none of these talk about anything like what we all saw?"

She stiffened again. "No! They don't! And if he's not doing any of this," she reached out and scattered the books down the table. Several of them thumped onto the floor. "Then what in all the hells is he doing?"

He could understand the girl wanting to know about the power that had spared her life. He wanted to know, and it hadn't happened to him. And she had a good point, too. If Tsegan was performing something they could call magic, despite the fact that magic in any form was supposed to have been dead and gone for generations, if it had ever existed at all, what was he doing? How was he doing it? And why did he have all these books with him if they had nothing to do with what he had done?

She leaned over and picked one up off the floor, closing it and showing him the spine. "You can't read this, right?"

He felt the heat rise behind his cheeks and looked away, shrugging. "No."

She nodded. "No, you can't." She flipped it, not noticing his discomfort at all. "You can't because as far as I can tell, it's gibberish. It's a bunch of nonsense symbols that look impressive, but it doesn't mean anything." She gestured to the others. "There are bits and pieces of actual words, but they don't say anything. A lot of them are like that. They look like something you would expect a wizard to have on his shelf in the fairy stories, but they don't mean anything."

His eyes narrowed. He liked Tsegan. He had come to trust the old man, and he didn't like where this seemed to be going. "I don't understand. You're saying he's a charlatan? But we saw what he did!"

She shook her head violently. "No, he's not a charlatan, Tyr. What he did was very real. It was too real, as far as I'm concerned. But it had nothing to do with any of these books. So why have them?"

He was in over his head. He knew it in his bones. But he felt like he needed to defend the old man. "Perhaps he likes to surround himself with things like this? He's supposed to be the only one left, Maiara! Maybe he's lonely? Maybe magic did work in all these different ways once, and these remind him of a time when he wasn't alone?"

That seemed to give her pause, and he had to force the smile of satisfaction from his face. She needed to understand he was no fool, if she was every going to respect him.

Then she shook her head. "No. It makes no sense. These are all trash."

That made him angry, although he could not have said why. He had felt a jolt when she proclaimed he could not read the words on the spines of the book, and it had built up in his chest through all her words since. Now it fueled a reaction he would have been hard-pressed to explain, if there had been anyone there coherent enough to demand an explanation. "How would you know they're trash? They don't stack up to farmer's scribbles or the children's tales you're used to?"

That brought her up short, and he could see he had hurt her. A part of him was ashamed at that, realizing full-well that it worked counter to everything he felt and everything he had wanted to do when he had followed her into the tower.

"Do you have any idea how many books I've read since we came here, Tyr?" Her beautiful face was cold. "Do you have any concept of how hard I have worked, day and night, since before you came?"

He shook his head. She was always reading, that was true. But he didn't pay too much attention to what, exactly, she was doing with those books.

"There are one hundred and seventy three books in that library downstairs. I have read every one of those books at least once." Her tone was getting harder. "More than twenty of those books were written for me, specifically, by him." She nearly spat that last word. "They are filled with questions, concepts, and challenges I have to puzzle through, and then he grills me whenever he's around to pay attention."

She was rising in her chair, and he leaned back, not sure how far this was going to go.

"My brain is so full of theories, philosophies, and unsolvable puzzles that I feel like it could burst at any moment." She settled back, a sneer marring her perfect features. "So yes, I think I have the right to say when a book is trash."

A cold, uncomfortable silence settled down over the room. He knew he should back off. He had had no idea she could have read so much. It seemed like an impossible task to him, and yet he didn't doubt her at all. But the anger was still in charge, and it was not ready to let go.

"Tsegan Aqisiaq is a great man. He may have lived more lifetimes than either of us can imagine, and he has used his powers for nothing but good since we met him. I believe he has nothing but the welfare of all the kingdom in his heart. In fact, he has nothing but the welfare of all fyrdar and oyathey in his heart! Why can't you trust him?"

She stared at him for long seconds as he sat there, waiting for the flames of her response.

She blinked, looked down, and then looked away, out one of the far windows. When she responded, her voice was low and soft, and he felt terrible. "I trust him. I just ..." One of her hands rose to brush against the center of her chest. "I just wanted to understand."

He was crushed. He felt like the worst kind of churl. For a moment, he wanted to reach out, to hold her hand, to beg her for forgiveness, and say that it was all his fault.

But it wasn't all his fault, damn it! The anger came surging back. Who was she that he should feel sorry for her? She was no better than him. She wasn't any kind of queen. Not yet, anyway. She had no right to question him, or Tsegan, or any of them. As far as he was concerned, they were all equals in this strange journey, until she ascended to the throne in Connat.

He rose; that small, rational part of his mind screaming silently into the rising tide of rage. Its sense went unheard.

"You are no one to question him, Maiara. He is a truly great man, who has given us this one opportunity to make something great of ourselves." He looked down at her, then at the books, with the best sneer his worst self could summon. "Best clean up your mess here and hope he doesn't realize what you've done. You're no princess yet, and he's the only one who can change that."

He pushed himself away from the table and strode toward the stairway. As he turned away, he saw her face, mouth open, eyes wide. She was more surprised than hurt, but that was good enough for the part of him that was now in control.

Who did she think she was, after all? And who was he, to chase after her, and then dance to her tune?

As he descended the stairs, taking his lantern in one hand and moving as quickly as he could, he ignored that part of him that shouted to be heard. He had said his piece, and she could analyze it at her leisure.

Who was she to tell him he couldn't read?

Chapter 18

The enormous blade whirred around his head, and Eirik could not stop himself from grinning. The feeling of the incredible weight of sharp steel under his complete control again was something he had not felt in a long time. It made him feel next to invincible.

Of course, Chagua was there, grinning as well, to prove how wrong that feeling was.

The islander was moving back and forth before him, a heavy wooden staff spinning easily from hand to hand. Chagua occasionally used his strange blade when they sparred now, but it was more of a handicap than a strength for training purposes; a weapon like that allowed for few nonlethal attacks.

That length of oak, however, was nearly as hard as iron. It could block a blow from the maekre blade without a problem, and would do little more than knock him senseless or leave him with incredibly colorful bruises when its blows landed.

But this time, Eirik thought he was ready.

The graceful pattern of the big sword sweeping back and forth was almost mesmerizing. But that was no longer the weakness Chagua had once shown it to be. Now, rather than establishing a pattern that a foe could use against him, it represented a never-ending array of possible attacks, so long as he kept his mind focused on the balance point and the placement of his enemy.

Coming up from a low pass, rather than bringing the blade up and over as he had done several times in a row, Eirik rushed the islander and brought the blade across, at chest height, with all the strength and speed he could bring to bear.

He had long since gotten over the idea that he needed to pull his blows against the islander. Even on those rare occasions when Chagua mistimed a parry or a dodge, the blow had not landed. If Eirik managed to disarm his opponent, or sent him sprawling out of the path of the enormous blade, he would always rise, hands up with a wry smile, and proclaim the contest over.

The massive sword blade whistled through the air as Eirik pulled it out of its original arc toward his tormentor. Everything he had learned as a young saemgard, everything he had relearned at the less-than-delicate hands of the islander, came together in a perfect moment of poise and execution.

The maekre blade flashed right through where Chagua had stood, over his head as the dark man dropped into a crouch, and the heavy staff was coming straight up.

Eirik saw what would happen next, but there was nothing he could do about it. He had committed to the blow he felt sure would win him the bout. The heavy sword pulled him around, into the rising stick, and all he could do was bring his knees together and hope he was in time.

He was not.

Intense pain rocked through his entire body as the staff buried itself into his groin.

Folding up around the pain, coughing and heaving for breath that wouldn't come, he had only a moment to reflect that Chagua was not pulling his blows either. Then he fell on his side, curled up around the world-ending agony that sent spasming waves of torment through his entire body.

"You over balanced." The voice seemed to come from far away as Eirik continued to rock back and forth on the ground. "You saw what you thought was an opening, and you struck with everything you had. That can sometimes win you a battle, but if you are wrong, it can cost you your life."

Eirik could barely make sense of the words, and the thought that Chagua was wasting one of his many lectures on pain-deaf ears was almost enough to wring a smile from the grimace of pain twisting up his face. Almost, but not quite.

Eirik didn't know how long he lay on the ground, concentrating on his breathing and trying to settle his body into stillness. The cold helped. He tried to focus on the clouds above, paying little attention to anything nearby. The fading light of the approaching sunset as it slanted into the valley seemed to carry a texture within it that he had never noticed before. He focused his attention on that and tried to ignore the queasiness rising up in his throat.

By the time Eirik was able to stagger to his feet again, Chagua had returned the weapons to their storage spaces and was leaning against the entrance frame of the stable. The horses made soft noises behind him as they demanded their evening's ration of oats, and the islander was staring off to the west, where the sunset was turning the sky a deep, angry red behind the distant mountains.

"Some would call that a low blow." Eirik approached the islander with a slow, limping gait, one hand still pressed to the wounded area.

Chagua smiled. "By what meaning of low?" He stretched, moving into the stable and toward the stairs. "It was certainly lower than your head, which I could have struck just as easily. Or your stomach, which would have meant a long, slow, painful death. If you mean low as in dishonorable, we'll just have to disagree on that."

At the doorway down into their lair, the islander turned, and Eirik stopped to see that the bright smile was gone. "Honor is something for a king's court, or maybe the fields of a tourney match. In war, there is no place for withholding a blow, no matter how you might feel about it. Once steel is bared in earnest, you fight for survival, you fight for victory, with every particle of your being, or you die."

Eirik's own smile slid off his face and a lot of the old resentments rose up to whisper behind his eyes. It was easy, apparently, for this man to forget that he had once been a member of the most elite fighting force the fyrdar kingdoms had possessed. He often cursed his vivid memories of the last days of the saemgard. He remembered his brothers and sisters dying all around, killed by coward hiding in the trees. Peasants swamped the survivors ten to one or more, pulling them from their horses and stabbing them half a hundred times with rusty, ill-kept blades.

There was nothing Chagua could teach Eirik about the indignities of battle or the proper place for honor and victory.

And then he understood. Comfortable in their battle-forged camaraderie, Eirik had started to see their latest matches from within that spirit of battle brethren he remembered from his early tourney days. He would never have struck one of his comrades with the blow that had just laid him low back then. But if he allowed himself to settle into anything resembling that comfortable mindset in a real battle, if he could not recapture his old battle-sense, how could he expect to protect Maiara if the old man's plan, whatever they may be, came to fruition?

Whatever Tsegan had contrived, it was going to be dangerous for them all; contending with an entire kingdom. There would be no room for delicate sensibilities there. He should not expect them here, in training.
With the pain of the blow still lingering, pulsing outward with each step, he only nodded.

Chagua returned the nod, turning back to the stairs and the warmth of the common room as the last light of day faded behind them.

*****

Eirik sat before the fire, contemplating the sparse scattering of bark and twigs beside the hearth. He hoped there was enough wood in the fire to keep it going awhile longer. Chagua was preparing the meal, which meant they were all going to be better off than when it was his turn to cook. Maiara was the best of them, of course. The girl had grown up in a guesthouse and had probably learned to cook at an early age. Tyr wasn't bad either, most likely because of the years when he, himself, had been too lost in his cups to do more than shovel a handful of horse's oats into his mouth at dinnertime before rolling over into oblivion.

He no longer shied away from the memories of those lost years. He understood, now, what he had become, and what it had cost him. The last of the drink burned from his blood months ago; he had not craved so much as a cup of wine for weeks. It would be easy to forget the man he had been. But he also knew, with a certainty that brought a bitter scowl to his lips, how easy it would be for him to lapse back into that pathetic sot again if he ever lowered his guard.

In fact, he had finally realized that many of Chagua's harshest comments were geared specifically to ensure that Eirik would not forget what he had been. They had hurt, yes; but that pain, like all the rest, served a purpose.

He flexed his hand. He would not fool himself. He had lost the speed of youth long ago, and, sadly, it had little to do with the drink. Even clean living could not undo the damage that time had caused. But what the mead, ale, wine, and spirits had taken from him was that solid core of his being, the rock-steady conviction that he was the best and destined for greatness.

The massacre at the ford, fleeing first the Vestan warriors and then the shadows of Astrigir who came hunting for him after, had shaken his faith in himself. The long, slow fall into obscure mediocrity, and then below that, had buried his self-confidence so deep he had not even noticed it was gone. But he had, now. And in brief flickers of momentary, lightning-like bursts, he was recapturing the feeling of power that had once been his constant companion.

Of course, then Chagua would dash him to the muddy earth, and he would learn the equally important lessons of awareness and humility all over again.

It was an interesting journey.

He took a sip of water and frowned. Someday, he thought, he might take a drink without that split second of mindless hope the cup might contain something other than water, but he doubted it.

He looked up and watched Chagua moving around the table beside the hearth, readying the evening's meal. None of their meals was anything you could call a banquet, but supplemented with what Chagua, Tyr, and occasionally Eirik himself could hunt down in the surrounding valleys, it would do. Their supplies were dwindling, and it was disheartening to think of the piles of empty sacks, casks, and crates forming outside the stable. But then, they had been in the mountains for nearly three months, and their sojourn here could only last so much longer.

Chagua was singing something under his breath as he worked, and Eirik settled back into his chair to listen. The man's voice was musical whether he was making scathing observations of Eirik's shortcomings or explaining the finer points of throwing sand into an opponent's eye. But these rare times when he sang, it was almost as if his voice became less musical and more powerful at the same time.

Unfortunately, Eirik couldn't understand a single word.

"What's that you're singing?" Things between them had loosened since the battle, and he felt more comfortable now asking such questions. He had realized, since the thawing in their relationship, that he knew very little about this man who was dragging him back to himself.

Chagua's singing stopped and he turned. "A song in the language of my people. We call it Garuna."

Eirik nodded, although the word meant nothing to him. He knew little about the islanders from the distant north. They were said to be even more refined than the oyathey, if that was possible. Only their merchants, and an occasional traveling philosopher or scholar, ventured far enough south to make an impression. Eirik tried to keep in mind that what knowledge he had came from a tiny sampling.

But it was clear, by Chagua's presence and his obvious skill, that there was more to the islanders than these intellectual pursuits. Eirik realized he had never even heard a name for Chagua's homeland other than the northern islands.

"Garuna." He said the word as if tasting it. It felt strange on his tongue. "Named after your homeland?"

Chagua had turned back to his preparation, but he smiled over his shoulder. "It is true, that one of the islands is called Garun, giving us the name of our language. But there are many islands beyond Garun. In fact, although in times long past that island was the root of our culture and heritage, it has since fallen out of favor, viewed as nothing more than a backwater by many." Something about the man's voice spoke more to Eirik than his tone, and he leaned forward. "But not by you?"

Again the bright flash of smile from within the dark tangle of black beard. "I have a special fondness for Garuna, as I was never allowed to visit it."

That seemed strange, reinforcing another recent realization. He might know little about the northern islands, but he knew nothing about Chagua. The man never spoke of his past, never mentioned friends or family he had left behind. He lived in the moment, in their little valley, and it was as if he had sprung into being here, with no existence beyond his role as teacher and instructor; and servant to Tsegan, of course. From what Eirik had been able to tell, the dark-skinned man from the north had built or repaired everything from the stable, storeroom, and common room, to the top of the old man's tower and whatever work had been done within it.

And Eirik suddenly realized he had no idea why the islander was doing any of it.

He put down the cup and sat up in the chair, ignoring the twinges of pain still radiating from his center. "Why are you here, Chagua?"

The other man stopped. "It is my turn to prepare the meal, Eirik. Would you rather me pawn that task off on one of the children, as I've noticed you do so often?"

That brought a smile to Eirik's face. "Don't act like it's not a relief whenever I manage to dodge cooking duty. You know the horses would make a better meal than some of the dishes I've put together."

Chagua smiled with a shrug. "True." He looked around the room, and Eirik noticed that his gaze settled on the shelves of books for a long moment before moving on. "Why am I here, in this valley so far from my home, working in secret toward a devastatingly unrealistic goal with a band of total strangers?"

Eirik stared at the dark-skinned man for a moment and then nodded. In the face of the bald statement, it was all he could think to do.

Chagua moved to sit down at the table after checking a small cauldron on the fire. "Do you know anything about the northern islands, Eirik Hastiin?"

Eirik shook his head, annoyed. He hated it when anyone forced him to admit to ignorance.

"Well, that's probably not true." Chagua settled back and waved a hand. "You know that my people are primarily dreamers, sages, and traders, correct?"

Eirik nodded.

"Although that is a skewed view, depending on the few of my people who venture this far south, it is not so far off the mark. Intellectual and scholarly pursuits are paramount to us. In fact, in the islands, great success and esteem may be gained by one who is accomplished in any of these disciplines, while the more physical pursuits are seen as necessities and obligations; not particularly noble pursuits in and of themselves. They are not things that might make a person great."

That was utterly alien to Eirik. In the fierce, warrior-dominated society of the tourney circuit, and before that, the warlike fyrdar court of King Einar, prowess in combat and strength of body were paramount.

"My people have traveled so far down this path, many of them scorn the physical disciplines. Several generations ago, it had become so bad that a noble family was disgraced by a child who excelled at athletics beyond the accepted norm. And if a warrior scion were to rise up within one of the high families? They were disowned outright."

Eirik felt as if Chagua was trying to spin a fantastical tale and found himself nodding along, even while believing less and less.

"My people are not alone in the northern seas, and defense of one's borders should be as important to any kingdom as the advancement of medicine, philosophy, or art."

Eirik almost stopped him there. Defending the realm should be as important as art?

"The dilemma, then: how to defend your realm when the highest levels of your society scorn the very traits that make for an effective warrior?" The big man's brow furrowed, his eyes distant. "There came a period of upheaval for my people; around the time your own fyrdar lords were breaking away from the empire of Kun Makha. We tried conscripting defenders from the lower castes, but who would lead them? The dangers of a conscripted army led by academics made itself quickly known. Mercenaries? The historical dangers of a state depending upon mercenary forces for its survival are obvious. But we tried it anyway and paid the customary price."

Eirik didn't know what history said about paying someone to protect you, but he didn't need to be a historian to realize it was a bad idea. Eventually, the people you were paying would realize you had no one to protect you from them, and there were easier ways of getting your gold than putting their life on the line. He nodded sagely, confidant that he had puzzled out Chagua's meaning.

"Eventually, it was decided that each of the noble houses, high and low, must contribute one child to the defense of the realm. These children would be raised from birth to the sword and shield. When others were learning logic, history, and rhetoric, those children given up to the defense of the islands trained their bodies, day and night; they learned strategy and tactics; they studied wars both modern and ancient. They dedicated their lives to being the best warriors they could be."

"The Swords." The word jumped into Eirik's mind, and he nodded. "When we first met, Tsegan said you were a Sword of the islands. That's what you are? Raised from birth to be a warrior?"

Chagua looked away. "Yes. Forever denied access to the pursuits my people truly esteem."

Eirik sat up straighter, looked back to the lines of books, then back to Chagua. "They didn't let you learn anything else?"

Chagua shook his head. "We were not even taught to read. It was thought that if we were given even limited access to those pursuits, our natural inclinations would take over and we would be weakened as warriors."

"But, wait." Eirik could read, although he wasn't certain about his squire. It wasn't seen as an essential skill for most in the fyrdar kingdoms, especially on the tourney circuit. He hadn't thought much about it before, and wondered, now, if this might be some sort of unconscious cultural reaction to the more intellectual nature of the oyathey of Kun Makha. He shook his head. "You said you studied history. If you can't read..."

Chagua's smile was thin, his eyes distant. "Lectures. Unending discourses on history, tactics, theory." He shook his head. "It was painful; torture. Like being tossed upon a bit of flotsam in the middle of the sea: dying of thirst, surrounded by water you cannot drink."

"You wanted more." Eirik was finding this all fascinating. To think that there was something he could do that Chagua could not was somehow invigorating.

"I did. I would sneak out to find books. I did my best to teach myself to read." His eyes flicked up to meet Eirik's, and the fyrdar warrior found that he could not look away. "Do you have any idea how difficult it is to teach yourself to read, with no help at all?"

Eirik had been taught by scholars engaged first by his father, then by his king for the purpose. It was something he realized now that he had always taken for granted; he had done precious little reading as a besotted tourney fighter. He couldn't even begin to imagine how difficult it might be to learn how to read without assistance.

He shook his head. "You did, though?"

Chagua looked away. "No. I tried. I picked up some things, but it was too difficult, given all of my other duties." He smiled, but there was no humor in the expression. "I failed, and worse, got caught."

The big islander was still, eyes fixed on the floor between his feet. Eirik tried to think of some way to break the uncomfortable silence without seeming like a thankless boor, but Chagua took up his story once again, without prompting.

"It would have meant the ruination of my family if word had gotten out. But then Master Aqisiaq appeared, looking to secure the services of a Sword, and my father and his scribes dug through the archives and contrived a shaky precedent allowing them to see me off and enlarge the family's coffers at the same time."

Eirik straightened. "Wait, they sold you?"

Chagua shook his head, sending the long main of coils shaking down his back. "Not sold. I cannot be forced to do anything outside the initial agreement, which was very specific." He turned his dark eyes on Eirik. "I was brought here to train you. Anything else, I may refuse."

Eirik looked around the room, he remembered the fresh construction above and all the other menial tasks he had seen Chagua perform in the past weeks. "But you're doing a lot more than that."

"Even the precedents my father's people could find would not allow an unwilling Sword to serve a foreigner. Master Aqisiaq had to convince me to go with him." His eyes flicked to the stacks of books and away, and Eirik understood.

"He said he'd teach you to read."

Chagua straightened and turned to face Eirik fully. "He did. And he offered me any book I might desire; the library is only the beginning. But before that, I was required to swear to perform any task he required."

Eirik nodded. Reading wasn't something that had enriched his own life overmuch, but he could see he had taken it for granted. He could also see that it was something Chagua greatly esteemed, and he understood working toward something like that. Especially now.

"So, has he? Taught you to read?"

The islander's eyes dimmed and he turned away. "No. He has stuck closely to the letter of our agreement. When we are done, and his own tasks complete, he will fulfill his side of the bargain." His voice softened. "Until then, as you say, I am little more than a slave, if a willing one."

He went back to preparing dinner, and then grunted as he tried to tease the fire back up in the hearth. "Tyr better be fetching firewood, or we shall be in for a cold meal."

Eirik wasn't too concerned with the fire, as his own body had not yet cooled down. At the reminder, he held his cool stone cup to his forehead and stifled an animal sigh of pleasure.

Footsteps rushed down the stairs and they both looked up as Tyr came crashing in.

"Is Tsegan back?" The boy was out of breath, and there was a harried look about his eyes that Eirik didn't like.

"You didn't get any wood?" Chagua's voice was harsher than it might have been.

Tyr gave the islander a quick glance then went back to scanning the room. "It's upstairs. Is the old man in the tower?"

Something about his squire's behavior did not ring true, and Eirik's eyes narrowed as he realized Maiara was still gone as well. "We haven't seen him. Why?"

Tyr grew even more agitated, although Eirik could tell he was working hard to hide it. "No reason. I thought I saw smoke, is all. I had a question for him, if he was back."

The words ran over themselves, making little sense. Tsegan had told them all never to seek him out. He had said that he would arrive whenever there was a true need. It was one of those self-important comments that kept Eirik from warming to the man. Although, when Einar's brigands had attacked—

But that thought, something he had gone over again and again in his mind, was still too dark to contemplate too closely.

Eirik thought he knew what was going on with his squire now, though, and he didn't want to embarrass the boy, so he shrugged and put the cup back to his forehead.

"Bring down some of the wood or dinner will be cold." Chagua spoke as he turned back to the food.

"Yeah," Tyr's eyes took one last fevered look around the common room. "Yeah, I'll be right down with that." And he was gone, turning with the speed of youth and running up the stairs.

As his footsteps faded into the stable above, Eirik put his cup down, his eyes resting thoughtfully on the doorway.

"Nothing good can come of this obsession." Chagua had turned as well.

"Which obsession is that?" Eirik tried to sound casual.

Chagua grinned. "The passions and energy of youth are wasted on them, I think. And I also think you are a better master than you sometimes pretend." His expression grew serious. "If the girl is a princess, and I have no choice but to believe this is so, and if Master Aqisiaq's intentions come to fruition, there will be no place in a queen's life for an infatuated young warrior. His feelings run deep. His heart will not escape this situation unscathed."

Eirik shrugged, pushing himself to his feet with a grunt. "He's old enough to make such decisions on his own. And who are we to deny those two a little happiness, if they can find it, before all of this luxury comes to an end?" He gestured to the ruin that had become their home.

"If things continue down their natural path, do you think Master Aqisiaq will be pleased if he has to push a princess into the middle of a war, great with child?"

"If Master Aqisiaq is that all-powerful, he can probably see that the girl doesn't quicken, if their little romance goes that far." He turned back to the stairs. "I don't think it has, and I don't think it will. Remember that was her childhood friend those bastards killed in the courtyard. I doubt she's in a frame of mind to pursue that kind of activity."

"Grief does strange things to people." Chagua sat down again near the fire.

Eirik paused, and then turned back to the islander. "So, you've been with him for a while?"

Chagua blew a breath out through pursed lips, his eyes floating up toward the ceiling. "Well over a year, now."

"And you've seen him do ... magic ... like he did the other night?" Eirik was still uncomfortable with the word, but he knew no other he could use that would do what he had seen justice.

Chagua's eyes narrowed. "I should really not speak of my master when he is not present."

Eirik waved that away. "Just in general, I mean. You've seen him use his ... powers ... before?"

Chagua's face became flat, his body motionless. "I have seen him do things neither of us could explain, yes."

Eirik nodded. "Have you ever seen him do anything like what happened to the ... arrow ... that almost killed the girl?"

The islander's face softened at that, and he looked away. "I have not."

Eirik nodded again. "I don't think he was in a position to see her, or the arrow. So, if he didn't do that, who did? And why would he say he had?"

Chagua looked troubled. "I do not know. We have no idea how long he was watching or from where. It could well have been his doing, and we would never know."

Eirik sighed. He remembered the moment vividly. It had haunted his dreams. He remembered reaching out, his eyes flaring at the moment he thought the arrow would hit. And then the arrow disappeared into a cloud of white that dusted the girl's body, doing no harm at all.

He shook his head. There were things in life that never got explained, he knew. Real life was seldom tied up with a neat bow like the endings of a children's story. But ever since he had awakened to find that strange old man staring down at him, it seemed nothing in life might ever be explained again.

He turned back to the stairs with a shrug.

"Where are you going?" Chagua called after him.

He turned with a smile. "If I know Tyr, there is a pile of wood right up there, but he isn't going to be right down with it. So I'll go fetch it." He started up the stairs. "I, for one, have no interest in a cold dinner."

He had to take control of the things he could control, after all.

Chapter 19

The room was cold and dark, with just the single candle to light the massive chamber, but she dared not use more, for fear of repeating what had happened the first time she had invaded Tsegan's tower.

And even a blazing fire in the hearth wouldn't have touched the cold that had settled into her bones, anyway.

Maiara had been nervous that first time, but she had been distracted to madness by Kustaa's death, the carnage that had been unleashed in the courtyard, and the mysterious events that had saved her from following her friend into the spirit lands. She had been desperate for answers, any answers, and Tsegan had left the valley again before she could ask him anything.

She often found the old man endearing, and she was definitely thankful for everything he had done for her already. Even if the rest was a fever dream, the prophecy nothing but a loosely woven skein of ancient babbling and wishful thinking, everything she had learned in the little valley had opened up her world forever. She still had not come to terms with the idea that she might be anyone special, never mind all the rest. She didn't feel special, she knew that.

But he had opened her eyes to worlds she had never known existed, and through their long sessions, when he was present, he had helped her to become so much more than she ever could have imagined. It had taken nearly every waking moment, and one of the most frightening things she had learned over the course of her studies was how much she had yet to learn ... but Tsegan had told her that that realization was more than most scholars ever achieved, and he had seemed genuinely pleased with her for making it. But for all the things he had taught her in these three months and more, he had neatly sidestepped the attempts she had made to discuss his powers. Since the battle, he closed down every attempt she had made to broach the subject. And the one time she had tried to use her newfound rhetorical skills on him, he had gotten genuinely angry, dismissing her with a snarl of contempt. It had been almost a week before he returned, taking up her lessons as if nothing had happened.

But something had happened. She still felt a stinging sense of betrayal that her mentor would not discuss something so important with her. The grief at Kustaa's death had not lessened; Tyr's coldness made her life among these strangers no easier. After the battle with the king's agents, Eirik had redoubled his efforts in the training yard, leaving Chagua little time to talk with a lost little girl with nothing much to offer.

Despite Tyr's dire warnings and her own vicious pangs of guilt, she had broken into the tower again. And then again. And then again. Now she felt like a regular visitor, and picking the lock in the door beneath the hill was almost second nature. Almost.

To hide these little moments up in the tower, she would often start by taking a walk out into the valley, stay in the woods long enough for the others to have forgotten where she was, then return by a different route, sneaking into the stables, and up into the tower.

During each of those hikes into the woods, she had felt that cold, powerful regard that had struck her the first time she had stepped into the valley, or she had run into old Wapa, as if he was waiting for her. She still wasn't sure why she had never told any of the others about the old man, especially after the attack, when their true peril had become clear to all of them. But he seemed so harmless, and he had never made a move to threaten her or discover anything about her companions or what they were doing in the little valley. In the end, however, she decided it was just because she liked the old man, and for whatever reason, she trusted him.

She had only known the others slightly longer, after all. There was just as much reason to trust a strange old man who lived in the woods as there was to trust the legendary warrior, the strange islander, or the petulant boy. That didn't make her feel much better, actually, when she thought about it that way.

The last time she had stumbled upon Wapa, sitting on a high rock between her valley and the next, he had seemed more subdued than normal. He had acted as if he had expected her, which he often did. But that last time, it had seemed as if her appearance had brought him some deep sorrow. When she pressed him, the man's dark eyes had welled up with tears. He had claimed it was nothing, and then waved her back a few steps. When he turned back to face her, his eyes had been clear and dry, and she couldn't be certain that she had seen anything at all.

They had spoken that day, as they often did, of the mountains he called home. They had spoken of the trees, and the winds, and the snows. He was often fond of talking about the moon as if it was a sentient being, although he denied that it was a god or a great spirit. He spoke of the water beneath the earth and of the animals that shared the high places with him. He had spoken of other things sharing the mountains with him; ancient forces he would only hint at. And when she asked about these, he would only give her a look and then claim she wasn't ready yet.

Sometimes, late at night as she was drifting off to sleep, often with a book half-open on her chest, she would think back on those conversations and realize with a start that she was learning nearly as much about the natural world with Wapa as she was learning about the twisted world of men from Tsegan and her books.

When they had said their goodbyes, there had been a heaviness about the old man she had never sensed before. He had reached out and took her hand as she turned to leave, and he had clutched it as if he would never let go. When he did finally let go, her hand sliding out from between his stick-thin fingers, he had stared into her eyes, and said something he had never said before.

He had told her to be careful.

She wasn't sure what he had meant, and when she turned back to him and asked, he had waved her off once again, smiled with an expression she thought contained just a little sadness, and then he had scampered off his rock and down the far valley, gone before she could call after him.

She had returned to the keep after that meeting instead of going up into the tower as she had intended. She found that often running into Wapa would distract her from her need to pour through Tsegan's belongings within the leaning structure. This time, though, it was those last words that haunted her thoughts.

Be careful of what? She was always careful, she thought. She had learned to be careful under the ever-watchful eyes of Vali and Turid. She had always known there was someone waiting to find fault with her behavior, or her work, or her appearance. If anything, she was too careful, she thought.

But somehow, Wapa's words had seemed heavy with some deeper, more frightening import.

Whatever he had meant, she had not seen him again. Each time she had wandered into the woods since, those last words felt more and more like a farewell.

The weather was getting warmer within the sheltered valley, and she knew, on some level she would not acknowledge, that her time here would soon come to an end. But she would make the most of what remained. If Tsegan was not going to help her, then she would help herself to whatever knowledge she could find.

Except that she hadn't been able to find any. None of her journeys into the tower had been any more successful than the first. Tsegan had a small library of books about magic, but each of them seemed as nonsensical and poorly structured as the rest. Not a single theory she had discovered came even close to describing any of the things she had seen or thought she had felt.

By now she had been through every room in the tower, most of them several times. She had been careful not to disturb anything, nor to leave any sign of her presence behind. There were countless ways a wary guest at an inn might try to secure their room, to indicate if some unwanted visitor had wandered in. She kept her eyes alert and always made sure to return every detail, from a single strand of hair to a tiny slip of paper, back to where she had found it.

Eventually, however, she had realized that Tsegan might have more resources at his disposal than even the most determined guesthouse visitor. What if he could use his powers to detect her presence? What if he could sense the aura of her passing, days or weeks after she had swept through?

That fear kept cold company with her own guilt. She had been taught never to invade anyone's private space. It was an essential element of being a good host, and Vali had beaten it into her at a young age. Those lessons were coming back to haunt her now, with each furtive journey up into the tower.

She knew that the anger and frustration she felt was being fueled by that guilt, just as she knew that it was a pathetic rationalization to decide that he deserved to have his privacy violated. A large part of her wanted to get caught, to bring it all out into the open. Maybe then Tsegan would be forced to give her some answers; any answers.

She found this sudden fascination with his powers disturbing. It had taken her focus off her other studies more and more as the weeks churned past. They had all seen Tsegan's powers now, and each of them knew there was something more than they could explain about the man. Even his name had ceased to seem strange.

But no one else was fixated upon this aspect of their situation. Given how strange it all had become, this was just one more facet of strangeness, right? So, why was she? Was it because of that arrow? Did it all come down to that one gods damned arrow?

They had all seen the missile dashed into crystalline dust, and none of them could explain it away. Yet none of the others saw that as anything more than one more dark mystery among many.

But she couldn't let it go. No more than she could lose the bone-deep chill that had haunted her since that night.

Here she was, yet again, bundled up in furs and cloak, squinting down at the dry, dusty writing of men and women long-dead by the light of a single, dim candle.

And it didn't matter at all.

She had poured over every book in the tower now for what seemed like a dozen times. Not a single tome had given so much as a hint at anything she would say was useful.

She closed the book and tapped the cover lightly. There was one book she felt could have been useful to her. She hadn't even thought about it until her fourth or fifth trip up those narrow sweeping stairs. But once she had remembered it, she couldn't forget it, and at least half of each journey up into the tower was spent looking for it.

The Burdren Saga was nowhere to be found.

Once she realized that, she had torn apart the common room as well. The book wasn't there either. In fact, the more she thought about it, she realized that she hadn't seen the old, worn little grimoire in a long time. It had been in the little library in the common room for a while, she thought. But she couldn't actually remember seeing it there since that first night.

For some reason, the book's absence bothered her more than she could explain. Why would he have taken the little book? Did he need it? Was he showing it to the leaders of his budding little rebellion?

That last thought summed it all up, she realized. The reason they had been brought together, thrown into this valley, and subjected to the terrible pressures each of them had endured, was for the sake of this rebellion Tsegan told them all was essential for the survival of the kingdoms.

She wasn't sure she believed in any of it anymore, if she ever had. And she felt almost sure the others harbored similar doubts. But here they were, and when it came time to leave the valley and venture back down into the real world, they would apparently be riding into the teeth of a war to supplant the king of Astrigir and put an untried girl in his place. To put her in his place.

Her eyes drifted to a window. It was still light outside, and the ringing of steel echoed up from the yard. She was no expert, but it seemed to her that Eirik was a new man when he fought now. He was able to move that giant sword of his as if it weighed almost nothing. And yet, as he got faster and faster, Chagua was still always one pace ahead. With men like that to protect her, she should have little to worry about, at least.

If he was going to convince others to take up her cause, he would almost have to take the book with him, right? There couldn't be many copies left, and he would need something to show those whose faith in the old ways, in the old words, might be weak.

She nodded to herself, dismissing her misgivings. The book was useless anyway. She had read it all. She was here, she was following the path that had been laid out for her, and she would do what needed to be done. The words did not give shape to the events, merely warned of them.

It wasn't as if she had specific lines to deliver, like a performer in a minstrel show. Tsegan had told her, many times when her self-confidence had flagged, that the saga spoke of her because of who she was. She could not fail if she tried. Things would happen as they were meant to happen, and she need not fear a misstep, as long as she kept to her studies and remained true to herself.

There was something about the logic of that last statement, his final argument each time she pushed back, that twisted in her mind, but she always dismissed it as further evidence of her own lack of confidence.

She was distracted from her deepening well of fear and doubt by a sound out in the courtyard. Or, rather, the lack of a sound. The ringing of steel had stopped, and the sound of hooves coming down the trail was strange enough to drag her to the window where she peeked out, careful not to be seen.

Tsegan usually left the valley on foot. In fact, only once had he ridden one of the cart horses, and that had been one of his shortest forays out into the world beyond their valley. This last time, as usual, he had walked out, heading directly north rather than taking the trail.

But he was riding back, on a magnificent white charger that put Hestir to shame.

She pulled back from the window, imagining him looking up, piercing the gloom with his dark gaze, eyes widening in betrayal.

Her heart pounded in her chest as a bittersweet taste flooded her mouth. She was afraid she was going to vomit, and wouldn't that have made a pretty mess for her to try to clean up, with Tsegan right outside?

She rose, grabbing the candle, careful of the wax, not letting it splatter onto the table or the book as she returned it to its place. She hurried down the stairs, stumbling several times, but finally coming up against the heavy lower door. She pulled it open, swept through, and then pulled it closed, as silently as she could, behind her.

She moved through the twisting tunnel as quietly as she could, putting out the candle as soon as she could make out the dim light filtering back through the stables. Out in the yard, she could hear the men talking, and without peeking outside, eyes clenched shut against possible discovery, mind whirring through half a dozen possible excuses she might give for being in the back of the stables, she swept down into their little common area, her lungs burning.

At the bottom of the stairs she sighed a great gust of relief, leaning against the cold stone of the doorframe.

"Well, hello there."

She jumped, a small, high-pitched scream just starting to escape her lips before she clamped them shut. Her eyes thrown wide, she scanned the room, terrified of what she might find.

Tyr was sitting in the corner nearest the bookshelves, a small book open in his lap. The smile he gave her had a cruel edge, and she knew in a moment that he understood where she had been.

She straightened her cloak and dress with an assumed, exaggerated nonchalance she wished she possessed, and moved smoothly into the room, taking one of the chairs at the long table.

"You found a book?" She nodded toward his lap, but at the flash of rising anger in his eyes, her shoulders sagged. She couldn't face another of their little squabbles now.

She let her head fall into her hands, elbows on the table. "I think I just almost died."

It felt good to be honest about things. She was certain there was a lesson somewhere in that jumble of emotions, but she didn't feel much like analyzing her own motives or reactions at the moment.

"What happened?" She heard him get up, the soft sound of the book sliding onto a shelf, and his footsteps approaching the table.

"You two down there?" Eirik's harsh voice echoed down the stairway. "Come up."

She lifted her head and looked into Tyr's face in time to see the suspicion rise in his eyes.

She ducked her head as she rose, moving around him and up the stairs after his master.

In the courtyard, Tsegan was standing beside the massive horse with a bright, warm smile on his face. "Ah, Princess!" He gave a slight bow that she found unsettling, then walked toward her, his mount moving with him. "I have a gift for you."

The old man pulled the horse's lead around so that it stood beside her, looking disinterestedly at her and then at its surroundings. In the stable she could hear the other horses whickering softly, and the big white horse's ear flicked once as if in disdainful rejection.

"A princess needs a fitting mount, you see." Tsegan handed her the reins and then stood back, lifting his arms as if presenting her for the first time to the others. "You must make a stunning image, to inspire your people to the greatness the age will require."

Behind her, she could hear Tyr coming out of the stables. She wanted to turn to him, to hear him say something that would break her out of the moment she felt coalescing around her, but his gaze was flat and distant. He barely acknowledged her at all.

"His name is Sannlir, beauty in the old tongue of your people." The old man's smile grew even wider as he raised a single finger toward her. "But he does not represent the sum and total of my gifts for you today!"

Tsegan moved lightly up beside the big horse and unlatched a large saddlebag. She saw, as the old man was bending down to open the satchel, that there was another just like it on the other side.

On one knee, Tsegan bent down over the bag, rummaging around while strange, gleeful sounds escaped beneath his breath. When he rose, it was with a grand flourish as he held out a flashing, billowing shape of slate blue. The color barely registered as she realized what he was holding: an elaborate confection of silk and lace.

He had brought her a dress.

And not just any dress, but a work of art. He held the dress by its slight shoulders, letting it drape down, where it was caught by the errant wind, ripples rolling down its shimmering length.

Then the color registered: it was the exact same shade as her eyes.

She didn't know what to say. She had never been given anything like that dress in her life, and her feelings on that were painfully mixed. It was a beautiful dress, there was no denying that. But what did she need a dress like that for? She was living a hard-scrabble life in the middle of the mountains. The dresses she had with her, most of which Tsegan had supplied when she arrived, were more than suitable for the life they were living.

Did this signal the end of their time in the keep? And if so, was this dress really fitting for the terrifying journey they were about to undertake? Countless hours had been spent honing her mind to the task ahead. She felt, if not ready, at least willing to accept the challenge. But what would this dress say to the men and women she tried to rally to her cause? Follow me because

I wear a fine dress well?

That felt like exactly the opposite direction she should be taking.

But how could she convey that to Tsegan as he stood there holding the dress in his hands, that look of child-like excitement in his wide eyes?

"Thank you so much, Tsegan." She began, not entirely sure where she was going. "But I don't know—"

He nodded. "I know exactly what you're thinking, Princess. And you are right, in a fashion. Your people must see in you more than a pretty face. They must hear your voice, look into your eyes as you tell them what you need from them. They must trust you with their lives, and more, with the lives of their children, and the children not yet born. Everything is at stake here, Princess, and the people must know that."

He looked more somber as he lowered the dress, careful to let it curl back into the saddlebag. "You will not be wearing this dress as a mask, my dear, but as a uniform. If you appear to be a queen before them, you will have them before you utter a single word. Men and women will respond to a person of regal bearing, but dressing the part is half the battle. It's not a lie, Maiara, it is the trappings of your new truth."

She stared at him, not sure what to say.

In the end, there was really only one thing she could say.

"Thank you."

The smile was back, and he nodded. "That's not all, of course." He turned to take them all in. "I have suitable clothing for the rest of us as well. As I'm sure you've been aware for some time, the turning of the seasons is upon us, and destiny marches on heavy, unrelenting feet."

The little man turned as they watched, taking in the tower, the stables, and the ruin on its hill behind them. "Alden's Tor has treated us well, but the time to leave has arrived." When he looked back at them, his face was hard and unyielding. "We leave in the morning."

That seemed to catch them all unaware, and the men turned toward each other with questioning eyes. But Tsegan was not finished. "We must reach Connat by the vernal equinox, and we have a great deal to accomplish along the way. Our sojourn here has been productive." He smiled at Maiara, then turned an approving eye on the sweat-slick Eirik, massive sword over one shoulder. "Everything is in place, and the time for action is now, before history outpaces us for the last time."

Maiara was shocked. It was one thing to know this day might come, to have lived in denial of its reality for so long, but now she felt like the last rabbit in a hutch, trapped in a corner with nowhere to run.

"You can't have laid the groundwork for a rebellion across the kingdom in the time you've been away." Eirik's voice was gruff, and she thought she saw a glimmer of something ugly in his eyes. "Astrigir is too large, the terrain too inhospitable, for you to have covered the ground that would require."

There was definitely a desperate edge in the big man's voice, and she almost felt sorry for him, except that she was now lost in her own terror.

"Nonsense." The word, flat and hollow, stopped Eirik cold. Tsegan looked the man up and down, shaking his head. "Your memory is of a young king in his prime; of a strong kingdom at the peak of its power. Astrigir is weak, its best strength spent over decades of fruitless battle. Einar is no longer the leader you remembered. He is feeble, lacking the resolve or the strength of his youth." The old man turned to Maiara, one hand outstretched as if summoning her. "The people cry out for something better, do they not, Princess?"

She shook her head, struck dumb at the request. She wracked her mind for information she had absorbed from over a hundred books, but nothing came to her mind.

Tsegan shook his head. "Think back to your time in Baedr, at the Fallen Oak. Were the complaints against the king not constant? Were the groans of the people, crushed beneath the taxes, not deafening?"

She remembered the people always complaining, that was true. Stur and his partners, forever talking about the king's share; old Achak, who might almost remember back to the time when Kun Makha was still one, who had nothing but contempt for Einar. For her ... father. Dumbly, she nodded.

"The people deserve better, Eirik, and fate has chosen all of you as its instrument in their salvation." Then he shook his head. "But all of that is meaningless before the prophecies of the Burdren Saga! 'A savior shall ride forth', it says! To protect her people from a rising doom! If we do not succeed, then all of Astrigir, and Vestan and Subraea too, are lost."

"I don't think—" Maiara could feel the weight of events pushing her down, and none of her schooling, lessons, or training mattered. But Tsegan was not about to let her voice her doubts.

"The history of the world pivots on this moment, Princess." When he said it, the word felt like it carried such weight, such concrete realism. "The path has been set, and we must place our feet upon it."

He turned to Eirik. "I have not prepared the entire realm, you are correct. If we can but take Connat and remove the king from his throne, the people of Astrigir will rise for us. When they realize that their salvation is at hand, the kingdom will be ours without further bloodshed."

The words were so sure, so confident. But Eirik shook his head, the broad comb of hair wagging with the strength of his doubt. She couldn't read the fire in his grey eyes, but she thought it might be a bitterness tinged with fear. "There are still those who are loyal; still those who will remain loyal."

Tsegan nodded, his voice calm, his hand up in a soothing gesture. "There will be, Eirik Hastiin, you are correct. But without an object for their loyalty, they will eventually come around to see the world as it is, rather than as they would have it be." The voice lowered slightly, and the dark eyes focused on the warrior. "Many people will experience that in the coming days."

The fire, whatever it had been, went out in the big man's eyes, and his shoulders bowed as beneath a great weight. There was no further resistance from him.

And the full weight of Tsegan Aqisiaq's black eyes fell on her.

"Everything I have prepared, everything all of you have done, was for this day. Light or darkness, milk or blood, will flow from every choice we make, starting right here. Do you trust me, Princess? Do you believe in me? Do you believe in yourself?"

And she did. At least, she thought she did. She trusted him, anyway, and maybe that would be enough to get the rock to the top of the mountain. And then, on the far side, the gravity of events would see them to the finish.

She nodded.

They spent the night preparing. They would only bring what they needed to get out of the mountains. Tsegan had planned accordingly, and supply caches would be waiting for them when they reached the plains. They would start meeting small groups of his rebellion's leaders soon, and they would see if the people really would rise up for her, whatever dress she wore.

That night, when all of her books, her clothing old and new, and her few personal possessions were ready for the morning's departure, Maiara slipped away to visit the barrow at the back of the valley.

She stood before the ancient stones, one hand on them despite the chill, and she cried at her friend's grave one last time. In the morning, she would leave him behind forever, and he would be alone in that cold little valley, until the end of days.

Chapter 20

Geir walked slowly down the middle of the street, trying to appreciate the feel of solid cobbles beneath his soles again. The low tenements of Connat's grima quarter rose up around him like sheltering walls, reminding him of his younger days, before his time as a foot soldier for Einar. Before his time as the king's bloody shadow.

There was no comfort to be had from the cobblestoned street, and there was no honest shelter offered by the hovels to either side. He glared at anyone who walked too close, one hand on a dagger at all times, defiant as his nerves urged him to pull his hood up despite the growing warmth of approaching spring.

He worked in the shadows. He thrived in the shadows. He knew that, understood it, and had, at times, even reveled in it. But these were his streets. He refused to hide from these wretches, and they were wise enough in their own way to give a man like him, with burning eyes and a long knife, a wide berth.

The apothecary was easy to spot, although the sign hanging out front had lost its paint long ago. The rough shape of a mortar and pestle were just discernible from the right angle; the window was filled with dead and dying plants, a few dried fish, and a tarnished set of ancient scales.

He pushed the door open to the accompaniment of a sour-toned bell. He tried not to flinch at the sound. The thing was battered and abused from decades of desperate entrances by loved ones looking for a miracle and the hurried exits of petty criminals clasping a few sad coins in their grubby hands.

The old man behind the counter was a strange inhabitant of the capital of Astrigir; an oyathey who called the fyrdar kingdom home. His long dark hair and wrinkled bronze skin would mark him out in any crowd, and yet the man had flourished on this little corner for as long as Geir could remember.

"Master Takoda, more of the same, if you please." He dropped two shining coins on the counter and then turned to watch out the door for anyone who might have followed him down the twisting, narrow streets.

Takoda scooped the coins up in a wrinkled hand and began to putter around behind his little desk, turning to a shelf of jars, bottles, and boxes, none of them labeled in any obvious way.

"Has it been working?" The old man's tone was vague and disinterested as he worked at the desk, mixing several powders together into a jar of white paste.

Geir grimaced, glancing back at the man before returning to his watch on the door. "A little. Not much." He grunted. "I don't know."

"I could be more helpful if you would bring her here." The old man gestured toward a curtain that blocked visibility into the back rooms. "From your descriptions alone, the wounds are grave."

Geir grunted again. "You're doing fine, Takoda. Just finish the mix and I'll be gone. I still have enough of the other concoction to last a few more days."

The old man looked up. "Remember, be careful with that. If you accidentally give too much, the patient is liable to pass into a sleep so deep, she may not return."

Geir nodded. "I know." But what he was thinking was that he had already set aside a large enough dose that, if things did not improve soon, he would end things purposefully on his own terms, not by accident.

The old oyathey slid the small stone jar across the desk. "This should last you a few more days if you apply it carefully."

Geir thanked the man, gave him an extra coin for his silence, and pushed back out into the street, ignoring the disquieting bell.

He slid the jar into a pocket within his cloak and moved upward, toward the edge of the grima quarter. He shouldn't, he knew, but then his life had not traced the path of a man gifted in keeping his own best interests in mind.

There were few watchmen in this part of the city, due mostly to the fact that it was the most dangerous area; but most watchman wouldn't mind the inhabitants killing each other.

But that all changed as he left the quarter behind and made his way up the hill. The change was gradual, the paint on the buildings to either side grew progressively less soiled, the colors seemed a shade brighter with each step, and then, eventually, everything around him was in decent repair; there were no obvious signs of decay or neglect. The people walked with more open curiosity rather than the humble, downcast glances of the grima quarter.

Here, he slid the hood up over his smooth scalp. Spring was still a little way off, although it was warmer than it should have been. But it would be better that someone on these brighter streets merely think a man strange for wearing a hood in warmer weather than someone recognize him from some of his less savory work in the past.

Geir worked in the shadows. He repeated that to himself over and over again. There were things that needed doing to keep a kingdom on an even keel, that the king could not be involved with. Lord Drostin and his network of shadow agents made sure that the rougher aspects of King Einar's rule occurred far from the king's court, casting no shadow on the king's name. It was part and parcel of the role he had been called upon to serve, and it rarely bothered him. He told himself that regularly.

But there were times that he longed for some sort of recognition for his efforts beyond the tacit approval the king passed through Drostin.

Geir had born no special allegiance to the men and women he had led into that little valley, other than Eydris, of course. But whatever had happened to them, whatever horrific force had been unleashed upon them, had been something no one should have suffered.

And now he was forced to watch firsthand as that suffering continued.

Geir moved upward, through the broadening streets, past shops, salons, and manufactories. The sun was high, and he was sweating beneath his hood, but he was used to ignoring discomfort. His disquiet would not be settled until he at least looked upon the Bhorg at the center of the city; King Einar's fortress. He had, of course, never set foot inside; although he had stood outside it many times.

He found that just standing in the courtyard outside the heavy main gates, staring out over the fortified bridge at the high granite walls, gave him a sense of attachment to the king that none of the written commendations, notes, or verbal praise passed along through his master could convey.

None of the warriors manning the guard posts would know him. There was no way he would ever get to the bridge, never mind the throne room buried deep within. But just standing before the symbol of his liege's power and authority was often enough to ensure himself that he was a part of something larger, something better, and that he made a difference.

This time, however, as he stepped out of the small side street and into the great courtyard before the Bhorg, he felt no great sense of attachment or fellowship with the warriors standing guard. The dark blue banners with their longships encircled by stars granted neither comfort nor pride.

Happeneding several times in the past, when a particularly terrible task had needed doing, or one of his assignments had gone horribly wrong. His sense of belonging to a greater, better purpose would fade, and he would hear the steady footsteps of retribution for all of his past deeds hastening their pace behind him. Those were dark days. And he felt their shadows closing in around him again.

He wished Lord Drostin had been near. The king's master of shadows had been missing for some time, now. The danger rising against the kingdom was dire, and Drostin and his shadows were away, maneuvering against this growing threat. There had been instructions left for him at one of the usual drops, along with a terse note of forgiveness for his defeat; but he wanted to speak with the man himself, not merely go on to his next task.

His mouth twisted at that thought. This new task was odd, to say the least. And although it did not require him to return to the spirit-forsaken mountains, and indeed allowed him to stay in Connat, he could make little sense of them. Often he knew his work was only one piece of a much wider puzzle, and there were times when he had been sent on an errand whose purpose would never be fully known to him. But this time, for some reason, it bothered him more than most.

It was probably just the chill of his failure in the mountains and its aftermath, he decided. He would always be a faithful servant of the king. And if the warriors guarding the Bhorg knew nothing of him, it was enough that the king knew his name.

He blew out a heavy breath and turned to make his way back to the quarter. She would be waking soon, and he needed to be there to administer the next dose of Master Takoda's anodyne.

He didn't want their neighbors troubled again by her screams.

*****

The muster house Drostin had set aside for him was on the edge of the grima quarter, on the outskirts of Connat, just inside the city wall. Just where the cobbles ended and the dirt of the outer streets held sway. In a district of the city known for its tumbledown shanties, pitiable inhabitants, and overcrowded tenements, their house at least had some modicum of privacy.

It looked like just another tenement house from outside, with most of the small windows boarded up, the rough wood of its construction holding only phantoms of an ancient whitewashing, and a chimney that looked as if it had collapsed decades ago and been rebuilt by a blind man.

Inside, the first few chambers looked little better. No self-respecting vagabond would take shelter in that house, filled as it was with filth, the wreckage of ages, and floors that creaked ominously with every step.

But deeper into the building, things changed. Not drastically; not enough that a casual appraisal by a desperate beggar would reveal any of the differences, but the floor was more secure, the filth was more contrived and less noisome, and the wreckage was distributed in a way that didn't impede movement.

In the back room lay a hidden trap. He pulled on the rope attached to the trap and it rose silently before him. A set of rickety stairs led to a small chamber in the basement, its walls solid and impenetrable save for a low door hidden in one corner. Through that door was the master's chamber of the muster house; Drostin's, had he been in residence. It was against custom for Geir to have used the room, but under the circumstances, he didn't care.

There was a table in the front of the chamber with ten comfortable chairs around it. The remnants of his last meal were still there, as well as the sheaves of papers revealing his newest task, and other pieces of information he would need in order to complete it.

He moved past the table toward a dark door at the rear of the room. Within was a comfortable bed, several small tables and chairs, and a chest of drawers. There was no sign of Drostin; he had left none of his belongings here, but that made perfect sense. There were several mustering houses about the city, and Drostin never stayed in any one of them for long.

Geir believed the Lord of Shadows spent most of his time in the Bhorg with the king and his other advisors, although the old man refused to speak of such things directly. These building were used by the king's agents when they were between tasks, or preparing for the next operation, or performing the rare duties they were called upon to perform in the capital itself.

She lay on the bed where he had left her. On her belly, the soft rise and fall of her shoulder blades was the only sign that she still lived. Anyone seeing her back could be forgiven their sense of surprise that she breathed at all. The flesh was a ridged and broken desert landscape, the surface dry and feverish, the depths of the cracks an angry red.

Whatever had befallen his mercenary bandits in that little valley had caught Eydris a glancing blow as she fled. He had not understood the extent of her wounds until the next day, when their silent, desperate flight had ended at the supply cache.

None of the others had escaped alive.

He had wrapped Eydris's wounds as best he could. The agony had been so intense she would lose consciousness each time he tried to move her. In the end, he had given up even trying to be gentle, hoisting her onto the back of their one pack horse and setting out on the long journey north.

She had nearly died several times. The damage to her back was the worst, but whatever force had struck her had wrapped around her neck as well, caressing her right cheek and jawline with its power. Her once striking face was shattered, the cracked and shriveled flesh pulling her eye down and her lip back in a parody of her old impish grin.

When she was awake, she was in constant pain. He had dosed her with prodigious amounts of wine and spirits on the journey north until they had run out. He had dared not stop at Bjornstad, knowing the questions that would cause should he show his face without a single member of his recent company. Instead, they had made due with the supplies from the cache, following the greenway north until they had come to the first of the small villages in the foothills. There, he had paid for a room with his dwindling supply of coin, ignoring the looks of the landlord and the other guests as he had carried Eydris's bundled form in from the cold and up to their little chamber.

It was then that he finally had leisure to explore the full extent of her injuries. Whatever force had been unleashed in that high valley had ravaged her flesh far beyond his ability to heal. He knew moving her further would jeopardize her life, but if they stayed in that little town, sooner or later, she would die.

And he had needed to report to Drostin. The young woman's survival would have repercussions, although he had no way of knowing what those might be. It was entirely possible that other agents would be in danger because of his failure.

The next day he had carried an unconscious Eydris out to the stable, put her back on the exhausted pack horse, and begun the last leg of their journey to Connat. It had been one of the worst experiences of his life, watching his colleague fade day after day, knowing there was nothing more he could do for her.

They had run out of spirits two days out of the guesthouse, making that last stretch of the greenway a truly hellish nightmare. And when he finally managed to recover Drostin's orders, and they had made their way to the muster house, it had been empty. He had gone directly to the old apothecary. The muster house had contained more than sufficient funds, among other things, to replenish their stores. He had hoped to get more help from old Takoda, but the man refused to leave his shop, he couldn't risk the streets, and Geir could not provide a satisfactory description of the woman's injuries for anything beyond a hurried diagnosis.

He put one finger into the stone jar and scooped out some of the paste. It was supposed to sooth the pain and promote healing in the ravaged flesh. There was no doubt in his mind Eydris had grown more quiet since their return to the city, but whether that was because of the efficacy of the apothecary's poultice or because she was fading away, he didn't know.

After he had applied the paste, he tilted her on her side to force another of her small pills down her throat. She coughed weakly, made a soft whimpering noise, and then subsided back into restless sleep.

Geir watched her sleep for a few minutes. They had never been particularly close. Their chosen paths made it hard to trust others, even their brothers and sisters, and they most often worked alone; it was rare that they spent any length of time with other agents. But among that dark family, he had been passing fond of Eydris, and he hated to see any fellow agent in such pain.

What had happened in that valley?

They had nearly won, he remembered that distinctly. Tore had never been very good with a bow at the best of times, but that last arrow had flown true; Geir would have sworn on it. But something had happened in the instant before it struck, and in a flash, the arrow was gone. The strange hooded figure had appeared, and those terrible shapes of dust and heat had risen up before him, engulfing his surviving warriors and tearing them apart.

It had been like something out of the ancient sagas; like some terrible unholy power from the dawn of time, reaching down to wipe his people from the earth.

Drostin must have known about the stranger in the hood. Whatever made that girl such a danger to the realm obviously made her worthy of protection such as he had never seen before.

Did her survival have anything to do with his new orders? He leaned back in the chair at Eydris's bedside and rubbed at his eyes with rough, calloused thumbs. Much of his life as an agent of the king had been relatively simple. He received his tasks, he went forth and performed those tasks or, occasionally, failed.

But this? A cowled figure in the mountains tearing seasoned warriors into meat and bone with conjured winds? Nothing had prepared him for this.

Geir checked one last time to make sure that Eydris was as comfortable as he could make her, then he eased himself out of the chair and back into the main room, where he settled into the large chair at the head of the table, Drostin's chair, and pulled the papers toward him.

They were the thin, filmy material upon which his orders were always written; easily swallowed, quick to burn. The first was fairly standard, the reference to his failure in the mountains and a warning that the other agents had been dispersed throughout the cities and towns surrounding Connat in preparation for whatever dire attack was coming. He was to perform the duties outlined in the following pages and then wait for further instructions.

He wasn't sure if this meant Drostin was in the north with the other agents or if he had stayed behind in Connat but would be out of contact for some other reason. Either way, he was alone at a moment when he most needed guidance and assistance. Drostin would be able to get more practiced medical help for Eydris, and it was possible that such help could be the difference between life and death at this point.

He had left requests for contact at all of their usual sites, but there was no way to guarantee the old man got the messages. Without knowing where he was, there was little chance Geir would be able to track him down on his own.

He peeled the top paper off and set it aside. The next several pages outlined the strange, unprecedented actions he was to take over the next few weeks and why the strong box contained so much coin. There were also two maps; one with two addresses marked out down in the merchant's quarter that he thought were probably storage houses, and another, of the entire city, with several different locations marked out in red. It was this second map that he found most puzzling, given his instructions.

The writing was not in Drostin's flowing, almost artistic script, but rather the chopped, efficient lettering of a clerk. He was to use the coin to secure those chosen locations, apparently boardinghouses, all of them located near the main gates in the city walls, none of them in particularly upscale districts, for a period of at least several weeks, starting as soon as he could. It seemed these were intended to serve as some kind of secondary line of muster houses around the city; not for the king's agents, but for his personal hearth guard.

And that was where Geir's confusion really began. The hearth guard, warriors sworn to the personal service of the king, were no saemgard. There had been no saemgard for nearly twenty years. But the hearth guard were still effective warriors. There were hundreds of them, sworn to protect the king against any threat. Why would the hearth guard need muster houses around the outskirts of the city? And they were the best-equipped warriors in the fyrdar kingdoms; why would they need stockpiles of additional equipment so far from the Bhorg?

Drostin must have known Geir would question these orders, because he had included more than his usual scant level of detail in an attempt to explain the situation.

There was a rebellion brewing, although the Lord of Shadows did not seem to know from which direction the attack might come. Judging from these preparations and the few details he had provided, he was expecting an insurgency that threatened to push the hearth guard right out of the Bhorg and into the city proper.

But if Drostin knew about the coming threat, couldn't he and the king just strengthen the cordon around the Bhorg itself and neutralize it? Why such an elaborate circle of redoubts away from the king's stronghold? He rested his head on one fist as he continued to stare at the map. The circle of red marks showing the chosen locations reminded him of something, but he couldn't put his finger on it. There was something familiar, somehow, about the arrangement of the defensive positions.

If they were expecting an invasion from outside the city, shouldn't they be planning on strengthening the city's walls? Or perhaps they meant to use the houses as strongpoints to direct the defense? But no; then he would be actually strengthening the boardinghouses, preparing them against an attack. Nothing in these instructions indicated that he needed to do that. Rather, he would be secretly filling them with the weapons, armor, and equipment from the two warehouses, almost as if Drostin expected the hearth guard to be forced from the Bhorg without their arms and armor.

He sighed, letting the paper fall to the tabletop with the others. It made no sense. What enemy could penetrate the Bhorg and force the hearth guard away from their stronghold? The Lord of Shadows must not know the actual plans of the enemy, or the preparations would be more specific and make more tactical sense.

But a lifetime of following the orders of his king made for a strong force of habit. He would do as he had been told. The grima quarter was filled with men and women, little better than thralls, really, who would work quickly for small coin. It would only take a few nights.

He pulled out another sheet, an inventory of the two caches he would be distributing. There were medical supplies in each as well as other equipment of war. Perhaps he could find something that would help him care for Eydris.

He looked over his shoulder to where he could see her, still as death, on Drostin's bed. He doubted there would be anything to help her, but he needed some hope. Defeated, isolated, and alone, he had never felt such separation before in all his clandestine service.

He looked down again to the map with its red markings, their pattern painfully, tantalizingly familiar.

Chapter 21

Beneath him, Vordr swayed back and forth with a slow, easy gait. He didn't have to focus on the reins, the horse merely followed the big white charger ahead, who followed Hestir in the lead. Behind him, he knew Chagua would be riding one of the wagon horses, while the other was laden down with supplies and other bundles the old man had told them they would need in the coming days. Tsegan, of course, was gone again, and hadn't been seen since their departure from the valley.

The old man had stayed behind, he said, to finish his own preparations. He didn't have a horse, so Tyr wasn't sure how he was planning on catching up with them before Maiara had to make her first speech, but they had learned not to question, and so they had all nodded somberly and turned their horses' heads to the trail without a word.

Tyr had not been prepared for the world beyond their valley. He had not realized how sheltering those high walls and hot springs had been. Beyond their sanctuary, winter still held the mountains in its icy grip. The temperatures were bitter each day, fogging breath whipped away by clawing winds; and each night, huddled beneath furs, blankets, and cloaks, the brutal cold was enough to steal that breath entirely.

There was nothing pleasant about their northward journey, and he was sad to see each of them reverting to the roles they had played in the earliest days of winter.

Eirik sat Hestir easily, with no more sway than that given to him by the horse itself. But he was somber and quiet, brooding on the gods alone knew what. Tyr had seen him, more than once, staring into a cup of water, and he was afraid he knew what his master was thinking as his brow furrowed and his grey eyes darkened.

Maiara sat uneasily upon her new horse, Sannlir, with rigid discomfort. It was painfully obvious she was not used to such an animal, and if she couldn't reconcile herself to it, there was going to be no selling her as some kind of war leader to a bunch of fyrdar, even if they were just peasants and thralls from outlying settlements. How she was going to develop such comfort on a ride like this, however, he couldn't have said.

Chagua's lapse was the most marked of all. In those early days, the islander had hardly spoken, other than to give orders or respond to questions with a grunt or a look. If anything, he spoke even less now. There was little need for him to give orders; Tyr and Eirik had more than enough experience traveling from their years on the circuit. Behind the islander's silent, stoic mask, Tyr believed he could detect a level of concern and fear the big man had never shown before. But in the face of Chagua's stubborn silence, there was no way to be sure.

And then there was Tyr himself. He could feel himself struggling against the isolation that settled upon the group, wanting more than ever to talk with each of them, to hear the islander's rolling laughter, to see Maiara's clear eyes glitter with mirth, or to listen as Eirik ruefully recounted his latest defeat. But nothing would drag them out of the quiet fears that separated them, cutting them off from one another. And in his confusion and helplessness, he was as quiet as all the rest.

Camp each night was easily established, even in the rough conditions of late winter. After the first few nights, each of them had settled into a routine that made it even less likely they would need to speak. Maiara took care of the horses while Tyr prepared the fire and the cooking area. Chagua and Eirik would wrestle with the single tent they now used to keep their body heat all in one chamber.

Lying so near Maiara had made it difficult for Tyr to sleep at all, but he would never have said anything to the others about that. They each had their burdens to bear as the future rushed up the greenway toward them. When he thought about it, he was embarrassed that his own burdens seemed to come down to getting a fire started in a foot of freshly-fallen snow and being able to fall asleep near a pretty girl.

He could feel the pressure building. The going had been terribly slow as they made their way from the valley back onto the greenway. It had taken nearly two weeks, in fact, and he had found himself remembering the valley with a fondness he had never experienced when he was actually there. But once they had reached the wide, white swath of the greenway, their progress had picked up. They were not going nearly as fast as they had when they first came this way, of course. Back then, there had been hardly any snow on the broad path itself. Now, the horses were pushing aside drifts that reached their chests on a bad day.

They would force their way off the path and beneath the trees to either side for camp. The snow was not as deep on the verge of the forest, which made their duties easier. On their way south, they had done so to keep away from other travelers and to hide from possible pursuit. Now, they could be tracked by a blind pig, so such precautions made little sense.

Tyr sighed and felt his bitterness deepen at the cloud it formed around the tight opening of his hood. When Eirik turned to the side, making for the deepening shadows of the forest, he closed his eyes in relief. He couldn't feel his fingers on the reins, and the thought of getting a fire going was almost enough to bring tears to his eyes if he didn't think those tears would freeze in place.

As they bustled about, silently preparing camp, Tyr felt his frustration grow until he could contain it no longer.

Chagua and Eirik were spreading the waxed canvas of their tent over an area they had cleared of snow; stakes, poles, and rope stacked to one side. Tyr stepped up beside Chagua and tapped his chest, then tapped the islander on the shoulder and pointed to the fire pit, already prepared and laid with kindling. He shrugged vaguely and gave an apologetic smile through the frost-rimmed opening in his hood.

Chagua looked back at the fire pit, then down at Tyr, then over at Eirik, standing with the canvas in hand, head cocked to one side. The Islander gave a brisk nod, patted Tyr on the shoulder, then turned away, moving toward the fire pit.

Tyr took the big man's place, reached down for the canvas, and gestured for his master to continue pulling the fabric taut. Once the bulk of the tent was laid out, he crawled inside and began to put the bracing poles in place one at a time.

"What was that all about?" Eirik grunted as he pushed a pole up against the heavy weight of the tent. "Couldn't get the fire started?"

Tyr grinned, wiping one chill hand over his forehead. He had forgotten that, despite the freezing cold outside, struggling beneath the smothering weight of the half-raised tent was hot work. "Just thought it might be nice if we could talk for a little, is all." He reached out to pull the canvas more in line with the pressure from the pole. "You haven't said much since we left the valley."

Eirik gave him a suspicious glance then looked away to secure the top of the pole. He tugged the tie one last time to make sure it was tight, then pushed his way to the next socket, reaching back with an open hand so Tyr could give him another pole.

After a moment more, it became clear that Eirik was not going to talk, despite being cornered. "What's wrong? Do you think we're doing the wrong thing?"

Eirik shot him a dark glance then went back to his work. "It's not my place to say if we're doing the wrong thing. If it's the wrong thing, then I guess it won't work, right?"

Tyr hadn't thought about it that way. It seemed like a rather dark way to look at the whole adventure. Was his master using this strange course of events as a way to make amends for the last two decades? If Tsegan was correct, he would be vindicated; if Tsegan was wrong, he would be dead? The fyrdar were a fey people, given to dark thoughts, gripped by fatalistic visions. Was Eirik using Tsegan's plans as an elaborate form of suicide?

That sent a shiver down Tyr's spine despite the oppressive warmth.

"I believe in her." These sudden, dark thoughts hit at the foundation of his own doubts. What if Tsegan really was just a crazy old man? What would happen to them? What would happen to Maiara?

Eirik stopped working and glared at him for a minute. "You believe in her." He repeated the words in a harsh whisper, grey eyes narrowed to slits. "Couldn't have anything to do with her pretty face, could it? Boy, you're too old to be led around by your stones."

It was a hurtful comment, not the least because he knew there might well be some truth to it. He stared into his master's eyes until Eirik broke away and turned back to the tent pole. "Three more of these and you can go back to the fire."

Tyr wanted nothing more than to leave his master to the work, but it was a two man job, and abandoning it now would only cause him more problems, as he'd have to give some kind of explanation to Chagua, at the very least.

They finished erecting the tent in silence, each shooting an occasional glare at the other. Tyr felt like he was back on his family's farm, a petulant boy forced to work through his pain.

When they were finished, Tyr went back out into the cold without a word, settling down next to the fire. Chagua and Maiara were nearly done with dinner. There didn't seem to be any more talking than necessary outside, either.

Tyr found himself staring at the girl from beneath his deep hood then looked quickly away. It didn't matter that she was beautiful. He believed in her anyway.

He cursed Eirik under his breath for casting his ill humor over Tyr's.

So much for trying to coax his master out of his black mood. He had only succeeded in darkening his own.

*****

Almost a week later, and nothing had improved. Tyr was fairly certain the weather should be moderating, but it was as if winter had followed them down through the mountains. The snow was not as deep, almost as if it had only started to accumulate again a day or so before they arrived.

All things considered, it was enough to make a young man paranoid that nature itself was out to get him.

He had noticed the last few nights that Maiara was keeping to herself, bundled up in her cloaks and furs, shivering despite anything the weight of clothing, the fire, or the muggy closeness of their tent could do to offset the cold.

None of them had talked much during their journey. That was part of the problem. And since his ill-fated attempts to speak with his master, Tyr had been unwilling to make another effort to break the silence.

But Maiara looked so lost, bundled up in layer after layer of winter gear, like a little girl caught up in something much larger than herself, that he felt a growing pull toward her. He had done everything he could to avoid the dark thoughts Eirik had placed in his mind. He did not want to think of their work here as nothing more than an elaborate, doomed dance with death.

But the more he tried to avoid those thoughts, the more they wormed their way into his waking moments.

He waited until the tent was up and the fire bright before moving beside Maiara. He saw what she was planning to prepare for dinner and moved to assist her without saying anything. The girl looked up at him briefly, smiled, then moved aside to give him room.

They worked in silence, paring down the stunted vegetables for the stew pot where the dried meats were already soaking. Little pots of spices were lined up on the plank beside them, ready to add their own mysterious effects to the cauldron.

"How are you feeling?" He tried to sound casual, but after days of little talk beyond that necessary to continue moving north, any casual conversational gambit sounded forced.

She smiled, acknowledging the awkwardness, and nodded. But he saw the slight shiver in her hands, despite how close they were to the fire.

"I'm cold, but then, we're all cold." She gave a more pronounced shiver, almost as if she were doing it with theatrical exaggeration, but Tyr thought he sensed that it was more genuine than the girl would have wanted to let on. "I feel like I've been cold all my life, now. Do you remember ever being warm?"

He smiled, but the tremor in her voice concerned him. "Of course! And we'll be out of the mountains soon. Spring is well underway down on the plains."

She shook her head, her smile fading. "I can't get the chill out of me, Tyr. Part of me really thinks I'll never be warm again."

It was cold. In fact, it seemed colder even than it should be. But he wanted to give her comfort somehow.

"Don't worry." He gave her arm a brisk rub before quickly removing his hand. "You'll be warm again."

They worked in silence for a while before Tyr could work up the courage for another foray. "Other than the cold, how are you?"

They were all nervous, understandably, he thought. But the old man's entire scheme rested upon the slim shoulders of this young girl. He couldn't even imagine what it must feel like with all that pressure bearing down on you.

Let alone what it must feel like, knowing that the whole plan revolved around killing a man who was supposedly her father.

Tyr's relationship with his parents had been trying, but his mother and father had always been there for him, and even allowed him, in the end, to give their hard-earned money to Eirik to help him pursue his dream. Dreams that seemed as distant as the plot which had ensnared them all.

Maiara shrugged as she settled down by the fire with the long spoon, giving the contents of the cauldron an occasional stir.

"I try not to think about it too much, to be honest." She idly took up a spoonful of clear broth and then poured it back into the mix. Her voice was soft. "I've never been comfortable, speaking in front of people."

He hadn't thought about that aspect of things. Tsegan's grand design intended for them to move through the countryside meeting with groups of rebel leaders, convincing them to follow, and then unleashing them all on an unsuspecting Connat.

He could see how that kind of pressure would wear on anyone, especially someone who didn't like talking to large groups.

"Nonsense." He tried to wave away her concerns, knowing that he, himself, would not want to have to perform those particular tasks. "I'm sure you're going to be wonderful. You've been preparing so hard!"

The little laugh she gave was more of a harsh bark, and he could see that he had done nothing to help the situation. "I've got not quite three months of schooling at the knee of a crazy old man who can't sit still for more than a day. I know enough to be dangerous to everyone, and not enough to help anyone."

The despair that gripped Eirik seemed to have gotten its claws into Maiara, as well, and he found himself wondering for a moment if Chagua, too, was drowning in silent darkness.

But there was one thing, if they believed, that they all did have on their side. And although he understood why none of them sought comfort in the strangeness, there were times when he believed it was all they had left.

"Well, you have all that training, and an ancient prophecy." He tried to give her a smile. "You can't forget that. The Burdren Saga has to be worth something, doesn't it?"

Her own smile was sickly. "Old words in an ancient book that might refer to us, or could equally have referred to half a dozen figures in the last hundred years, or some lucky people who haven't even been born yet."

He sighed, shoulders sagging beneath the weight of his furs. Somehow, where all of his reassurance couldn't reach her, his distress did. Maiara reached out and patted his shoulder, her smile sad.

"Don't worry, Tyr. Pretty soon none of us will have anything to worry about, one way or another."

The fatalistic words fell like lead weights into his stomach. Eirik wasn't the only one with this brutal, fatalistic streak of their people, it would seem.

He gave her a weak smile and turned back to the fire. He would try his best, for however much more time he had with these people, not to try to cheer anyone else up.

*****

The snows dogged their steps all the way out of the mountains. Even as they began to see signs of civilization at the verge of the foothills, it seemed like the area surrounding them was refusing to give way to spring.

Tyr started to wonder if there might not be a spirit or god of winter who was angry with them for avoiding his fury in the sheltered valley and now sought vengeance.

At first there were only scattered farmsteads; newly constructed homes and outbuildings established by brave settlers seeking to take advantage of the retreat of the ancient glaciers. That brought a smile to the boy's face when it had occurred to him. Their recent weather certainly wasn't an indication of a mild winter; that was for sure.

A few days after they first spotted the glow of windows off in the gloom, they came to a fairly large town that they had all avoided on their journeys south only a few months ago. It was an entire settlement of new construction. The warm light spilling from the windows of a small inn was too much temptation after the long, cold journey.

Tsegan had warned them to stay away from people during their journey north, and each of them had dutifully nodded their heads at his instructions, conscious of the delicate array of forces the old man had set in motion down on the plains.

But that had been in the relative warmth of their familiar common room. Here, after days of sleeping huddled together in a freezing tent, after hours upon hours swaying on the backs of their plodding, near-frozen horses, those words carried little weight.

They came to a quick accord, despite Chagua's determined insistence that they stick with the plan. In the end, the islander had refused to join them and had taken the two pack horses farther down the road, to make camp in a stand of trees they had seen about a half mile north of the town.

Tyr felt bad as he watched the islander disappear into the cold fog, the others already turning their horses into the courtyard of the inn. He didn't feel bad enough to join the big warrior in his cold and silent exile, however, kicking Vordr into a trot to keep up with the others.

As it turned out, he had been right about the town. Ivituut, unimaginatively named The Green Place in the ancient fyrdar tongue, had been built directly beside the greenway only a couple years ago. This high up, the fertile seasons would not have been long enough to sustain even so modest a town as this just a few years ago, but the oyathey sages appeared to be correct. Ivituut had been able to hang on, each year apparently easier than the last.

At least, that's what the men and women in the cramped little common room were saying, before they would then look out the windows at the chill fog and mutter to themselves.

Eirik had bulled his way through the tightly-packed crowd to a corner table, dropping into a small chair and waving for a cup of mead before Tyr caught his eye with a single upraised eyebrow. The big man had the grace to look embarrassed, and when the landlord arrived with the mead, he mumbled something about a misunderstanding and asked the man for three cups of tea instead. That earned him a dark look before the innkeeper gave a sharp snort through his mustaches and turned without a word.

Tea was not a popular drink among the fyrdar, although the oyathey had been drinking it long before the ancient raiders had crossed the sea. A place like Ivituut would have some, no doubt, but it wouldn't be ready, and it wouldn't be easy to prepare.

Tyr relaxed a little as he watched the man waddle away through the crowd. This was a complication he had not even considered. It had been easy keeping Eirik sober in the mountains after Chagua had poured the last of his spirits into the dirt. But here, where all the big man needed to do was sneak around a corner and run to the nearest mead hall? It was something they were all going to have to be aware of. Eirik was like a different man since Chagua had recalled him to himself, but just the way the big man was staring at the cups of the other patrons seated around them was enough proof for Tyr that the process was not complete, and might never be.

The tea tasted like grass soaked in warm water, as fyrdar tea often did. But he was thankful enough for the warmth and held the cup close in both hands as he sipped. Maiara, too, was clutching her cup, although she hadn't done more than give the contents a quick sip followed by a politely concealed grimace. Eirik did not drink but looked morosely into the cup, then back out over the sea of mead, ale, and spirits that flowed all around him.

They settled down in the warmth and Tyr tried to relax. He could see Maiara glancing around the room, her shoulders tense, most likely imagining trying to address a group like this in the near future. Eirik could not take his roaming eyes off the various drinks that moved through the room in an endless, enticing dance.

Tyr shook his head and settled back in his chair. All around them, the people of Ivituut were having conversations that would have been at home in any ale house in any of the fyrdar kingdoms. As he listened, he realized that this was his first chance to put Tsegan's words to the test, to try to determine the depth of dissatisfaction the people might feel for King Einar.

He cocked his head to one side, the better to hear the table off to their left. The men sitting there had looked vaguely displeased when he first scanned the room. That should have made them the best place to start, looking for discontent.

But as he listened, all he heard were sentiments regarding the sudden downturn in the weather and what it might do to their plans for early planting. None of the men were talking about taxes, or wars, or anything else to do with Einar and distant Connat. But they were only one table, and the room held probably ten or more.

He listened to the others around them, thankful for once that his companions had become so distant.

But none of the tables around them seemed to be grumbling about the king. He heard complaints about the weather in plenty, and complaints about wives and husbands. He heard one man, certain a neighbor had poisoned his cows, threatening to return the favor.

What he didn't hear was a single mention of Einar.

He became desperate, and thought that, if he was able to cast his net a little wider, he might find something he could use to reassure both Eirik and Maiara. He made some noise about having to relieve himself and pushed away from the table, giving the girl a warning glance that managed to take in both Eirik and his cooling mug. She smiled slightly and nodded.

He made his way to the back door, beyond which he figured should be the trench the place used for privy business. Sure enough, a few frigid steps beyond the doorway was a trench dug into the frozen earth. There was no one there, so he was able to continue his charade without having to expose himself to the bitter cold.

When he returned, he did so by a slow, meandering path that took him past tables he had not yet been able to study. More talk about the weather, more talk about crops, and yield. He paused by one table when he heard someone mention Kun Makha and the oyathey. But the conversation appeared to be about some new agricultural processes, and he began to move away. One of the old men then muttered Einar's name, and he stopped.

It was a complaint, as it happened, but not one Tyr had expected, or one that might be expected to start a revolution. Something to do with Einar's being too close to the new ruler of Kun Makha and pushing these new techniques on the high farms.

The man was on to other complaints soon enough, and on the journey back to his table, Tyr heard no more.

Eirik was sitting as straight as an arrow shaft with a sullen look on his face, Maiara's glare was hard when it turned from the old warrior to Tyr's own. She shook her head, and the boy knew in a moment what had happened. Eirik had tried to get his hands on something stronger than tea, and the girl had stopped him.

Tyr sighed. So much for the strength of character of the last saemgard.

Tyr gestured for the landlord and arranged for a room for the night. Together, he and Maiara managed to get Eirik up the narrow stairs despite several sorrowful glances down into the common room, and into the big bed where he fell almost immediately to sleep.

There was only one other bed.

Tyr moved quickly, tossing down his cloak in front of the door and lowering himself to the floor without a word. Maiara watched him, her face a mystery. When he was as comfortable as he was going to get, he rolled over with a muttered "G'night."

There was no sound behind him for several breaths, then a soft sigh that he could have done without. "Goodnight, Tyr." Her voice was soft, and he heard her roll into the other bed; the light from the room's one candle was blown out, and then there was silence.

He told himself this was the only way that made sense, because now when Eirik tried to sneak out and back down to the common room, he would be in the way.

He stayed awake for a long time, staring at the door less than a foot's length from his nose, trying to quiet thoughts that had nothing to do with Eirik.

Chapter 22

The night in Ivituut haunted Maiara for days afterward. She had listened intently to the conversations raging around her, and she had heard nothing to suggest deep unrest in the kingdom. Her desire to stay in the little guest-house had been entirely innocent, but as she had settled down with her cup of weak tea, she had listened to the tables around her, hoping for some confirmation that Tsegan was right about the people's state of mind.

She had heard nothing.

They left the next day, and she felt even more isolated and alone. In the night, Eirik had risen from his bed with as much stealth as he could muster, and then he had tripped over Tyr, lying before the door. The boy had muttered something, Eirik had grumbled incoherently, and then had collapsed back onto his bed.

She had lain awake for hours after that, staring up into the impenetrable darkness, terrified with visions of rooms full of farmers listening to her prattle on about kings and destinies, and then shouting questions at her about terraced farming, seed yields, and crop rotations.

She had awakened to the scrabbling of a fresh blizzard at the windows, the cold light of a winter dawn leaking through the thin curtains. They had had a quick breakfast in the common room, wrapped up some sausage and bread for Chagua, and ventured out into the blowing wind.

Chagua had been waiting for them where the greenway swept up and around his little copse of trees. The islander had seemed in a disgustingly good mood, all things considered. He claimed the weather had been much warmer than usual, and he had sat looking up at the stars, without a cloud overhead, before falling asleep under the open sky.

No matter how temperate the little copse of trees might have been overnight, winter had struck it full force by the time Maiara and her companions arrived. The four of them moved off down the greenway hunched against the cold and the blowing snow, the warmth of Ivituut nothing but a distant dream.

The blizzard lasted all that day and into the next, and even when the snow had died away, the temperature continued to fall. She worried for the horses, huddled together beneath their blankets outside the tent, waiting desperately for morning.

By noon of the next day, the wind died down, and as they topped a high hill, the sun broke through the black clouds to bathe the valley below in warm light; an overdue promise of spring.

Even more surprising than the warm sunshine, however, was Tsegan Aqisiaq, patiently sitting an old farm horse on the far side of the hill, waiting for them.

"Greetings, my friends!" The old man's white hair was windblown, but his smile was as bright as ever. "A timely arrival, indeed!"

Eirik seemed annoyed by that. "You expected the journey to take that long? We should have been out of the mountains over a week ago. It would have been nice to have some kind of warning."

Even Chagua looked frustrated, but the old man merely put his hands up in a placating gesture. "I had no way of knowing how long it would take, Saemgard." The title seemed to carry more weight than it had before, and Eirik looked like he was sitting up straighter having been so addressed. "But my preparations for the next step in our journey have just been completed, and so you are just in time." He shrugged. "It took me longer to prepare than I had anticipated, and so it was good fortune, or fate, that you were detained by the unseasonable weather." The old man smiled, but then looked back at the storm clouds looming in the distance south, and Maiara thought he looked genuinely bothered.

Then the old man shook himself and turned to her. "Your Highness, I trust you are ready to meet with the first delegation of your future subjects? The king and his minions have not been idle while you were ensconced in the mountains, I'm afraid. We must move with matching speed, now."

She felt the chill in her heart, always lurking since the night that Kustaa died, rise up, threatening to choke her voice away. She fought for breath, her eyes widening, and the tremors, also near-constant companions since that night, took hold.

"It's okay." She heard Tyr's voice as the boy nudged his horse up next to hers, gripping her shoulder quickly. "You know what you need to do. You'll be perfect."

She tried to smile as Tsegan moved toward them, giving the boy a strange look before turning back to her. "You will, indeed, be perfect, Princess. This is the role fate decreed for you long before you were born. You have the mind, you have the blood, and you have the weight of prophecy behind you." He flipped one hand vaguely, his smile widening. "My own training may not stand you in poor stead either, of course."

In the heart of the valley below was a large farmstead, a big house, two long barns, and several good-sized outbuildings. The land all around had been partitioned into grazing meadows and crops by neat, well-maintained fences. Whoever ran this farm took great pride in the details. The people of Baedr would approve.

"Our friends are gathered in the far barn, my dear. They are ready when you are, although you should feel comfortable taking some small amount of time to prepare."

She felt the ice choking her again and shook her head violently. "You've never even told me what I'm supposed to say! Who are they? Who do they think I am?"

The man's eyes turned kindly, and he grasped Sannlir's reins and pulled her gently away from the others, one warm hand on her leg before pulling it away. "Gods, girl, you're freezing!" He rubbed vigorously at her leg for a moment before continuing. "My dear, they are merely farmers, innocent workers of the soil, who deserve more loyalty from their liege than Einar can be bothered to give. As the king drowns Astrigir in debt pursuing his petty wars, these are the people most hurt by this foolishness, and the first who will die when the darkness arrives to burn the kingdoms to ash."

She looked down at him, unhearing, amazed that none of this should have occurred to her sooner. The thought of telling their strange tale to groups of strangers had terrified her since the beginning. But never once had she even contemplated what she might actually have to say, or what she was trying to do!

"You will hear their grievances, and then you will assure them that a brighter day is dawning. By your very existence, you will provide them with hope that something better is on the horizon, and that their sons and daughters will no longer be dragged into Einar's bloody skirmishes. You will let them know that they no longer need to fear that their neighbors will disappear from their beds, torn away by Shadows of the king, never to be heard from again." The old man's eyes were afire as he finished. "You will tell them that the age of fear is over, and the age of hope has begun."

It all sounded grand when Tsegan said it. But could she speak with even a fraction of his energy? She shook her head, throat still closed with cold fear.

"Princess, we will go down to the barn now. I will introduce you to my friends, and you will speak to them the words that rise into your heart. You want what is good for them, do you not?" She nodded, eyes wide. "You want peace and justice to prevail in Astrigir, do you not?" She nodded again. "And you understand that all of this, as important as it is, is secondary to the need for the fyrdar to be unified when the darkness comes for us all?"

She closed her eyes. She thought she nodded, but she couldn't be sure. The looming, existential threat was too much for her to grasp, even after all of her lessons and training. But she could understand the more universal concepts of peace and justice for the common people, for her people; and she decided to focus on those, and try to survive, for now, one breath at a time.

Tsegan led them, not to the barn, but to the large house. "Before we go in, you must all understand, this is the beginning of all we have discussed. We must look the part."

He carried two heavy saddlebags into the house and gestured for them to follow him inside.

*****

The dress felt even more amazing on than it had looked draped in Tsegan's hands. The color perfectly matched the blue of her eyes. The fabric was a quality of silk she had never encountered before, backed with a soft cotton that made the dress feel warm and comforting against her skin. The bodice was cut lower than anything she had ever worn, and even with the lace detailing plunging down from the neckline, she felt terrible self-conscious showing so much skin. The skirts of the dress hung down to her ankles, but there was a slit on the right side higher than she liked. It made walking in the tight dress easier, and it fell closed when she stood still, but it was one more unfamiliar note among all the rest.

The house had a large gathering room before the front door, and as she descended the stairs, she stopped as she saw the others waiting for her. Each looked as if they were wearing a costume from some baroque minstrel show. And yet at the same time, each of them seemed to look exactly right.

Tyr was the least-adorned of the three, wearing his normal leathers, but without the usual fur mantle. Instead, over the leather armor he was wearing a tabard of rich blue with silver details and a wide white belt. It was obvious the boy had tried desperately to comb his hair into some semblance of order, with indifferent results. The look on his face as he stared up at her was embarrassing, and she quickly looked away.

Chagua wore loose robes of a light ivory, with the same dark blue picking out the edges of his collar, cuffs and the trim of the hood that hung down his back. The color complimented his dark skin and the long coils of his hair nicely. He looked up at her with a warm smile, but nothing like Tyr's dumbstruck look.

Eirik Hastiin was by far the most changed. He still wore his armor, more metal than leather, but the metal now gleamed in the sunlight. He, too, had lost his fur mantle, but instead of a mere tabard, the former saemgard was wearing an elaborate surcoat that reached down to his ankles, slit just below the waist for sitting a horse. The blue was repeated in his clothing as well, as was the white and silver in a simple pattern repeated all around the fringes of the garment. On his chest a single crimson wing swept up and to the left.

It took her a moment to realize that the blue featured in all of their new clothing was the same shade of her dress. When they entered the barn, the connection between them would be obvious.

Eirik looked miserable, but he was staring at her with the same look that haunted Tyr's eyes, and she found that even more disconcerting. She moved quickly down the steps, trying to ignore the unfamiliar swish around her ankles and the cold wind on her leg. As she turned toward the front door, however, she stopped again. It appeared that she and her three companions were not the only ones to receive a fresh look.

Tsegan stood there in rich black and white robes, their pattern dizzying to the eye. He held a staff she had never seen before and looked like nothing so much as one of the wizards from her story book, stepped from those old pages and into a life cast into upheaval and chaos.

But his smile was still there, still the same warm, open expression he had always worn, and in fact, his eyes seemed slightly sheepish, as if embarrassed by his own transformation.

"We must all look the part, sadly." He lifted his arms and looked down at the fall of the elaborate robes. "Please do not gaze too long on my own costume, the damage to your eyes might prove permanent."

He indicated the front door and they moved toward it, but stopped when he held up a hand. "When we enter, I will go in first. Then the lad," Tyr looked unhappy with that but gave the old man a grudging nod. "Chagua will enter next, followed by the princess' saemgard." Eirik straightened, but the lost expression never left his eyes.

"When you hear that all talk has ceased, my dear, make your entrance. You will see that I have prepared a dais for you. Remember, this was the part for which you were born. Be yourself and you cannot fail. I have carefully selected these people. It is a small group already inclined to hear your words favorably. Speak from your heart, tell them how you feel; tell them of peace and justice and fairness. Tell them how you feel about senseless war, and all the costs that it brings. Your studies should help you there, I think."

He looked into her eyes. "Be honest with them, and you will have them."

She nodded, trying to answer his smile with one of her own, but the ice still gripped her throat, and she had to concentrate on breathing.

"Very well, then, my friends. If you will follow me?" The old man opened the door and swept outside. Each of them, after looking at her one last time, followed. Tyr tried to look encouraging, she thought, but his eyes dipped to her bodice, he blushed fiercely, and she wanted to slap him instead. Chagua nodded to her with a reassuring smile and she felt a little better, and then Eirik walked past, his hollow eyes searching deeply into hers for something she couldn't name. Whether he found it or not she could not have said as he walked past, and it was time for her to follow.

The walk to the barn was the longest she had ever taken. The small side door swallowed first Tsegan, then Tyr with one last backward glance, then Chagua, and finally Eirik. And then she was alone in the dirty yard, listening in cold terror to the soft murmur of voices inside. She stood beside the door, her fists clenching and unclenching, her breath coming in ragged gasps as she fought with the icy panic threatening to silence her forever.

Then the barn behind her grew still. Not a sound emerged, and she knew it was time. She could run, but not far in that dress. And that would leave her friends alone in the barn full of strangers; that would mean she had failed.

But to step through that door was to truly set in motion the course of events that would end with the death of the man that, if she believed all of this, was her father.

She turned and began to walk away.

She kept her head down, cold, silent, icy tears coursing down her cheeks. She couldn't do it. She couldn't face them and tell them their king was evil, or that she was the one to bring peace and justice back to their lives. Who was she to say such things? It was ludicrous.

She picked up the pace, intending to run straight to Sannlir and ride right out of that valley and continue until she fell from the horse's back in exhaustion.

But when she ran around the corner of the house, Tsegan was waiting for her.

He didn't look angry or surprised. He wasn't even out of breath. How had he gotten here before her? But there was no pity in his eyes, either. His gaze was flat and hard, and he took her by the shoulders in hands so warm they seemed to burn, before she could move.

"I understand fear, Princess. I understand terror, even. But you do not understand the fear, the terror, that awaits us all if you cannot overcome your own dread today." He pointed back in the direction of the barn. "If you do not pass through this trial, every person you have ever met, and countless more you will never meet, will pay the consequences." He bowed his head, dark eyes boring into her from beneath his lowered brows. "This is no game we have been playing. And the stakes are higher than you could ever imagine. Remember: we fight far more than the inequities of a single misguided man." He shook her gently, once, to emphasize his words. "Without you, here and now, nothing but death and misery lay in store for all the realms. There are many things King Einar may once have become, but the man he is today is a terror, and a scourge to his people."

The silent tears became a flood as a sob wracked her body, her face turning back and forth as if to deny his words, even as she felt the weight of them crushing her down.

His grip tightened, not painfully, but with a gentle implacability. "There is no turning from this course now, Maiara." She couldn't remember the last time he had called her by name. "As surely as the stars wheel in their set courses, you have already walked into that barn, spoken to those people, and turned them to our cause. It is fate. You cannot deny it."

She shook her head again, but this time she felt the conviction drain from her, and she rested against his warm hands. Her breath calmed slowly, and she was able to bring the wracking sobs under control. She looked at him, his face blurred by her tears, and tried to apologize.

The wizened old man only smiled and shook his head. "There is no shame in fear, only in allowing that fear to overcome your other senses." He reached out and wiped one cheek. "Thankfully, you are a woman blessed with the proper coloration for tears. Wipe them away, and no one will be the wiser."

Together they walked back toward the barn. When they were at the door, he turned away, smiling again. "I have to go around to sneak back in the way I came. No one will have noticed my leaving. Give me a moment, and then enter." He leaned toward her again. "Do not fear, my child. We are all with you."

And he was gone. She stood again, in the same place that had broken her only a moment before. But this time, she would not give in to the formless terror; she would not give way to weak sentimentality. She stood straighter, pulled the lines of her dress into a more comfortable fall, and walked with back straight and chin high, into the dusty barn.

Inside it was dark, the only light the cold sun filtering through the chinks and gaps in the barn and the door through which she had just entered. She could see a small crowd of people standing in the middle, waiting patiently. They reminded her of Baedre, and that familiarity eased something in her chest. She tried to smile as she moved around to the small raised platform Tsegan had had constructed and was surprised by the nervous smiles the men and women in the shadows returned.

She saw Eirik standing to one side of the platform, his massive sword held before him, its point buried in the floor. Behind him, Tyr stood with his thumbs hooked behind his axes. On the other side of the platform stood Chagua, his thin, curved sword in a pose almost identical to Eirik's. And behind the islander was Tsegan, almost lost in the darkness.

As she moved to the center of the platform, the old man joined her at a dignified pace, and she realized he, too, had assumed a role for these people.

"My friends, thank you for coming together here today." The old man's voice was much more aged than normal. "Especially considering the unreasoning rage of our king."

The people in the barn nodded, many looking to either side, as if finding strength within the small group.

"I have spoken to each of you, and I have listened to each of you. I have heard your tales of sadness and loss, about what the brute-king in Connat has taken from you, and I have wept with you over those wrongs." Tsegan bowed his head, gave a heavy sigh, and then looked back up again.

"And yet I have told each of you that all hope is not lost. I have spoken of a new power rising in the land, to sweep the old king aside and take its rightful, just place on the throne. I have told you of the heir the king himself denies out of greed and jealousy. The daughter he renounced and cast aside, the child he would have killed, had kinder forces not prevailed."

He turned and gestured with a feeble-seeming hand toward Maiara, his eyes glowing. "I wish you now to meet this scion of the house of Jalen, trueborn daughter, in secret, and rightful heir of Einar of Astrigir."

He stepped away then, one hand still raised toward her, and she turned to look out at the upturned faces, watching her expectantly.

The faces were familiar. They looked just like the men and women who had come into the House of the Fallen Oak every day of her life. She saw on those faces the trials and losses of people who wrested their living from the land. She knew many would have lost family members to accidents and injuries, many others to illnesses the country folk could not cure or treat. She saw those loses, and others besides, in their eyes as they stared at her, wanting with all their being for her to be the savior Tsegan had promised.

And then she blinked. How many of these men and women truly could blame Einar for their ills? Taxes? Everyone paid taxes, and most complained about them even as they counted out the coins. All the rest, the regular difficulties of these people's lives, could they really be put at the feet of the king? Wars? Many of Tsegan's most fiery words touched on the subject of Einar's unjust wars, but she had found little evidence of anything more than border skirmishes occurring in the last fifteen years.

But then she remembered the rest of what Tsegan had said. The disappearances, the hardships forced upon these people by the agents of the king. She had seen little of this in Baedr, but then, Baedr was far from the borders, or Connat. The true ravages of the king would not reach so far into the hinterlands, she thought, as she watched the men and women before her, eyes bright with belief.

"Has the king wronged you?" She wasn't sure why she had said those words, but they felt right, and the people immediately responded with nods and low, muttered words of agreement.

"Has the king taken your people, your wealth, your safety?" She felt as if her voice was coming from a great distance, almost as if it wasn't her own, and yet she recognized the words. They were words she had encountered time and time again in her reading. They were rearranged, certainly, but they were the root cause of almost every rebellion in every history she had read.

And the people responded. Again, they nodded, and this time their agreement was louder, as a dark anger rose in their eyes.

"Do you wish for a better day, a brighter day, when the bounty of your hands is yours to keep, when the agents of the king are a distant memory, and your children are left to you, to forge their own destinies and not to die on some cold field far from home?" Her voice rose, deepening, growing louder with each point, and she felt the people respond. She felt the moment rising up to sweep her away. Her own confusion and doubts faded before the rising fire in her mind.

"Will you fight, now, one glorious battle, for safety from all future, needless fighting? Will you stand with us today, so that you can stand on your own two feet tomorrow? Will you vow to rid the land of Einar and his foul betrayal of the ancient trusts, and allow me to lead you into a brighter future, where you are left to live your own lives, to pursue your own goals, and to enjoy the fruits of your own efforts, forevermore?"

They were hers. They cried out with one voice, raising their hands in tight fists, shaking them against the tyrant in distant Connat. She smiled, nodding, feeling the energy of the small crowd flow into her like warm sunshine. For the first time she could remember, the cold inside her withdrew. She was dizzy with the power, dazed by the trust these simple people placed in her as they shouted wordlessly into the rafters.

She couldn't remember being led out of the barn, the people reaching out to touch her as she passed. She didn't remember mounting her horse, or riding from the valley, her companions stunned into silence around her.

She could only remember thinking she wanted to feel all of that again. She wanted to stand before people filled with belief and purpose again. She wanted to stand before more people, bigger crowds, louder crowds.

Their adulation had pushed back the cold in her own heart; pushed back the darkness that had haunted her for so long.

She wanted to hear them roar her name again.

Chapter 23

Eirik stood frozen, looking out over the sun-dappled glade at the crowd that had assembled to hear Maiara speak. He wanted to shake his head, but he knew his role. He would remain still unless anyone threatened the princess, and then he was to unleash the maekre blade in swift and brutal action.

He wanted to shake his head, nonetheless.

This was the seventh stop they had made since that first little barn where Maiara had almost ended the whole charade by running away. But Tsegan had somehow talked the girl around; she had gone into that barn, and her words had stirred them into a frenzy, looking to overthrow Einar and install Maiara as Queen of Astrigir.

It was madness. The girl was a waif from a piss-pot, nowhere village, no matter how much learning the old man had forced into her head. And Einar was not the bloodthirsty madman they proclaimed him to be. He couldn't be, could he? The king Eirik had followed, the man he had called friend all those years ago, could not have changed so completely in the intervening time.

But what if he had never truly known Einar at all, even back then? A devious voice in his mind told him to look at how drastically he, himself had changed. Would Einar have believed it, if someone had told him Eirik Hastiin would end up as nothing but a sodden tourney fighter barely able to keep his seat?

His eyes narrowed. Hadn't Einar hunted him for nearly two decades? Hadn't his agents tried, over and over, to kill Eirik for nothing more than surviving when all of his brothers and sisters had died? His entire life since had been running from this king that now played the role of villain in their little drama.

He had to have been running from the king. If not, what had he been running from?

The man Maiara described in more vivid detail each time she addressed the growing crowds sounded more and more like a man who might have hunted a former friend across the decades. The man she blamed for every travail of the common people could well be a man that would set heartless killers to hunt down his childhood friend out of mere spite.

His mind walked in familiar circles. He found, when he was standing before Maiara, blade in hand, that his thoughts found this rutted paths and ground them deeper with each gathering.

These meetings, at first in barns, then taverns, and now in a wide clearing beneath the warm spring sky, always went the same. Tsegan rode on ahead and prepared the people, the four of them would don their new finery, and they would enter; first the old man, then the squire, then the islander, and lastly, him; the sole surviving saemgard, lending a mysterious weight and validity to the claims of the strange, pale-skinned, dark-haired girl with the fierce blue eyes.

By the end, Maiara would be in a daze, breath coming in soft, shallow gasps, eyes locked on the distance.

Whatever was happening to these crowds, it was happening to her as well. And the old man seemed well-satisfied with the results. Eirik didn't know what effect these meetings were having on the kingdom beyond the little pieces they saw, but obviously Tsegan believed their situation was gaining strength as they grew ever-closer to Connat.

That was the true fear in Eirik's heart, wasn't it? Returning to Connat? He had not seen the capitol since the morning he had ridden out of the Bhorg and onto the bloody fields of Merrick Ford.

He had avoided circuit tourneys anywhere near the capitol, spending more time in Vestan and Subraea than he did in his home kingdom, for fear of Ainar's wrath.

Behind him, he heard Maiara's voice rising to its final, ringing indictment of the king, and the answering roar from the crowd was like a wounded dragon, the volume of their joined voices battering at him with physical force. He knew his role now. He turned, hopping up onto the platform Tsegan had ordered prepared, and put one arm behind the girl's back, sliding easily over the shimmering silk, and helped her down off the back of the platform and to their horses. Chagua and Tyr helped the girl mount, and then the five of them were off, with the crowd chasing after, crying Maiara's name to the heavens as they fell farther and farther behind.

How they had not been caught yet was just another mystery to pile at Tsegan's feet, he thought.

Usually, the king would have crushed such a movement as theirs long before it reached this level. Where were Einar's Shadows?

They stopped in a quiet glade an hour's ride from the meeting place and went about the many mundane tasks of making camp. Tsegan would not let them change from their new clothing as long as there were any witnesses about, and so that was usually the first thing they did when making their camp after such a meeting.

With the warming spring nights they were now raising two tents; one for Maiara and one for the men, although Chagua usually slept outside beneath the stars, leaving the tourney tent for Tyr and Eirik. Maiara sat before the small cook fire Tyr had lit, staring into the dancing flames as her eyes slowly came back into focus, her breathing settled, and she returned to herself.

It seemed to be taking longer and longer as the crowds got bigger, and Chagua had expressed concern to Tsegan more than once. But the old man seemed pleased; the girl was performing admirably, and so they left it alone, watching from the corner of their eyes as she settled back into herself with a little more work each time.

"Hungry?" Tyr offered the girl a carrot as he prepared dinner. She jerked slightly at the sound of his voice, then nodded.

"Yes, thank you." Taking the carrot, she held it in both hands in her lap for a moment before raising it to her mouth to take a vague, disinterested bite.

That was another thing. She was always hungry after one of these speeches and could seldom wait for dinner before she began to complain.

Tsegan was gone again, of course. The man never stayed with them for more than an hour or two after the latest gathering. He would take his leave long before they stopped to make camp, going ahead to prepare for the next assembly.

Eirik found himself wishing the old man would stay longer. The paths down which his mind tended to wander as Maiara was speaking were leaving him with more and more questions and a stronger sense of misgiving than he had had since that first meeting in his old tent.

But he was gone before Eirik could marshal his words, and he would not appear again until immediate preparation and action were required.

Still, Eirik resolved that there would come a time when he would talk with the man before their plan reached its final stage. He would demand an audience if that's what it took.

The others ate in near silence. Even now that they had escaped the mountain winter's last, clasping grasp, their dark moods seemed to have lingered. Maiara was no longer quiet and sullen, but rather wandered about in a dazed state of mild euphoria. It looked familiar to Eirik, although the others disagreed. Still, he recognized it.

He recognized it even more as he was seeing it in himself again. Each time they passed through a village, he felt the draw of every alehouse, inn, and tavern door. And when he saw a patron stumble from one of these establishments, he felt a painful twist in his gut that combined contempt, pity, and envy in an unpalatable mix.

Maiara was becoming intoxicated on the reaction of the crowds, no matter what the others wished to see. And if there was anyone in their company who was an authority on the dangers of such things, it was him.

Both the shy girl they had first met and the strong, independent woman she had become were gone now, replaced with this fiery creature who shouted into crowds for the sheer pleasure of the roaring echoes that returned.

Would they ever get that little girl, or that woman, back again?

He rested his head against a rock and looked up at the stars as the others settled down around the fire after the evening meal. He was also sick of stews and soups. It was the best they could really do on the road, but they had been traveling for a long time now. He would gladly stand through a score of Maiara's speeches for a slab of beef or mutton. Hells, he'd even listen to two or three for a chicken.

He knew they didn't have long to go, now. The countryside was growing familiar, and Connat couldn't be too far away. Soon, he would once again gaze upon the city that had been his home. And then there would be fighting unlike anything he had experienced in half a lifetime.

And then maybe, if he was lucky and the gods and spirits agreed, he would be able to have some fresh meat.

He sighed. Maybe then, but certainly not before.

*****

Connat was not a beautiful city. It lacked the gentle, sweeping architecture of the oyathey cities to the north. It was not seamlessly integrated into the natural beauty around it, as those cities were. But Eirik liked to think that Connat and the other fyrdar cities had a strength those airy northern cities lacked.

It was not a tall city. The buildings seldom stretched over a couple stories high. But there was a permanence in their stocky stone construction that the polished, gleaming wood of the oyathey could never match. The streaked grey walls had been constructed for function, not form. And the heavy oaken gates that would bar the enemies of the king of Astrigir had repelled countless assaults through the centuries, although never the dreaded Utan against which they had undoubtedly first been built.

It had been many years since he had last ridden through any of those gates. The circumstances of his return twisted in his mind.

From their perch on the high southern hill overlooking the capital of Astrigir, they could make out the somber lines of the Bhorg crouched in the center of the city. Its squat towers were dark and menacing as they stared at the rest of the town over the deep ditch surrounding the king's stronghold. The hard grey lines of the internal streets around the Bhorg, paved with native granite, made for a sharp contrast to the brown smudges of the outlying thoroughfares.

To be honest, it was a dirty city when compared to the gems of Kun Makha. But it had been his home, and seeing it now twisted a knife in his gut that was equal parts fear and loss.

"Connat. Einar's seat of power, and the turning point of a new age for fyrdar and oyathey both." Tsegan gestured down toward the city, dirty smoke hovering over the early morning scene.

The group was silent as they each took in the sight. Eirik could feel them all around him, knew he should be trying to judge their own reactions, but he was too overcome with his own. That was his home down there, and they were preparing to bring war and destruction upon it. No matter how necessary Tsegan said that was going to be, the people dead and injured as a result would be no less so for all that.

"It seems so ... peaceful." Maiara's voice was soft and broke into the maelstrom of Eirik's thoughts more surely than a shout or scream ever could have.

"They have no idea what's coming." Tyr sounded sad, and Eirik finally found the strength to look away. His squire's eyes were wretched as they shifted from one side of the city to the other, taking everything in. Eirik realized that the boy had probably never seen Connat before, and he felt a pang of guilt that he had kept him so isolated for all their time together.

"They live beneath the yoke of a tyrant and will welcome freedom from Einar's grasp no matter the cost." Tsegan's voice was gruff and imperious as he shifted in his own saddle. He turned the horse about until he was directly before Maiara, and he looked at her with hard, dark eyes. "You have seen the results of Einar's cruelty and caprice. You have spoken yourself with the victims of his rule. They rise up behind us like a gathering flood, and you cannot abandon them now."

The girl shook her head as if coming out of a dream and focused on the little man before her. "I wasn't— I didn't –" For a moment she was the girl they had first met in that distant valley, she looked lost and alone, and he wanted nothing more than to reach out, put his arm around her, and protect her from the old man's rising anger.

But then she stiffened, rose higher in her saddle, and looked down her straight, regal nose to Tsegan with a brief jerk of a nod. "There will be a price to pay for what we must do, but history will judge us, and those who weather the storm will emerge the better for it."

They were words straight out of her latest speeches, and he didn't like the cold way she delivered them. Her shining eyes dimmed when she spoke like that, and he almost had the impression she lost something of herself, giving in to the old man's vision.

It seemed to satisfy Tsegan, and he nodded. "Yes, of course." The old man's horse shifted slightly so he could join them in looking down on the high plateau of Astrigir. "The darkness that approaches will not bow down before Einar. It will sweep him and his kingdom away, and then Vestan and Subraea will fall, and then Kun Makha itself will be ground beneath the force that comes to destroy us all. Only with Maiara seated within the Bhorg will the fyrdar be able to withstand the dread enemy that approaches and lead us all to the glory and radiance that only a victory over the darkness can achieve." Around him, Eirik could feel the others rising higher in their saddles. To either side of him, he watched as Maiara and Tyr tilted their chins up, the light of resolve burning in their eyes.

And he could no longer sit idly by and watch this all happen around him.

Eirik was putting his heels into Hestir's flanks before he fully re-alized what he was doing. He moved the horse out of line with the others and brought it about to face them all, directly before Tsegan's little mountain pony.

"No." He shook his head, glaring first at the old man and then at each of the others in turn. "This cannot be right." He made a broad sweep behind him with one gloved hand, indicating the city and the plains beyond. "Those people have done nothing to deserve this fate. They are our people," he turned to regard Maiara. "They are your people, if all of this is to be believed. They do not deserve to be swept away by your plots and plans, old man!"

He spoke of the common people, but he knew he wasn't thinking of them at all, and the shame of that stoked his anger even higher. It was Einar's face he kept seeing, rising out of the red mists in his mind, staring at him accusingly. Never mind that it was a young Einar, twenty years gone, that he saw. It was his friend, and the idea of ousting him from his throne, of seeing him humiliated, thrown down, killed, was no longer some strange, distant abstract. It was here, and the time was now. As sure as he could smell the morning smoke of Connat on the air, he could feel his old friend's approach-ing doom; the realization that he was bringing that doom himself had proven more than he could bear.

Eirik braced himself for the old man's wrath. The others, round-eyed, shied away as if they all expected Tsegan to blast him on the spot. Truth to tell, he expected something along those lines himself, and it took every ounce of his courage not to flinch.

Instead, the old man laughed.

"Do you honestly think you can avoid your fate now, Saemgard?" The dark eyes narrowed and Tsegan leaned out of his saddle toward Eirik. "Do you think a prophecy is something to be so lightly cast aside?"

And that was what had been bothering him, aside from the imminent assault on his childhood friend, for so long. If this prophecy was, in fact, fore-ordained, why did they need to spend so much time and effort fulfilling its convoluted requirements?

"If it's a true prophecy, won't it come true no matter what happens?" He felt the truth of his words give him strength his anger could have never provided, and he stared into the hard darkness of Tsegan's eyes. "If you're prophetic saga is so prophetic, won't all of this come to pass without our hav-ing had to spend months locked in the frozen mountains?" He tossed a hand at Maiara. "If she's fated to be a great queen, wouldn't that have happened without all of the study you forced upon her? Look at us! We're nothing but a company of fools! The future of all the kingdoms revolves on us?"

He looked at each of his companions in turn. He saw the doubt in Tyr's eyes as the boy looked at the girl and then away, he watched as Chagua refused to meet his gaze, and then, reluctantly, he looked to Maiara. Did the girl feel the doubt that had come crushing down upon him? Did she have the strength of character to set all of this aside if it meant she would no longer be a princess? That she would never be a queen?

Maiara stared back at him, her brilliant blue eyes wide, her jaw working silently. But before she could say anything, Tsegan laughed again.

"Saemgard, thank all the gods your part in this has little to do with your brain." The man dismissed him with a glance, turning back to stare at the city below. "The forces of time are as a mighty, undeniable river, pressing ever onward. When such a force bears down upon you, do you truly believe you can escape it by burying your head in the sand?"

He wheeled his little horse and regarded each of them. "Even if you were to run back right now and hide in our little valley, this prophecy would rise up behind you to sweep you right back to this moment." His expression softened slightly as he continued, his voice dropping low. "Can you possibly imagine the damage that kind of power bearing down upon the world would cause? The waters will rise, fate will be satisfied, and when the waters recede, having returned you all back here in the end, the destruction they will have visited upon the land will have been beyond your imaginations."

They all stared at him, none of them moving, none of them speaking. The sincerity flowing out from the old man was palpable, and Eirik could only blink back, the strength and conviction of his refusals dying within his chest.

Einar had been a friend. No matter what had happened in the intervening years, they had shared so much when they were young men, when the world had not yet forced its imprint upon them. Could he cause his friend's death even now? If the circumstances arose, would he be able to look his old friend in the eye and raise the maekre blade against him?

The answer he felt rising like a solid weight in this throat both shamed and relieved him.

"There is another way." Maiara's voice was deeper than normal. It lacked the high, airy quality it had taken on of late. It sounded more like her own voice.

"Nonsense." Tsegan snapped, his gaze hardly wavering from Eirik's. "There are many paths you may take, all of them against my advice, but they will all deposit you on this hillside, I assure you. And no matter the pain and suffering your intransigence will cause, it will be as nothing when a further weakened Astrigir must face her next dark trial."

Each word felt like a spike in Eirik's heart, another arrow sinking into the flesh of his childhood friend. The old man's words brooked no argument; Einar was going to die.

"That's not what I meant." Her voice lacked the power of her most recent speeches, but it was low and strong. Facing down the old wizard at the height of his anger was the most impressive feat Eirik had yet seen the girl perform.

"There is no need for King Einar to die, if all you say is true. The people rising up behind us should be more than sufficient to swamp the defenses of the Bhorg. If we neutralize the king, take him prisoner, he will be no further threat to us, to the kingdom, or to the future."

Eirik's grey eyes were still locked with Tsegan's, but he felt them widen. He watched the old man wrestle with the girl's words. He watched the desire to disagree with her war with the need to secure their wavering resolve. And then the full weight of the old man's gaze bore into his once again, this time gauging his own tenacity. He had the impression that strange calculations were grinding away behind the old man's gaze.

Tsegan then blinked, nodded, and relaxed back into his saddle. "That is not ideal, and there is plenty of precedent to give us pause, but if that is the clearest way forward, perhaps we can forestall the worst and deal with the ramifications later."

Eirik felt the knot of tension loosen in his chest. His growing distrust for the girl eased.

There was at least a hope, now, that Einar would live.

He looked at Maiara thankfully, but she looked quickly away. She had just tried to spare his best friend, but he suddenly realized she had just tried to spare the man who could, if this whole insane situation was to be believed, be her father as well.

An uncomfortable silence fell upon them, and Eirik swallowed what remained of the fear and guilt, clearing his throat and nodding toward the city.

"Then what's our next step?" He turned to look at Chagua and Tyr. "I don't know about you, but I could do with some solid food in my gut before I have to fight my way through the entire garrison of the Bhorg."

That brought tight smiles from both men, and Tsegan nodded as if grateful for the distraction. "Yes. Our next step." He wheeled the little horse around again and indicated the near side of the city, one of the more affluent sections of Connat. "There is a small house on the outskirts of the city, near the gate, there, that has been prepared for you. Chagua knows the way. If the four of you ride directly there, a servant will meet you to take care of your mounts. There is a stable with a fenced-in yard in the back. Prepare yourselves, and, when the time comes, ride out for the Bhorg with all haste."

Eirik scanned the route the old man had indicated. "That's a long way. What kind of distraction have you prepared? If things get too chaotic, we might never make it to the Bhorg."

Chagua rode up beside Eirik and joined him in surveying the city. "There might be a way, Eirik. There is an avenue that meanders around the back of the hill, but makes straight for the Bhorg, otherwise. The wealthy inhabitants of that district will not have been brought into the princess' plans. The distraction, whatever it will be, should start far from there. With a little luck, we should have a straight route to the stronghold."

Tsegan nodded, staring down into the silent morning scene. "The distraction will be an all-out attack on the southern edge of the city. It will draw the defenders down and away from you, leaving your path clear. You will get to the fortress, and you, Eirik, will lead the others into the Bhorg." He turned back around, and once more the intensity of his gaze was for Eirik alone. "Once Einar is secured and the princess is on the throne, things will begin to calm down. The fewer deaths that result, the better things will be tomorrow for everyone."

The old man turned toward the princess and reached out to touch her shoulder. "Have no fear, Princess. Your people are well aware of you. You know them. You have spoken with them. They will accept you as their queen. The prophecy, no matter what any of us believe, will not be denied. You will be queen, and you will lead your people to victory over the darkness. You will be the shield of all the fyrdar people, and Kun Makha besides." His expression softened, and even Eirik felt the warmth and the regret. "Your road is a hard one, child. I know. Much will be lost along the way, and when your journey is complete, you will hardly recognize yourself. But you are the savior. You will save your people, and all of us, in the end. You must believe that."

That set something itching in Eirik's mind again, but he shook it away. His mind had always plagued him with foolish notions just before a battle, and he would not allow it to cast shadows upon him now, when Maiara needed him at his best. And besides, something else rose up to demand his attention.

"Wait, you won't be with us?"

Tsegan had never stayed with them for more than a few hours at a time; he was always riding off to prepare the next step in the prophecy's infernal dance. But he had always been with them at the moment of decisive action. Was he going to leave them now, on the eve of battle?

The old man shook his head. "I will enter the city through the far northern gate. You enter through the near entrance. There are many preparations that I must complete before the attack can occur. Today is the vernal equinox. We must act before the moon rises, or we will be lost."

A cold chill blew down Eirik's spine as it all became very real. This was going to happen today. Before they next slept, everything would be resolved. Somehow, he had assumed they would be attacking tomorrow, after they had time to prepare. He hadn't realized that when the old man had said tomorrow, he had meant tomorrow.

"The distraction will begin just before sunset, so be prepared." Tsegan turned, heading back down the northern slope of the hill. "Everything will be in readiness for you." He turned back to them, glaring from beneath his raised hood. "Do not be seen entering the city. Hoods up, each of you." One last glare and he was gone, riding off toward the distant city.

The group stood about in silence for several uncomfortable heartbeats. When Chagua turned his own mount down the hill without a word, Maiara and Tyr followed, although his squire had the good sense to shoot him a cowed look first.

Then Eirik kicked Hestir into a trot, bringing him around and after the others. No matter what the night held for them, the prospect of having a roof over his head for even a little while was too appealing to pass up.

And anyway, maybe there was a chance this servant could make them something other than stew before all hell was unleashed.

Chapter 24

The men moved down the middle of the street, brazen despite their ragged clothing and unkempt appearance. They were peasants and thralls, unskilled field hands who should never have been in Connat in the first place, but there they were. And they weren't being shy about it, either. They strode down the muddy lane, chins up, eyes curious, staring at any person unlucky enough to cross their path.

They were brutes, strong from their field work and lacking any sort of education to smooth their rough edges, and they didn't care that they didn't belong. Most of the city folk they passed averted their faces, took sharp corners onto small side streets, or just hurried past, trying not to catch the men's attention.

Geir would have liked to catch their attention, but he knew they were only a symptom of something far more dangerous building within the city. If he confronted this group, he knew that four or five more were within shouting distance, and would descend upon him before he had time to take care of this crowd and escape.

All day long these strange little clusters of hard men and women had been moving into the city. They didn't seem to have much in common with each other beyond the fact that they were not Connat citizens. They were farmers, merchants, servants, and thralls from the outlying territories, and on any normal day, a single group of them would have been nothing more than an object of mild ridicule by their city-dwelling peers.

But Geir knew that there was a deeper significance to their presence here. He had noticed newcomers wandering the streets for some time now as he made his way around Connat fulfilling Drostin's commands. He had been quick to connect his work with these shiftless good-for-nothing peasants, and an inkling of what was coming, and of his master's plans, had been building in his mind for days.

At first, the old man's orders had troubled him. If there was going to be an attack on the Bhorg, why would they not merely reinforce the fortress itself? Why establish these caches of weapons and armor on the outskirts by the gates, as if preparing for an elaborate siege? Where were the warriors to man the outer walls? Where was the strength to make use of these added supplies? His instructions had been entirely lacking in sufficient explanations. He had been left to his own devices in establishing a framework in which all of this made sense.

The best he had come up with was that a trap was being laid. Someone was riling up the peasantry, and a storm was about to burst upon them all. If Drostin thought there would be a need for the king's fighters in the Bhorg to retreat to prepared defenses on the outskirts, then he was anticipating a strong attack, indeed. But if such an attack occurred, and the fighters, rather than hold the line and be crushed by waves of peasants, retreated, gave up the center only to fall back upon them in their own time? Well, then, it was quite possible that a far larger force could be trapped in the fortress, where they could be dealt with at leisure.

Ahead of him, the peasants turned a corner, one giving a raucous laugh as a pair of maid servants hurried by. He scowled, settling back into a doorway, fading into the shadows. He fiddled with the ties of a bracer to give himself an excuse to stand.

He looked up from beneath his brow, but there were no further clusters of strangers in the streets. The maids moved past, looking no more comfortable with him than they had passing the brutes a moment ago. He felt a surge of annoyance, but he knew, with his gleaming head covered in traditional fyrdar markings, his long, plaited beard, and his dark clothing, he hardly looked like a man an innocent maid would talk with in the street.

As the girls passed, he followed them with his eyes, then checked around again. There were no more farmers, and he sighed. With every group he had noticed, he had felt a growing need to do something. But without hearing from Drostin, he dared not take any action at all. Such restraint did not come easy for him, knowing the city was filling with the king's enemies. He had learned to trust the Lord of Shadows over the many years of his service, however, and so he pulled his hood over his head and put his feet back on the path toward the run-down tenement.

He had seen no sign of other Shadow agents since his arrival, and he was beginning to feel a vague sense of concern. If they were all out trying to stop whatever was developing in the hinterlands, they had obviously failed. And yet if his brothers and sisters had failed so magnificently, he felt certain he would have heard something from Drostin.

Instead, there had been no further communication, and he had spent the last weeks preparing the caches and looking after Eydris. She was better, but still too weak to stand. If it had not been for master Takoda, he was certain the woman would have died.

Aside from looking after Eydris and pursuing his duties, he had made time to sneak short visits to the courtyard before the Bhorg every few days. He wanted to get a sense of how the guards were handling the building pressure. The mindset of a man or woman willing to stand stock still hugging a poleaxe for hours at a time was entirely foreign to him. But if he was any judge at all, the guards seemed to have no inkling at all of approaching danger.

Geir had always held a special contempt for such soldiers. He would not call them warriors. He often entertained little fantasies of breaking into the palace to prove to the king his own abilities in the face of those who wore Einar's colors openly, demanding his monarch's recognition for a lifetime of service that would put the workaday efforts of those guards to shame.

Not that he would ever do such a thing. Geir would be invited into the palace one day, he was certain of it. After a lifetime of service and sacrifice, there would come a time for him to step forward and be recognized. One day, the king would look into Geir's eyes, would clasp Geir's hand, and everything he had ever done, every action that haunted him in the darkness of the night, would be made right.

He did not go directly into the tenement, resurfacing from his daydream outside the old wreck of a building. He walked past, watching that he was not being followed, and that no one was paying undue attention to the ruin. The street was empty, as it should be at midday, and so he doubled back and slipped into the building with one last glance up and down the street.

Moving through the labyrinth of misdirection and garbage, Geir made his way down into the security of the safe house proper and stuck his head into Drostin's chamber to check on Eydris. She was sleeping the deep, untroubled sleep of exhaustion, and he softly backed away to let her continue her repose.

The big table in the main room was clear, as always. If the Lord of Shadows arrived and needed to conduct a meeting of every Shadow agent within a thousand miles, the safe house would be ready.

The only object on the surface was a crude copy of king's table, the pieces looking as if they had been carved and painted by a child. It was the best he could procure without attracting the wrong kind of attention in the grima quarter, and in the end, it had been a useless risk anyway. Eydris, even at the best of times, had never been much for games. The few times she had relented to his unceasing attempts to distract her by setting the game up on a small table dragged to her bedside had been total disasters. The woman had no concept of the abstract nature of the game and insisted on rushing toward the middle of the board when on the attack or running as swiftly as she could for the edge of the board when on defense. She had lost each game, presented each loss as proof that she had been right all along, and then collapsed back into bed, claiming she was too tired to talk with him anymore.

He had taken to playing himself in the dark watches of the night. His mind refused to stop spinning, always dragging the worst images and events from his past before his eyes.

Each of those games had been no more successful than the matches against Eydris. He had spent nearly all winter thinking about the damned game. He knew all of the opening moves in attack and defense that he had devised during those long nights in the Bjornstad trading post. Each move he made was immediately met with the most obvious countermove, revealing nothing as the game ground down to its inevitable conclusion. The attacker had the obvious advantage of numbers, and given all other factors as equal, these matches all ended in a victory for the attacker.

It made him long for the painstaking matches with Vidhar as the mercenary learned the game, or even his pathetic routs of Tore.

He remembered the insights he felt were just out of reach in those days, staring at the board, watching his opponents deploy their pieces and move them about. And then he would remember their deaths, the terrible power unleashed upon them, ending their lives with horrible, dream-haunting screams.

Geir collapsed at the big table and dragged the board toward him. The pieces were as he had left them, set up for the next game. He told himself he wanted to be ready, in case he was able to entice Eydris to just one more play. But it was more than that. When he set up the board, he was closer to those old games than at any time after the opening move. And now he stared down at the pieces, remembering the various, childlike opening gambits each of those men had tried against him, and a tired smile crossed his rough features.

By watching Tore's deployment and his opening moves in defense, Geir could always tell where the king would make his inevitable bid for freedom. There were spaces on the board that created patterns, and within those patterns, the future movements of his opponent became clear.

He stared down at the pieces, at the defenders arrayed around the king, at the attackers menacing from every direction.

And at the spaces between them, where both sides must eventually cross.

Why would any player...

He began a new game, but this time as the attacking pieces hovered around the edges, giving nothing away, he sent the defenders into the middle ground in a pattern that had become familiar to him over the last several weeks. He watched as the first few attackers struck the defenders, bogging down, removed from the board as they were caught between defending forces.

But there were many more left in reserve, moving toward the center, past the embattled defenders. By this current theory, the strategy should have revealed the eventual path of the retreating king.

But there was no such path.

With the strategy currently laid out on the board, there was no path to freedom. The king would be trapped in the center despite the strength of his warriors that remained, defending the middle ground. The king would be trapped and killed by the more numerous attackers, and those defending redoubts would serve no purpose at all.

No purpose at all.

The door upstairs gave its soul-wrenching creak, and Geir jumped out of his seat. A small axe fell from his belt into his hand.

The soft creak of footfalls overhead marked a steady, confident pace. With the rising ball of ice in his gut, Geir straightened and moved toward the stairs.

*****

Geir's confidence rose with the dread that froze his heart. He made no attempt to hide as he came to the top of the concealed stairway, moving around the detritus hiding the entrance to the safe house, toward the sound of footsteps in the outer hall.

Drostin was standing there, his usual smile in place. Geir found himself relaxing but forced himself to remain on guard. His new insights below told him nothing could be taken for granted. He was used to operating without full understanding of the bigger picture, but something was very wrong with the situation in the capitol and his current instructions, and he needed to keep that in mind.

"Ah, Geir, good." The king's Shadow master moved forward with the sure steps of a much younger, stronger man. "I trust everything is in order? My instructions were clear?"

Geir nodded, but stayed where he was, keeping an old, overturned chair between him and his master. "The caches have been prepared. Everything is as you ordered."

The man nodded, glance flicking behind Geir to where the entrance to the safe house lay hidden behind the garbage. "Good, good. Is there any particular reason I'm being greeted up here, amidst the ruin and the stench?"

Geir looked around the room. Under normal circumstances, he would never have run up the stairs to greet his master in the middle of the collapsing tenement. He would have remained below, wary and prepared, but assuming the person above was a Shadow agent welcome in the safe house. The rooms below were designed to give the defender every advantage, including narrow corridors, awkward jogs and angles to provide concealment and ambush points, and multiple paths through the rooms.

Instead, he had taken the stairs two at a time and confronted Drostin here, among the wreckage, without consideration of what it might mean or how it might appear.

And nothing was reassuring him that he had been wrong.

"I was on my way out." The lie came easily after a lifetime of navigating the shadows. "There was some unusual activity around the northern cache this morning." He realized that he had been keeping the small axe low, behind his leg and the chair, without being aware of it. "I was going to check on it again."

Drostin shook his head. "It's fine. I went by them all on my way here. Are you sure you are well? You appear to be out of breath."

The old man made to move toward him, his dark eyes open and honest, although a little wary. And why wouldn't he be, a voice in Geir's mind muttered? His agent just came running up the stairs with an axe hidden behind his back.

"I'm fine. I just wanted to make sure everything was ready." He cocked his head to the side as if hearing something strange, and then looked back at Drostin. "Where are the others?"

The older man smiled again, but there was a tension that hadn't been there before. "These are dangerous times, Geir. A rebellion has been kindled in the hinterlands. Traitors are spread throughout the surrounding countryside, and they will be moving very shortly on the Bhorg. The other agents are out collecting as much information as possible, trying to head off the attack before it can begin. With luck, we will never need your preparations. But if the others fail, we need to be ready."

That made complete sense. It fit everything he knew about the current situation, everything he had observed, and everything he had ever known about Drostin and the work of his Shadow network.

But the king's table board below kept rising into his mind. The avenues, the open spaces, the clusters of defenders drawn out of position.

No escape for the king.

"I need to understand something." He put a lifetime of evasion into his tone, keeping it as calm and nonchalant as possible. He didn't want to alert his master to his own doubts and suspicions.

"Of course, Geir." Drostin looked around, but there was nothing he could possibly rest against that wouldn't stain his dark clothing with dust or worse. He settled for resting his shoulder lightly against the wall with a vague air of distaste. "What is troubling you?"

Geir realized that he had probably never been in as much danger as he was in at that moment. Drostin was old, that was true. But he had been the king's Lord of Shadows for longer than Geir had been alive. There was little to be known about killing a man that Drostin did not know. He would compensate for the little loss in speed and strength age had taken from him with a lifetime of experience, training, and a vicious natural instinct for the quick kill.

He cleared his throat, his grip on the hand axe's slender shaft uncomfortably slick. If his fears were true, the moment for action would come quickly. If he wasn't ready, he would be dead before he realized he had missed his chance.

"The placement of the caches..."

Drostin's face was curious, but no touch of suspicion or anger marred the calm of his smile. "Yes? What about them?"

"It struck me..." Geir swallowed. This man had been a friend and mentor for most of his adult life. His trust in Drostin, while submerged in a world filled with lies, betrayals, and death, had been the one constant that had kept him sane in all that time. That and his faith in his king. If Einar and Drostin needed something to be done, there was a good reason for it. The benefit to the realm would surely outweigh the guilt and horror that rose up in his own mind in the darkness.

If he couldn't trust Lord Drostin, there was no one in the world he could trust.

"Why are we preparing for the guards to retreat from the Bhorg, when we could have used the supplies in the caches to shore up the defenses? We should never have needed to set up secondary defensive positions. The king would have been defended, never put in danger, and the peasants could not possibly penetrate the outer walls."

Drostin blinked, and the smile widened slightly. "Peasants? Why do you say peasants?"

Geir cursed himself. But he needed to give the old man every opportunity before he let his steel fly. "Groups have been wandering into the city from the countryside for the last several days. They don't belong. I assumed they were the rebels you're talking about. With a little warning, the gates could have been closed to them days ago."

Drostin's smile was fixed, his eyes still. "They are. They are the rebels, Geir. Of course." The old man shrugged, leaning more heavily against the wall. "If we closed the gates, they would fade into the countryside. We would never know how many there were, or when they might strike again. Yet if we allow them to combine their forces, there may be too many rebels for the king's hearth guard to stop. If we lure them in, however, do as much damage as we can along the way, and then the hearth guard maneuver through the streets, fall back on your caches, and rearm, they will be ready to return and crush the rabble. The enemy will be trapped, the warriors of the king will sweep back in and destroy them at our leisure." He pushed off against the wall and crossed the room quickly, taking Geir gently by one shoulder. "You will be a hero, Geir. The king will know it was you who saved his throne." The smile widened. "He already knows I intend for you to be my successor. This will cement your position."

Something in Geir's chest broke. An hour before, if he had heard this man say those words, it would have meant the world to him. Now, following the casual summary of a plan that was patently false, he felt it might shatter his heart in his chest.

Before he could move away, Drostin's fingers tightened. "Where is Eydris, Geir? Did she return with you? She was supposed to find me after you were finished in the mountains, but she never contacted me. Is she alright?"

"No." The word jumped from his lips before he had time to think, and he tried not to let the surprise show on his face. "No. She died of her wounds as we moved north."

Drostin nodded, his face thoughtful. "Well, that makes what comes next a little easier, anyway."

Geir pushed himself away from the Lord of Shadows, brought the hand axe up, and slashed down at the old man's face.

Drostin eased back, letting the lethal wedge of metal flash past, and then put a foot on Geir's chest and pushed him over.

The old man's smile never faded.

The force of the kick was devastating, far more than a little old man like the Shadow master should have been able to produce. He crashed into the furniture screening the entrance to the basement, grunting with the pain of bruised or broken ribs as he tumbled through the wreckage. He rolled to his feet in a cloud of dust, ready for the next blow, but Drostin had not followed him through the room, instead straightening, watching with an amused grin.

The axe rose again and flashed down, spinning through the air at that smug, wrinkled face. There was no way Drostin could avoid the blow; it was coming too fast to dodge, the steel too heavy to deflect without a weapon of his own.

The old man's hand rose in a gesture that was almost insulting in its nonchalance. The room echoed with a dull clang and the axe bounced away, spinning through the dust-filled air to clatter to the floor somewhere behind Geir.

"You sad little fool." Drostin shook his head. "You have been dancing to my tune your entire life. I can read your every thought and impulse like a children's story book."

Geir was not listening to the words. He had fought too many of the king's battles to be distracted by banter. The words barely registered. Another small axe appeared in his hand and went spinning through the air as he moved sideways, looking for a defensible position amidst the wreckage. He wished he had grabbed one of his fighting axes before rushing upstairs.

"Geir Muata." The old man's voice was harsh. "Geir the Shadow agent. Geir the special. Geir the loyal."

Again, the old man deflected the axe with a gesture. How was he doing that? Was he wearing some kind of half-gauntlet that Geir had missed in the dim light? He only had two axes left, and he didn't want to lead the old man into the cellar where Eydris slept. If he spent the last two axes to no effect, he was going to have to take this fight out into the street.

In fact, that didn't seem like such a bad idea. Drostin would follow him, he had no doubt. And no matter how spry the old man was, there was no way he could keep up with Geir in an all-out sprint to the palace. He would demand the hearth guard admit him into the Bhorg and tell the king what was happening.

But what was happening? Was Drostin betraying Einar and his Shadows? Was it just Geir he was double crossing? Had Geir done something to earn his master's displeasure?

Was this about what had happened in the mountains?

Suddenly, running to the king seemed like less of a sure answer.

Across the room, Drostin laughed. It was not the old man's customary dry humor, but a full-throated, light-hearted laugh, as if a grandfather had just witnessed a grandchild in the middle of some silliness.

"You're not bad, Geir." Drostin had made no move to attack him after that initial kick, and suddenly, as he recognized the tone of finality in the old man's voice, that realization terrified him. "You learned your lessons passably well."

Geir could tell that Drostin was building to something, and he had no intention of letting the old man reach that moment.

Both of his remaining axes came up at the same time, and his arms slashed down, releasing each with careful precision.

The axes flashed through the air with all the accuracy a lifetime of fighting could muster, aimed just to either side of the center of the old man's chest. He would need to move in one direction or the other to defend against one, and when he did, the other would have him.

No matter what trick Drostin had been using to deflect the earlier attacks, there was no way he could address two at once.

The old man raised his hands with the speed of a cat, shoulders jerking slightly as he was surprised by the double throw.

But both axes clanged away and buried themselves in the ceiling over Drostin's head, showering the old man with dust.

"Enough." Drostin snarled, and Geir braced himself for the coming attack.

He was hit in the chest by something that felt like a falling tree, his breath snatched away by a sudden, blazing heat.

Whatever had struck him burned through his clothes as it sent him crashing backward through the wall and into the next room. The pain was horrific; he could feel his skin tightening, snapping and cracking as it withered in the burning heat.

He tried to scream, but the arid wind flashed down his throat and into his chest, drawing forth the last breath there in an agonized wheeze.

He rolled to a stop in total silence. His mind crashed about, trapped in his head, desperate to know what had just happened to him, to understand what had just happened to him. He was in agony, his clothing hung from his shoulders in dry, dusty tatters. He forced himself up to his hands and knees, ignoring vicious stabs of anguish from his claw-like hands.

Despite the torment of his fingers, he could feel the dust on the floor. It was far harsher than he would have expected. Thicker, too.

Then, squinting to see through shriveled eyes, he gasped to see that the floor was covered in sand.

Geir tried to whip his head back up, to stare through the hole his body had punched in the wall, but he moved like an old man, the pain slowing him to a stiff, shaking turn.

He could just make out Drostin's shape through the hole, sunlight from the front room surrounding him in a halo of hanging dust, and something screamed at him through the torment wracking his body.

"You?" He croaked out, his throat raw and pained.

"Me." The word came to him through a rising haze of shock as darkness began to eat at the corners of his vision and the world began to recede away.

"It was always me."
          And then there was nothing more.

Chapter 25

The house was a run-down manse nestled against the southern wall of the city. It might have been a wealthy merchant's home once, or a low-ranking thane's, but it appeared to have been abandoned for many years.

Eirik could tell the others were troubled by their surroundings. Maiara, in particular, looked as if she had wandered into a brothel as she led her horse, a blanket draped over its broad white back, through the muddy streets. They had all done their best to hide the nature of the chargers and Tyr's big work horse by loading them up with supplies and covering them with large blankets. Chagua, at least, got to ride his mount. No one was going to mistake the broken down old cart horse for anything that might threaten the king's peace.

Looking back at the expressions on their faces, on Maiara and Chagua especially, he smiled. If only Tsegan had arranged for them to stay in the grima quarter. Then the little princess would really be able to see how the other half lived.

He tamped down that reaction and took a deep breath. His mind raged with what the night would bring, but there was no denying that Maiara had stood with him before the old man. She had offered to try to spare Einar. That didn't make sneaking into his own city as a filthy rebel any easier, but it was a slight salve to his tormented conscience.

He led Hestir up to the old, faded gate and waved the others over. "Tsegan said there would be someone here to look after the horses, but let's get them behind the wall as quickly as possible first."

He pushed on the gate, but although it sagged against the pressure, it didn't give; barred from behind. He banged on the wall with a balled fist, longing for the gauntlet stashed away in his saddlebag. He had always found knocking on things with a steel-enclosed fist more satisfying than going without.

The old hinges creaked, the gate shuddered, and then opened just a shade, a single blue eye glaring out at them. "What?"

Eirik looked at the others, but no one seemed ready to step forward, so he shrugged and turned back to the doorman, trying his best to smile through his thick beard. "We're friends."

The eye blinked but made no other response.

He felt the old anger rising within him, but he did his best to temper the response. They were here in secret; knocking the door open and sending the man sprawling into the dirt might feel good, but it would definitely cause a stir among the neighbors.

He leaned in closer, his smiling growing a bit more genuine as the man leaned away. "Look, friend, we were sent here. There are four of us, right?" He leaned back and let the man see the others behind him. Chagua had slid from his horse, and now they were all standing, doing their best to look casual in their long cloaks and deep cowls. "You're expecting us, I believe?"

The blue eye darted over the group then flitted back to Eirik. "How do I know you're them?"

This was getting to be a bit much. The maekre blade was slid behind his saddle's straps, hidden beneath the blanket, but it would only take a moment to fetch it and batter the gate down.

He felt a pressure behind him and Maiara gently moved him aside. He looked down at her with a frown, but if the girl thought she could do a better job of shifting the gate guard, he was happy to let her try.

He moved to stand by Tyr, who shrugged loyally, before they turned to watch Maiara.

"These are frightening times, I know." She spoke in a low, soft voice. Not menacing like a whisper, but warm and reassuring. "We are here to help you." She turned slightly to look back at them, gesturing them forward. "I know he told you there would be four of us, and that we would come today."

She turned back to the man, leaning into the gate.

"Are we not how our mutual friend described us to you? Two warriors, an islander, and a girl?" She made a show of looking up and down the street and then turned back to the blue eye with another warm smile. "I don't see any other groups quite like ours. Maybe you can let us in and we can discuss it?"

The man paused for a breath or two, more to make a point than due to any further doubt, Eirik was sure, then the gate squeaked open and they led their mounts inside.

The courtyard was not big, and the horses and their riders, along with the quaking doorman, took up nearly the lot of the space between the gate, the small stable, and the looming bulk of the house. The servant shrank against the wall beside the open door, not looking directly at anyone.

"Thank you." Maiara brought her mount around and stood before the man, gesturing gently toward Chagua, who nodded and moved to close the gates. "The less time we spend on the streets the better. Did master Aqisiaq leave any further instructions?"

The man flinched at the name, and Eirik's eyes tightened. The old man seemed to be less and less inclined to use his kindly voice on people lately; and they had all seen what he was capable of when he decided not to be polite.

"No, mistress." The man was staring at the mud of the courtyard, re-fusing to look up. "Nothing more." He pointed over his shoulder at the house. "There is food and drink waiting for you. I shall care for the horses as you ... while you are inside."

Eirik realized that the man probably had no idea what was going on. He knew that if he was planning a rebellion, the man who had to stay behind and hold the horses would not be high on his list of confidants.

Then he realized what the man had said. There would be food inside. And drink.

Eirik felt the shaking before it could actually manifest, and he tight-ened his fists against the rising need. Not now. Not today. Not this of all days.

He felt a hand on his shoulder and looked up to see Tyr standing there, clearly concerned.

He forced a smile and a shrug, then turned to pull the blanket from Hestir's back, rolling it up to put over the animal's neck. He bustled about the packs, pulling straps and undoing buckles, ignoring the looks he knew Tyr and Chagua were exchanging behind him. When he had pulled his own sad-dlebags free, he turned to see everyone else ready as well, and Maiara turned back to the cowed man standing by the gate.

"This way?" She gestured with one heavy leather bag to the stairs leading up to the side entrance of the house. "You'll take care of the horses?"

The man nodded with a nervous jerk but made no attempt to speak. Maiara nodded herself then turned and led the way up to the door. It opened easily as she pulled on the handle, and they slipped inside.

The faded glory of the home's past owners was even more on display in the entry hall. Dust and cobwebs were everywhere, but beneath the dirt and clutter, the sheer scale of the room spoke of a powerful presence from the distant past.

A dining room was visible from the entryway and they moved in that direction. Eirik dropped his bags on a rickety-looking chair, his attention fixed entirely on the table.

Someone had dusted the furniture here, and the table, although old, was clean. And on that table were platters of meat and fish, bowls of vegeta-bles and sauces, and several jugs of various shapes and sizes.

He stared at the jugs.

Chagua pushed past him, losing all sense of decency in his rush for the table. He piled several slabs of meat onto a plate, followed by a mound of greens, and then reached for a jug. He stopped, looking over his shoulder at Eirik.

"I'm sorry, Eirik. I didn't think." He backed away, casting one last, longing look at the jug.

Eirik shook his head, waving one hand at the table. "Please, Chagua, you don't think I can handle myself? Don't worry. Take a drink." He turned to them all. "Please, don't worry about me." He rubbed his palms on his pant legs, looked around the room, then sighed. "I'll check out the rest of the house,

I think."

"I'll go with you." Tyr had just picked up a plate but put it back as Eirik moved toward a doorway in the far wall.

Eirik shook his head. "No, you won't. You'll stay here and get something to eat. I'm not hungry right now, I'll get something before we head out."

"Eirik, you can't." Maiara was standing in the door, still holding her own bags. "We all need to eat, and I think we should stay together. We only have a little while left before we need to leave. I don't think we should scatter at a time like this."

He smiled. "I won't be gone for long." He tapped the wall with a fist. "I'm just going for a quick walk. We all need to get into our minstrel's costumes, as well, so don't waste too much time eating." He smiled at them all, although the expression felt brittle, and left them to the food. And the drink.

He had been wanting something more substantial than stews and soups for weeks now, and he had just walked out of a room full of what had smelled very much like beef. His mouth worked, flooded with bile as he wrestled with the memories of what else had been on the table.

He knew if he had even a taste of wine or ale, there would be no stopping. He remembered the feelings that had wracked his body as the spirits had leached away in the first painful weeks of the valley. He remembered shaking; he remembered how weak he had been.

The drink had mastered him. He knew that. And he would never let anything have power like that over him again. He had almost succumbed in that tavern on the road, and the battle would most likely last the rest of his life. But he was determined to do whatever he had to do, to keep his hand steady and his vision clear until the day he died.

But did that mean he was going to have to leave any room containing wine for the rest of his life? He moved through the house, finding a narrow set of stairs leading to the second floor, and he climbed into the humid darkness without thinking.

He was fairly certain he would be able to sit at a table with his friends someday and bear his misery without having to leave. Just not today, with everything else piling up around him.

The dim light in the upper level came from windows that had been covered with sheets and heavy curtains years ago. Bars of solid light, heavy with floating dust, fell across the hall and into the rooms on either side. Whoever had cleaned downstairs had not made it up here, and he trailed footprints behind him in the dust. At one end of the house, he found a small bed chamber with a narrow window, its covering half fallen away. He almost sat down on the bed, then paused, thinking better of the impulse.

Pushing on the cot, he heard an ominous creak, then the entire thing fell gently inward, a rush of dust washing out over the floor. He cleared his throat and moved to the window, resting one arm against the wall and looking out into the street.

It was still nearly empty, although occasionally he saw small groups moving about, all of them striding purposefully north, toward the center of the city. Most of these wore cloaks much like his own, and he found himself wondering if they were the vanguard of Tsegan's peasant army.

He was in Connat again. Not in a triumphal homecoming as he had dreamed so often over the past twenty years, but to tear down his king and replace him with a little girl. Tsegan's words had been all well and good up in the mountains or huddled together in some clearing far from civilization, but here, where reality met fevered fancy, the thought of what they were about to do was enough to make him crawl out of his own skin.

He saw another band wander past the house, walking down the center of the street, brazenly challenging two women who crossed to the other side to avoid them. There was no subtlety in that crowd; their anger was something he could feel from his high perch overhead. He had seen men and women like them on the tourney circuit. They were working themselves up for a fight.

He pulled the sheet farther away from the window so he could follow the group until they turned a corner toward the center of the city, striding out of his field of vision. He looked up at the sky, off to the left, where the sun was just starting to dip toward the hills and distant mountains on the horizon.

Tsegan's rising river looked to be outpacing them after all. If they didn't leave soon, he was afraid they wouldn't be able to get near the Bhorg at all.

*****

The others were around the table, sitting gingerly on chairs that looked like that should have collapsed years ago. There was still plenty of food, although the whole table looked like it had been ravaged by a determined army. Tyr, Chagua, and Maiara each had a cup close to hand. Both Tyr and Maiara flinched away from theirs as he walked in.

He sighed. He was going to have to deal with all of this eventually.

"There are groups moving toward the Bhorg." He reached out and grabbed a slab of meat from the decimated tray. "I think they're Tsegan's, and that might mean the old man's schedule has stumbled a bit. There's still some time before sunset, but if we leave now, we should be in position in plenty of time for whatever he has planned."

Maiara looked sick; her bronze skin pale. "We need to leave earlier?"

Tyr smiled at her, and Eirik felt a rush of sympathy for his squire. For him, the night could not end well; dead, captured, or infatuated with a woman who would be his queen before sunrise.

"Yes, I think so." He glanced at Chagua for support, but the islander looked like he was lost in his own doubts. "Chagua, do you think we should leave soon?"

The dark man started as if just waking up. He shook himself, coils of hair swinging, and shrugged. "Tsegan Aqisiaq did not have a formal schedule, but rather an order of events he wished for us to follow as closely as possible."

A shout from the street caught their attention and they all turned toward the windows.

They couldn't make out the actual words, but the tone of angry challenge was unmistakable. An answering voice, a murmur of rationality, was drowned out by a further surge of anger, and then a great tumult of screaming and shouting, a cry of pain, and then a triumphant roar that faded away up the street.

They stood in silence for a moment, looking at each other, and then Chagua nodded. "Lacking more specific instructions, perhaps we should leave earlier than planned."

Each of them took their bags into an unused room to get dressed for the assault. Eirik watched them all leave, then stood by the table, staring at the cups and jugs before grabbing another slab of meat and moving off to find his own place to prepare.

Eirik settled the fine cloth of Tsegan's surcoat over his armor, shifting his arms until it fell properly. He was wearing his old fighting leathers, augmented with a coat of chain and plate; the weight felt right as it settled onto his shoulders, sending his blood singing as it hadn't in many, many years. The song was almost enough to drown out the doubts still haunting the back of his mind.

As he settled the surcoat, his fingers brushed against the wing and he shivered. He had spent so long hiding from that emblem, from what it represented, what it had meant to him and to his family. To wear it openly as he stormed the Bhorg was just another twist of destiny's knife and more than enough to dampen any song in his heart.

Coming back into the dining room, he stopped as he saw the others assembled. His mind, already troubled, started at the war gear. But then his step faltered and his eyes widened. The fighting men faded into the background beside Maiara, and he stopped in mid-stride, his breath catching embarrassingly in his chest.

She was stunning, literally stunning. It was always his first thought each time he saw her in the gown. The color matched with her eyes was uncanny, and the shimmer of the fabric gave the entire dress a dreamlike, otherworldly air. Her long, dark hair was braided and wound up into a circlet, a single strand falling down her neck.

She wore no other crown, as they had all agreed that would seem premature. But woven into her hair he saw threads of silver holding a single sapphire in place over her forehead. It would be more than enough to suggest their intentions to anyone with the inclination to see.

Eirik cleared his throat, ducked his head, and moved into the room, putting his equipment bag down on the table with a muffled clank.

Chagua's ivory robes were the same, but now he wore a suit of fine mail beneath that Eirik had never seen before. It was not bulky enough to change the fall of the robe, but this close, it was easy to notice. The graceful, sweeping sword hung at his side on a belt of old leather that should have looked out of place with the rest of the finery. Instead, it gave him a serious, martial appearance.

Tyr was back in his leathers with the blue tabard, but a wing sigil had been added to the chest, in black rather than his own crimson. The haft of two fighting axes swept up past either shoulder, held in place with a baldric settled beneath the tabard. The boy looked nervous and eager at the same time.

"Well, we make quite a display, at any rate." He tried to force a little levity into his voice, but he could feel it falling flat before the words had left his mouth.

"I'm not sure we'll be sneaking up on anyone, dressed like this." Maiara gestured to her gown, then at the costumes the rest of them wore.

"We look like minstrels performing an old saga." Tyr tried to sound annoyed, but Eirik could see the boy standing taller in his tabard than he had ever stood in the mud-stained leathers of a tourney squire.

Eirik turned to Chagua, but the islander's gaze was distant, his mind far from this strange moment. "What do you think?" He tapped the table before the other man, bringing him back to the present. "Should we at least wear cloaks to approach the stronghold?"

Chagua shook himself then jerked a quick negative with his chin. "No. Master Tsegan's directions were specific. We are to approach the Bhorg as we are."

Eirik paused as he turned back to the table, looking at the man through narrowed eyes. He didn't know what it meant, but Chagua's island accent had turned flat and dull.

"Well, I don't think he had intended for the peasants to take to the streets quite so soon, either." Tyr jabbed a thumb over his shoulder at the window behind him. They could hear more shouting in the distance.

Eirik walked to the window and pulled the sheet aside. The sun was slanting in from the west, the shadows lengthening across the muddy avenue. He turned back to the others, meeting their eyes, seeing his own confusion and fear reflected back at him, then looked at Chagua. The man refused to look up.

"I think Tyr's right. We'll put the cloaks on and get as close to the Bhorg as we can. Easier to take them off later if we don't need them than to find something suitable if the mob becomes restive."

The islander bowed his head, and the others went to collect their riding cloaks, moving toward the door with slow, hesitant steps.

"I'll make sure the horses are ready." Tyr lifted the door latch, pulling his hood up over his head and went to step out, but Eirik reached out to stop him with a hand on his shoulder.

"If we ride from here, we'll have to abandon the horses before we get anywhere near the Bhorg. We'll be better off on foot. Horses are little more than a hindrance in a city anyway."

Chagua started to speak and then stopped. The dark head nodded, although his gaze was still distant.

"Then what do we have them for?" Maiara had been silent for a while, and the plaintive, childlike tone in her voice now was a harsh reminder that she was still a young girl thrust into a strange, perilous nightmare.

"I think the horses served their purpose out in the countryside." He turned toward her, but the others were listening as well. He tilted his head toward Tyr. "He's right. We're dressed like we've stepped out of your old fairy story book. The horses were part of that image. Now that it's been set in their minds, no need to endanger them tonight."

He looked to Chagua again, and after a moment, the islander nodded with a shrug, looking away.

Eirik nodded in response. "We'll walk. It will give us more flexibility and help us sneak as close as we can before the ruse is up."

Or begins in earnest, he thought to himself with a bitter shake of his head.

"We must be in place for moonrise." Chagua's voice was dull as he waved at the door. "Master Tsegan's river will not be denied."

Eirik shook his head. "I don't believe that. There's nothing mystical about sunset, or moonrise, or any other time of day." His mind still rebelled at the entire notion of fate and prophecy, but if he was going to do something, he was going to do it right. By the sounds in the street, the attack had already begun, and if they waited too long, they would never be able to move through the press of bodies to the Bhorg and whatever awaited them there.

He shrugged. "But you're not wrong about waiting." He sighed. "Let's go."

*****

The streets were nearly empty, aside from an occasional, huddled form lying in the mud. They quietly moved past those, not looking too closely. As they continued toward the center of Connat, more and more people joined them. They were dressed as field workers, farmers, and merchants, but they wielded sharp, gleaming axes, swords, and shields. Many of them had found bits and pieces of armor that looked good enough for the king's own hearth guard.

It felt as if they were in a river, being pushed along toward the fortress at the city's center by the force of a bloodthirsty current. The thought did not sit well in his mind, reminding him of Chagua's earlier words.

Yet, as each side street passed, disgorging its own flood of angry, well-armed civilians onto the main thoroughfare, the thought was more and more apt.

They heard the screams long before they saw any sign of fighting. They were surrounded now by a surging, angry mob, their faces locked in mindless expressions of fury and hatred. Their voices were raised in hoarse, throat-scouring roars, but few actual words emerged to give form or sense to their emotions. It was like nothing so much as a nightmare, being swept along at the speed of others regardless of his own intentions, surrounded by mindless, hate-filled faces.

He reached over his shoulder and adjusted the baldric holding the maekre blade to his back. The hilt stabbed up over his shoulder, over his head, but the familiar blade was hidden beneath his cloak. It meant that he could not wear his own hood, but his was not a well-known face in Connat after all these years, and the presence of a maekre blade would be far more inciting to this crowd than his own ugly visage.

Tyr and Maiara, both hooded, were directly behind him as he broached through the crowd, Chagua taking up the rear, eyes ever-watchful for mischief. They were jostled, pushed, and shoved as the rising tide of rebels swept ever upward, but there was no malice directed toward them as far as Eirik could tell; nothing more than the formless rage of a mass of people whose resentments and frustrations had been stoked to a fever pitch.

The screams ahead took on a harsher, more pained tone; it was akin to the sounds Eirik was accustomed to from his countless tourney melees. But beneath that familiar drone was a spiking keen that touched something much farther back in his mind. It was the sound that had echoed through his nightmares for years beyond counting; the sound that had driven him into countless cups, bottles, and jugs in his endless attempts to escape.

The sound of death.

The crowd around them surged forward as it heard, and the low buildings hemming them in on either side fell away. They were in the square before the Bhorg. Time seemed to drag while the crowd trapped him, not unlike a nightmare again, and he lost all sense of where he was. In a panic, he jerked his head back, but the others were still with him.

Maiara was obviously out of her element, surrounded by the surging mob, but her eyes were clear and her face firm. Tyr's face wavered between frightened and furious. Chagua's eyes were flat and cold, scanning for threats like a hawk scanned for prey.

Before them, above the surging heads of the crowd, the squat towers of the Bhorg rose up like the bulwarks of a seawall. The dark granite loomed over them, stirring already agitated memories that threatened to crush him with their weight.

From each tower flew the blue on blue banner of Astrigir, the long ship rippling proudly in a cold wind blowing down off the mountains. The sight of that ship over the heaving throng, knowing how much of that night's blood would be on his hands, nearly forced him to his knees.

But before he could fall to his inner demons, his foot came down on something soft and rolling; he almost lost his balance, flailing out with one hand to grab a man beside him to keep himself upright. Glancing down he couldn't be sure, but he thought he saw an arm disappearing beneath the mob behind him.

Then there was space. The crowd, entering the wider area around the front gates, spread out. The sight of blood and bodies before them only fueled their anger. Eirik had seen battle before. He had surveyed countless tourney fields after a melee, the fighters strewn about the ground in still or moaning heaps, the ground itself churned to a muddy soup.

Once, on a distant field, before being driven into the river, he had seen a real battlefield, littered with the bodies of the dead and dying, screaming, crying, or lying terribly still beneath the lowering sky.

The courtyard before the Bhorg was infinitely worse.

Although it was hard to discern, with many of them armed and armored with the equipment Tsegan had somehow procured, he thought the majority of the dead were the civilians he had helped to bring here.

Scattered through the piled dead were several of the king's palace guard, but there were far fewer of them. Clearly, Maiara's rebels had struck here, thinking to overwhelm the guards with superior numbers, and found out firsthand what such a victory cost.

They had forced the gateway in the end, and around the shattered wooden gates were heaped the crowd's answer to the initial slaughter: the bodies of scores of guards, with several of the heavily armored hearth guard intermingled with even more civilian dead, piled up against the walls, staring sightlessly up into the fading light of evening.

There was still fighting around the edges of the square, but things seemed to have moved past the gate. He could hear clashes and screams from within the Bhorg, but the crowd around them milled about aimlessly, the sight of the dead dampening their bloodlust.

Eirik turned and pulled Maiara and Tyr close, Chagua following along from habit more than conscious volition. The islander's gaze seemed to wander over the blasted scene, drifting over the piled dead as if he couldn't quite comprehend what he was seeing.

"We need to get the princess into the Bhorg." He jerked his head toward the shattered gates. "Waiting out here serves no purpose."

They all looked at the darkening gloom of the gatehouse, its towers reaching up to either side and the light of the bridge beckoning beyond. But what really held their attention, on the far side of that bridge, was the entrance to the Bhorg itself, filled with deep shadows and the echoing screams of battle.

"We're not going to be able to force passage if the hearth guard within have rallied." He stood taller, looking about them, trying to decide the best course of action. "If we can get these people to come with us, to force the defenders back if they gather themselves, we'll have a better chance of reaching the throne room." He looked at Tyr, who nodded, and then Chagua, who still looked lost and alone.

"What does the prophecy have to say about this, islander?" Eirik's emotions were in a surging torrent of chaos, but a tendril managed to slip free and lash out at the only representative of the architect of the madness swirling all about them. "What would Tsegan tell you to do, if he was actually here?"

"And where is he?" Tyr gave voice to the real question Eirik wanted to ask. All of this was happening because of the old man, but he was nowhere in sight. In the boy's eyes the big warrior saw an echo of the growing chill of abandonment that was swelling in his own chest.

Chagua shrugged. "I do not know."

Eirik nodded. "Right, so we have no choice." He turned to Maiara, her face hidden deep within the shadows of her hood. "You need to reveal yourself, Princess. We're only going to be able to get you to where you need to be if we get these people to help us."

She nodded, hands floating up to take the hood on either side and slowly slide it off her silken hair.

The effect on the crowd around them was not immediate. Those closest noticed her first, eventually reaching out to silence those around them. A growing circle of silence spread out from the four as the grim-faced fighters, all eager for guidance in the face of all that death and blood, realized who stood in their midst.

Cries of 'Princess!' and 'Lead us!' rang out in the sudden stillness. And he watched as she straightened, her eyes hardening and growing distant, the veil lowering over her face with the recognition of the crowd.

"We're almost there!" Her voice, that voice that was both hers and not hers, rang out over the square. The last fighting outside the Bhorg had died away, and all was still and silent but for the moaning and cries of the wounded and the dying.

"A tyrant sits his throne within!" She whirled, letting the dirty cloak fall and revealing her magnificent gown, pointing with one bare arm into the depths of the Bhorg. "He defies the will of Astrigir and spits upon your courage and sacrifice! Will you surrender now, returning to your homes and farms and awaiting his cruel and petty vengeance? Or will you come with me, demand justice, and make this kingdom the jewel of the fyrdar realms it was always meant to be?"

Eirik knew she was just a girl, and even with their familiarity, he felt his blood rushing to answer her call. He could only imagine what the men and women in the crowd felt. He saw the wavering resolve strengthen in their faces, he watched as they surged ahead, each wanting to see the princess, those nearest reaching out to touch her. He pushed them back, as did Tyr on the other side. But she reached her own hands out in turn, brushing the grasping, dirty claws with her fingers as she moved toward the broken gate.

"Then come with me, and let us demand justice!"

The roar was painful as it rose up all around them, and it was all he could do not to flinch as it echoed off the dark stone of the Bhorg. The crowd rushed forward like a floodtide, although now there was a small region of calm around the princess herself. She strode through the broken gates, and he followed.

Weapons flashed before them in the last gleams of daylight as they crossed the fortified bridge to the king's stronghold. The crowd pushed ahead, screaming and shouting once again, and once again he could make no sense from their cries. Glancing back he could see Maiara making a conscious effort not to look down at the bodies they passed, but in the gleaming fury of her eyes, he thought he could see the shimmer of an unshed tear.

Then the shadows of the Bhorg closed in around them. They were through the main gate and into the arming yard beyond, more bodies scattered around them. The hearth guard had tried to make a stand here, but the sheer weight of the peasant revolt had doomed them, crashing down upon their barricades and dashing them into the stone of the floor. Wide halls led out in three different directions, and Eirik quickly decided that their best course was to take full advantage of the chaos of the attack and move straight for the throne room at the heart of the fortress.

He turned back to the others as they walked, directing them toward the hallway before them, and so was not looking when the counterattack came crashing in from either side.

The hearth guard bore thick, heavy shields, while those behind struck out with long, wide-headed spears. The coordination was unmistakable, and he realized that Einar's defenders were not as defeated as they might have seemed.

Eirik tore his maekre blade free as he spun back toward the attack, seeing Tyr and Chagua each draw their own weapons. He cried defiance, the eerily familiar chamber only deepening the sense of nightmarish dislocation that had haunted him since his first glimpse of Connat from the hill above. He had no sense at all what he was defying.

The battle crashed into them, and all was chaos. He kept close, denying the howling beast within his chest its desire to rush forward into the fighting. He needed to stay with the princess, to keep her safe, and to force a way through this and into the dark hall on the far side.

The rebels all around them had no knowledge of the fortress's layout and were merely swinging wildly at any hearth guard that came too close. Once they had pressed the attackers away from the central hall, the king's defenders had broken their formations to leap into the angry mob, attacking it from within and sowing even more chaos and confusion.

And then he heard Maiara scream.

He spun around, only to find that he had moved farther away from the girl than he had thought. Or perhaps, somehow, she had moved farther away from him. Chagua was defending against three hearth guard, while Tyr finished off an opponent and looked about, trying to find Eirik.

Maiara had picked an axe up off the ground and was holding its haft as if it was a staff, but the warriors around her were paying little heed as they struggled to get to grips with each other.

"Maiara, wait!" Eirik screamed, his voice harsh in the low confines of the arming hall, but as he moved toward her, Tyr shouldered him aside, one heavy axe coming up to deflect a spear thrust from a hearth guard who had thought to take advantage of his distraction.

Eirik spun about, growling, and brought his enormous sword around in a flat, whistling arc. The hearth guard met his gaze, his own fury burning hot, and then for a moment those eyes widened as they flicked over his face.

The maekre blade took the man in the chest and sent him crashing back into the surging mob before the revelation was complete.

Eirik turned again, but the distance between him and his companions was even greater now. Tyr was battling two hearth guard, Chagua had spun up and over the battle to land behind his foes, dropping each of them with a single slash.

But Maiara, pushed by the cruel confusion of the battle, was nearly lost in the shadows of a side hall.

"Maiara, no!" Eirik reached out to her, and their eyes met for one, brief moment, before she was swept down the tunnel by the surge of the battle.

He charged after her, screaming incoherently as the entire purpose of their attack was stolen away. He caught a glancing blow on his shoulder, the armored pauldron ringing, and threw himself to the side to avoid the warrior's next slash.

All around him the battle raged, expanding as rebels and hearth guard surged in and out. He dispatched two more attackers and looked back, trying desperately to pierce the gloom and the flood of bodies.

But Maiara was gone.

Chapter 26

A man reared up out of the shadows before her, an axe blade gleaming behind him as he raised it into the air.

And another man, wearing almost identical armor and a long, shining sword, crashed into him, sending him smashing into the wall and stabbed him repeatedly with an incoherent growl as the axeman staggered, mouth agape, and then slid down to rest with his back against the wall, gaze dull and lifeless as bright blood ran down the wall behind him.

"Princess, come with me!" The man with the sword shouted in a voice only slightly less animalistic than his earlier cries.

He had to be a friend, though, right? Einar's hearth guard would have no idea who she was.

She nodded gratefully to the man, her own weapon heavy in her hands, and looked back the way she had come. They were in a narrow hall with wooden doors leading off to either side. Light was provided by lanterns set in the high walls, but many of them had been knocked down, leaving puddles of oil burning fitfully on the floor.

The man with the sword, unsatisfied with her speed, reached back to grab her wrist, and she looked down. He left a smear of blood behind when he let her go with a muttered apology.

She wanted to tell him that it was alright. She wanted to tell him this was all her fault and not his. She opened her mouth to say just that, when another warrior, this time in the heavy armor of the hearth guard, rushed toward them and split the man's head with a short, heavy axe.

Blood and worse splashed back against the wall as the sword fell to the floor with a dull clang and the body slumped down, eyes staring mutely up at her as he dropped away.

The man with the axe turned, raising the weapon so quickly that blood sprayed across the ceiling, but then stopped when he saw her. His grey eyes swept up and down her body, noting the dress, the detailing, her hair. They widened in confusion for a moment, then he shook his head.

"You need to get deeper into the keep, my lady." He grabbed her roughly by the wrist, the same wrist her fallen savior had grabbed, leaving more blood behind, and tugged her further down the hall, in the same direction the man with the sword had been leading her. "Head for the throne room, there will be more guards there to protect you."

She didn't know what to say, stammering out half an apology and half an explanation, entirely incoherent, but the man had already rushed off the way she had come, leaving her alone.

She looked after the hearth guard, then down at the man he had killed, the man who had saved her life, and she began to shake.

This was all her fault. The first body she had seen in the wide court-yard outside had stared accusingly at her with a dead look, and she had known what it was trying to tell her. Without her, that woman would still be alive. Without her and Tsegan's foolish prophetic saga, this man and all of the others would still be alive.

She felt the hot trail of tears down her face as she fell to her knees next to the body. She stared at the ruin of his face, remembering the apologetic look he gave her as he realized that he had grabbed her; grabbed her to save her. And now he was dead.

She wrapped her arms around herself, squeezing with all of the manic strength that welled up within her, and wanting nothing more in that moment than to be back in that sheltered little valley, laughing with her friends, or talking with Wapa, the crazy old man in the hills.

It wasn't Baedre she remembered, or the House of the Fallen Oak, or Vali or Turid or even Kustaa, although that realization sank yet another dagger of guilt into her already-bleeding mind. No, it was that mountain valley. She remembered the icy winds, the clear skies, and the warmth of the springs behind the ancient ruin of Alden's Tor. She remembered the silent regard of that ancient place and how she had never felt like she was alone.

A sob wracked her body, sending a tremor down through every limb as her throat burned and her heart clenched painfully in her chest.

It was all her fault.

It was all her.

And who was she to believe that she warranted any of this suffering? Even if she was the secret daughter of a king who had brought his realm to the edge of destruction, would she be able to do any better? She had studied as hard as she could for months and had found that not only did she have a knack for such study, she enjoyed it. But what were those three months when compared to the years, decades, and centuries of traditions that supported Einar Jalen's claim to the throne? King Einar ... her father...

A sudden wave seemed to wash over her, the light of the corridor dimmed, sounds faded away, and she felt as if the world, the horrible nightmare world, was withdrawing from her. She was nearly overwhelmed with a strange certainty that she had somehow outlived her usefulness.

A shout brought her up out of her misery and she rose on unsteady legs, looking up and down the corridor. She couldn't tell where the cry had come from, but something told her, even in the depths of her despair, that she couldn't stay here.

She looked down at the body and whispered a silent apology. One hand fluttered out as if she would reach down and touch the man, but then she shied away and moved past him. She needed the wall for support as she moved, careful not to brush against any of the doors, hurrying past the darker sections, but the corridor seemed to stretch on forever, and now she thought she could hear distant shouts both in front and behind.

Her hands tightened into fists and she looked down in shock, realizing that she had left the long axe behind. She shook her head at the thought of returning. The weapon had been next to useless anyway; it had been far too heavy for her to wield as a staff, the only weapon she was even passingly familiar with.

Finally, she came to an intersection, and for a moment was simply relieved that she had made any progress at all. But then she realized she had no idea where to go next. She stopped, trying to pierce the gloom in any direction, but without any real hope.

She was about to continue on straight when an explosion of noise erupted from the left. Two men came stumbling around a corner that had been hidden in the shadows, defending themselves desperately against a tide of men coming up behind. In the fitful lighting, she couldn't tell who they fought for. Was this the remnants of Einar's hearth guard being driven to destruction? Was it a counterattack that would finally push her own people from the Bhorg once and for all?

One of the defenders staggered to one knee and she slipped back behind the corner, although she could not take her eyes off what was happening.

The man's companion, seeing his brother fall, stopped retreating and moved before him, bravely holding out a heavy double-handed axe to bar the way. The first attacker to reach him was struck in the throat and another spray of blood painted the wall. But there were too many coming up behind, and even as the lone defender wrenched his weapon clear, two spears stabbed out of the onrushing mob, taking him in the neck and chest and pushing him over onto his back with a tortured scream.

The man who had stumbled rose up, a small fighting axe in either hand, and spun into the mob like a windmill, striking left and right with his heavy blades.

It was horrible to watch, not knowing if it was friend or foe dying, enemy or ally making such a valiant last stand.

And not knowing what either outcome would mean for her.

Maiara began to move back down the hall the way she had come, but even as she lost sight of the battle, there was a terrific scream, an answering roar from many throats, and the mob came sweeping around the corner, bloody weapons upraised.

She fell backward, raising one hand hopelessly to ward off the first blow, and the woman at the front of the line came to a skidding halt, putting her arms out to either side to stop her companions.

"Are you blind, you fools?" The woman screamed, her voice hoarse and rasping.

The men and women behind her stopped as well, glaring around the woman with cruel, menacing eyes.

When they saw her, however, the hardness in their faces eased, and several whispered her name or the word 'princess'.

"Princess, it's not safe here for you. Where is your defender?"

Maiara tried to make sense of the word, but clarity would not come.

"Where is the knight protector?"

She shook her head, not knowing the significance of the question nor the answer.

The woman looked in each direction and then back at her. "You better come with us. We're going to the throne room. We'll keep you safe."

And with that the woman, assuming Maiara was right behind her, raced off in the direction she herself had just come.

Maiara shrunk against the wall as the men and women passed, each nodding solemnly to her as they rushed by.

She wanted to shout to them, to tell them they were going in the wrong direction. Her mouth worked silently, her throat pulsed with the need to scream, but nothing came out, and the host raced past, those to the rear hardly giving her a glance as they went by.

And then she was alone again.

She couldn't breathe. The air was hot and heavy all around; it felt like she was moving through tepid water with every step.

She bowed her head, her hair falling around her face like a curtain, and concentrated.

Nothing she could do would save the man with the sword. Nothing she could do would bring any of the dead, on either side, back to life. The dead would stay dead, the wounded would feel their agony and loss for the rest of their lives. And those left behind would mourn the fallen for years and years to come now no matter what she did.

But she could give those deaths, that loss, meaning, if she could gather her senses and force herself to continue through to the throne room. She had to, no matter how she felt, lost in that warren of stone, or all of the sacrifice of that bloody night would be for nothing.

She raised her head once more to the intersection of halls before her, trying to ignore the blood, the bodies piled up around her.

The Bhorg was not a building as she understood the term, but more like a low pile of heavy granite with a maze of passages carved into it. She thought she knew which hall to take here, but what about the next juncture? Her courage would mean nothing if she wandered around, lost and confused in the halls of the Bhorg until her friends were all killed or captured.

But it meant even less if she stayed still. In fact, she thought as her eyes narrowed, her indecision could easily be nothing more than her cowardice offering an excuse for avoiding the danger that her mind might be fooled into accepting. The orphan girl from Baedr would never have been able to wade through the blood of this night.

She had to be more than that lost little orphan girl. She was more.

She straightened up, clenched her teeth, and moved purposefully between the two passageways to either side and forward, deeper into the fortress.

Occasionally, she heard fighting off in the distance, but none of it came close enough to threaten her or give her an idea of where she should go next. At the next intersection she was offered the choice of left or right, with nothing but a blank stone wall before her; something she had been afraid would happen.

She wanted to punch the wall in frustration, but obviously that wouldn't solve anything. She looked first one way then the other. The same dark, low halls, with no hint that would recommend one over the other.

Did she really need to be in the throne room? After all, Tsegan's plan called for Eirik and Tyr, and she supposed Chagua, to move on the throne room with all the fighters they could rally, to secure the throne and the king, and then stage a coronation before as many members of Einar's court as they could gather. There was really no need at all for her to be there until the chamber was secure.

And what about the timing? They had had only a short time before sunset when they crashed into the Bhorg. Did they need to have the king secured by moonrise? Did she need to be sitting on the throne by moonrise?

Her head began to spin and she reached out with one hand to steady herself. Was Eirik right, could it be the timing didn't matter? But if that was the case, and the timing didn't matter, how much more of the prophecy was unimportant?

A spike of pain drove through her right eye and she flinched down in agony, pressing a palm to the socket, feeling the hot pulses against the skin of her hand. The throbbing eased then faded away. She needed to get to the throne room no matter what else happened.

But even her bolstered resolve was not enough to puzzle out which way she needed to go.

An eruption of shouting and the clash of metal rose up on her left, above the general, distant clangor of battle. She had no interest in getting tangled up in another bloody fray and so decided to move swiftly to the right. A scream, a rumbling growl of victory, and the sounds faded away.

She felt her face harden and she stood tall for the first time since entering the Bhorg. She had had enough of hiding. As she continued down her chosen corridor, she began to open each door as she came to it. She thought she might find noncombatants cowering in a corner somewhere or some other indication as to where she should head next.

Each of the rooms was empty of anything useful. Most were storage chambers, filled with bags and boxes that she had no time to sort through. She found no torture chambers or rooms lined with the skulls of innocents, which seemed like an oversight on Einar's part. Her smile tightened further and she reined in her imagination.

She was about to leave yet another storage room when she noticed a stack of freshly-plaited brooms in one corner. She took one last look back into the corridor and then ducked into the room. She picked up a broom and tested the bristles. They were fresh, and she felt a pang of guilt at what she was about to do. In the face of everything happening around her, she realized how foolish that guilt was, but it was simple, it was mundane, and it was familiar. It actually gave her a small touch of comfort.

Without further worry, she put the head of the broom against the floor, pushing until she felt the shaft strike stone, then brought her heel down sharply.

She screamed.

Then she cursed, limping in a circle for a moment, then turned back to the broom with a vindictive light in her eye.

She grabbed the broom back up and put the head down again, concentrated on it, and raised her foot.

She felt a sudden chill run through her, the temperature in the room seeming to drop, and brought her foot down.

The broom shaft snapped neatly off at the head, leaving her with a short, serviceable staff.

She went back to the door, checked for anyone outside, and then moved back out into the passageway and continued on the way she had been going. It felt warmer again, the cold of the storage room left behind.

Soon she was standing at another intersection, the hall splitting off to the left and the right, and she listened to the distant sounds of fighting. The screams and shouts rose up on the right and she turned toward the left-hand passage, then stopped.

She was never going to find her way clear of this spirit-cursed fortress if she kept avoiding people.

She shrugged her shoulders within the dress, a dress that felt less and less appropriate with each moment she spent lost in the hell of battle, and headed toward the sounds of fighting.

The corridor opened out into a common area that was so much like the big room just off the entrance that she was afraid she had come full circle.

But there was no doorway leading to the outside here. By the splintered wreckage of tables and chairs, it might once have been a dining area, but now it was a slaughterhouse. Men and women struggled against each other, stumbling over dead bodies; the walls and ceiling were splashed with blood.

If she never saw another drop of blood, it would be too soon.

Here the lighting was a little better, with most of the lanterns hanging higher than in the low corridors and thus having survived the worst of the conflict. The ornate armor of the hearth guard was more easily visible here, and she could see that in this area, at least, the attackers seemed to have the upper hand.

The fighting was savage, with the farmers and merchants in mismatched armor pushing the surviving hearth guard back against a long far wall. There were six of her rebels left, holding three defenders at bay. Attackers and defenders alike looked exhausted, hair plastered to their foreheads, shoulders sloped, hands shaking with fatigue. But their faces were twisted into animal snarls, and it was obvious that no quarter was being asked for or given.

Unless someone stepped in.

These were all going to be her subjects. Each death, on either side, would mean the kingdom was weaker when the sun rose. It was her duty to save as many of these fighters as she could.

"Wait!" She moved into the room, stepping over the dead and dying, trying not to see them. There was too much for her to do already to become bogged down once more in regret and guilt.

"I said wait!" She used the voice she had developed with Tsegan in the valley over the winter, perfected before all those angry crowds since coming down out of the mountains. And the voice worked.

The attackers looked back at her, hesitant. One of them obviously recognized her; she knew that look, now. The man put up a hand, stopping his companions, and they stepped away from the hearth guard, keeping a wary eye on the defenders.

"You're not supposed to be here. You're supposed to be—"

The three warriors against the wall, knowing that their time was short, attacked at some unspoken signal. Axes rose and came crashing down as her people staggered away, raising their own weapons in defense.

The bloody clash lasted only a moment, but all three hearth guard were dead, as was the man who had tried to address her. She stared down at him, blood pooling on the floor beneath his head, and wanted to scream.

And then she realized that the surviving attackers were looking at her.

And none of them had that familiar look in their eyes.

They didn't recognize her. They didn't know her. Whether they were new recruits to the cause or had just followed the first wave of rebels into the Bhorg, she couldn't know. But they were tightening their grips on the shining weapons, moving slowly toward her in a sideways creep that seemed to be gaining speed with each step.

"Stop!" She used the voice on them, and they hesitated. "I am Maiara, rightful ruler of Astrigir!" She stood tall, shoulders back, and rested the butt of her makeshift staff on the floor before her.

They resumed their advance.

"Wait!" A ball of freezing anger was building in her gut, powered by every terrible sight she had seen, every terrible thing she had caused to happen that day. "I am your princess!"

They didn't care. It might have been simple bloodlust; it might have been that their own minds had been shattered by what they had seen and done that night. None of that mattered, though, as they came toward her. There were four of them, two men and two women, all holding swords and axes that were just as menacing for all their apparent lack of skill.

Two went wide, moving around to take her from either side, as the others continued to advance on her, their expressions flat.

"No!" She raised the staff before her, backing up, and the icy fury continued to rise. She thought she saw the man before her pause as his breath came out in a puff of steam, but then his head jerked forward and he fell limply to the ground.

The woman beside him looked down at the body as if waking from a nightmare, eyes narrowing as she saw the fletching of an arrow protruding from the back of the man's head. Another arrow struck her in the side and she went to her knees with a grunt, her sword falling.

The two others glared back behind them at a flood of fur-clad warriors pouring in from a small side door. At their front was a tall man with red hair and a long beard, handing a short bow to someone behind him.

The redhead drew a long-handled fighting axe from his belt with a dark grin and moved into the room.

"The lady said no." He took a running start, winding up with the axe, and struck with a blow so strong it knocked the raised weapon of the defender clear across the room. Before the man could say anything, the hearth guard's return blow caught him in the side of the head, crunching into his skull and dashing him to the floor.

The last remaining attacker shrieked as her companion fell and raised her own axe in reply. Maiara screamed out for it all to stop, her own breath billowing out into the freezing room, but two more men crashed into the peasant from the doorway, bearing her down, axe flying, knives flashing as they silenced her.

And then Maiara was alone with a room full of Einar's most loyal warriors.

The red head, clearly the leader, scanned the room, but found no further threats. He turned to Maiara, still standing with her staff held in a guard position across her body, and raised one open hand to her in a calming gesture.

"All is well, my lady. They're dead." He looked down at the man he had just killed. "They don't seem to lack for courage or numbers."

He gestured to the rest of his warriors, and the men and women scattered through the room checking for wounded. Attackers were given the final mercy of a quick dagger thrust, while three wounded hearth guard were dragged to another door and placed in a line, tended to by several of their brethren.

"My lady?" The redheaded hearth guard looked down at her, concern in his light eyes. "My lady, if you'll come with us?"

She shook her head slightly. The chill was gone, and she wasn't entirely certain she wasn't going mad. "I'm sorry?"

"This area is still dangerous, my lady." He gestured back at a small body of warriors waiting by the door with the wounded. "I must report back. You will be safer if you come with us."

She shook her head again. "Come with you? Come where?"

"To the throne room, my lady."

She felt lightheaded. She held her breath, afraid that if she tried to breathe, she would scream instead. It was a nightmare. It had to be.

She nodded silently, her eyes fixed on the corridor beyond.

Chapter 27

Tyr battered his way to a wall, threw his back flat against it, and tried to catch his breath. He was still in the arming chamber just inside the Bhorg, but most of the fighting seemed to have moved away. A trickle of rebels in their mismatched gear was still coming through, fighting past the remaining hearth guard in the room and plunging deeper into the fortress.

He doubted most of them even knew why they were here. The room was filled with bodies, horrible sword and axe wounds gaping in wet, obscene mockery of the bruises and broken bones of the circuit tourneys. The men and women in their fresh armor, shining new weapons in their untrained hands, were utter strangers to this horror, and it was breaking their minds as surely as the weapons of the hearth guard were breaking their bodies.

He wiped a sheen of sweat from his forehead then hefted his massive axe and pushed back out into the center of the room. The three corridors leading away all looked the same at first glance, but they were very different. The one to the left was darker and narrower; he assumed that led away to the supply rooms beneath the fortress. There would be little reason to venture into that darkness, and so he turned to the others.

The straw matting strewn about the floor of the arming chamber continued on down the right passage; wider and taller than the others. The stables would be in that direction, and probably the garrison and the living quarters of the lower-ranking guards. That might, eventually, lead him to the throne room, but not directly.

And that left the hall before him. The vast majority of fallen warriors and hearth guard were gathered there; the lamps on those walls were more ornate and more numerous, their flames the bright yellow of refined oil.

He hefted his axe and moved forward, keeping a wary gaze all around.

The fighting was over here, but that didn't mean anything. The hearth guard were probably retreating to more defensible positions deeper within the Bhorg; a counterattack could come at any time. The righteous fury driving the rebels might gutter and fade at any moment, especially when confronted with the brutal realities of war. If the king's warriors timed a counterstrike well, the entire attacking army would shatter like poorly-tempered steel.

His chosen hall was wide and brightly lit; the deeper he went, the louder the sounds of continued combat became. His heart was racing like it had never raced before, beating against his ribs as if desperate to escape. He tried to swallow and found his throat swollen shut with fear and disgust. The dead were everywhere, sprawled all along the corridors, heaped up at various intersections. The deeper he got, the more dead defenders he was finding. The tight confines of these halls went a long way to compensate for the peasant army's lack of training.

No matter who won this battle, the kingdom would pay the cost for years to come. Astrigir would emerge from this night weaker than it had been in many, many years.

Eirik had ranted against the king since long before Tyr had entered his service. He was famous for it, in fact, among the fighters of the tourney circuit.

But something had always bothered him about those tales. Would a king as ruthless as Einar Jalen was said to be, filled with hatred and vitriol decades old, truly have been unable to find one lone tourney knight?

It had never made much sense to Tyr, but his faith had been unshakable back then; if Eirik thought he was being hunted by agents of the king, then Tyr had been more than happy to believe him. Einar was a bad king. Enough of his subjects believed it that it could very well be true. There were wars, that was true enough. And there were taxes, that was undeniable. And to those with a more well-developed distrust of the oyathey, it was said that the king's rapport with Kun Makha was far too close for a loyal fyrdar sovereign.

But this night's bloody work, with the untrained people of the kingdom dashed against the king's own personal guard, would leave scars that would take a generation to heal.

Tyr shook his head, stepping over yet another body, and moved deeper into the fortress. At the next intersection, he kneeled by the wall and looked carefully around, trying to judge how near the shouts and crash of battle actually were.

They were far too close, he realized, as a limp body fell past him to hit the stone with a dull slap.

He straightened and put his back against the wall, axe across his chest, and watched for the next person to pass.

It was a hearth guard, fur cloak over his rich armor. The man was being forced back by two strong looking youths in shining helms with long spears.

There was no way the hearth guard was going to survive this match, as the two rebels coordinated their strikes to keep the man off balance.

Every death here would weaken the kingdom, no matter who sat the throne come dawn.

He was stepping forward before he realized what he was doing.

The massive axe rose as if of its own volition. It fell with the heavy inevitability of fate. It cracked the hearth guard on the back of the head and sent him crashing to the floor with a dazed grunt. He shifted once and then slumped into stillness.

Tyr hoped he hadn't killed the man.

He had little time for such thoughts, however, as the spear-wielding rebel on the left lunged. The glittering metal spearhead seemed to float toward him, and for a moment he felt as if he was caught in a dream. Then he brought his axe up, caught the spear shaft just behind the head, knocking the weapon up and away.

As he parried the blow, the other spearmen put his own weapon up and sent a straight arm slamming into the other man's chest.

"No! He's with the princess!" He pointed to Tyr's tabard, with its distinctive blue and silver. "He was with her in the grove, remember?"

The other man shook his head, but the dull gleam left his eyes, and he seemed to come back to himself. He stared at Tyr, unseeing, but didn't make another move to attack him.

"My lord," the second spearmen caught Tyr by surprise at that. He was no lord. "You should come with us. We're going to the throne room, to meet up with the protector and the princess."

The protector and the princess; Eirik and Maiara. And Chagua, the teacher. And Tsegan, the ancient ... wizard?

No one had ever bothered to tell Tyr what his role in this insane saga was supposed to be. He had followed Eirik as he always had and helped in any way he could. Tyr had spent so much of his life believing in the man's potential, trying everything to rekindle that flame. It was burning now, and more brightly than he would have ever imagined. His childhood hero was reborn.

But now what, for him?

'Lord' sounded pretty good, to start.

"Which way?" He had no way of knowing how long he had been wandering through the Bhorg and felt the pressure of Tsegan's timetable roaring behind him, pushing him forward.

The two men looked at each other, and then the second man pointed down the way he had come, back toward the arming chamber at the front of the fortress.

"I think it's down that way, my lord." But there was nothing but doubt in the man's voice, and Tyr shook his head.

"I just came from there. That's not it." He turned back to the junction. Had the unconscious hearth guard just stirred?

"It isn't down there." He pointed with his axe down the hall the man had just run out of. "And I don't think it's in that direction." He shifted the weapon to indicate the left-hand passage. "I don't see why we shouldn't head straight in?"

The men shared another look, and the spokesman shrugged. "We'll follow you, my lord." He stabbed his spear vaguely down the hall behind Tyr.

"If it's not that way, then we don't know where it is."

Tyr nodded, took a tighter grip on his axe, and continued on down the way he had been going.

Just a short way past the intersection, they heard the rising crash of battle. Turning a corner, they found another junction, this time giving the choice between straight or right. But first, they would have to work their way through a fierce knot of fighting.

It was a savage snarl of men and women, so tangled together it was impossible to tell rebel from guard. The floor was littered with several bodies, blood pooling in the recesses of the floor.

The two young spearmen seemed to lose themselves, charging into the fight without a thought. One slammed his weapon into the back of a man who dueled with a red headed woman wielding paired axes, but as the woman looked up to thank the spearman, her eyes flared and she sent an axe spinning into his chest.

Tyr's companion fell without a sound, spear clattering to the floor.

He could make no sense of the fighting. Most wore furs, and beneath the ragged coverings, the equipment Tsegan had secured for his rebel army looked nearly identical to the armor of the king's warriors. There was no real sense that the fighters themselves knew who they were fighting. They lashed out with abandon, attacking anyone within reach.

He could do nothing in that madness, he realized. Every death could be friend or foe, and he would probably never know the difference. In fact, if Tsegan was right and Maiara was the ruler of Astrigir with the rising sun, they would all be her subjects, and dead all the same.

Tyr paced through the fighting, axe raised across his body. One man spun toward him, having just sent a blonde woman collapsing to the floor, and slashed at him with a longsword. Tyr couldn't tell if the man was inept because he had never held a sword before or exhausted from the constant battle. Either way, though, the blow was clumsy and slow, easily knocked aside with the haft of his axe.

He brought the heavy weapon back across again, head reversed, and struck the swordsman a glancing blow across the top of his head. The man spun into a wall, crashing to the floor with a strange half-smile on his face.

Tyr was almost across, into the next stretch of hall, when a shriek erupted behind him. He turned to see the redhead, once again with an axe in either hand, striding toward him.

She threw one of her weapons and it flashed at his chest, his axe coming up to deflect it at the last moment. She was right behind it, however, her other axe falling toward his head. His own weapon was out of position from deflecting her throw.

He leaned back, lost his balance, and went crashing down to the floor, the woman tumbling down on top of him, growling and spitting like an animal, twisting the small axe around between them, trying to bring its razor-sharp blade up beneath his chin.

With a grunt, Tyr brought his knee up and around, catching the woman in the side and sending her rolling away with a cry. Before she could recover, he rolled over himself, bringing his heavy axe down onto her forehead. He winced at the crunching sound. He hadn't wanted to hit her that hard, but she'd hardly given him a choice.

Tyr rolled away and up to his feet, glancing back quickly at the chaos roiling within the intersection. No one else seemed to have taken any notice of him, and so with one last regretful glance at the lone surviving spearman, fighting for his life amidst the churning, directionless mass of men doing their honest best to kill each other, he rounded a corner, not looking back again.

Why had the red headed warrior been so sure of his own allegiance? He slowed to a halt. The woman had been vicious but skilled. He didn't know any farmers who could wield a fighting axe in either hand. Although it was likely that their cause had attracted a few seasoned fighters, the chances were still better that the woman was a hearth guard. And in the heat of that frenzied battle, she had singled him out for attack.

Why?

He looked down. The ridiculous tabard. He had seen no one in the Bhorg wearing such a garment; and especially not with the sweeping wing of Hastiin emblazoned upon it.

He grabbed a bunch of the tabard with one filthy hand and began to pull it over his head.

But what about the prophecy?

Would things turn out badly if he ran into the throne room without his minstrel's costume?

He pulled it over his head quickly, looking to either side to make sure no one was near. He balled the fabric up and tossed it onto the floor beside the wall, adjusting his grip on the great axe.

He had walked less than a dozen steps when he returned, picked up the tabard, and rolled it into a tight ball that just barely fit into the satchel he wore on a cross-shoulder strap.

Having survived the bloodiest battle Astrigir had seen in nearly two decades, he wasn't about to face an enraged Tsegan Aqisiaq without the proper attire.

He continued down the hall without a look back.

*****

It was a grueling trek through the halls of the Bhorg; without his tabard, he was equally likely now to be attacked by friend or foe at every turn. More than once, he had been forced to stand and defend himself. He wiped the sweat from his face again, thinking fondly of the distant valley and the winter cold. He would give almost anything for just a breath of that freezing mountain air.

He refused to admit it to himself for the longest time, but eventually he had no choice. He was completely lost. Defenders and rebels were chasing each other back and forth through the fortress, and he had tried at every opportunity to avoid battle where he could. He had left several still forms behind him, hoping that they would wake up with nothing more than a terrific pain in the head. But he knew, in the heat of battle, more than a few of them were probably more seriously injured; maybe even dead.

But he had done his best, and he had to be satisfied with that.

He rested against the wall, looking backward and forward. The place hadn't looked that big from the hill above. How could he still be lost?

Which made him doubt, for the first time, the wisdom of their goal. How did they know Einar would still be in the throne room? Did it make any sense for the hearth guard to keep the king in such an obvious location, when there was only one real reason the rebels could have for attacking the Bhorg?

But if King Einar was not in the throne room, it would take a wiser head than Tyr's to puzzle out where he might be. Hells, Tyr had never even been in the sprawling fortress before. He was having a hard enough time finding the throne room, never mind finding Einar if the man had been spirited somewhere else.

And that was the problem he had to solve; how to find the throne room in this maze of a stronghold in time to make a difference.

Whatever difference he was supposed to make.

He couldn't very well stop a hearth guard and ask politely. He had looked in at several chambers along the way, thinking he might find servants or thralls hiding under a bed somewhere that might be persuaded to point him in the right direction.

But someone in the Bhorg had been prepared, and when the rebels had struck, the non-fighters had been withdrawn away from the fighting.

There was a scream up ahead, and he stopped. Fighting spilled around the corner, with several men scrambling backward, trying to escape the fury of a trio of men each fighting with two long-handled weapons that looked as heavy as stone but with no apparent blade.

The men were bronze-skinned, long black hair flying free behind them as they howled a vibrating war cry. They wore soft leathers and fine chain that did nothing to hamper their graceful movements as they heaved their strange weapons in wide, sweeping arcs.

Oyathey.

He had seen renegades and exiles fighting in the tourney circuit a few times. He recognized the armor and the blunt weapons, but the difference in skill between those tourney fighters and these three was like night and day.

It was said that an oyathey warrior had no need of an edge to best his opponents, forging victory from his own strength and skill. These three screaming demons went a long way to proving that to be true.

But what were oyathey warriors doing in the Bhorg?

One of the men scrambling away from the oyathey caught a glancing blow to the ribs that tossed him into the air. The man smashed into the wall with a pained grunt and tumbled to the floor where he rocked back and forth, hugging himself in agony, oblivious to whatever might happen to him next.

The other two oyathey hooted in appreciation of the blow as all three continued tearing down the hall after the remaining fyrdar. One struck the whining man with a casual backhand blow that cracked his skull against the wall and toppled him over, dead.

The lead oyathey slowed when he saw Tyr, and his dark eyes narrowed.

Then the man's companions ran past, and with one last blink he followed after them, leaving Tyr alone.

When the sounds of their footsteps and ululating cries had faded, he slumped back against a cold stone wall with a low, soft whistle.

What in the names of all the gods and spirits were oyathey warriors doing stalking the halls of the Bhorg?

After only a moment's reflection, he realized that it didn't really matter. The leader of the three had assumed he was a friend. Were they fighting for Tsegan? The old man clearly had his fingers in nearly everything, and he was unmistakably oyathey himself. Somehow, it wouldn't surprise Tyr if he had infiltrated an entire warband of oyathey howlers into the fortress. But why would the old wizard not have mentioned them?

Did that mean they were fighting for Einar? That would seem to confirm the king's deep ties to Kun Makha, but why, then, did they spare his life?

He shook his head, pushed off from the wall, and with one last glance after the strange warriors, took off at a steady jog, retracing their steps.

Warned again by the clangor of battle, he slowed before turning the next corner, and found himself peering around at the last moments of yet another skirmish. Most of the survivors wore the unmistakable fur mantles of Einar's hearth guard, while the heaped dead were unidentifiable in their contorted, final rest.

One of the hearth guard, a short, squat brute with a long blond queue, lashed forward with a bearded axe, catching his foe with the long, sweeping edge on the back swing and spraying blood into the air. As the rebel fell, eyes wide in pained disbelief, the hearth guard looked around for another foe, and his cold gaze fell upon Tyr.

It happened before he even had time to think. He had nowhere to go and had already been mistaken for a hearth guard, or at least for one of Einar's loyalists, twice.

He stepped out, putting on his most desperate face, and singled out the bloody warrior that seemed to be in command.

"Come quickly!" He panted, doing his best impression of a minstrel show's mummer in the throes of a panicked plea. "Please!"

The hooded looks of the hearth guard all turned to him, distrustful in the midst of the night's bloody business. But the man with the blond tail stood straighter, looking at Tyr from beneath a single arched brow.

"What?"

He couldn't let that lack of faith burn away his intensity or knock him off his path. "It's the king! They've made it into the throne room! We need to rally to the throne room!"

The other hearth guard began to mutter to themselves, their concern obvious. The squat blond stared at Tyr for a moment longer then turned to the others.

"Quick, go. We're done here anyway." As they began to file out, moving down a corridor Tyr thought he never would have chosen, the man turned back to him and put one broad hand on his chest. "Not so quick to turn aside, there, sunshine. You'll be coming with us."

It took everything Tyr had not to grin; he maintained the terror-stricken look. "Yes, my lord." He dipped his head, not wanting to spend another moment looking into the man's green eyes.

"If I find you've turned us from our path with lies, your death will stand out even in the tale of this treasonous night."

The man pushed him against the wall then nodded toward the corridor. "Now, move."

Tyr moved. He had no idea what the situation in the throne room would be like when he arrived; having a suspicious, angry hearth guard standing behind him would probably be a detriment, but he was moving in the right direction, and that was an improvement.

Now all he had to do was keep his head down and hope the whole thing hadn't fallen apart before he got there.

What if he arrived in the throne room, and no one else was there?

Chapter 28

All was darkness and pain. The bright pulsing agony did nothing to illuminate the darkness; only accentuating its boundless depths and profound weight. The darkness encompassed the agony, and yet the agony was all.

It would have posed a pretty puzzle if the torture had given any leisure with which to think.

There was no passage of time. Both pain and utter black were eternal, stretching forward and blotting out the future, stretching backward and erasing whatever past had led to this place.

There was nothing but darkness and pain; there never had been, and there never would be.

A thousand years past, or a moment. A light entered the darkness in a piercing brilliant shaft that burned away the black but intensified the pain immeasurably, transforming it into a screaming, shrieking, echo that filled the world.

Suddenly there was only the torment and a desperate prayer for a return of the darkness.

But the darkness did not return. The light, that single burning spear, flickered, then steadied. And for another eternity, there was only the pain and the light.

And then, far off, buried deep beneath the suffering, behind the brilliance, and from a place out of time, came a voice.

The sounds were distant and indistinct. There was no sense or pattern, but with the noise came a new concept: words. There were no words hidden within the noise, but somehow it seemed to bring a form of comfort that could not be explained. The pain was still ever-present; would always be present. But somehow, the sound of the voice soothed.

Slowly, within the surf-like rise and fall of the voice's senseless droning, a word did emerge. It meant nothing at first, but then, repeated over and over, a sense of something important attached itself to the sound.

"Geir."

It was a word that should have been recognized. It carried with it a lifetime of meaning and emotion and weight.

But nothing more came, and the agony rose up to engulf all once again.

It might have been a moment, it might have been a year, but the voice returned, insistently repeating the word.

"Geir. Geir. Geir!"

There was a sense of movement within the pain and the light; a rocking sensation that seemed to set boundaries to the once limitless universe of agony and illumination.

The light brightened. The rushing sounds intensified. The word hit like a metal spike to the middle of the forehead.

Or a maekre blade to the spine.

"GEIR!"

And he screamed.

He screamed as if all the demons and dark spirits of all the hells were chasing him from their domains and up into the agonizing brightness of day.

His scream went on and on and on. And with that scream came a whole new raft of pains as he felt his face crack and shift, wetness running down rough, numb cheeks.

He felt his hands tightened into fists that snapped and popped, sending new bursts of pain shooting through arms that were already rivers of torture.

He felt his body convulse, and his back split, sending fresh waves of wet agony flooding through him.

The scream continued.

And rising up out of the flashing cacophony of pain were flickering images that reinforced the misery. A face rose up before him. An old face; kindly face; wrinkles of age radiating out in deep smile lines from around the mouth and eyes. It was a familiar face; a face he had trusted for most of his life. He knew the owner of that face better than he had known any other living person.

Or he thought he had.

The scream slowly took on form as he felt his head whip back and forth in a hellish denial. From out of the pained, animal howl, a word arose.

"No!"

It stretched on and on. Unrecognizable as his own voice, distorted as it was by the agony of his torn and desiccated throat.

He was panting; injured, tortured lungs barely able to keep up with the need to feed that single screamed word.

But limited by the confines of his tortured, physical form, there was only so long such an agonized scream could last.

He collapsed against a rough surface, panting and gasping for breath, throat scratched and burning.

The light dimmed to slightly more tolerable levels and he tried to look about him. The pain had not lessened, it was an eternal presence that accompanied his every breath and move. But it no longer shackled his mind to its crushing reality. He knew his name now, thanks to the voice. And Geir knew that, as long as he breathed, there was still something to be done.

That was when he realized that he was blind.

He could see the light, with vague, indistinct shadows flickering across it, but that was all.

Panic rose up within him, momentarily tamping down the pain. If he was blind, then he really was helpless, and hopeless. There would be no chance for him to atone for a lifetime of misplaced loyalty.

A sob wracked his pain-filled body. His king. He had served his king all his life. That was the only thing that had made the horrible things he had done bearable. His loyalty had been unquestioned and unwavering. He had done everything that had ever been demanded of him. He had not balked at the darkest, most foul deed.

A new flicker of images rose up before his blinded eyes, but this time it was not a single man, but rather a succession of images, each dissolving with a scream as the next rose to take its place; men, women, and a long, long sequence of children, young and terrified and innocent. And then, at the end of the blurring string, that single, kindly face once more.

Lord Drostin, the king's Lord of Shadows.

The king.

That brought him back to the torture of the moment, and he tried to rise. His limbs did not work properly, his arms shook violently as he tried to push himself to his feet, his legs offered no stability at all, and he fell back down. Every single movement of every part of his body sent bright sword blades of fresh agony stabbing into him.

"Geir, slow down."

That voice again. The soothing voice. But now it seemed nearly as pained as his own. He almost recognized it, despite its own quavering, tortured tones. He reached out in the blurry, formless light and felt a weak hand touch his own with a faint, tentative caress that scored a burning fire across his skin before it was withdrawn.

He hissed with this new pain, flinching and drawing away.

"Who—" It came out as a weak croak, but he didn't know how to finish the question anyway. "What—" Again, the croak, this time faltering into stillness.

"You need to lie back on the floor. You need to rest. Let me get you some water." That word, more than all the others, brought comfort. Water; he needed water. More than anything else.

He nodded, despite the pain, and tried to settle back onto the hard wood of the floor.

A floor. He was on a floor. More of his recent past came back to him. Drostin at the door, talking nonsense about the weapon caches hidden around the city. Almost as if he had no interest in protecting the king.

The king.

He saw a game board; king's table. He saw the spaces between the attackers and the defenders, he read those spaces.

He saw the death of his king in those spaces.

He scrambled to rise again, desperately casting about, hoping that the world would resolve itself into a visible pattern he could navigate to follow Drostin, to stop him.

The pain flashed out again and he collapsed with a cry. There was no comfort even from settling back against the floor, as every pressure caused new, screaming torment.

A shadow passed before him and the voice returned. "Take this."

There was pain and weakness there, but he found comfort in the voice nevertheless.

And another image returned to him.

"Eydris?"

"Who else would it be, you fool?" A clumsy hand tried to tilt his head forward to accept the cup, but he was smiling slightly, despite the painful cracking that caused, and water dribbled down his chin instead.

"You truly are a fool, do you know that?"

"He betrayed us, Eydris. He means to harm the king." He drank then pushed the cup away with one clumsy hand as the ache in his jaw became too much.

"Who?" She settled back, her shadow receding. She must be resting up against a piece of rotted furniture.

He wanted to sob. His throat felt cored out, but he forced the words past parched, cracked lips. "It was Drostin. He did this to me." He tried to point to where he thought she was. "Just as he did it to you, in the mountains."

"No." The word was flat and final. "How? Drostin has served the king for..."

Geir nodded. None of them knew how long Drostin had served the king, because none of them had ever been allowed to know the full history of their dark society.

"And he's been a traitor all this time?" There was doubt in her voice now; a doubt that echoed his own. "How could that be? If he was a traitor, why not do this years ago? Decades ago?"

He started to shake his head but stopped when the pain, inside and out, flared anew. "I don't know." His voice was barely a croak. "None of it makes any sense."

Her blurry shadow shifted. "Maybe it wasn't Drostin, but an imposter?"

He gave his head the slightest shake, wincing at the pain. "I was as close to him as I am to you." He paused, mindful of the irony. "It was him."

She lapsed into silence, and he remembered her own injuries. She had been bed-ridden for weeks on end; only returning to consciousness in the last few days.

"You should be in bed." He coughed out the words, wishing suddenly for more water.

Her laugh was a dark, ugly sound. "You should be dead."

That was probably true enough. They had both seen the strength of this strange power. It had killed nearly a score of hardened mountain folk with barely any effort.

"I feel dead."

"Well, there's nothing more we can do." Her voice sounded weaker, more distant, although her shadow had not moved. "Either he'll win and come back to finish us off, or he will lose and we'll most likely die here before anyone even knows to look."

That couldn't be the end to it. Not after everything they had done. Not after everything he had done, he had thought, in the name of his king.

"No." He steeled himself for the pain, and then pushed himself off the floor.

In a lifetime of battle, torture, and havoc, he had never experienced such pain. But he rose, teeth gritted and blind eyes tight, refusing to surrender to the agony.

"No." He repeated as he stood. He was dizzy with the pain, and he knew he must look like a terror if the corpses in the vale were any indication. He vividly remembered Eydris's wounds, and from his own agonies, he knew he was even worse off than she had been.

But if he surrendered now, he was damned. There would be no forgiveness for a man who had done the things he had done. Neither gods nor spirits would care that he had been fooled. All that blood was on his hands, and there would be no peace for him in this world or any other.

As he stood, panting from the effort, the room around him began to emerge slightly from the haze. He saw hard lines first, dim light streaming through the windows at a severe angle, the wreckage strewn about the room. Then, as if she were approaching through a think bank of fog, he saw Eydris. She was slumped against a broken chair, and although he could make out few details, she looked exhausted.

"We need to follow him. We need to stop him." No one would ever recognize his voice again. He hardly recognized it himself. He could barely speak above a whisper. "We can't let this happen."

The blurry form of Eydris shook its head weakly. "I'm not moving. I can't move."

Her voice cracked, and he imagined the guilt and self-loathing she must feel for her weakness.

He nodded. "Stay, then. I'll send help."

She shook her head again. "Geir, how can you possibly be standing? You're dying. You must be. How can you even think of walking to the Bhorg? You'll never make it there, never mind stopping him."

The procession of images once more flashed past his mind, once again the children standing out in sharpest relief. He whispered, "I have to." And he pushed away from the wall, unsteady on his burning feet. "I have to."

She muttered something then. It might have been "Please, stay." But he couldn't be sure, and he couldn't stay, anyway.

He would come back for her, if he could.

*****

The journey to the front door seemed to last another eternity. Every step was an agony, every obstacle something to be cursed with all of his remaining strength. His vision was still hazy, more a blur of shadow and light with vague, indistinct details emerging and then sinking back down again.

But he got to the door and pushed it open. It was stuck, and he had to shoulder it aside; a whole new world of anguish, but his mind was focused on one thing as all other concerns fell away. He saw before him Drostin's smiling face, heard the old man's voice as he said, 'It was always me.' And behind the man, flickering in the fires of the deepest hells, the faces of countless children, their voices silenced forever.

That focus allowed him to push through the pain, force the door open, and stagger out into the street.

The quarter was nearly silent, which was odd considering the lateness of the day. He heard some distant shouting, nearby the crying of a child, and the barking and howling of dogs in the middle distance. But there was no one in the street. Around him the buildings were dark with an abandoned air he had never known in the grima quarter.

He oriented himself, the entire world strange and new through his damaged vision. He turned uphill, toward the center of the city and the king's stronghold at its heart, and stopped, his mouth falling open.

A column of smoke, thick and dark enough for even him to see against the dimming sky, rose from the direction of the Bhorg. Someone had set fire to the king's citadel. His face tightened, the pain fading a little with this new affront. As he peered around him he saw other, lighter columns as well. It was as if the entire city were alight.

With a grunt of pain, he pushed himself off, limping up the hill toward the distant tower of smoke.

As he turned a corner, leaving the quarter behind and stepping painfully into that shadowy border land between poverty and plenty, he saw the first bodies.

He stopped, stooping down with a grunt, to turn over the nearest corpse. It had been a woman, a civilian by her dress. Probably an innocent caught up in the fighting.

But who was fighting? What force had Drostin brought to bear against the king? Scanning the other bodies he saw no warriors, although there were several axes and a sword that would never have been left lying for long if the denizens of the grima quarter had been active. He reached out, flinching with the pain, to grab one of the axes, hefted it in his claw-like hand, and nodded.

When he caught up with Drostin, he would need a weapon.

He continued moving, seeing more bodies, other signs of violence, as he went up the hill. There had been looting here, several shops with their windows smashed out, their doors knocked askew. Perhaps the children of the quarter were active after all, just hunting larger game than an occasional fallen blade.

Still he saw no warriors among the dead. Then he began to see the occasional body of a hearth guard; piled around these was usually a drift of dead men and women in the garb of farmers and merchants.

Just like the crowds he had seen wandering the streets before Drostin's arrival.

The city looked like it had been sacked. How long had he been unconscious after Drostin's attack? He hadn't even thought to ask Eydris. Was this the same day? Was it the next?

Judging from his parched throat, it could have been hours, maybe a day or more. But no more than that.

Plenty of time, either way, for Connat to have fallen to a ragged mob of traitors, apparently.

How? How could this have happened? Maybe the Bhorg was still in loyal hands. Maybe the smoke he had seen was from some other structure in the center of the city. Maybe the stronghold itself still stood.

He grasped the axe head, using the weapon's haft as a cane, ignoring the screams of his tormented muscles, and tried to pick up his pace.

What could he do when he reached the Bhorg? The guards there would not know him. He was no servant of the king as far as they knew, no matter that he had thought he'd spent his entire life in loyal service. He was nothing to them; they would not welcome his help in defending the king.

Defending the king.

It all came back to that. All of the bloody actions of his life came back to that. If the king survived this day, then at least there would be that to balance the scales. It was not much. It would never be enough given all the innocent blood on the counterbalancing pan. But it would have to do.

He came across another pile of dead rebels and stopped, staring at them. In filthy tunics and loose trousers, the gleaming helms, shirts of chain, and round shields they bore stood out in a sharp contrast. The weapons gleamed, as if they had arrived fresh from the forge.

He had known, of course. Part of him had known from the moment he had looked down at the king's table board in the safe house and realized the significance of the placement of the pieces.

He looked down at his own axe, just to be sure. Flipping the blade delicately, he looked for the maker's mark on the blade. He found it at last, peering through the lowering fog of his new vision.

The forges of the Bhorg. The weapons had come from the king's own armory.

The caches that he himself had established had armed the rebels now burning down his city.

He stood, swaying in the middle of the street, before the pile of broken and bleeding bodies. He doubled over with a violent fit of coughing that sent a fountain of blood spraying out over the cobbles.

His mind swam, dizzy with pain and guilt, and he rested his elbows on his knees rather than straighten too quickly. When he did rise, his distant gaze drifted once more over the corpses before him, over the equipment he himself had placed in their hands.

The transgressions continued to pile up upon his soul.

The face smiled in his mind. The children melted into screaming red shadow. The roiling smoke rose up into the sky.

He needed to reach the king.

He limped past the pile of dead, breath hitching in his chest, damaged eyes focused on the smoke.

He needed to reach the king.

Chapter 29

He had followed Maiara, screaming her name, as the battle swept them apart. He had watched, helpless, as she had been forced out of the arming chamber and into the service sectors of the Bhorg. He had tried to keep up, but his surcoat marked him as an enemy of the king; no hearth guard wore such finery. They had shunned any of the trappings of the saemgard after that last battle and to be dressed this way now was an offense none of them were likely to forgive.

At every turn, he was set upon by heavily armored, fur-mantled hearth guard, their axes and swords thirsty for traitor blood. None of them knew for certain how this could have come to pass, but they were more than willing to blame the tall man in black, bright blue surcoat gleaming, who held the weapon of their order's disgraced forerunners.

The maekre blade was not a subtle weapon. As the first hearth guard charged him in the hall, he tried to be gentle, pulling his blows, striking with the flat every chance that he had. But even being hit with the flat of the enormous weapon meant being struck with a huge weight of steel swung at a prodigious speed.

He learned the hard way that using the dull back edge made almost no difference to his opponents.

Forcing his way through the defenders would have been nearly impossible without harming the men and women who sought to stop him. He did his best, but he needed to find Maiara, to reach the king, to put an end to all of this, to save as many lives as he could.

Including the king's.

With gritted teeth he forged his way deeper into the Bhorg, seeking to avoid confrontation when he could, to minimize damage where he was able, but ultimately focused on finding Maiara and keeping her safe.

Battle raged all around, Tsegan's rebels pushing the loyal warriors and hearth guard back into the fortress with the sheer weight of numbers despite their lack of training or even familiarity with their weapons.

The storehouse section of the Bhorg was a warren. He had not spent much time here in his youth, there was little reason for one of the king's elite warriors to wander around the storage rooms, kitchens, and broom closets.

But he had ventured here enough to remember it as a labyrinth.

The tangled passages were ramped softly, placing most of the actual storage chambers beneath the main level of the Bhorg. It was a little known fact, but the king's fortress in Connat actually took up a great deal of the hill upon which it stood, and most of that subterranean level was given over to storage, preparation, smithing, and servants' quarters. A person unfamiliar with the Bhorg could end up in the lower levels with no knowledge that they had sunk beneath the earth at all.

He could wander for days in the depths of this quarter and never find Maiara. He needed to make some decisions quickly before he was trapped down here, wading through hearth guard blood, while the prophecy played out somewhere far over his head.

The corridor swelled out into a sorting chamber, where orders and supplies were catalogued and prepared. The tables had been pushed aside or crushed beneath the weight of battle, with bodies scattered across the floor. Blood gleamed dully in the dim lantern light. He moved through the slaughter, trying his best not to focus on the blood splashed across the once-familiar granite of the walls, or the staring eyes of dead who might, if he were to look at them closely, been equally familiar.

He was nearly through the chamber when a shouted challenge rang out behind him.

"You! Rebel whore! Turn and meet justice!" The voice was higher pitched than the words might warrant, and when Eirik turned around, sure enough, it was a very young member of the hearth guard, leading several lower-ranked warriors through this section of the Bhorg, clearing out the rebels as they went.

In many ways, the whelp reminded him of Tyr.

"Leave, boy, and live." He had no interest in killing any more of Einar's subjects. His argument was with his king; his warriors were nothing more than pawns. But he was done tiptoeing. If these men wanted a fight, they had found one.

The boy coughed a laugh. At least, Eirik thought it was supposed to be a laugh. The boy's eyes were nervous, their whites glowing in the lantern light.

"Put down the sword and come with us."

That didn't seem likely. In the middle of an invasion of the Bhorg, they weren't going to be taking prisoners and leading them around. He would put down the maekre blade, and that would be the end of him.

It was hardly an honorable course of action. The child must have been as poisoned as his master, to suggest such a thing.

And that made killing him just a little bit easier.

With a roar, Eirik ran at the small cluster of warriors in answer.

The boy's gaze widened further and he took a quick step back, bumping into one of his henchmen, who staggered back, out of the way.

Eirik's first blow was with the flat of the blade, striking one of the warriors in the shoulder and smashing him into a wall where he collapsed, screaming, grabbing at his mangled joint.

The boy was no coward, Eirik would give him that. Rather than send his fighters after the big invader, the boy drew back with his long axe and rushed forward, his face twisted into a vicious snarl.

Eirik saw two others coming up fast behind their young commander. That was going to make dealing with the boy more difficult. He had wanted to bat him out of the way as he had the first man, but such a blow would leave him overextended, his side open to attack before he could bring the maekre blade back in on guard.

He rushed the boy, clashing with him much sooner than the lad could have expected, catching him in the chest with one shoulder and lifting him up into the air. He punched out with the hilt of his enormous sword, catching one of the other men in the jaw and smashing the bones of his face. The last man was caught flat-footed as Eirik carried the boy commander into him, sending them both crashing to the floor.

The man who attacked from the side caught Eirik completely by surprise. The axe head struck him in the ribs, and although the chain there held, the pain was intense. He thought he heard bone snapping.

With a growl, Eirik brought the maekre blade around in a swirling arc that caught the other man's axe, snagging on the beard of the weapon and tugging it from his hand. The axe landed amidst the splintered clutter of a shattered sorting table. He turned about to scan the room for further threats, and the boy was already up and rushing at him, two more warriors with him.

They were not going to allow him even a sop for his honor.

Eirik began to spin his huge sword in a blurring circle, weaving a defensive barrier around himself that could not be penetrated by the lighter axes of the attackers. Several attempts to strike through the whistling design resulted in harsh clangs that sent the axes skittering across the floor. When only one man was left with a weapon, he snaked his sword out of the defense maneuver and struck at the man with the pummel, catching him in the center of head and sending him staggering backward with a dazed, empty look on his face.

And then the boy stabbed Erick in the side. With a triumphant howl, the young hearth guard pulled the thin-bladed dagger free, a spray of Eirik's blood coming with it.

Eirik felt himself grow instantly weak. The wound wasn't mortal; only a finger's length or so of the blade glistened red. But he would bleed like a stuck pig, now, his strength running down his side in a hot red tide.

Another man rose up on this other side, heavy axe raised to strike, and Eirik had no choice. He speared the man through the chest. His foe stumbled to a halt, axe falling harmlessly away, staring at the length of thick steel sunk through his body. With a soft noise, he slid away, eyes glazing over.

Eirik growled low in his throat, turning to see if their friend's death had dissuaded the others. If anything, they were even more determined now. With a howl, they fell on him, leaving him no room for mercy. He punched out with the hilt of his sword, crushing one man's face, and then slashed around, taking another man across the face, sheering the top of his head clean away with the weight and momentum of his blade.

The boy, the only foe left standing, roared defiance and rushed at Eirik, an axe high.

The old anger boiled up within him as he parried the falling weight of sharpened steel, trying again and again to strike a blow that might spare the lad. The boy was no match in skill or strength, but he was good enough to deny such an opening. Eirik's rage continued to rise as it became more and more obvious what he would have to do, and when he finally struck, abandoning all pretense at avoiding a fatal blow, he roared in fury.

The maekre blade lashed out and removed the boy's head from his shoulders, sending his body toppling to the blood-slick floor.

He winced in pain as he imagined Tyr's features on the tumbling head.

Eirik roared like a wounded beast, holding one hand to his side and glaring at the bodies strewn about him.

This was all Einar's fault. If the man had not failed in his own promise, if he had become the king he was meant to be and not such a wretched tyrant, each of these men would still be alive, and this brave boy would have a full life ahead of him. Each drop of blood spilled in the city above or in the halls of the Bhorg itself owed only one man for the spilling.

This was no one's fault but Einar's, and the man had to be stopped.

Eirik was in a twisted nightmare, a dark, haunted realm of past visions and present blood. And one man had chased him into this shadow world where nothing good could survive. One man had hounded him from his first defeat, throughout the fyrdar kingdoms and the squalor of the tourney circuit he had retreated to, and even up into the mountains where he had searched for the illusion of forgiveness and redemption.

He looked down at his blood-drenched blade. There was no redemption for him. He had failed, and the king he had lost everything for had hounded him like a beast of prey throughout his sad, pathetic life.

Einar had proven himself, long ago, an unworthy king. And the fruit of that betrayal quickened now in the halls of the Bhorg.

Fate had chosen him as the instrument of justice. Prophecy be damned, Einar deserved to lose his kingdom. And if, in the process, he lost his life as well? Well, that outcome didn't seem so terrible to Eirik now, wading through the blood of innocent men and women whose only crime was the same he had committed all those years ago; trust in a faithless king.

Maiara would have to find her own way to the throne room if fate wished it. He stalked from the juncture hall, glancing to either side to gather his bearings, and headed back up into the main level of the stronghold.

If destiny wanted him to confront Einar in his own den, who was Eirik Hastiin to deny her?

*****

The halls were like a slaughterhouse, with bodies stacked in every corner, sprawled across the floor, splashed with blood and gore. The heat and the smell were creating a horrible brew that made it hard to breathe, and he found himself hoping that the upper regions of the Bhorg had better ventilation. He had never really had occasion to wonder about such things when he was younger.

As he moved through the halls with silent, bloody intent, his gaze fell to the bodies he passed. Many of them, even here, were hearth guard or Einar's lesser warriors. Many more, however, were Tsegan's rebels, and he found his anger building with each young body he passed, twisted in the agonies of a violent death that he knew would never have been visited upon them if it weren't for Einar's rule.

It was amazing, all those years spent running from the king, that he never noticed how bad the man's reign had become.

But an insidious little voice whispered in the back of his mind in counterpoint to his pulsing anger … was there not enough guilt to spread around?

He passed a young girl clutching a shining new axe in her cold hands, eyes staring blankly at the ceiling with a vague, worried expression. Was that girl here because Einar was a bad king? Had he done something to her or her family that had driven her from her safe home on some farm, or in some merchant's house, to come and die here in the basement of a dark and foreboding citadel?

Or was she here because of Tsegan and Maiara?

Eirik had been present at every one of the old man's meetings. He had a good idea how many people the girl had spoken to. And he knew that just counting the dead he had seen here, never mind the men and women still running rampant through the Bhorg, there were more than all the people who had attended those meetings.

How many people in the fortress that night had died, would die, for a girl they had never even met?

He had no evidence of Einar's wrongdoing other than his own experience of being the man's hunted quarry. But none of this would have happened if he were not a tyrant; he knew that. He had to know that. He clung to it, ignoring all else, and it stoked his anger to new heights.

As he came back up into the main level of the fortress, there were even more bodies thrown throughout the halls. How many had already died? Scores? It had to be more than that. There was more than a score in the arming chamber alone. Hundreds? Easily, given all the bodies he had passed in the storage level.

Thousands?

It seemed horrific, but if he looked back at the crowds they had fought through in the streets, and the bodies he had seen just in the sections he had walked through ... if he multiplied that to fill up the rest of the Bhorg with this horror?

It could very well be thousands dead and dying at this very moment.

He shook his head grimly, looking to either side as he began to jog down the main entrance hall toward the living quarters, the king's meeting chambers, and the throne room at the center of the structure.

Astrigir bled tonight, and it would be years in the healing. Years.

The trust of the people was paramount for a ruler to rule effectively. And a ruler needed to be able to trust the people as well. There was a compact between the ruler and the ruled, especially in fyrdar society, that could not be broken without shattering the entire structure.

He passed another grotesque display, this time two men, their allegiance unclear by their dress and equipment, embraced in agonized death, each with a dagger buried in the other's stomach.

That trust had been shattered here, and it would be a generation or more before it could be fully repaired.

And that was the moment he realized what he was seeing.

Twenty years ago, as a young man, he had ridden forth from these halls for his friend and king to defeat the last defenders of Vestan and begin a new era of strength and power for his kingdom, and all the fyrdar. Instead, he had been present for the worst defeat any of the Broken Kingdoms had ever known. Astrigir had never fully recovered. Even today, as he strode through the halls of the Bhorg, striking down any man who dared to challenge him, it was but a shadow of the realm it had been on that morning of his youth.

If that battle on the banks of the Merrik had torn down this once mighty land, how much worse would this night's toll be?

His pace slowed as he realized the price Astrigir would pay. The fruit of a generation of warriors lay contorted on the cold stones of the Bhorg. Who would be left to defend their borders should the other fyrdar realms, learning of this folly, choose to attack?

What hope would they have if Kun Makha, gods and spirits forfend, decided to bring Astrigir back under its domain?

No matter the outcome, Astrigir was going to be vulnerable for a generation. Nothing could stop that now.

And no matter how much blame there was to spread about, there was only one man who had made this night necessary.

Someone dashed out of a side corridor toward him and he made no effort to spare them. The maekre blade slashed out as he gave them a sidelong glance. The weapon took the figure full in the chest, knocking it back down the passageway with a shriek.

He was in the long receiving hall now. He had many fondest memories of this place, before time and Einar's venom had turned them to black regrets. He shied from the splashes of dark blood on the walls, stepped over twisted bodies littering the floor, and felt his anger rise with every step that squelched through the noisome mire.

The stonework became lighter as he strode down the hall. Grey granite was supplemented with polished marble; the lamps growing brighter and more frequent, mercilessly illuminating the horrible red price of battle.

And then he was there. The grand entrance to the throne room with its abstract dragons, traditional lintels carved into the marble, was before him. The stations for the honor guard were empty, of course, the torn and ruined bodies of defender and attacker alike scattered across the mosaic floor.

Both sides equally betrayed by their king.

He swept into the hall. Dim, crimson flashes flared around the periphery of his vision as he scanned the large chamber. A band of Tsegan's rebels had made it this far, but they held back at the rear of the hall. They were clearly readying themselves for another charge, based upon the high-water mark of dead and dying that lay scattered across the middle of the room.

Overhead, wide skylights let the final, fading light of sunset wash through in heavy, dust-filled bars of crimson.

Across the hall he saw them, then.

Cowering down behind a barricade of overturned benches and side-tables was a line of hearth guard, their weapons held at the ready. He was struck by how young they looked. Were there no older warriors to give their king guidance?

But then, of course, there weren't. Eirik's generation had been thrown away on that feckless battle twenty years ago.

Behind the line of defenders cowered a small group of men and women dressed in the finery of nobles, with another escort of warriors standing nearby. A smaller group stood there as well, apart from the earls and thanes, with their own honor guard separating them from attacker and defender both. There was something different about those men and women, their clothing and weapons strange, long straight hair black as midnight.

But Eirik was hardly thinking at that point. All of the blood and the pain he had seen were churning inside him, deafening him to any thoughts but the cries for vengeance and justice echoing in his mind.

And then he saw him.

Einar Jalen looked very much as he had on the morning of the battle, all those years ago. The intervening time had been kind to the king; his blond hair and beard only slightly touched with the grey that had long ago claimed Eirik's own temples.

His blue eyes were not cowed, but alight with fury and indignation as he muttered commands to those around him, a long sword clutched in one hand. His other hand was around the shoulders of a tall woman standing beside him, her own face regal, gaze clear of any fear.

By her clothing and coloring she had to be from the empire of Kun Makha. She stood tall and straight, her bearing as stately as any queen.

Perhaps it was too late. Perhaps Kun Makha had already come to claim Astrigir.

The rage within him flared, burning away all doubt, all guilt, and all concern for anything beyond the man who had hounded him for decades.

Eirik hefted his maekre blade, the weapon identical to the ceremonial sword his king had given him so long ago. His vision narrowed until he saw nothing but Einar, standing amidst his last remaining defenders and the oyathey warriors of Kun Makha.

He had no room for thoughts of Maiara's offered mercy for the king. Einar Jalen must die.

With a scream, he pushed past the rebels milling about the doorway, knocking several of them to the blood-slick floor in his haste to get to the king.

He saw movement, vaguely perceived through the fog of his rage, as defenders moved to intercept him, but the months and years of training and native ability were his once again, and the enormous blade wove back and forth, defending from blows that rained in from all sides, counterattacking with slashes that sent the men and women of the hearth guard staggering away.

And all that time, he did not look away from Einar.

And so he was staring into the man's face when the king saw him. He watched as those familiar blue eyes narrowed sharply and then widened in recognition.

A lightning flash swept across the cold determination of that face.

For a brief moment, gone before it really registered, it seemed as if Einar had almost smiled.

It was not the smile of the hunter bringing his quarry to bay. It was not the smile of an evil tyrant whose infernal plans have finally come to fruition.

For a moment, just a moment, the merest sliver of time, a smile of relief and glad surprise lit the king's face.

Eirik was blinded by the rage that smile ignited behind his eyes. The expression on the king's face was gone before he could even be sure of what he had seen, replaced with rising horror and sick surprise, but that one moment burned itself into Eirik's mind, and ignited a wrathful fire that put his earlier fury to shame.

"Einar!" He screamed, his booming voice echoing through the space. "Einar, search no further, brother! I am come!"

The rebels behind him backed away, the defenders around the king stared at him in awe as recognition dawned on their blood-streaked faces. Only the oyathey were unmoved, readying their long weapons, expression calm and calculating.

Eirik charged. He felt a blow against his shoulder, ignoring the flare of pain. He felt another strike his hip, felt something tear, a hot wetness running down his leg, and it didn't even slow him down. His burning gaze was locked on Einar's face as it began to twist slowly in surprise and fear.

Two hearth guard, a tall man and a powerful, low-built woman, leapt in front of him, each wielding a long, flashing spear.

Eirik laughed.

The maekre blade had been designed, in part, to answer the Vestan tendency to arm their lesser warriors with long spears. The weight of the weapon made it perfect for shifting the long shafts out of line when they were in the hands of weak, untrained fighters. When they were properly wielded, the heavy sword did even better than that.

With one prodigious swing he smashed the two spears, their heads spinning away into the shadows, and with the return swing, his momentum unchanged, he removed the hearth guards' heads from their necks.

The bodies tumbled to the floor on either side, a flood of hot crimson washing out of them and over the smooth stone.

Eirik stood between the two bodies, panting, and grinned a blood-spattered smile at the man who had once been his closest friend.

And then he charged.

"Eirik, no!"

It was a familiar voice. A voice he had not expected to hear again. He heard it through a fog of rage and pain and gave it no more heed than he would a bad dream after a night of drinking.

He continued to close the distance between himself and the tyrant king.

"Eirik, wait!"

But he wouldn't wait. The hearth guard before him were closing ranks. They saw their deaths in his eyes, he knew that, but they prepared to defend their king anyway. They, at least, would die having fulfilled their duty.

And then something crashed into him from the side, bearing him down beneath a flurry of slapping blows that drove his heavy sword to the side. They rolled when they hit, tumbling across the floor, splashing through puddles of blood and gore, and came to rest in the empty space between the two poised forces.

Eirik's head whipped around, looking for whoever had had the gall to interrupt his vengeance. Tyr was crouched nearby, looking up at him, disbelieving.

The entire room was steeped in silence, and Eirik rose slowly, maekre blade dangling from one hand, to look all about him.

Everyone in the room was staring at him.

He saw recognition in many of the faces. That was to be expected from the rebels, many of whom had followed him into this hellish maze, or seen him during Tsegan's ridiculous gatherings. But the expressions on the hearth guards' faces were far more difficult to fathom. He saw recognition and awe. He saw terror and respect.

But mostly what he saw when he looked at them was confusion and surprise.

And that confusion and surprise was compounded a hundred-fold when he turned back to glare at Einar.

And that, finally, stopped him.

There was no anger on that face. It was not the expression of a tyrant, finally confronted by his righteous, aggrieved servant. There was no shame there, or fury, or fear.

Einar looked surprised, and confused. The ghost of that smile still lingered on his lips, although his eyes were now dark with concern.

And there was nothing right with any of that at all.

Chapter 30

Tyr scrambled up, grunting with the pain. He had smashed his knee against the stones and several of Eirik's armor plates had dug savagely into his skin as they rolled. But at least it seemed as if he had broken his master's momentum.

Well, at least he wasn't alone anymore.

Eirik was standing still above him, staring at the knot of men and women at the far end of the hall. The small group of hearth guard Tyr had followed to the throne room were staring at him and the old warrior, frozen in place at the small side entrance to the chamber.

Tyr looked back behind them to where a contingent from Tsegan's army of farmers was standing in their newly-acquired gear, no more willing to move in the sudden stillness than anyone else.

The throne room had not been spared the bloody marks of battle. Bodies were strewn all over the intricate designs of the floor. Several of them showed the unmistakable signs of violence left behind by an expertly-wielded maekre blade. The fading red light washing down from overhead bathed the entire scene in crimson. The moaning of the wounded was a soft counterpoint to the silence throughout the chamber.

And as Eirik stood, gaze locked on the opposite end of the room, Tyr finally turned and, for the first time in his life, saw the man who had hounded his master for more years than he himself had been alive.

Einar Jalen stood before his heavy wooden throne; he was a big man, bigger even than Eirik in his full war coat and fur mantle. His blond hair showed only the first strands of encroaching grey. He did not shave the sides of his head as Eirik did, but kept it in a full, wild mane. His beard was more neatly kept than Eirik's, and his face not nearly so scarred or world-weary. Otherwise, the men were eerily similar.

After spending the last five years of his own life running from this man, he would have expected those piercing grey eyes to be flaring with hatred, the noble features twisted with fury at this invasion of his stronghold.

Instead, all Tyr saw was confusion and surprise.

If Einar had been hunting Eirik all this time, why would he be so surprised to find him leading the rebellion?

The doubts that had begun to churn in the depths of Tyr's mind surged up again. So much of this made no sense, given what they thought they knew.

Einar should be screaming in rage, foaming at the mouth, demanding his remaining guards scour the rebels from his halls. Instead, he was standing there, staring at Eirik with a dazed, questioning expression.

Tyr took in the rest of the scene around the king. The throne was enormous, its arms and back carved with entangled dragons whose strangely geometric designs were mesmerizing. Several of the people standing around Einar were jarls or hearth guard champions. But what of the warriors in light leather and chain? And who was the tall oyathey woman standing beside the king?

The woman was dressed in a gown of vibrant reds and whites, her long black hair hanging low over one shoulder. Her features were even more regal than the king's, and she surveyed them all with the proud bearing of a woman more annoyed and offended than concerned.

What was going on?

"What is going on here?" The voice boomed from the back of the chamber, echoing painfully down the length of the throne room, rolling back over them from the far wall.

It was a voice he had never heard before a few months ago, but a voice he would never now forget.

Tyr turned slowly, along with almost every other person in the hall, to look at the crowd of rebels in the rear of the chamber. They parted slowly, turning as well, to reveal a kindly-looking old man in dark robes standing there, glowering at the scene laid out before him.

"What in the names of all the gods and spirits is happening here?" He moved forward, glaring to either side, where the rebels shrunk back from him, mouths agape.

Waves of power seemed to roll off the old man, and there was no denying his immense presence as he strolled forward.

"Protector, do your duty!" Those dark, baleful eyes fell upon Eirik, and Tyr felt himself sag with relief that Tsegan was not looking at him. "Destiny must be fulfilled, Saemgard, if the realm is to survive!"

Eirik's eyes tightened as he stared at the old man, and Tyr felt sorry for his master with a pity stronger than he had ever felt before, even in his master's deepest despair.

Eirik's look darted from Tsegan to the king and back again. Following that gaze, Tyr was looking at the king when the man saw Tsegan for the first time.

The man looked as if he had seen a spirit walk straight out of the wall.

Einar Jalen's eyes were wide, his mouth hanging open. Around him, the older nobles looked the same, staring at Tsegan as if the old man was some kind of monster, writhing in from the darkest sagas.

The king's jaw worked soundlessly, and for the first time, the woman beside him looked concerned, reaching out with one hand and whispering something in his ear.

And then Tsegan's gaze fell upon the woman. He smiled one of his kindly smiles and sighed. There was something about that sound that caused the flesh between Tyr's shoulder blades to crawl.

The room, close and humid before, seemed stifling now.

Tsegan turned back to Eirik, his expression bright, his face firm. "Protector, your entire life has led you to this moment. Your journey ends here." He twisted slightly to point toward the cluster of hearth guard standing around the king. "There is the wellspring of your life's pain, Eirik Hastiin. There is the man who took all the promise of your youth and twisted it into something dark and vile and empty."

The old man turned fully toward the king and his voice rose until it shook the very stones beneath Tyr's feet. "There is the tyrant who has taken the kingdom you love, your home, the realm you pledged your life to defend, and brought it all to the very brink of doom!"

Tyr glanced back at the rebels but saw that the old man's voice had had the same effect on them. They were shrinking back, toward the entrances to the throne room, all eyes wide.

Eirik, however, stood firm.

The old warrior's face was hard, his teeth grinding together within the tangle of his beard. It looked almost as if he was shaking, fighting some terrible battle within his own mind.

Around the king, the earls were whispering to each other in a violent hissing, pulling at the king's clothing as children desperate to get their father's attention. But the king stared only at Tsegan, now, and for the first time in a long time, Tyr found himself wondering once more about the old man's identity. The king and his court were certainly acting as if the old man had stepped out of the ancient sagas and into this blood-splashed warren.

"Saemgard, do your duty to the realm!" Tsegan pointed to the king with one claw-like finger, and his voice seemed to carry the weight of a hundred years and more behind it.

Sweat trickled down Tyr's face, and he wondered if it was just the tension of the moment, or if it really was starting to burn like a desert in the dark, stone room.

Eirik stared at Einar and his shaking subsided. The big man took up his maekre blade in both hands, twisting a tortured shriek from the leather in his tightened fists. He took a step toward the king, and the hearth guard between them shifted their focus from the old man to the larger, more obvious threat. The warriors that had led Tyr to the throne room shifted their own positions, moving across the floor to stand between the king and the warrior stalking down the hall toward him.

The squat hearth guard with the long blond tail cast a warning glare at Tyr, and he stared back, no idea now what was supposed to happen.

None of this felt as he had imagined on the long journey north from the mountains.

Where was Maiara? There was no guarantee, given the savagery of the fighting within the Bhorg, that she was even alive. That thought set a chill settling into his stomach that was almost enough to ward off the rising heat. She couldn't be dead; she couldn't be. His mouth twisted as he asked himself what would happen to all their grand schemes if they went through all of this, tore down the king, but had lost Maiara?

And where was Chagua? The fight in the arming chamber had separated them all, but even then, after the initial attack, the islander had seemed eager to avoid battle, skirting the fighting as the surge of bodies pushed them all apart.

There was no way the islander was dead. Tyr refused to believe anyone in the Bhorg, no matter their numerical superiority, would be able to defeat the warrior from the northern islands.

Maybe Chagua had found Maiara, and they were safe together? Just because Tyr had had no luck finding her, didn't mean a man like Chagua, with far more experience and training, had failed as well.

So, instead of the four of them standing bravely side by side before a shrinking tyrant, the light of imminent justice flickering in his gaze, he was lost in this tangled mess. The king was hardly the picture of a bloodthirsty despot, abandoned in the last moments by mercenary guards. Instead, he seemed confused and surprised. Understandably angry, of course, but still in full possession of his mind. Scarcely the raving madman Tyr had imagined him to be.

And instead of Eirik standing bravely before him, challenging him to a duel right out of the ancient sagas, his master was torn, shaking and miserable, needing Tsegan's goading to do what needed to be done.

Maiara and Chagua were gone; lost somewhere in the maze of the Bhorg amidst the most horrific, bloody fighting imaginable.

And then there was Tyr himself. Loyal squire, devoted follower, and the man who had tried to tackle his master in the final moments of his grand charge.

None of it was as it should have been, and he felt tears of frustration rising in his eyes as the full muddled reality of their situation, whatever it was, struck him at last.

"Master, wait!" How long had it been since he had called Eirik master out loud? Their relationship had changed so much over the past few years, as the once-great warrior had fallen farther and farther into despair, farther and farther from the promise of greatness whose echo had called to the young, impressionable boy Tyr had been.

But here he was now, the very image of a hero. And it was all wrong.

Eirik paused in his advance, looking over his shoulder toward Tyr, his craggy features twisting once more as the rage within him surged up to overwhelm his doubts.

Tsegan glared back at Tyr, and for the first time, there was no sign of the kindly old man at all.

Tyr had seen Tsegan annoyed and frustrated, he had often seen the old man's face tighten with irritation during their long winter together. He had heard sharp words directed at every member of their band, aside from Chagua of course, more times than he cared to count. In fact, if he had been pressed, he would have had to admit that he found Tsegan Aqisiaq to be a bit on the grumpy side, on the whole.

But he had never seen the expression that contorted the old man's face now.

Tsegan's eyes burned with contempt as he glared at him, and he felt the temperature rise all around, as if someone had lit an enormous fire right behind him. There was no sign of the kindly old man at all. The very lines of Tsegan's face seemed to writhe and change. The familiar gleam of humor was gone, replaced with utter and total scorn.

"Master, wait." The mocking words dripped with biting sarcasm, whispered with a derision that chilled him despite the rising heat.

The old man took a step toward him, and behind his white halo of hair, Tyr could see Eirik, watching them both with a wild expression.

"Master, wait." This time a contemptuous whisper, soaked in malice.

Tyr stared back at the old man, resolved not to retreat a single step.

But he remembered, in a brilliant flash, the devastation the old man had meted out in the mountain valley against their mysterious attackers. He remembered flesh blasted from dry, splintered bone. He remembered the howls of agony from within the swirling curtains of sand and dust.

He remembered the temperature rising to a desert blast as those men and women had died screaming.

And he took a step back.

Tsegan smiled, but it was not the familiar, kindly smile of a grandfather, or even an old mentor, amused by the antics of the younger generation.

Tsegan smiled at him with the expression of a cruel child who has just brought down a squirrel with an arrow and realized the little creature was still alive; still within the scope of his cruelty.

Tsegan continued to approach; the only movement in the entire room, and finally Tyr felt the wall behind him. The stone was not cool as it had been, but rough and dry and hot, as if it had been out in the sun on a scorching day.

Tyr would not look away. He refused to allow Eirik's last view of him to be that of a coward pleading for his life before ... whatever this creature they had all taken as a friend had become.

There was a commotion at another side door. Everyone, the old man included, turned to see what was happening now.

Chagua rushed in, gasping for breath, his thin-seeming sword clutched in one tight fist. The islander scanned the long room in a moment. His attention settled on Eirik, then Tsegan and Tyr. He was splashed with blood, his light robes streaked with red. His expression was hooded as he met Tsegan's glare, and Tyr felt another shift in the world around him.

If they couldn't trust Tsegan, how could they trust Chagua, the man who had served him with such unquestioning loyalty?

The islander had lost a great deal of the reserve that had made him seem so alien and strange during the early days of winter. They had never discussed it, but he knew that he, for one, had begun to think of the big dark-skinned man as a friend. He knew Maiara felt the same, and even Eirik seemed to have thawed, after the worst of his training was behind them.

He ignored the twist of pain at the thought of Maiara, and the realization that she wasn't with Chagua after all.

Realizing he might not be able to trust the islander meant that might be a moot point anyway.

If Tsegan was truly an enemy, and Chagua was his servant, was it so out of the realm of possibility that the islander had already killed Maiara, taking advantage of the chaos of battle to remove her from the equation? Might that not be her blood, splattered on his fine robes?

"Why?" He blurted the word without thinking about it. He seemed to be doing that a lot lately.

Tsegan turned back to him, and for a moment, Tyr had to wonder why, indeed? Why had he shouted out a question that would bring the old man's attention back to him when only moments ago he would have given up a kingdom to have him look away?

But instead of cowering back, he asked again, "Why?"

The old man raised a single eyebrow. "Why?"

It came surging up now, as if Tyr had downed too much mead and was losing his dinner. "Why all of this?" He gestured wildly with his hands, realizing suddenly that he had lost his axe somewhere along the way.

He didn't care. It was all too elaborate, too involved. No matter who or what this man was, what could he possibly be hoping to accomplish with this elaborate scheme? It seemed like a lot of trouble to go through to kill a king, considering the hellish powers this man was able to command.

"Why?"

A completely different smile oozed across Tsegan's wrinkled face. "Why." He repeated, looking Tyr up and down as if surveying a thrall for purchase. "Why, indeed."

The old man's gaze shifted back to Chagua, then to Eirik, still standing like a statue, locked between the silent, terrified rebels and the king's wary guardians.

"You are oyathey. Why do you do this?" The new voice was strong, ringing out from beside the king and startling several of the hearth guard.

The tall woman standing beside the king watched Tsegan with a wary expression, her face a stony mask of noble indifference. "Your silence does not become you, old man. Answer your empress, if you will not answer the boy. Why?"

Tsegan's gaze flashed with dark amusement as he turned once more to face the king and his retinue. "Why do I do this? Why, as an oyathey, would I go against my empress like this?"

He turned to the rebels, the amusement bubbling over. "A better question, my friends, might be why is Aiyana Rayen, Empress of Kun Makha, here in the very heart of the Bhorg?"

A low, suspicious muttering swept through the crowded rebels. They understood very little of what was happening, but they knew Einar was a tyrant, and many of them had suspected his ties to the empire. If that was the empress of Kun Makha, it only served to prove their suspicions.

Tyr watched the man play the emotions of the mob like a master minstrel on an old, familiar lute.

Chagua still stood by the door, sword in hand, staring now at the king and the empress through dark, narrowed eyes. Eirik was still between the forces as if locked between his present and his past, vibrating violently with the tension between the two. The mob of rebels at the back of the room, growing larger as more and more of their fellows found the throne room, shifted uneasily, almost as if they were gathering themselves for a charge no matter what Eirik did.

Then Tsegan shrugged. He gave a little chuckle that was so familiar to Tyr, he shuddered to hear it in this new context.

"Why." The old man repeated yet again, but now turning away from the mob, past Eirik, and looked down the hall to the cluster of hearth guard and jarls.

"Why, why, why, why, why." The old man rubbed his wizened hands together, his shoulder raised as if in anticipation.

"It always comes down to that, does it not, Aiyana? Why are you here? Why did your father die so young? Why could you not have been a better daughter?" He shifted his attention to Einar. "Why couldn't I realize my father's dreams? Why did I throw my kingdom's strength away? Why, why, why, why, why?"

He laughed a vile laugh and continued. "And I shall forgive you this once the insult, my dear. I am no more oyathey than your fellow sovereign, there." He gestured with one hand toward the tall king and then withdrew his hand, cocking his head to one side with another cackle. "Considerably less than he, even, when you think about it."

Something seemed to break within Einar, and he surged forward, held back only by two burly hearth guard. "Chogan! Betrayer! You abandoned me! Who are you? What are you?"

That seemed to amuse the old man even more. "Indeed. Sorry. An array of questions I didn't even think to add to the list."

He shrugged, working his shoulder muscles as if preparing to lift something heavy. "Sadly, it is the lot of mortal man to die with so many of his questions left unanswered."

With a single gesture of his hand, a leaping, swirling snake of living sand erupted from the floor by his side.

The temperature within the throne room flared as every drop of moisture was wicked away by the driving heat.

The rebels screamed as one, shying away from the specter, with no idea what it might mean. Tyr flinched as well, more from knowledge than ignorance, however.

The wild, hissing rumble of sand was met with shouts and yells from the hearth guard as they closed ranks, and then cries of surprise and screams of pain as the old man's power hit the first line of defenders. It swept along their position, tearing weapons and shields from hands, sending helms sailing back into the people behind them, ripping at their furs and scratching against the leather and chain of their armor.

The men and women cowered away from the impact, including several members of the group who had led Tyr to the throne room. The squat man who had led them was one of the first to feel the true fury of Tsegan's sand storm, as his deep-throated shouts turned to high-pitched screams of pain, his flesh flensed away by the scouring wind.

The men and women around the chamber screamed as if echoing the man's pain, and surged away from the violent, impossible force tearing the defenders down. The rebels pushed back, trampling one another as they tried to flee. The surviving hearth guard pushed the king and the empress against the far wall, holding weapons and shields bravely, if senselessly, before them.

The wind continued to howl. The dying continued to shriek in agony.

And above it all, cold despite the driving heat of the desert, the old man laughed.

Chapter 31

The pain was all-consuming. Every step sent jarring waves of gut-twisting agony through his tortured body, but Geir would not stop, could not stop. If he paused, even for a moment, he would never move again.

He had found the gates to the Bhorg smashed open, their guards dead or gone. There were bodies everywhere, contorted in the infinite poses of violent death. They had been thick in the courtyard before the stronghold, piled in drifts at the front gate, and then scattered across the bridge before the dark, broken-toothed entrance.

All of this, seen through the distant haze of his ruined eyes, was like nothing so much as a nightmare come to life as the sun set in a blaze of crimson glory in the west, behind distant mountains who threw their long shadows across the kingdom in jagged slashes of darkness and red light.

He had stumbled over the bodies, often falling to his hands and knees to continue his progress. Within the gates, he had found himself in a wide chamber that had hosted an entire bloody battle all its own. The light was dim, rendering his failing vision even more cloudy and indistinct, although the cool of the dark, ancient stones was a relief to his tortured skin.

The king.

The only truly coherent thought running through his mind now, under and over and through the waves of pain that set his entire body shaking, was that he needed to find the king.

Geir had never been in the Bhorg, of course. He had always believed Drostin's tales of a thankful king forced to distance himself from the darker, but no less necessary, tasks of trusted Shadows. He had often stood in the courtyard beyond the gates, staring at the Bhorg, dreaming of one day being welcomed by his king, thanked for his service, and accepted for his unwavering loyalty, even as he knew none of those things could ever happen.

He choked on a sob as the weight of the flickering visions threatened to bear him to the floor. His throat was raw, hollow with an aching sorrow that demanded he shed tears his ravaged eyes could no longer shed. There was wetness on his cheeks, but he knew now it was blood, seeping through the cracks in his burned and shrunken flesh. He had dressed Eydris's wounds enough to imagine the nightmare visage his face had become.

The halls were empty. Distant shouting caught his attention, but in the huge room, its far walls hidden in shadow and the swimming fog of his own vision, he couldn't tell where it was coming from. It seemed to echo all around him, offering no guidance at all.

He wandered the hall, hands outstretched like a blind beggar in the street. The contempt with which he had looked upon such men throughout his lifetime came back to haunt him now. Such men had always seemed to him to be utterly useless; useless to themselves, to their families, to their king. Again he sobbed, the dry, hacking sound mocking in his ears. He knew, now, how useless they were.

He went right first, for no reason he could have explained. He found a high, wide entrance to another system of halls. He could feel the hay beneath his feet and figured that there might be stables down that corridor. He didn't think the king would keep his stables near the throne room.

He moved along the wall, touching it when he needed reassurance that he had not drifted too far away, until he found himself before a brightly-lit corridor. It was not as wide as the first, but here more lanterns glowed within his personal fog as the passage fell away into the distance. This seemed the most likely, to him. Directly across from the main entrance to the fortress and better lit, it made the most sense that this would be the hall down which guests and jarls and earls would come.

The concentration it took to put one foot before the next, not to topple over and collapse in pain and exhaustion, was all that kept the cascade of images from overwhelming him. But the well-lit corridor was easier to manage, with most of the dead having been pushed to the walls or piled up in various intersections, and that gave his mind too much time to focus; to see; to remember.

It had made so much sense when he was younger, desperately seeking guidance and a role to play within the kingdom he had loved all his life. After the Battle of Merrik Ford, when wise Chogan's assured victory had turned to blood and dust, his anger had been all-consuming. He refused to continue as a mere fighter in the king's service, to retreat to the darkness of the Bhorg as the world spun out of control beyond the kingdom's borders. Astrigir had been dealt a terrible blow by dark, dishonorable forces that had nearly brought the realm to ruin. Obviously King Einar's enemies had infiltrated the saemgard and led their brethren to the slaughter.

He had desperately needed to strike a return blow against those who sought to bring his kingdom down. When Drostin had found him, hunting down rumors of a survivor among the saemgard who might lead him to the architects of that terrible massacre, he would have been willing to believe almost anything.

Drostin had taken him into the ranks of the Shadows, explained the needs of every king to have men and women willing to do the unthinkable in the name of the realm's stability, and he had taken to it without a second thought.

It had seemed so simple a prospect. Of course it made more sense for a single man, or family, to die quietly than have them ignite a bloody rebellion that would kill hundreds of their neighbors and shake the foundations of the now-fragile kingdom. Of course, it was better that a child with a terrible affliction die than the disease spread throughout a region.

He had hunted the king's enemies, infiltrated rebel cells, tracked down dissidents and insurgents who threatened Einar's rule. He had even spent months at a time set to hunting down the last surviving saemgard, although he had never found the man.

Aside from these many fyrdar threats, he had spent years hunting oyathey scouts moving into the southern mountains. Drostin was convinced something was happening in the mountains involving these strange agents of Kun Makha, some mysterious project years in the making, and Drostin was certain it threatened to bring the entire kingdom down.

He staggered to a halt. Except that Drostin was no true advisor to the king. He was no Lord of Shadows, watching out for the king's best interests from behind the throne, helping to keep Astrigir healthy and hale.

And that meant that every task Geir had done for the beast had to be doubted. Every death, every moment of torture he had visited upon the oyathey he had found in the mountains; everything had been in service, not to the noble king he loved, but to a demonic creature who served some dark, evil purpose all his own.

Through his own need to serve, Geir's entire life had been twisted to the purposes of a terrible enemy of the realm.

The sounds of distant fighting swelled to the left as he approached an intersection, and he shied away. If he was dragged into a battle now, he would never survive to reach his goal.

He needed to find the king.

He shrank into a shadow, huddled there like a child hiding from an angry father, and soon the sounds faded away. No fighting erupted around the corner, no angry warriors came running by looking for someone to fight.

When he was confident they had moved on, he rose, hissing through clenched teeth and bleeding lips at the pain, and set off again.

It was a group of rebels, not the hearth guard, who finally overtook him in the hall. He flinched away from their raucous shouting, raising one hand as if to ward off a blow as his shoulder settled against the cool stone of the wall.

"Please—" He hissed in his ravaged voice. But he doubted they could hear it above their own shouts. There didn't seem to be any foes about, and even as he peered up at them, he couldn't tell if they were hearth guard or rebels.

When he noticed one of the figures in the back carrying a heavy, shining candelabrum, he realized they had to be rebels, taking advantage of the chaos to loot the king's palace.

He gritted his teeth as his eyes narrowed, but he knew there was nothing he could do. If he attracted their anger in any way, they could kill him without effort.

He collapsed against the wall, the weight of his failure combining with the flickering images that were never far from his thoughts now. He was at the mercy of a mob of traitor thugs and thieves, and no closer to finding his king.

"By the gods, what happened to you?" The voice was aghast, and Geir nodded as much as his tormented skin would allow. He remembered what Eydris had looked like after she met with Drostin's rage in the mountains, and that had only been a grazing blow to the woman's back. He could only imagine how he looked himself.

He paused with that thought. Drostin had been up in the mountains. He had not pieced that together until just now. He had been behind the attack that had torn his people apart, that had almost killed Eydris.

Why?

He coughed, peering up at the circle of faces staring down at him. Even through the fog, he could see the horror on their faces.

"I—" He couldn't talk. His throat felt as if it was coated in sand.

"Was there a fire?" The tone and volume of the question made it clear the woman wasn't asking him.

"I don't know." Another person in the crowd replied. "He looks like someone tried to cook him."

Someone else hushed the two and leaned down. "Do you need help?" This voice was kinder, softer. The person reached out to touch his shoulder but drew back when he hissed in pain. "I'm sorry. What can we do? Do you want to come out with us? We're leaving. You probably should too. There's something dark happening in the throne room."

That brought his head jerking back up, and he hissed again at the new pain.

"Yeah, come with us." Another voice said, taking his reaction to mean he wanted to go with them. "There's nothing much left, now."

"The ... king?" He waved them back again. Did this mean the rabble had already killed Einar? Had Drostin already won?

"Back in the throne room." The kindly voice said. "But come with us. We can take you to an apothecary or a healer. How are you even walking?"

He took a deep breath, closing his eyes against the coming wave of nausea and pain, and forced his legs to straighten. In his chest something snapped, and he cursed with a jagged, animal sound, but he stood, using the wall to steady himself and looked down at the peasants around him.

He knew he must seem like a monster. His clothing must be hanging in tatters, plastered to his body with the blood and serum seeping from his wounds. There was nothing left of his rich, black cloak, or his inlaid fighting axe. He was dressed in rags, with nothing more than a dagger hanging from a dried, cracked belt, to even tell he was a fighter. Even the axe he was using to support himself was more a woodsman's tool than a weapon. There was nothing that would identify him as anything more than a terribly wounded member of the rabble. And that is exactly how they had seen him.

"Where ... is ... the ... throne room." They had said they had been there. They could tell him how to go, and end this nightmare wandering. These fools could lead him to the king, or where the king had died. And to the man who sought to kill him.

"Down back that way." One of the voices from the back of the crowd faded as the man turned away to point down the way they had come.

"But you don't want to go there, brother, honest." Another voice. "If there was anything worth seeing, we'd have stayed."

"It'll be worth your life to go there ... not that you got a lot left to lose." That voice was harsher than the others, already moving away down the passage.

"You don't know what's happening any more than the rest of us." Another man said, and it seemed as if they were taking up a conversation that had been interrupted by his appearance.

"Did you see that old man? Did you see the princess's protector back away?" The sour voice was fading away, but Geir could still catch the hint of fear beneath the arrogant tone.

"And what about her?" Asked a third man as they moved farther away. The response was lost in the distance.

"You really shouldn't go back there." The kindly voice was still nearby, although the others were filing past. "I don't know what's happening in that room, but it's like something out of the sagas. The hearth guard ... the protector..."

"And where is the princess?" Another strange voice asked. "We were here for her!"

"And that old man? Who was that?" One of the passing rebels stopped to add her own comment to the litany. "Was that the princess's advisor? It looked a little like him, but not really. He seemed to have everyone backing off!" And then she was gone.

Geir nodded. He had an idea what was happening, but he knew who that old man must be. If Drostin was already in the throne room, he had already run out of time.

He put one claw-like hand on the stranger's shoulder, doing his best to ignore the pain. "I ... need ... to—"

He couldn't continue, his voice grinding down into a pain-filled cough, but the blurred face nodded. "Alright, alright. It's each man's fate to find his own way." The man turned and pointed.

"You're almost there. Follow this hall until you get to a wide receiving area. Turn left, follow that passage, and you will arrive at the throne room." The figure moved to touch his shoulder but stopped himself, again. "Good luck in whatever drives you, friend."

There was a crash down the opposite hall, and they both jumped. Then the man turned to him one last time. "Good luck." And he was gone.

Geir hurried down the new passage as quickly as his wounds allowed. If Drostin was already in the throne room, this would all be over very soon. He didn't seem like a man who cared to linger over the killing blow.

A wide swelling in the corridor that must have been the receiving area was dark, most of the lamps fallen, the candelabras gone. Aside from the few remaining lamps, the only fitful light was provided by burning puddles of oil on the stone. He stopped in the center of the chamber, listening carefully, and heard the mutter of distant voices off to the left.

He hurried in that direction, dragging himself with willpower alone as his body demanded he surrender to the darkness.

The voices ahead grew more distinct. One resolved itself into a lecturing tone, rising and falling in a pedantic rhythm that he recognized from Drostin's countless meetings, listing objectives and assigning them to Shadow agents.

Not Shadow agents. Geir stopped the line of thought. Traitors. Unwitting traitors, but traitors all the same. Every last one of them. Every last one of us, he amended in his mind.

Somewhere not too far ahead, the man who had made his entire life a terrible, treasonous lie was talking as if nothing particularly important was happening at all.

That fueled Geir's will with a fresh infusion of anger, but it also gave him hope. If Drostin was lecturing someone, it meant that things were still occurring somewhere up ahead, and that the king might not be dead after all.

As long as Einar lived, there was hope for some slight chance he could make amends before he finally let himself die.

The air grew noticeably warmer as the walls on either side faded away, the hall opening into a wider area, probably an entry hall before the throne room. Strange shapes loomed out of the fog and shadows. Beasts, they looked like. Dragons? The carvings he had heard so much about, from men and women he had plied with mead and spirits in his youth.

Again, he wished he could cry, as he realized he was entering the chamber that had figured so prominently in his dreams. And he could see nothing but vague shapes and shadows, with a distant red glow dimming overhead.

"Sadly." That voice; that now-hated voice, dripped with sarcasm. "It is the lot of mortal man to die with so many of his questions left unanswered."

Geir felt a pulse that seemed terribly familiar. Every inch of his body tensed away from that pounding rhythm and he hissed, collapsing to one knee in the entranceway to the great room.

The sound seemed to resonate in his bones. As if his body remembered something his mind had chosen to forget.

And then he heard the screams. The howl of a terrible wind tore through the hall; the same horrific sound he had heard up in the mountains as his warriors had died before him.

A sound with a far more recent, and agonizing, association.

He rose and peered into the room, pushing against the waves of heat that sought to force him back, in time to see it happen again. A tight cyclone of burning wind and sand roared across a group of hearth guard standing in a defensive line across the hall. He watched, as best he could through his ruined vision, as their weapons and armor were torn away, then their clothing and flesh, sucked into the arid, screaming monster storm.

Finally, the wind faded, leaving cascades of sand drifting to the floor all across the hall while the dry clatter of splintered bones rattled across the hall.

A group of men and women were standing around him; rebels who had been too curious or foolish to flee when the confrontation began. They were screaming now at what they had witnessed, their voices a faint echo of the rage that had filled the hall only moments before.

In the far corner of the hall huddled a group of figures that had been revealed by the dying of the mystical storm. A tall shape rose up behind the men and women gathered there; the throne of Astrigir. And standing before the throne, regal and proud despite the horrors swirling around him, was Einar Jalen, king of Astrigir. The man Geir had served faithfully all his life, even if that service had been twisted to a terrible purpose.

Geir had never seen Einar this close before, only ever having been able to watch from afar. The king was even more impressive now, despite the swirling fog that ruined his vision. He was tall and noble; a man any warrior would be proud to serve.

And then Geir noticed the woman standing beside his king. She was nearly of a height with Einar, but her dress and long black hair identified her as a noblewoman from Kun Makha, and his confusion only grew. He had always held a special place in his heart for the empire, and for the culture the fyrdar had spurned so long ago. Even as Drostin set him to hunting them across the mountains. But why was a noble oyathey woman standing beside the king now? She wasn't alone, either, he noticed, but surrounded with her own defenders, who stared forward in the wild disbelief that gripped their fyrdar companions.

They stared at the center of the wide chamber; at a person standing at the middle of the throne room.

They stared at Drostin.

Geir felt a growl swelling in his savaged throat as he recognized the ghoul that had made a mockery of his entire life. The strange old man with his biting sarcasm and terrible powers was standing right there, before him. And so was his king. And that meant that Geir was not too late.

He took a staggering step forward, and then another. He tried to raise the heavy axe, but it slipped from his ruined fingers. One claw-like hand settled over the dagger at his belt, trying desperately to pull it free. It felt as if it had fused to the leather of the sheath, never to emerge again.

As he took another step, pulling again with a pained grunt, he noticed another man standing in the open space before the court of Astrigir. The old fighter from the mountains, maekre blade dangling from one hand.

And as his tortured gaze settled on the man's face, he stopped. It couldn't be. There was no way even the tangled web of fate could have become so terribly snarled.

Eirik Hastiin? The last saemgard? Even after joining Drostin's Shadows, Geir had hunted Hastiin when his duties allowed, on his own and alone, always figuring that one day, if he could bring the traitor down, he would gain the recognition from the king he had always craved.

Hastiin was here, now, with Drostin. And it all made a terrible sense.

A lifetime of hunting had led him here, to this. The big man was before him, staring at the old man and the king. Even his plate and chain would be no use against a dagger thrust through the back of the neck. He would be bleeding out before he knew his day of triumph was at an end.

He pulled harder on the hilt, hating the whimpering noise that escaped his clenched teeth. This couldn't be. He couldn't be this close to Hastiin only to have his strength fail him in the end.

But then he paused. If he killed Hastiin, the other rebels would know him for a loyal follower of the king. The strange reprieve his wounds had conferred upon him would be over, and he would never get close enough to Drostin to kill him as well.

But if he was able to kill the old man, then the king's hearth guard would make short work of the traitor, and his duties would still have been fulfilled.

He needed to kill Drostin; the rest would take care of itself.

Drostin and Hastiin were standing close together, the entire room frozen by the explosion of mysterious force and violence the old man had called forth. He had to strike now, while that distraction lasted, and before someone saw what he was doing.

He raised his off hand and took the hilt of the dagger in both as he began to walk once more toward the old wizard's back. He pulled, but this time, he pulled with all the strength of those flickering images. Each child's face gave him more power, each life he had ended, crying out for vengeance, fueled his efforts.

He felt the skin of his palms peeling away, and he ignored it.

He felt fresh blood wash over the hilt, making it slick, but only clasped harder, pulling with every last ounce of strength he could muster.

The dagger, freed at last from the desiccated sheath, leapt out into the hot air as if eager to taste blood.

And Geir smiled, ignoring the pull of his tight lips and the taste of blood in his mouth, as he raised the weapon high in shaking hands.

He would save the king, and then he could die.

Chapter 32

It felt as if she had been with this troop of jarls, wives, and hearth guard for eternity. At first they had made quick progress, the hearth guard taking them through a circuitous path that seemed to avoid the heaviest fighting. She had heard the sounds of battle throughout their journey, but always at a distance; and when it seemed to be closing in on them, their guards had taken them in the opposite direction.

They had run into small groups of warriors several times, but the hearth guard they met exchanged whispered comments, hooded glances back and forth down the halls, and then they would separate, her group would be ushered deeper into the Bhorg, and the others would move off. Chasing the battle, she assumed.

When they ran into her own rebels, her heart would rush into her throat. She was terrified someone would identify her, would cry out against her apparent treachery and reveal her to the men and women ushering her toward the throne room. Even when that didn't happen, when in the dim light and chaos of battle she most likely appeared like just another noncombatant, she was forced to watch as her people were slaughtered or set to flight.

In short order she found herself feeling as if she had fallen from one nightmare into another, in a swirling vision of blood that would never end.

The hearth guard kept telling her to drop her makeshift staff, but she refused; clinging to the splintered shaft for reasons she herself could not have explained.

Eventually, the distant sounds of battle faded away. She tried to imagine why, all at once, the fighting would wind down. She couldn't think of any good reason. Perhaps Tsegan's peasant army had dispersed itself so thoroughly through the stronghold that there were too few of them to continue the fight. Perhaps they had won, and most of the hearth guard were either dead or had been forced back to the throne room.

Perhaps they had lost, and Tsegan's prophecy was doomed.

Once that thought had wormed its way into her mind, it wouldn't let go. She began to dread what she might see when they arrived in the throne room. Would Einar stand there, triumphant, over the bodies of her friends?

As they continued to move through the cool shadows, she could not shake the vision of Tyr lying entangled in a pile of corpses, staring sightlessly up at her with wide, dead eyes. Or Eirik, his strength, power, and resolve drained away. Or Chagua, his lilting voice silenced forever.

And as she saw each of them, they slowly turned to her in her vision and became Kustaa. Kustaa, her friend. Kustaa, the first friend who had ever known her. Kustaa, the first casualty of the old man's prophetic crusade.

Kustaa, who had never hurt another person, and who had never been anything but kind. Kustaa, of all people in this crazy, violent world, was dead.

As she continued to shuffle down the corridor in eerie silence, a tear tracked its way down her cheek. In the whirlwind tumult that had become her life since leaving the Fallen Oak, she had had so little time to mourn her friend. She had taken so little time to mourn him, she corrected herself.

If Tsegan's teachings had taught her nothing else, she had learned the importance of accepting responsibility for her actions; and her inaction. She gripped the broom handle tighter as her throat became raw. It was everything, she knew, as she wiped angrily at the tears. Her knee caught in the slit of her dress and she pulled it violently. Whose idea was it to send her into battle in a dress like this, anyway?

It was all too much; the death, the bloodshed, the fear.

And Kustaa, who had followed her all the way up into the mountains only to be killed by that madman and his crew.

The hearth guard ahead slowed down and put their heads together, mumbling in a nervous, senseless murmur. The nobles around her pushed closer together, trying to draw her into their protective knot. They looked at her with suspicious expressions when she shook them off with a hiss, and moved toward the head of the group, where the warriors were talking with more and more animation.

"—have a duty!" One woman, blonde hair piled atop her head in a heavy braid, was saying.

"And part of that duty is to keep King Einar's subjects safe." That was from a short man who shied away from the woman's glare.

Maiara could tell at a glance that the man was a coward.

"I'm going forward." She pushed past the two arguing hearth guard without looking at either of them.

"Will you be shamed by a jarl's lady in a formal gown?" The woman's hiss dripped with scorn, and Maiara missed his mumbled reply as she pressed forward.

"Come on." The woman's voice was louder, addressing the other warriors in the hall. "Move."

"My lady, thank you." The woman muttered as she passed Maiara, and she felt the guilt of her ploy added to all the other weight dragging her down into the deepest hells.

The warriors filed past, skipping and jogging to move ahead of her in the hall as they approached a wider portion of hall, a grand doorway on the far side.

"The throne room is through there." The woman who had taken charge of their escort said in a hushed tone. "The king and his retinue will be through the door and to the right. We will make sure the room is safe, then move you to be with the others. If the king—"

A chorus of horrible screams rose to a heinous, nightmarish shriek all too familiar to Maiara, through the doorway before them.

"No." The short man's voice trembled. "No. No, no, no." He turned and fled without looking at any of the others. Three more hearth guard, casting apologetic looks toward the woman leading them, followed after him.

Around Maiara, several nobles began to cry, shrinking away from the terrible sound.

The sound of Tsegan's magic at work.

The temperature in the room spiked, and Maiara found herself struggling for breath in the oppressive heat. The others were discomfited too, but no one seemed as affected as she was. They had started without her. Did that mean they thought she was dead? Or was her presence not as integral to the prophecies as Tsegan had said?

Many of her doubts about the old man came sidling back into her mind, even as she moved toward the door.

The hearth guard with the elaborate braid watched her companions in disgust. As their footfalls faded into the distance, followed by the low, dying moans in the throne room, she shrugged, turned toward the doorway hefting her axe, and moved cautiously forward.

The other warriors joined her, and they moved cautiously through the door.

Maiara was right behind them, looking over their shoulders as they made a small defensive line just inside the throne room.

The temperature within was even worse. It felt like an oven, but with an unnatural, greasy feel. The failing light of sunset shown down through long banks of windows set into the ornate ceiling, the dull light glowing in the shimmering heat.

Sure enough, the old man himself was standing in the middle of the grand chamber, confronting a knot of men and women standing around a big blond man who must be King Einar. She stared at the man, searching that broad, noble face and those bright, flashing eyes for anything that might feel familiar. There was nothing; no paternal magnetism called to her through the shimmering air. She found that lack more distressing than she had imagined she would.

A line of hearth guard stood nervously in front of their king, eyeing the piles of broken, splintered bones that must be all that remained of the first line of the king's defenders. Standing with the king was a tall oyathey woman in a gown not dissimilar to her own, but in vibrant red with black detailing.

What was an oyathey noblewoman in a formal gown doing in the middle of the battle?

Tsegan was standing there, his hands raised as if to cast another hellish wind wyrm at the king. If Tsegan could kill the king himself, why the entire, elaborate charade? And hadn't she begged everyone to spare Einar, to ensure Eirik did not abandon their cause?

A little distance behind Tsegan, standing alone by a side door opposite her own, was Chagua. The islander stood watching the old man with his dark, impenetrable gaze. He had his sword in one hand, but his stance was rigid, not at all the relaxed, ready pose she knew from the yard of their mountain keep.

What were the two of them doing here?

Maybe Tsegan was clearing the defenders away, which would mean… And she saw them; Eirik and Tyr were very nearby, behind Tsegan. The boy had his hand outstretched, as if pleading his master for something, and Eirik looked like a man trapped between terrible truths. He was shaking with the strain, and both of them were glistening in the heat, sweat pouring down their faces and into their beards.

And then, beyond Eirik, she saw him. It was as if he had stalked out of her nightmares and into this hellish landscape as he hobbled slowly forward, holding a bent and twisted old dagger in both hands, high over his head.

She looked more closely, and recoiled from what she saw. The man showed all the signs of having been struck with Tsegan's terrible power, but he had not died. His clothing hung from him in strips, melted into his flesh in several places. He looked like a red and black statue of a man, with entire areas of his body charred, bone visible through the cracked meat. And where the skin was split and cracked, the raw flesh beneath wept blood and a clear, viscous liquid.

He was a terror, but by far the worst thing about the man was his face. He was barely recognizable, with his remaining hair burned away. His ears were red, raw stubs on either side of his head, his nose was sunken, like that of a corpse buried for years. There were no lips that she could see, and his eyes were vacant, white orbs, with just the hint of shade behind the fog, flickering with a blind man's meaningless, jittering motions.

But it was him. It was the mercenary who had attacked in the mountains. The man who had led the killers into that valley with the sole intention of murdering her and her friends.

The man responsible for Kustaa's death.

The scream that tore from her aching throat tried to encompass all the loss, the fear, the doubt, and the guilt that had been heaped upon her shoulders for months. She held the broom handle across her body as she had been taught, bearing down on the burned horror sneaking up behind Tsegan.

No matter what doubts or fears she harbored, Tsegan was a friend, and this man, this thing before her, had killed Kustaa.

Everyone in the room spun about to stare at her, but she didn't care. She didn't care that she had never been in a throne room. She didn't care that this was supposed to be her throne room, when this night's work was through. She didn't care if the king staring at her was her father or not.

All she cared about was that this creature before her had come, in a moment's flash of irrational insight, to represent every terrible thing that had been forced upon her over the past winter and more.

The man's halting gait stopped as she burst out of the small cordon of hearth guard, her staff held high. His ravaged face turned toward her, rheumy eyes widening in shock as the tear of his lipless mouth gaped opened.

He staggered back, one hand letting go of his dagger so that he could try to fend off her attack.

That was never going to happen.

Maiara knew the man had no hope of stopping her, even before she began her first strike. And she didn't care.

The staff whistled down, weaving past the man's descending arms, to slap into the bare, tortured flesh of his side.

The melted dagger clanged against the floor. The mouth split open with a terrible scream and he spun away from the impact, the torture of each step clear in his milky gaze.

She struck him again, bringing the broom handle cracking against the mutilated killer's knee.

Then she struck him in the arm.

Then she struck his side again.

Then she caught him in the side of the head, sending him spinning backward, toward the far wall.

And each time she felt the hard wood of the staff strike flesh, she saw a flash of Kustaa's face, cold and lifeless in the snow.

"Maiara, no!" She wasn't sure who that was. Tyr, maybe? She didn't care.

There was a laugh, too. She thought it might be the old man, but again, nothing mattered to her but the monster cowering before her.

When the killer, now bleeding and broken from countless crushing strikes, hit the far wall, he curled up against it, one arm over his glistening scalp, the other held to his chest at an odd, unnatural angle.

She brought the staff up over her head, ready to finish this, and met his gaze as he turned to stare at her with his cloud-filled eyes.

They were wide, empty, and hopeless.

And that stopped her blow.

The man fell down against the wall, sliding to one knee with a whimper, his one raised hand shaking.

Those eyes were so terribly empty and lost that she stopped, lowered her staff, and could only stare.

Those eyes seemed, even in the depths of her own despair, to make a mockery of her losses.

And that terrible laughter rang again through the hall. Maiara turned to see Tsegan, facing her and her fallen foe, the old, familiar smile on his open, friendly face.

"Ah, Princess! You've arrived!" It was Tsegan, but there was something wrong. It was the old familiar voice, but at the same time it was very, very different.

And she didn't like the way he has said the word 'princess' at all.

The white brows came down with concern, the thin lips pursed. "Oh, my dear. It's all very confusing, I know."

The words were concerned; the tone of the mentor with the favored student. But beneath them was something darker.

The old man's gaze shifted to glance at the killer she had beaten into the corner, and he smiled.

And something in her mind clicked at that expression. The man who had shepherded her from sheltered orphan to … whatever she was now, would never have smiled at another's suffering like that.

Not the man she thought he was, anyway.

"You really should not have stayed your hand. If anyone in this room deserves to die, it is that man."

There was a commotion behind Tsegan, and she looked up to see a hearth guard wielding a massive black axe emerge from the group surrounding the king and run at the old man from behind.

Off to her right she saw Eirik, too, tense as if he was ready to charge.

To charge the man attacking Tsegan? Then why was he staring at the old man's back?

Tsegan's facial expression did not so much as flicker. A hand struck out, almost negligently, and a small, narrow bar of heat and sand seemed to emerge from his palm, striking the charging warrior in the forehead.

The man's body continued to run for several strides despite the fact that it no longer had a head. The axe tumbled from the dropping arms, and then body and weapon drove into the floor in a tangled heap of loose limbs and heavy iron.

Eirik stopped, mouth open, and stared at the headless body.

"Just a warning, everyone." Tsegan shifted to turn back to the king and his retinue, shrinking back against the big throne, and then farther to take in Eirik and Tyr. "I will no longer tolerate your barbaric lack of manners."

He turned back to Maiara, and despite the baking heat of the room, she felt a chill sweep up her back at his expression. "As I was saying, Princess, please, do not allow yourself to be dissuaded by this poor wretch's current condition. The man has more blood on his hands than you can possibly imagine." The old eyes narrowed, the familiar laugh lines taking on a more sinister aspect. "Far more than your little friend from the inn, Maiara, although that death, too, can be laid at his feet."

That quenched the chill, and she turned to look down once more at the ravaged body of the man who had caused so much pain. He wasn't looking at her, though. He was staring at Tsegan, and the hopelessness was etched so deeply upon his ravaged face that she could almost feel sorry for him.

Almost.

The man whispered something, those unseeing eyes somehow fixed on Tsegan. The lipless mouth twitched, blood running down his chin from the cracked flesh as he tried to talk.

"Enough." Tsegan held up one hand toward Eirik, and the big warrior, who had seemed on the verge of moving toward Tsegan gain, stopped, although his face was rigid with anger.

What was happening?

"Geir, thank you for all of your loyal service." The words made no sense, but this was lost in the gathering storm of confusion building within her. "But now, as with all the rest, our time is done."

The hand Tsegan had raised against Eirik shifted until it faced the man on the ground, palm up, fingers extended as if summoning the man to stand.

"You represent the very best of the fyrdar race, Geir Muata." The old man's voice lowered, becoming little more than a growl. "Which is to say, you were a loyal, mongrel dog."

The hand clenched into a tight, shaking fist, and Maiara felt a strange, insistent surge in her mind. This time, the wind did not howl through the high hall like a rampant monster, but rather rose softly, almost gently, swirling among the different groups arrayed around the chamber until it formed a slowly-gathering circle around the pitiful wreck at Maiara's feet.

The man looked down to where the dust of the floor was stirring, forming a slow, gracefully spinning circle around his bloody feet. He began to shake violently, his ruined head moving jerkily from side to side, denying what he saw forming around him. He looked up again, first at Tsegan, a mute plea clear in his expression, and then at Maiara.

What he wanted was clear, and it shocked her more than it should have.

"Do you think any of the men and women in your books of history would have hesitated with that final blow, princess?" Tsegan's voice was vague, distracted. "I expected better of my best pupil. Allow me to show you how it is done."

The wind began to speed up, the dust whirling around the man seemed to thicken, its color lightening to that of coarse desert sand.

Maiara didn't truly understand what was happening. She didn't understand the growing tension between Eirik and Tyr and Tsegan. Chagua had not moved, his face unreadable. Was their plan still in effect? Were they still trying to remove Einar from the throne? Who was this man before her? Some agent of the kings who had gone into the mountains to try to stop them, at the very least.

But how had Tsegan known him?

She knew only one thing in that moment; she didn't want to see this happen again. Not even to this man.

Maiara raised her broken staff high, ignoring the hollow that seemed to be forming in her stomach, and brought it down toward the fallen killer's upraised face. The man closed his eyes as if accepting a blessing.

And the staff stopped as if it had hit the wall.

"No, that is not how this ends."

Tsegan's voice was still calm, with a slight vibration of effort, but there was an unmistakable cruelty behind it, as well.

The staff shook in her hand and then shattered, scattering splinters in all directions.

Maiara cried out, shying away from the blast, and while she looked away, a new sound arose in the tomb-like silence of the throne room.

The wind, which had been quiet and gentle, made a soft hissing sound as the dust continued to thicken. The whirlwind around the man Tsegan had called Geir rose up around him like a translucent, shimmering curtain.

The man was lifted to his feet, and then slowly, painfully, he rose into the air.

This time, Tsegan maintained rigid control over the winds he had summoned. Rather than letting them tear this man to tatters in moments, as he had up in the mountains during the attack, he moved his hands in slow, rhythmic gestures that seemed almost dancelike, and the ebb and flow of the wind and sand followed the movements, flowing over the floating man, caressing his tortured body.

The man's screams were hellish. Slowly, the demon wind scoured his flesh away as everyone in the chamber looked on in horror.

The entire room was frozen, as if in a dream, as the temperature continued to rise and the swirling wind dug deeper and deeper into the body of the dying man.

He was dying, certainly, but it was a long, slow process. Blood and water were drawn from the man's body even as muscle, tendon, and bone were revealed by the now-howling wind. Somehow, against any kind of logic, even as the man's face was reduced to little more than a wet, red skull, the screaming went on and on and on.

When the high-pitched shriek finally faded away, swallowed up by the roar of the contained storm, Tsegan clenched his fingers into tight fists, bringing them clapping together, and the cyclone condensed itself with a soft cough of displaced air. There was a snapping, crackling sound, and then the wind was gone. Dust and sand swirled downward in a spinning cascade as dried and splintered bones fell through it to clatter on the floor.

Chapter 33

Tsegan sighed with satisfaction as he watched the yellow bones come to a rest amidst the scattering sand and then turned away from the girl and toward the rest of the hall.

"Now, where were we?" Eirik was coming to hate that voice.

If he was going to admit it to himself, he had always hated Tsegan's voice. But now that reaction was bone-deep.

Eirik hadn't known the man with the dagger. Maybe he would have been familiar, once, but with his skin burned away and his clothing in tatters, there had been no way to identify him. He looked at the pile of old bones; he certainly didn't recognize him now.

He didn't know what was happening. Who was Tsegan? What was his true purpose here? Why had he manipulated all of them into this complicated ploy? He knew none of these answers, but he would be damned to the darkest, hottest hells if he was going to let this strange old man dictate whatever came next.

And clearly, Eirik was not alone in that sentiment, as he watched two of the warriors around Einar raise short war bows and loose their arrows at Tsegan.

Tsegan's death would mean many of their questions were never answered, starting with what they were supposed to do with the king, but he was willing to live with that lack of knowledge if it meant that he and his friends would live.

With a start, he was reminded of the battle up in the mountains as he watched the two arrows shatter into trails of dust as Tsegan made one offhanded gesture.

Another hearth guard, a woman with a pile of intricate blonde braids atop her head, hefted a massive fighting axe and charged, soundlessly, from the group Maiara had entered with only moments before.

Eirik tensed himself, gripping the maekre blade tightly, and shifted his balance. If the woman could distract Tsegan, perhaps an attack from two directions would be enough.

But the old man twisted again, gesturing with one palm toward the blonde warrior, and she shattered into a torrent of sand and bone that washed across the floor, a yellowed skull coming to rest at Tsegan's feet.

The old man returned the skull's empty smile with an evil grin, and then cast about again, as if trying to remind himself what he had been doing before he was interrupted.

His gaze swept over the king's guards and retinue, all silent and wide-eyed, and continued to move about the room, taking in the other group of hearth guard, Eirik and Tyr, Chagua standing alone across the room, and the large crowd of peasant fighters at the back.

And then he stopped facing Maiara.

"Princess." The word came out in a malevolent hiss, contempt dripping from it like the sweat that stung his own scalp.

He shot a glance at the old warrior. "Your princess. Had you ever realized that was the price of your integrity, Saemgard? A pretty face?" The old man nearly spit. "Princess. Do you know what she truly is, you pathetic fool? I tore her from a filthy street halfway around the world! A dirty infant I plucked from a hovel and carried across the sea to drop on the doorstep of two greedy, gullible innkeepers."

The girl looked as if she was being physically struck with the words.

"She is literally less than nothing to you or anyone else on this side of the world, you old fool. Princess?" He laughed with a cruel, vicious stab back at the girl. "She's not even fyrdar or oyathey. No more than I am."

A single word, from the shadows of his people's distant past, rose up in his mind. Eirik was stepping forward before Tsegan could continue.

"No further need of you, my dear." His hands came up again, forming strange, disturbing shapes that flowed one into another. "Your story has taken on a life of its own, now." The sound of rushing sand rose up in the silence. "Time to start taking care of the loose threads."

The girl stood immobile, the shattered stump of a broom handle clutched forgotten and useless in her hands. Anger burned in her crystalline eyes behind the tears. She took several slow steps back, showing no fear, but then she faltered as her foot slipped on the bones of the dead mercenary.

"Let's end this, shall we?" Tsegan murmured, stabbing his hands forward.

"No!" The scream erupted by Eirik's side and he started, looking around in stunned surprised as Tyr tore past him, axe raised high.

The lad had never wanted for courage. But what he thought he could accomplish now, rushing into the evil old man's field of vision like a madman, Eirik didn't know.

The smile that stretched across that old, wrinkled face was horrific. He had expected one of them to do something like this, that much was clear. And Eirik didn't think it had mattered to the old man who it might have been. He was playing with them now, like a cat with a mouse.

Tyr had never had a chance.

Tsegan's gestures shifted slightly to face the onrushing boy, and the old man's hand shook slightly as he pushed them forward.

They had all seen it happen too many times to doubt what would happen next. There was no way to beat the old man when he could dash any foe aside with a gesture of his wrinkled hands.

Eirik screamed, reaching out with one hand as if that futile gesture would have any impact on anything, and watched miserably as a solid ram of wind and sand struck his squire in the middle of the chest.

Tyr was engulfed in the storm, arching back into the wall, surrounded by a blinding cloud of dust. He may have cried out, but the roaring of the winds would have drowned out even the most soul-wrenching death scream.

Eirik thought he saw Maiara reach out toward Tyr, but only in hopeless, helpless reflex. The gesture had no effect on the terrible scene unfolding before them.

The boy's body tumbled across the floor and struck the wall with a heavy, ugly sound. Once more the dust swirled away, scattering across the floor, and the still body lay there like a pile of discarded rags.

Eirik could only stare. The boy who had believed in him, who had saved him from himself time and time again, was as still as any corpse, sand piled up around him in dry, hot drifts.

From where she stood amidst a murderer's bones, Maiara gave a sharp, painful sob, staring at Tyr's limp form through the drifting dust.

The vast chamber dimmed as the last bars of dying sunlight faded from the windows high overhead.

"Ah," Tsegan held up one finger as if everyone in the room had been moving to challenge him. "I believe that would mean it is just about moonrise, does it not?" He spun slightly to look from Maiara to Eirik. "The moment of our great triumph is upon us, no?"

The bark of laughter was harsh and violent, and many hardened warriors in the room recoiled as it echoed up and down the hall.

"Idiots, every last cursed one of you." He spat the words as if they tasted vile. He paced in the center of the room, glaring at each group in turn, sharing his contempt equally among them all. "A lifetime's work, and hardly worth the effort."

"I don't know what your purpose is in returning, Chogan, or whoever you are, but one thing is certain. Astrigir is stronger than any one man; even you." Einar pushed his way past his defenders, stepping out of their protection to stand alone amidst the bones of his fallen warriors. Behind him, the tall oyathey woman stepped up beside him, her regal head tilted disdainfully as she stared at Tsegan with enigmatic black eyes.

"You could undoubtedly kill us all." Einar indicated everyone in the room with one arm, and Eirik felt a stirring of something deep in his chest at being included in the sweeping gesture. "But you will be hunted by those who come after. To the edges of my realm and beyond you will be hunted."

"And beyond." The woman beside him repeated, putting one hand on the king's shoulder.

Tsegan's arms dropped, and for a moment it seemed as if the threats had given him pause. Then his shoulders gave a little heave, and then another, and another.

The old man was laughing.

"'Astrigir is stronger than any one man?'" The old man shook his head. "Astrigir is weaker than you can possibly imagination, your majesty." He spun about, indicating the silent, terrified crowd cowering in the back of the hall. "Do you not see what I have done to your precious kingdom today? Your people were more than willing to hate you, Einar, to see you torn from your throne and supplanted by a simple orphan girl in a pretty dress."

The old man indicated Maiara, tears streaking her dusty face, with a disdainful wave of his hand. "A servant girl, Einar. They followed a servant girl into rebellion. A simple minstrel's show; a good story, a pretty face, some costumes, and a hint of prophecy was all it took to rouse them from their tragic, colorless lives and rebel against the dynasty that has ruled them for over a hundred years."

Eirik felt something break in his chest. He had known it wasn't real. Even that night in his tent, when Tyr had roused him from his drunken stupor and Tsegan had burned the spirits from his body with the promise of redemption, he had known it wasn't real.

But to hear the words, in that voice steeped in disdain, it broke him.

"Your people have risen up against you, Einar." It continued. The voice, droning on and on, as if a lifetime of patience had run out in that stifling, death-filled chamber.

"Your people do not trust you. They believe they have tasted freedom, and that will only spread from here to the farthest reaches of your realm. And your jarls, those who survive this night, will not trust those subjects, and with cause. War will wash over all you know. War without end, as your people rip each other down. Your land will tear itself apart until there is nothing left but devastation and ruin."

The old man's voice seemed to be gathering strength as he spoke. "And do not believe for a moment that the sickness unleashed here this night ends at your borders, King EinarKing Einar. It will spread to the east and the west; Vestan and Subraea will fall as surely as Astrigir has fallen, and the strength of the fyrdar people will falter, and it will fail, and it will fade."

Einar was pale beneath his heavy beard as the strange old man's bleak prophecy rolled over him. He reached up without seeming thought and placed one rough hand over the oyathey woman's, still resting on his shoulder.

He jerked slightly when Tsegan let loose another bark of laughter. "Oh, please, Einar. Don't believe there is salvation to be found to the north. Kun Makha has been a shadow of its former glory for more generations than even you know! Do you think a strong empire would have allowed their fyrdar subjects to fall away as old Maquilla did a century ago?

"No, Empress, I do not know what grand schemes your father set in motion in the mountains. I've tried, God alone knows I've tried." The old man laughed, but there was a brittle edge to the sound. "None of my agents were ever able to break your people. I suppose I owe you congratulations on that score." His face hardened. "But no; whatever his plans might have been, no matter how grand your efforts to continue them, nothing your people could possibly accomplish in the mountains now will stave off the inevitable."

The old man began to pace before his audience, secure in the knowledge that none of them would move against him.

"Oyathey blood has been thin and weak for centuries. The only strength they could claim was with the infusion of fyrdar stock." The old man leered at Eirik, and he twisted his hands on the hilt of his maekre blade with frustration. "And now, thanks to my friend, the fallen Saemgard and his band, the last of that strength will be gone as well."

The consequences seemed dire; Eirik couldn't puzzle his way through half of what Tsegan had just said. Tsegan, or Chogan, or whatever the man's name was.

But Eirik could see what the implications were for the kingdom. He had been haunted by fears of just such an outcome as he stalked through the halls of the Bhorg, haunted by his memories and his guilt.

The strength of Astrigir was shattered. The heart of her power, the king's hearth guard, lay dead or dying, strewn about the stronghold like the discarded wooden soldiers of a petulant child. Those subjects of the king with the bravery to stand before such power were dead themselves or scattered now back to their homes.

Astrigir was vulnerable; vulnerable to invasion from any of the surrounding realms, vulnerable to starvation, with so many of their farmers dead, scattered, or torn with distrust. Vulnerable to any other plague the gods and spirits might see fit to send against them, with a generation of their strongest laid low.

What the old man might mean by all the rest, though, Eirik had no idea, and he could not marshal the strength to care. He had been used, manipulated, led by his own fears and guilt and paranoia to be an instrument against the realm he loved.

His gaze moved to find Einar, but the king was staring in disbelieving horror as the old man continued.

"I was relieved to see that your habitual gathering on the vernal equinox has continued, your majesty." The old man gave a mocking bow to the king, then a deeper but no less sardonic gesture to the woman. "Empress Aiyana, you may lack your father's vision and strength, but your presence in Kun Makha would prolong the inevitable beyond my willingness to allow. Thank you for saving me the time it would have taken to seek you out as well."

Eirik's jaw worked silently, his hands twitching on the enormous maekre blade. The enormity of the old man's plot knew no bounds. To be at the center of the entire affair, to the utter destruction of anything that had ever given meaning to his life, felt like an enormous pressure being applied to his entire body at once. He shook with rage he had no way of releasing.

And the old man wasn't done yet.

"There will be nothing holding this entire side of the world together, once you fall." Tsegan's words were like sand rushing across an open wound, and he turned, looking past Eirik, to where Chagua stood, his dark face frozen, glistening with sweat.

"And none of it could have happened without you, my friend."

Those old, dark eyes flickered over to Eirik. "Did you believe him your friend, Saemgard? Did the bonds forged in battle convince you of his sincerity?"

That horrible, poisonous laugh rang off the high, vaulted ceiling.

"It was a steep price to pay, for such an ephemeral item as trust. But what other option was there, you were being so stubborn? What was the final count, over a score dead in that little valley? No one of any consequence, of course; just a collection of mountain vagabonds. I did lose one of my trusted agents, which is vexing. But still, well worth the price, to keep your dense mind distracted, wouldn't you agree?"

Eirik writhed inside, rage and hatred churning within him. He never should have trusted the damned islander. He had always known it. He glared at the old man, but Tsegan wasn't even looking at him.

The old man was looking at Chagua, who was still, like a statue guarding the doorway, staring back.

And as Eirik watched, he saw that the islander, too, was shaking.

"What's wrong, Master Emeru? Was not your compensation equitable? Did my library not please you? Did you not have access to all the knowledge you asked and more?" That vile old face twisted again as the smile tightened. "I do apologize that we never had the opportunity to sit down so I could teach you how to read it, of course, you savage. But these are busy times. You understand."

The islander's face shifted ever-so slightly. It was like watching a hillside in the mountains moments before an avalanche.

"Or, no?" Tsegan sidled closer to Chagua, one hand making idle motions, sending a small fountain of sand spinning from his palm. "Perhaps your true discontent is in knowing that your name will forever be connected with these terrible events? When the histories of this time are finally written, your northern islands will have proven to take a hand in the destruction of your entire world." He took another step closer to Chagua. "How will the council feel, when it is discovered that one of the greatest Swords in the history of your nation was an unwitting tool in the annihilation of all you hold dear?"

Tsegan stared into that dark face for a long, painful moment, the smile twisting further, and then turned away with a shrug.

"Nevertheless, the concerns of a collection of effete scholars squatting on their little islands is really of no consequence here today, wouldn't you agree, your majesties?"

Tsegan dropped his hand, the tiny cyclone dying away, sending sand drifting down around his feet. "No. We have the destruction of a continent's hopes and dreams to complete. We have a once great civilization's final collapse into obscurity and irrelevance to preside over." He shrugged, looking at Einar and the oyathey woman with a tilted head as he approached them with his shifting, oily gait.

"With your deaths, the history of the entire world will be sealed. There was a time when your ancestors, Aiyana, believed that the coming of the fyrdar was the greatest event that could have happened to your ancient, failing empire. Those who survive the coming cataclysm will see that it was nothing short of your final doom, arriving upon your shores to seal the fate of Kun Makha once and for all, tracking them from the far side of the world."

Eirik trembled with rage, watching across the room as Chagua, dark eyes following the wicked old man, did the same.

But neither of them seemed capable of breaking out of the horror of the moment.

And yet somehow, in the depths of his own misery, his gaze fell once more upon Maiara. The girl looked lost and hopeless, staring at Tyr's crumbled form, tears streaking her beautiful face. There was something in those usually bright, crystalline eyes that made the depths of his own despair feel trifling in comparison.

Chapter 34

It had all been a lie. Everything she had been told, everything she had learned, everything she had been led to believe since the moment they pulled her away from her life in the Fallen Oak had been a lie. Even beyond that. Her entire life had been a lie. Something broke inside Maiara, and she felt herself falling to her knees.

She was nothing. She was no one. A pathetic little orphan girl with no family, no friends, and no future, and she had allowed the old man to convince her she was so much more.

She was no princess.

As the depths of her guilt rose up around her, she had to be honest with herself: she had never truly believed she was a princess. There had been something wrong about the word from the first time she had heard him say it. It had chafed, like an ill-fitting dress, and it had never grown more comfortable.

He had tried so hard to convince her it was real, but in the end, she had allowed him to convince her. She had ignored everything she knew and felt and believed, in favor of a future where she would mean something, where she would be important, where she could make a difference.

But it had all been an elaborate hoax.

Tsegan— No, this man who had assumed the name and mantle of Tsegan Aqisiaq from the stories, he had used her to carefully create this moment. He had built a story around her that would have been a perfect fit for her book of fairy stories. He had used that story to stoke the usual resentments of farmers, merchants, workers, and thanes into a burning flame with the promise of some fantastical world without taxes, war, or want.

The old man had woven an improbable tale for all of them, taking strands of ancient prophecy, tying them into the everyday grievances of the common folk, and offering them a bright, shining future that had seemed as if it had come straight from the ancient sagas.

And none of that would have been possible without her to tie it all together. She had allowed herself to be manipulated and used like a minstrel's showpiece, and now, somehow, the entire kingdom would fall.

One thing had not been an illusion. She had been a good student. She had been an exemplary student. And no betrayal by her mentor could take the knowledge she had learned from her now, no matter how much comfort there would have been in ignorance.

She knew exactly what was going to happen to Astrigir now. And the other fyrdar kingdoms would soon follow into the chaos of rebellion and death. Even if they somehow managed to stop the old man, there would be no saving the realm. How many warriors had they lost in this night's misguided rebellion? How many of the rebels now lying dead in the streets outside, or strewn throughout the halls of the Bhorg, were the leaders of their communities?

They had lost a generation of their best, on both sides of the conflict, and who would be left to save the survivors from the famine and disease and disorder that had to follow?

Astrigir was doomed. Her home was lost. The realm she had been taught to revere, that she had been convinced she would save from some phantom destruction through a convoluted, twisted prophecy, was doomed.

There had been so many signs, and she had ignored them all. She had ignored them all because she had believed in the man who offered to make her so much more than she could have ever imagined she could be.

Kustaa was dead, buried in the ancient crypt up in the mountains. Tyr was gone, nothing but a broken pile of rags. She had reached out to him as he was struck, but she had no power. She could not pull her gaze away from his still form. The boy had tried so hard. He had been the least involved in any of this, and yet his faith, in his master, in the old man, even in her, had been the strongest.

And now he was dead.

And so many countless others. The king's hearth guard had been decimated. The common folk who had risen up at her command ... how many of them were dead?

She dragged her eyes away from Tyr's body and turned slowly, with each tiny motion of her body bringing a screaming, raging agony, to stare at the old man, now gloating before the king and the woman he had called the empress of Kun Makha.

Who was he?

He had claimed to be Tsegan Aqisiaq, the last wizard of Kun Makha. And they had believed him?

But he was oyathey. Everything about his appearance said that that was true. He had never claimed to be that Tsegan, but he had left them to believe it. And what choice had they had, when he had revealed such incredible powers?

Magic had been dead in Kun Makha since the time of the fyrdar splintering from the original empire. The old wizards, sorcerers, and wise men and women had faded away. Every scholar had, over the decades and centuries, come to believe that the power had somehow faded from the world.

But this man wielded that power. Who else could he be, if not ancient Tsegan, no matter how ridiculous that sounded?

All of the tales from that ancient book of child's legends came back to mock her now. Life was no fairy story, and her experiences at the hands of Turid and Vali Sayen in the House of the Fallen Oak should have proven that to her.

But she had seen his magic!

Something broke inside her and her shoulders fell. She felt as if she was a house, falling apart from the inside as its supporting structure gave way one beam at a time. She was an empty shell. She was a vessel this man had filled with fancies and pretty pictures and then used to convince the people to follow him into destruction.

"Who are you?" She barked the words, her aching throat giving them a harsh, biting sound. It came out as an accusation and seemed to set the shimmering air around her swirling with her anger.

The old man looked at her over his shoulder, and the smile on those thin lips was grotesque.

"Who am I? Who am I?" He spun about, arms raised, as if presenting himself to the room. "Why, I am Tsegan Aqisiaq, of course! Who else would I be? A figure stepped out of legend, to shepherd my sad, lost homeland back onto the path of the mighty!" He raised his hand again, and again a tiny figure of heat and sand danced on his palm. "I come to restore magic to your shores! To bring the power of the ancients back to the glens and dales of the realms!" The smile become a skull-like rictus. "I came in fulfillment of all the prophecies!" Those dark, burning eyes narrowed. "No?"

Her mouth dried even as she felt the overwhelming desire to spit. Contempt washed off the man in waves like the heat radiating through the room. His words twisted inside her, taking every petty doubt and fear she had ever felt and turning them against her.

She was a fool. She was a foolish child, and this man had used her foolishness to bring down a kingdom.

His barked laughter stung despite the pain and humiliation already piled upon her. "Who am I." It was a statement, and it was cast to the room at large, not just toward her.

"Your majesty, who am I?" The old man turned back to the king and his remaining defenders. "Who am I to you?"

Einar said nothing, standing taller, chin raised in defiance.

The old man turned back to Maiara. "Ask him who I am. Ask him who I have been."

Then he turned to Eirik. "Do you remember me now, Saemgard?"

She watched as something dark and ugly dawned on Eirik's face.

"The last time we saw each other in these hallowed halls, I was bidding a fond farewell to your entire cadre as they rode out to defeat the invidious Vestan at Merrik Ford." The old man turned back to the king. "And it seemed like such a clear-cut decision, did it not, your majesty? Take Vestan in the flank, have your most powerful warriors roll up all the enemy's strength, and win the day. Vestan would fall, Subraea would follow, and then the fyrdar would treat with Kun Makha as equals. Your place in the history of the fyrdar would be assured, your father's shade would look down upon you with favor, and your faith in yourself would be vindicated for good and all.

"What could possibly go wrong, eh, Hastiin?" Eirik shook, tears of rage tracking down his cheeks, but he made no move toward the old man.

"So, princess, who am I?" The poison she felt in that word was indescribable. "Am I the most trusted advisor to a young and foolish king? Am I a figure striding out of myth and legend to save the fyrdar from themselves, to forge a new, powerful realm that will withstand the looming threat of prophecy?" He lowered his arms and stared at her from beneath the wide, sweeping white brows that had once seemed so benign. "Or am I the worst enemy of the fyrdar and the oyathey both? Am I the agent of your destruction? Who was it that orchestrated the destruction of every bloodline born to mystical power? Who murdered men, women, and children for the merest hinted rumor of arcane ability? Was it me who has shaped a generation of the most malicious, directionless men and women into a shadowy nightmare that will haunt any successor of this fallen king to the last, bloody days of the realm?"

This time his laughter rang around the room like a great bell, vibrating deep within her stomach. She could feel her gorge rising in her throat. The words would have meant nothing to her just a few short months ago. But she had studied the history of Astrigir along with all of her other subjects. She recognized the events he was describing now. She even remembered the name Einar had screamed. Chogan.

Chogan had been a key advisor to the king in the years after his father's untimely death. A man of oyathey decent, he had risen quickly in the young king's favor. The books had been vague, however, on how their time together had ended. And there had been no mention of Chogan and the battle of Merrik Ford.

But then, if Tsegan, or Chogan, or whoever he was had assembled that collection of books just for her, why would he include any source that might implicate him?

What other holes might there be in her knowledge?

"The answer to your question is actually quite simple, girl." The old man stood tall, his hands on his hips, and his chin raised in regal disdain for all about him. "I am Utan."

She blinked, uncomprehending. Her mind felt numb. But around her, others were reacting far more strongly. She saw Eirik's eyes widen in surprise and disbelief. She slowly became aware of the others in the hall, from the king and his retinue to the rebels massed in the shadows opposite. The sound he had spoken repeated itself in her mind, its meaning emerging like a terrible monster from a dark sea.

The Utan. The Others. The mysterious force that had driven the fyrdar from their home realms in times now lost in legend.

But they were myths, weren't they? No one believed the Utan were a real people, no more than they believed monsters wandered the world, or that magic was real.

But of course, that last was a bad example today.

Or perhaps the best example there could be.

"We could be finished here, you know." The old man turned back to the king. "I will have to kill you, Einar, but every other person in this room could live to walk away, and it would make no difference in the outcome. The series of events we have set in motion here, coupled with the Shadows who will believe they avenge you in every atrocity they will now commit in your name, will ensure that Astrigir will fall. It will be unable to defend its borders, and Vestan and Subraea will not be able to deny the temptation to be the power that topples your realm. The smart money will be on Vestan, of course. Resentment from your ill-conceived attempt to subjugate them still burns in King Iver's heart, and the hearts of all his subjects. But Jerrick of Subraea is no man's fool when it comes to the main chance."

He shrugged. "No, nothing will save you from what is coming." The smile had twisted into a vicious mockery of a grin, now. "And so, you might ask, why bother sullying my hands with further death tonight?" He brought his hands together and cracked his knuckles as if preparing to lift a great weight.

"I have suffered for over forty years in this benighted, filthy, squalid backwater of a realm. I have worked tirelessly for longer than most of you have been alive to bring about the downfall of Astrigir and all the rest." His breath seemed to be coming in short, sharp gasps now as his voice lowered to an angry, rumbling growl. "I have returned to my homeland only once in all that time. I left wives and children behind me, sacrificed for the cause. And for that, you grimy degenerate barbarians, every last one of you is going to die."

There was no warning. No grand gesture or pronouncement came with the next attack. The old man waved his hand and the entire troop of hearth guard that had accompanied her to the throne room died.

There was a strange pulse as the wind tore up off the floor and swept around them. She felt a tugging in her chest that seemed to pulse in time with the writhing of the storm-driven sand. The screams of the warriors who had fought to bring her to safety caught in her soul and wrung yet another shoulder-wrenching sob from her aching chest.

But even as the power engulfed the warriors and tore the flesh from their bones, she felt something cold rising up in her stomach. It throbbed with the ebb and flow of the old man's power, filling her with a heady, ominous sensation of portentous weight that felt strangely familiar.

Chagua, who had stood silent and still, trapped in his own nightmare, could take no more and charged the old man. His curved sword flashed in the lantern light and an ululating bellow escaped his lips, nearly drowning out the dying cries of the hearth guard.

Maiara knew what was going to happen before the man had completed his first step. She cried silent tears of pain and frustration as she watched the old man's hand rise, not even deigning to turn toward the man who had served him faithfully for so long; a man whose thirst for knowledge had led him to betray his people, only to be betrayed himself.

The power struck the islander a glancing blow. His sword, that had always struck her as fragile-seeming and had yet withstood every blow landed upon it, shattered, sending the hilt spinning from his hand. The blast sent Chagua tumbling back, arms and legs flailing, to slam against the back wall with bone-breaking force.

Before the old man could even laugh, Eirik was upon him, the maekre blade flashing and spinning as if it weighed nothing at all.

The man who had called himself Tsegan fell back before the sudden, vicious onslaught. He used small, controlled bursts of his power to deflect each blow as it fell, but it seemed all he could do as Eirik pressed the attack, hauling the full weight of his enormous weapon through its arcs, pulling it down upon the old man time after time after time.

The hateful creature was forced back one step at a time, shuffling through the dust and bones of his victims and past the frozen, wide-eyed survivors of the king's hearth guard.

Bursts of howling noise swept up and down the hall as each blow was deflected, sending a spray of dust and sand showering out at each ringing parry.

The entire time, Eirik roared like a wounded animal.

And with each parry, Maiara sensed, rather than saw, a pulse run through the room.

She watched, her gaze fixed on the old man's face as it began to grow tight and wan beneath its usual bronze tone. His dark eyes narrowed, and it almost seemed as if Eirik had overwhelmed the wizard's ability to focus his power into anything more than the defensive shield he was weaving with each deflection.

And then Eirik's foot came down on a large bone that rolled beneath him, and for just one moment, the endless pattern of whirring attacks faltered as he regained his balance.

And that was all that was needed.

With a triumphant wail, the old man brought a hand up and struck the warrior's chest with his palm.

Eirik screamed as something snapped with echoing volume, and his body was blasted back across the big hall. A fountain of howling sand followed the big man's flight, swirling around him and tearing his beautiful blue surcoat to tatters. The maekre blade was hurled back to clatter across the floor, coming to rest beside Tyr's still body.

Eirik was still moaning as he fetched up against the doorframe, curled into a tight ball of agony.

Other than the old saemgard's sounds of pain, and the quiet sobs from the king's retinue, the hall was utterly silent.

"Now." For the first time, the old man seemed angry. "If we are finished with the foolish heroics, maybe I can complete my work and be on my way? The stench in this room is nearly overwhelming."

He held his hand out toward the king and the woman beside him. They held each other now, all pretense of staid propriety gone.

But Maiara didn't care about Einar or the strange empress. Her gaze twitched, from Eirik to Tyr to Chagua. She scanned all of the bodies and scattered bones littering the floor of the throne room.

It had all been done in her name. All of the destruction, all of the bloodshed, the devastation that would reach out from this room to engulf the entire realm and beyond had all been done in her name.

And she was nothing. She was alone. There was no one left alive who cared whether she lived or died. She certainly had no concern on that score. She was worth nothing. The prophecy, that had promised so much, was a sham. She was no savior, no princess, no figure from legend come from the shadows.

And he was no wise councilor and mentor, striding out of the pages of history to guide her and the kingdom into a brave new future.

He tensed his hands, fingers tightening into vicious claws, and the nerve of the king's defenders finally broke. She saw it was true, then. The best of the hearth guard were dead; those that remained were damaged, broken souls who could no more protect the king than they could fly.

The old man's arms lashed forward and a thick rope of wind and sand lashed forward, pulsing with brilliant light and fell energies.

And she felt that pulse in her stomach, in her heart, and that strange presence rose up within her, cold radiating out from her chest. She felt almost as if some enormous creature loomed over her, somewhere to the south. And she howled herself, shrieking in a throat-tearing scream as she stabbed her own hands out at the old man's back, fingers curled, and imagined him lashed into oblivion.

Nothing happened.

Of course.

Her scream slowed, lowered, and faded away. Her hands fell to her sides as the old man, his attention caught at last, turned to face her with a single, upraised white eyebrow.

And then she growled again, one foot snapping down in an aggressive stance, both hands lashing out again. She could almost feel the power. She felt the rising cold within her. She tried to freeze the traitor where he stood. She tried to pick him up with furious, mountain winds and dash his body to the stones. She tried to conjure a spear of ice to flash through the air and impale him upon its length.

The power was there. The power was right there. But it was elusive. She grabbed for it with her mind, but it slipped through her grasp time and again.

And the old man smiled.

"Well, this is certainly unforeseen." He straightened, giving her a new, appraising look as if seeing her for the first time. "So many years spent ensuring that this would not happen here. So many lifetimes making certain that the power would never rise on these shores again. So many children dead, so many lives shattered. And yet here you are."

He shook his head ruefully. "To think that I carried you here myself. This explains your damned eyes, at any rate. No one among our people has ever had such eyes. And yours were black, like mine, when I left you with those damned landlords."

His own cold, dark eyes narrowed yet again, his nostrils flaring with frustrated anger. "Plenty of time now to remedy my mistake."

His arms pushed toward her as his teeth flashed in a grimace within his tangled white beard. She felt the pulses building, heard the distant roaring of desert winds. She fell back, raising her own hands again, desperate to fend off the power she felt bearing down upon her from some great, burning distance.

He was going to kill her. Like he had killed so many people already. He was going to blast her with the same power that had thrown down Tyr, and Eirik, and Chagua. She felt the heat rising all around her, ducking behind one upraised arm as if that was going to help at all.

He was going to remove her from this world, and then, when she was gone, he was going to finish his work. This man who had taken everything she had ever had, every little bit of happiness or satisfaction she could claim, and replaced it with shame and guilt and sorrow, was now going to take her life, and there was nothing she could do about it at all.

Her misguided faith had brought her here, and it would end with her, here.

The floor between them writhed as the dust rose up, joining sand from a blazing desert an unimaginable distance away. Somehow, he was channeling all the primal force of some immense desert and harnessing it to his will. And those winds would scour the flesh from her bones.

It began to swirl around her and she cried out. She fell to one knee, a scathing, burning pain rushing over every inch of skin, tearing the beautiful dress to ribbons. She raised one arm up over her face, knowing that nothing could protect her.

Her tears were whipped from her face as the power of the mighty desert pulled at the life within her, drawing it from her mouth and nose and eyes, even as her skin felt the first burning caress of the killing sand. She sobbed, and coughed on the dry heat that sucked at her breath, filling her mouth with sand.

Something behind her cracked and shifted. It felt as if the wall itself had broken open; a cool breeze reached her through the shrieking whirlwind. She glanced backward but there was nothing but dark stone seen through the swirling curtain of coarse, burning sand.

And yet, that breeze was unmistakable.

She could almost sense, as she shied from the pain, the crisp air of the little mountain valley.

She could feel the winter sun on her face, the cold, biting wind. She could see the snow falling on the jagged peaks all around. She could see the skin of ice on the little rivulet behind the ruined fort of Alden's Tor, with the cold water burbling just beneath. She saw Tyr smiling at her, frost riming the fur lining of his hood. As her body was ravaged by the desert winds, she saw Chagua and Eirik, steam rising from their bodies after a brutal match, smiling at her through twirling flakes of falling snow.

She saw Wapayekha, the crazy old man of the mountains, smiling at her, his ancient eyes kind. In her mind, she could see a single tear make its way down his creased face as he watched her body writhing in pain. His entire face tightened, then, urging her to something she could not understand through her agony.

Through the flashing visions, burning sand, and roaring of the desert wind, she could just hear the man who had been her mentor laughing at her pain.

She unclenched one fist, opening her hand against the pain, and pushed with every last strength left to her.

Behind her, again, she felt a massive shifting, and the cold winter wind blew stronger against her back. Where it touched, she felt the soothing caress of those far off winds against her desert-ravaged body.

The laughter faltered.

What was behind her? What was beyond the wall and the twisting passages of the Bhorg that lay all around? She wasn't sure, there was no way to be certain, given how lost she had become before the hearth guard had found her and taken her as one of their own.

But for some reason beyond logic, she suddenly knew that her mountain valley was somewhere in that direction. Calling out to her, burning along a connection that had been forged months ago, in the heat of a terrible battle, back when she had had something to believe in.

She pushed again with her hand, and the wind around her changed in texture and tenor. The temperature all around her fell, plunging from the parching desert heat to the brutal cold of winter, but it did nothing to harm her. She took strength from that wind, feeling snow and ice skitter over her burned body, smoothing away the damage of the sand.

She looked up, from beneath her upraised hand, to where the old man stared at her in confusion and alarm.

He pushed toward her with more focus, his shoulders bunching with the effort. The desert winds, which she could see engulfing her own winter storm, tightened. Bursts of heat lightning flashed through both clouds as the storms collided.

The cool blues and whites of her own mountain winds began to change, turning harsher, more yellow, and the temperature around her began to rise.

She felt the unmistakable presence of the mountains now, looming up in the distance, lending her the strength of rock and wind, snow and ice. The cold curtain wall clouded, almost as if the air around her was freezing into a solid wall of ice. She could see the shifting brilliant yellow of the sand storm buffeting the other side, but for a moment, it could not reach her.

She sobbed again. How was any of this possible? What was she doing?

She could not have put it into words, but Wapa's face once more rose before her, and it seemed as if he blinked with relief and nodded wordlessly to her. She felt, without knowing why, that he was looking on with approval at some long-anticipated event.

Somehow, he had known this was going to happen. And for some reason, that thought comforted her. Enough, anyway, that she could put her fear and confusion aside for now, and address what needed to be done.

She took a deep breath and looked down at her hands. The horrible damage she had felt being inflicted upon her flesh was no longer there, although strange, wave-patterned lines of pale scar tissue wended their way beneath the smooth copper skin. She straightened, feeling the strength of the mountains flow through her, replenishing the energy she had lost throughout this night of horror.

On the far side of the wall of ice, through the refracting crystals and the swirling sand, she could see the old man standing, arms out as if to embrace her, hands like claws as he forced them together against some terrible force.

And she realized with a start that she was that force. The old man was trying to crush her, and her burgeoning power, with his own. There was an ominous snap that seemed to fill up her world, and fissures began to appear in the wall around her.

If she did nothing, his power would engulf hers, and she would be crushed despite the wonders she had just performed.

Wonders that made no sense at all, but seemed to fill this bitter old man with fear.

She looked down at her hand again, tightened it into a fist, and looked up through the ice and sand at the man who had revealed himself to be her true enemy.

She gritted her teeth, knowing, somehow, that what happened next was going to hurt terribly, but knowing she had no choice.

She plunged her hand into the wall of ice, which opened to accept her, and out into the roaring sand storm that was consuming her frigid barrier.

She felt the sand bite into her flesh, immediately wearing away at the winter's protection, digging into her skin. She ignored the pain, opened her fist palm upward, and sent her will forth with a savage twist of her lip.

She imagined the howling winter winds, the heavy crack of lake ice in the cold of a brutal winter night. She imagined the blinding, driving snow of a terrible mountain storm, and she sent it all into the blurred figure trying to crush her.

The pain flared in her hand and was gone. An enormous, deafening roar filled her ears, shattering her little haven and throwing chunks of ice into the scorching whirlwind that surrounded her. The swirling chaos flashed hot and cold, blue and white, as the powers of the desert and the mountains clashed.

But that was all secondary to what was happening between Maiara and the old man. His eyes were wide with shock as he let his killing storm collapse, withdrawing all of his power into a tight defensive cordon around himself as a column of freezing wind, ice, and snow blasted toward him from her outstretched hand. It burned within the wreathing icy cold, but she ignored the pain, concentrating on the power running through it.

His own hands were raised high, palms toward her, shaping a lens of wind and sand, a shield that absorbed the blast of mountain winter and sent swirls of snow and chunks of steaming ice careening off into the hall all around them. High above, the long windows shattered, adding glittering shards of glass to the hellish storm raining down across the hall.

She pushed harder, imagining the freezing winds penetrating the shield and dashing the old man to the ground. But he roared in incoherent rage, the sound almost swallowed up by the competing storms that filled the large chamber. His hands were clenched, tendons standing out in rigid, painful relief as he pushed back with all the power of the desert.

But the desert was far, far away. The source of his power was half a world distant. And the mountains were right there, behind her. The power was raw and immediate; ample compensation for her unsure hand and lack of experience.

In fact, as she stood taller, bringing up her other hand and concentrating more and more power upon that shield, the mountains were all around her. She felt connections forging, springing out from her chest to countless peaks and mountain valleys. Winter still ruled in the high places, and somehow, through some mystical connection she thought she might never understand, it lent her its power now, to deal with this invader, this murderer, this thief that had helped unknown forces to rob generations of fyrdar and oyathey their birthright and power.

She screamed, and even in her own ears the sound was painful, a low, ominous rumbling that included the power of blizzard, avalanche, and winter thunder, and sent it rebounding from the surrounding walls.

Her arms shot up, open, and there was a horrific, echoing crack as the floor of the throne room shattered. An enormous spear of ice, thicker than the body of a strong man, erupted from the rift, lantern light flashing from razor-sharp edges and jagged points.

The fury snapped into the shield, plunging through wind and sand, losing none of its power or edge as it sank itself right through the old man's chest.

The howling desert winds died in an instant. Sand and dust settled quietly to the floor, blown fitfully by the slowly dying winter winds.

Maiara's breath heaved in her chest, her shoulders rising and falling like a fevered bellows. The ragged echo of her breathing was the only sound in the entire chamber.

The old man stared at her with wide, disbelieving eyes over the enormous spear of ice that transfixed him, supporting him as his legs gave way, sinking him further along the massive shaft. Dark blood stained the ice, running down rifts and channels in the ice to spread out over the frost-lined floor.

She dropped her hands and felt the tremors begin. She was in a daze, she knew, but couldn't shake it. She looked around at the devastation of the room, at the king and the empress, staring at her from before the massive wooden throne. She saw the rebels, staring from the shadows behind her. She saw Chagua push himself into a sitting position, clothing tattered, raw burns across his face and chest, staring at her without a sound.

There was more movement off to her right, and she saw Eirik stir, shaking his head, levering himself up onto his hands and knees, and turning to stare with fascinated horror at the old man's body, propped up by the jagged spear.

And then she looked at Tyr.

The body was still, unmoving, its covering of dust and sand turning to mud as snow and ice melted on him.

The snow and the ice were melting on him.

That had to mean something.

And then she felt as if the floor had opened beneath her. She was falling.

And everything faded into a cool, comforting darkness.

Chapter 35

Everything was dark, but for some reason, that was alright. The stifling heat was gone, replaced with the comforting, familiar cold of the mountain valley. It was soothing on flesh that had been ravaged by the heat and the sand, giving comfort where it had felt no comfort would ever be felt again. And the darkness felt protective, somehow, rather than threatening.

Slowly, all around but at some great distance, sounds infiltrated into the darkness. Whispered voices hissed, discussing matters of great import in words that had no sense attached to them.

And then one word that did have sense. A name. His name. In a voice that had come to mean everything to him over the years.

"Tyr. Up, boy. There's work to do."

That hardly seemed fair.

He pushed himself up, toward the voice and a growing sense of vague, diffuse light. As he rose, pain slowly blossomed all around. With the light and the words came a sudden realization that wherever he was, he was in a great deal of pain.

Tyr coughed and lurched upward, reaching out with one hand at blurred shapes that seemed to dance in the fog.

It was Eirik, of course, and the look of concern he could slowly make out on the man's face took all the sting from the words that had drawn him out of the darkness.

"Wha—" He coughed again, nearly doubling over with the pain. His throat felt as if it had been scoured to the bone. When he thought about it, his entire body felt as if it had been scoured to the bone.

And then, in a flash, he remembered those last moments, before he hit the wall and everything spun into darkness.

He screamed.

He screamed despite the raw pain it awakened in his throat. He flailed, pushing away Eirik's attempts to restrain him as he tried to scramble away from the big warrior, looming up now in his still-blurry vision like some figure out of a nightmare.

"Tyr, calm down." Big hands clamped down on his shoulders, pushing him down to the cool stone of the floor. "Calm down!" The hands gave one shake, rattling his teeth in his head. "Everything is alright. It's over. He's dead.

He's gone. You're going to be alright."

He stopped struggling, focusing on the old warrior's tone as much as the words. He settled back, listening, and could hear no sounds of fighting or struggle.

"Honestly, you need to come back now. We should leave soon."

He opened his eyes again, focusing on Eirik's rough face. The broad crest of hair had been mostly singed away, giving an odd appearance coupled with the shaven strips to either side. His beard, too, was patchy, with areas of his face burned and blackened, blood seeping from open wounds. But those sharp grey eyes were clear and full of concern.

He nodded, wincing from the pain the movement caused. "I'm alright." He shook his head a little, wincing at the pain. "I'll be alright."

The old warrior smiled, nodding. "You will. You will."

He sat up, helped by one strong arm from his master, and the first thing he noticed, at first glance, he took to be a statue.

When he realized he was looking at a human body, suspended by a glistening pole transfixing it through the chest, rising up from a ragged crack in the stone floor, he almost lost what little food might have remained in his stomach. He had seen many terrible injuries during his time with Eirik, and the battle just passed had added countless images that would haunt his sleep for the rest of his life. But seeing the man before him impaled upon what appeared to be a giant's spear of glittering ice was very nearly too much.

Until he realized who it was.

"What...? How...?" He pointed to the body, turning to look up at Eirik with raised eyebrows. "What...?" He repeated, unable to put the horror and confusion into words.

Instead of answering, Eirik cast a hooded glance across the hall to where a lone figure lay, wrapped up in a hearth guard's fur mantle and cloak. "I don't know how." Eirik's voice rumbled low in his chest. His gaze flicked away from the body to the king's party at the far end of the hall, then down at the floor. "What seems to be obvious, at first glance."

They both stared at the old man's still body, and at the still shape of Maiara on the floor not far away.

That reminded him where he was, and he jerked upright, looking around with alarm. The last he remembered, they had been in the middle of a battle. That battle seemed to be over, judging by the rows of still forms beneath cloaks, mantles, and sheets lined against one long wall. A cluster of men and women stood around the throne, and the king, the man they had come to overthrow, sat disconsolately in the enormous wooden chair. He was clearly uneasy, one forearm resting on a knee as he listened to one of the jarls talking with sweeping, animated gestures.

The rebels that had gathered at the far end of the throne room were gone, although several men and women he thought he recognized from their ranks were standing nearby, keeping a wary eye equally on the king's retinue and the girl apparently sleeping on the floor.

He found Chagua, sitting with his back to the wall nearby, holding a long hilt, its blade shattered at the crosspiece, in his lap. The man's tangle of thick locks was matted with sand where it was not burned away, giving him the appearance of a great wounded lion. He gave Tyr a weary nod, and Tyr nodded back, not sure what else might have happened after he had been knocked out of the fight.

"Why is Maiara over there, alone?" He gestured with his chin, still trying to move as little as possible. "Is she alright?"

The girl didn't seem to be wounded, although she was muffled in the big cloak; there was no telling what the heavy garment might be hiding. She was still, lying on her back, but her chest rose in fell in deep, even breaths.

"She'll be fine." Eirik looked up at her, then away.

Something slid into place in his mind, and Tyr looked back at the body of the man they had all called Tsegan. A chill swept up his back and he nodded toward the impaled form.

"Her?"

Eirik glanced at the figure and then away. "Best I can gather. I was as out as you." He nodded toward Chagua. "He saw most of it; says it was her." The big man looked quickly at the girl, then it seemed as if his gaze darted quickly toward the far end of the hall.

Tyr stared at Maiara's still form. "But, how?" He asked the question knowing Eirik would have no answer, but then provided one himself. "The arrow."

Eirik nodded. "That must have been the beginning."

"Nothing since then?"

Eirik shook his head, his gaze drifting back to the throne and the crowd around it. "Nothing that I had seen, or Chagua. We need to leave soon, Tyr. We won't be welcome here much longer. It's only a matter of time before the shock wears off."

The row of long, narrow windows high overhead were starting to glow with the bright orange light of dawn, broken glass cutting the light into solid-seeming beams that caught the floating dust in sparkling, phantom columns.

"All of us?"

It had only been months, but he couldn't imagine leaving her here alone, no matter what had happened, or what she had done. All of the dreams and plans they had been fed over the winter were as dead as the rows of victims against the wall, but Maiara had lost as much, at least, as the rest of them.

"I will be taking my leave." The lyrical accent of the northern islanders was jarring amidst the death and destruction strewn about them, but Tyr was happy to hear Chagua speak, even if it was a whisper.

Eirik nodded, standing. "I think we all need to leave before Einar decides to try to stop us." He spoke in an answering, hushed tone, glancing at the throne.

The islander stared at Eirik for a long moment, absently twisting his hands around the hilt of the broken sword, searching his face for something. Eventually he said, "What of your anger?"

The big warrior looked back up the hall and eventually shrugged. "I don't know, anymore. But there has been more than enough death here tonight."

Chagua nodded slowly then knelt beside Tyr. "You will be coming with us?"

Every surface of his body ached, as if he had the worst sunburn he had ever suffered, but he nodded, moving to try to push himself to his feet. It took several tries, and both of the big men eventually had to help him.

Once he was steady, he took a few tentative steps across the floor, pointedly ignoring the still form standing nearby, wide-eyed, a spreading pool of water and blood at its feet.

"Where are you going?" Eirik's harsh whisper caught him off guard, as did the rough jerk on his elbow as his master caught up to him.

"We're not leaving her." He indicated Maiara, still motionless, apparently unaware of their approach. He turned to look full in Eirik's rugged face. "I'm not leaving her."

Eirik searched his face for a moment and then nodded at whatever he saw there. "You're right. Of course, you're right."

Chagua moved up beside them, slipping the hilt into a bag at his waist, and the three of them together crossed the hall.

Maiara's eyes were closed, her face beautiful in peaceful sleep. She did not move when Tyr reached out to lay a gentle hand on her shoulder.

"Hey." As far as conversational sallies went, it was pretty weak. But then, he was pretty weak, too, so he decided to go easy on himself.

The girl's smile seemed to deepen a little, but other than that, she gave no sign that she had heard him.

An uncomfortable silence stretched on as Eirik cast anxious glances down the hall to the group around the throne and Chagua stared in silent appraisal at Maiara.

Tyr looked away, not sure what to do next.

"I will carry her." Chagua leaned down, gathering the girl up in his muscled arms.

Tyr wanted to argue, to take her in his own arms, but he could barely stand. Besides, she was asleep. She probably wouldn't remember any of this anyway.

"We need to leave now." Eirik tried not to look toward the distant throne, but it was painfully clear that he could not stay much longer.

They turned toward the side door, Tyr casting a quick, darting glance back at the body propped upright in the center of the throne room.

They were at the door, Tyr helping Chagua navigate past a tangle of fallen weapons, when the king's voice stopped them.

"Saemgard." The shout rang down the hall, echoing off the ancient granite and marble.

Eirik stopped, straightening, and then slowly turned around. The others joined him, forming up behind the big warrior. They watched as the king, having leapt from his throne, approached warily, attention constantly flicking toward Maiara's still form.

Behind the king came a group of the surviving hearth guard, casting dark looks equally divided between Maiara and Eirik. Following the king and his guards were the jarls, keeping a safe distance behind, and the oyathey woman, striding aloof and alone.

Eirik did not seem inclined to stop, however, and immediately turned again, his eyes hard and narrow, and nodded to the door, ushering them out and away.

"Eirik, please." The tone of the king's voice was hardly imperious; it was more plea than command. "Please, wait."

Tyr stopped, looking over his shoulder at his master.

Eirik's face was a stony mask as the muscles of his jaw clenched and unclenched beneath the patchwork beard. His mouth was thin and hard, but he closed his eyes, took a deep breath, and turned to face the man they had come to depose.

The king stopped as if, having kept Eirik from leaving, he didn't know what else to do. He searched Eirik's face, looking for something he apparently didn't find there as the big warrior stared back, his own expression hard and unmoving.

The stretch of silence was brutal, and it seemed to last an eternity as the two men stared at each other. The hearth guard and the jarls, meanwhile, glared at Eirik, Tyr, and Chagua, their gazes shying away from Maiara. The empress alone seemed to have the courage to look at the girl and was appraising her with open, cool curiosity.

Eventually, it was Eirik who spoke first, surprising Tyr after all of the pain and torture he knew the man had suffered through the years, hounded by the king.

"What do you want, Einar? I think it's best if you just let my friends and I leave." The voice was flat and cold.

The king looked as if the words hurt him, and he continued to stare at the old warrior for a few moments more before shaking his head. "After all these years you return, bringing dissent and devastation in your wake, and that is all you have to say to me?"

That seemed to strike a nerve, and Eirik's faced twisted into a snarl as he took one menacing step forward. It bothered Tyr, for reasons he couldn't place, when the hearth guard behind the king took an answering step back, rather than moving to defend him.

"You hunt me through the years, hound me like an animal down every muddy track and through every insignificant village, and then you expect me to have something more to say to you?"

The cold grey eyes moved then, sweeping over the destruction of the hall, the bodies covered in their drapes, and the final body, uncovered and standing behind them. "I am sorry, Einar, that things came to this." His voice seemed to catch in his throat, and Tyr was shocked to see tears starting in the man's eyes. "We are all victims here, each of us used to the ends of a vicious, evil power. I will be forever shamed by the way that creature manipulated my resentment and my fear, pitting me against the realm I would give my life to maintain. But that shame and guilt will be my punishment. No king who has so abused me will exact any further retribution."

Einar's face was blank, his fine brow furrowed. "Abused you? Hunted you?" There had been no pain in his face before Eirik had spoken; Tyr would have sworn to that. But there was pain there now; a pain to match Eirik's own. "What of you, my noble Saemgard? What of your duties to your king in his hour of need?"

This was confusing. Tyr watched the two men, almost forgetting Maiara despite the glowering looks they were still getting from the hearth guard and the jarls.

Eirik's anger rose another notch. "My duties to you? What duties do I owe a king who hunts me like an animal?"

"I never hunted you!" The king screamed the words, his hands balled into fists in obvious frustration. "You disappeared! I thought you were dead! I had warriors search up and down the Merrik valley, on both sides of the border, searching for months for you, to bring you home!"

Eirik's rage faltered at that, and Tyr's own eyes widened. The one central reality of their lives had always been the king's ceaseless hunt for his fallen saemgard.

Einar's voice lowered. "Do you honestly have such little regard for me, you believe I could not find you if I wished?" He shook his heavy mane. "By the time my people tracked you down, you were living the life of a vagabond, wandering from tourney field to tourney field. You fled from anyone I sent to bring you home." He shrugged, exhaustion written all over his broad face. "I knew you blamed me for our defeat, for the deaths of your brothers and sisters. I left you alone. But I kept all your property in trust. Always hoping that one day you would come home."

Eirik shook his head furiously, a building fear in his wild eyes. "No. That is not how it was. You cannot have that, Einar. Your people pursued me across the three kingdoms, hunted me like a rabid animal, and never gave me a single night's sleep in all those twenty years."

The king waved his hands in sharp denial. "No warriors of mine have hunted you for more than a decade! No servants of mine hounded your steps!"

"They were his." The voice startled Tyr, until he realized that it was his own.

He pointed with a hesitant hand at the body of the old man. "They were his, and they hunted us, never quite catching us, for all that time." His voice turned bitter. "Keeping us ripe for his lies, for when he judged the time was right."

"   As he played us all." Chagua nodded, his calm gaze moving between the king's and Eirik's faces.

The king looked at the islander, then nodded himself, bowing his head.

"He knew his business well, whoever he was." Chagua continued, as he glanced back to the body. "He must have been plotting this for decades."

"And he was not alone." The oyathey woman pushed past the hearth guard and her own honor guard to join the king. "His kind have haunted Kun Makha and the fyrdar realms for long decades, always staying to the shadows, behind nearly every rebellion and disruption the old empire and the Broken Kingdoms have suffered."

Einar shook his head, still staring at the floor. "You can't know that, Aiyana. It is too easy to attribute every misfortune to phantoms if you grant them that power. Your father was a great man, and I honor him by honoring our agreement. But not every fear of his was founded."

"He had power." Eirik muttered, nodding to the impaled form behind them, and then the row of bodies.

The empress put a hand on Einar's shoulder. "You heard his words. Do they not prove my father's fears were well-founded?"

The king nodded, but he did not look up. His shoulders slumped, as if the weight of events had finally caught up with him.

"What are we to do now?" He whispered, raising his head; his eyes haunted. "Chogan, or whatever his name was, was not wrong in his moment of triumph. The price of this night will be dear."

"You are not alone." The woman said quietly in turn, moving him to face her. "You will have all the aid Kun Makha can give. You have always doubted my father's fears, and the agreement our fathers came to before we were born. But you allowed the work to continue. Surely you see, now, that he was right?"

Tyr felt, once again, that the conversation was soaring high over his head, but when kings and empresses argued in front of you, you couldn't help but feel that the place of a squire was to keep his mouth shut and his head down.

Luckily, Eirik felt differently, or believed that the last of the saemgard was owed a little more than that.

"What in the names of all the spirits and gods are you talking about?" He grunted the words, louder than their whispers, and both of the rulers looked quickly back at the group of jarls standing behind the line of hearth guard.

"My father was a wise man." Empress Aiyana straightened, her chin rising in a familiar attitude. Tyr knew the old emperor had been highly regarded, even in the fyrdar realms. He had supported research in agriculture, architecture, and engineering. He had been a patron of artists, scholars, and philosophers. Even fyrdar farmers and merchants who resented the source of the knowledge used many of the techniques Kun Makha had been offering for over a generation.

But he had never heard of any collaboration between Astrigir and the empire. Even the hint of undue influence had been enough to turn many of the less educated commoners against the king. What kind of agreement could they be talking about? And what would such a man have feared?

"My father believed there was a power working against the empire and the Broken Kingdoms." There was some muttering at that from the jarls; few fyrdar appreciated the term. But clearly the empress did not care much for what the lesser nobles might appreciate. "He had seen signs growing in Kun Makha even when he was young. Some malign purpose was moving in the shadows, maximizing the impact of each misfortune, inhibiting any attempt to mitigate disaster."

"Him?" Tyr blurted out, still struggling to follow. He pointed in the vague direction of the old man's body, not caring to look at it again. "He did all that?"

Einar shook his head, giving the tall woman beside him a sidelong glance. "It could not have been. Chogan was a much younger man when he advised my father, and then me when my father died. He was just a man." A shadow passed behind his eyes and they flicked off toward the body. "Well, he aged as one, anyway."

"He was one of many, sent here from afar to undermine the old empire, to keep us all weak and struggling amongst ourselves." The empress' voice faded away, but the fire remained in her gaze.

Einar looked back at Eirik, the plea plain on his face. "I need you, Eirik. Please, don't leave me to deal with this alone."

That didn't seem to please the Empress Aiyana, but she remained silent.

Tyr turned to watch his master, aware that Chagua watched as well, Maiara's sleeping form cradled gently in his arms.

Eirik stared at the king for a very long time. It seemed mad, to think that they had come to the Bhorg to overthrow this man, and here they were, his master considering rejoining the royal court. But then, they were all victims of the old wizard. Perhaps it wasn't entirely mad after all.

"No." The word dropped into the silence like a heavy stone. Eirik, at least, still saw the madness in their situation. "I can't, Einar." His voice shook as he spoke, and he could not meet the king's gaze. But he forced himself to continue. "Perhaps I can return, I don't know. But not now." He adjusted the baldric that held the maekre blade to his back with a shrug. "I must see to my people first. When I have met my obligations to them, perhaps I can return to Connat to revisit my obligations to you."

Einar searched the old saemgard's face, his own eyes hard. "I could stop you." His chin lifted, but with what seemed to be more from petulance than strength. "You came here as a rebel. It could all end for you here and now."

Eirik stared at the king, his face still. "You could. But you won't."

The king almost seemed to flinch at that then nodded, stepping away.

The empress stepped back with him, and when one of the oyathey warriors moved to speak, she silenced him with a glare.

Eirik turned to Tyr and Chagua, nodding back toward the door. "I think we should leave, now."

The others nodded, and Eirik moved past them, taking the lead back into the dark corridors.

Tyr waited until Eirik and Chagua had passed, then turned to leave. He turned one last time to look back at the still, slumping body of the man they had called Tsegan.

He stood there alone for a moment, the rest of the room fading away. He could not look away from the body of the old man.

He walked back into the throne room, past the king, the empress, the guards, and the jarls, until he was standing before the man who had nearly destroyed them all. His head fell to one side as if he was studying the dead, cloudy eyes, then he bent to rummage in the bag the man had always worn at his side.

He straightened with something in his hand, back to the door where Eirik and Chagua stood waiting for him.

"Let's go." He moved past them without looking back.

Chapter 36

When she awoke in the stale old house on the outskirts of Connat, they told her she had been asleep for three days. She had no memory of any of that, of course, but judging from the hunger that awoke her, it could easily have been true. They had forced her to stay in that musty old bed for three more days before they allowed her to stand on her own, to navigate the rickety old stairs, and join them at the big table.

Each of them had treated her as if she was made of glass. They had watched her every move as if she might stumble and fall with every step.

Of course, at the same time they seemed to have a shade of fear in their eyes, but she didn't like thinking about that.

She couldn't remember much about the events in King Einar's throne room, but she remembered enough. She remembered the agonizing caress of the desert and the strength of the mountain that had come to her rescue.

The days she had been confined to her bed had given her ample time to reflect on those shimmering, refracted memories. She had tried, with what little strength she could muster, to connect with those powers again. She had been unable to so much as summon a cool breeze in the close room.

The gaping emptiness she felt within her, where the touch of the mountains had been for those brief, incredible moments, was more painful than any of her injuries or her crushing exhaustion. She had promised herself she would stop trying to touch the power, but as she fell into restless slumber, several times a day, she would reach out.

And feel nothing.

She tried to tell herself it didn't matter. Maybe the power had only been lent to her for that one battle. Maybe it would come again when she needed it. Maybe she would wake up and it would be there for her again. But a hard, burning doubt had settled into her stomach and nothing she told herself would make it go away.

Eventually, on that third day, they broke the news to her. They were leaving. Chagua needed to return to his island home. Some heavy burden bore down upon the man, calling him home to answer for a shame he would not discuss. Eirik and Tyr would accompany him to the port city of Hamon. They wouldn't talk about what would happen after, but she had the distinct impression that they might just take ship with the big islander and put Astrigir and the fyrdar kingdoms behind them both.

The thought that they might leave her behind in Connat was a physical pain, and she had refused to let them. It had taken all the strength she possessed to mount the enormous white charger that was the only gift of the demon's that remained to her. They had asked her if she wanted a different mount, but she had looked into the horse's liquid eyes and shaken her head. The man had been a foul stain on the world, but that shadow could not stretch to the innocent animal. She had almost convinced herself that it was true.

And so the four of them had ridden through the southern gates of Connat. They had passed under the closed, hostile glares of the king's guards. There had been fire in those eyes; hatred, accusation, and disdain, to be sure, but there was fear as well, especially in the gazes that lingered longest on Maiara herself.

She would not let those eyes define her, and so she rode with her friends through the gate, back straight, and she had not looked back.

*****

Beneath her, Sannlir swayed in an easy gait that had seen the rolling foothills flow past them for several days. The others had been nothing but kind, treating her as if she were a fragile sculpture that could fracture at a harsh word. But things were different, obviously. Very different; and each of them had to struggle to find their place in the new relationships that were being forged to replace the old.

And no one's place had changed as drastically as hers.

Eirik's past had been ripped open like a wound gone bad, letting the corruption leak out. Hopefully, healing could now begin. He was no longer a hunted man, if he ever had been. His relationship with the king was not renewed, it was not healed, and there was much blood between them that would need to be addressed. But there was the possibility of healing now, and that would mean the world to the big warrior, when he was able to face it.

She had heard that the king had asked the old warrior to stay, and knowing Eirik and his sense of duty, she felt certain he wouldn't be able to stay away forever. There would come a time, sooner or later, when the dire situation of the kingdom would summon him to Connat once more.

The kingdom was balanced on the verge of collapse, trust was a rare, precious commodity everywhere, and the revelation that the Utan were not only real, but were not yet finished with the fyrdar was enough to plunge each of the Broken Kingdoms into chaos, if the knowledge spread.

Einar would need Eirik, eventually. And the last remaining saemgard would not be able to deny his king when that rally cry came.

Tyr rode beside her for much of the journey, and as they stopped to make camp each night, the four of them worked with quiet efficiency. There were many smiles, but little talk. She wasn't sure about the others, but there was too much in her heart and mind now to make trivial conversation of what they had all gone through. The weight of those events still bore down upon her every day, and it felt almost disrespectful to discuss them. But there were still conversations to be had. Memories from before they had all come together in that mountain valley; an observation on the quiet spring, the beauty of a sunset, or the smell of the distant sea.

Tyr was quiet as they road, but he seemed more confident and comfortable with himself than he ever had before. The world stretched out before him, and his destiny was very much his own. Loyalty, alone, might tie him to his old master, now. Eirik could make no deeper claim on Tyr, who had fought, alone, through the battle of the Bhorg and made it to the throne room on his own. But the boy obviously did feel a great deal of loyalty toward the old warrior; he also felt an obvious sense of responsibility for the man he had been caring for since he was fourteen years old.

And probably with good reason. If left to his own devices, there was no telling how long Eirik might last before he fell into the nearest cup of wine and didn't emerge for days.

She cast a fond gaze back over her shoulder at the two warriors riding side by side. They rode in amiable silence, but she did not miss the occasional glance Tyr threw at his former master out of years of habit; making sure the man was keeping his seat.

Leading their little band, Chagua rode ahead, usually lost in thought. He shared the smiles, and even the occasional banter. But there was a shadow over the big islander that had not been banished by the revelations in Einar's throne room. In fact, the darkness behind his eyes owed a great deal to those events. The islander had retreated into the quiet, contemplative shell that had surrounded him when they had first met. She had seen him place the broken hilt of his strange sword into a saddlebag, taking it out several times a day since the battle to hold it in his lap, bending over as in prayer, seeming to commune silently with the shattered weapon.

Their current journey was expressly because the dark-skinned warrior needed to return home. It had taken a great deal of effort from Eirik and Tyr to coax the reasons out of him, but it had something to do with the broken sword and his family's agreement with the creature they had called Tsegan Aqisiaq.

And so they found themselves following the coast road. They had left the greenway yesterday, taking this smaller trail west toward the port city of Hamon, where Chagua should be able to secure passage aboard one of the coastal merchant ships out of the Kun Makha port of Shawmut. Long haul merchant ships left from the ancient harbor for the northern expanse of the empire and the farther islands almost every day.

And with the gold they had found in that old, dilapidated house, none of them would need to worry about money for a little while, at least.

"Are you alright?"

She jumped. Her nerves had been short since battle, and her companions had made a concerted effort not to surprise her. She liked to think it was out of kindness. They did the same, so it was the least she could do.

Tyr had pushed Vordr up beside her, and the big animal was hardly a stealthy horse. It had been more her wandering mind than any carelessness on Tyr's part, that had allowed him to approach unnoticed.

"Hmm?" She said, more to give herself time to think than anything else.

"How do you feel?" He wouldn't look at her, but that wasn't new. All three of them seemed to shy away from her gaze since they had left Connat.

Not that she could blame them, given what she had done.

She felt fine. She felt more than fine, in fact.

After her first night's sleep out on the open road, she had felt more rested and energized than she could remember ever having felt before. That feeling had only grown with each subsequent night. While she slept, she felt as if her body was filled with all the energy of the world. When she closed her eyes, she could hear the roaring winds of the mountain winter. She could feel the cool caress of snowflakes on her skin. When she awoke, she was always cool, but never cold.

She felt wonderful. And yet, the power did not stir within her breast.

She shrugged with a slight smile. "I feel fine. You?"

He laughed. "I'm sore. The old man might not have killed us; he might have been distracted or getting tired, but he still managed to savage my hide."

She smiled, and it felt good. She had spent a great deal of time thinking about that. Somehow, her three friends had been shielded from the worst of the old sorcerer's power. Blasts that had torn the flesh off other targets had struck them down, certainly, and ravaged their bodies with the terrible power of the dessert. But they had survived where so many others had died. She knew they thought she had something to do with that. She had denied it, of course, but she knew they didn't believe her.

She had not told them that she believed it had been the sight of their bodies, still and broken, that had pushed her over the edge into the well of power she had discovered tying her to the distant mountains.

When they were each struck down, she had had no more power than they had.

But something had saved them, that was certain. Otherwise, there was no reason any of them should be alive.

But they were. And she didn't know why.

"Well, you don't look much the worse for wear." She gave him a smile then turned back toward the trail. The silence became profound, and she cursed silently. Why couldn't she just talk to him?

"What will you be doing in Hamon?" Changing the subject usually worked, when she had accidentally stunned him into confused, self-conscious silence.

"I don't know. I know Eirik wants to go north with Chagua, but I don't know if he'll let himself."

She nodded as if she knew what to make of that. "Do you think he will?"

He smiled, but his forehead was rough with doubt. "I don't know if he's quite ready yet to return to the Bhorg." He shrugged, urging Vordr a little closer to her own mount. "He's been running from Einar for longer than either of us has been alive, and I'm not sure he's comfortable with the idea that he doesn't have to run anymore."

She nodded at that, her face solemn. She thought she understood just a little bit about running. She felt she might be running from what had happened in the throne room of the Bhorg for the rest of her life.

"At least he seems to be staying away from the spirits."

They had all been sensitive about the old warrior's fixation as they rode toward the coast, but eventually they had stopped at a roadside tavern, when no better option was available. Eirik had been jittery, but he had settled down, ordered tea with a grand gesture, laying double the price on the old bar, and that had been that.

"He still finds it hard." Tyr's voice grew softer, a little distant. "I think it will always be hard. He had fallen pretty low before ... well, before all of this."

And that was the problem, wasn't it? All of this?

They had been manipulated and used by a terrible creature serving some unknown masters that seemed to have come lurching at them out of the distant past. The Utan were hardly a known threat, more like some terrible cultural nightmare the fyrdar had been whispering about for centuries.

Could the man who had assumed the mantle of Tsegan Aqisiaq truly be a servant of the Utan, as he had claimed?

But if not, who had been behind the terrible things the man had done?

There were times, often late at night, when she wished she had not killed him. There was so much she needed to know; so much she was afraid only he could have told her.

She felt the small book in her pocket. That had told her a little, but had left more mysteries than it answered.

And then, unbidden, another age-ravaged face rose up in her mind. Wapa seemed to gaze calmly at her from within a swirling white mist. He was smiling. But then, he so often smiled.

And suddenly she realized that she would be returning to that valley, the source of all of their promise, and of their pain.

But if the rest of them were heading north, did that mean she would be going alone? Could she make her way up into the mountains without them?

Did she want to?

Sannlir plodded on, content to move at the lazy speed set by Chagua's overworked cart horse. It gave her more time to think, and more time to worry.

*****

The town of Hamon was not large, but it was a very active port. In fact, there was little farmland around Hamon; most of the inhabitants derived their living from the sea.

The buildings were mostly low, built from the white granite of the surrounding hills. As they approached through the wet lands wrapped around the back of the town, clopping across long bridges from one small island to the next, they could see countless masts rising up from behind the line of buildings. It was a busy harbor, although most of the ships would be small fishing vessels. The journey north to Shawmut, and then on to the distant islands, would start in this small, innocuous fyrdar town.

The streets were dirt, still muddy with the spring rains. They were filled with people going about their business. In the doorways and stalls, beneath awnings or taking advantage of the warmer air, children and old folks mended nets, men and women cleaned or dressing the morning's catch. Factors and merchants were on the move as well, strutting importantly from one appointment to the next, buying and selling from the hard-faced fisher folk.

Nearer the waterfront they found long wooden storage houses and shipwrights' halls. There was very little of the hectic busyness she had expected of a major port from her studies.

Chagua led them to an inn one street up from the docks. A pair of boys came out to take their horses with bored efficiency. Hamon saw more than its fair share of travelers, it appeared. Even with the big warhorses, they were nothing special here.

Chagua had grown quieter the closer they came to the port town. The burden of his return home obviously weighed heavily upon him, and he had been feeling it more and more for the past several days. He had spent most of that day riding slumped in his jury-rigged saddle, holding the broken hilt to his chest.

Without a word or a backward glance, the islander swept up the front steps of the Oar House Inn. Eirik cast a glance at Tyr and Maiara, shrugged, and followed him inside.

She could tell from the way Tyr tensed that he still worried about Eirik and the big man's drinking. The boy hurried after his old master, doing a very poor job of appearing nonchalant, and went in without looking back.

Maiara stood in the courtyard, alone, for several moments. She looked from the dark wood of the door and then up into the cloud-free sky. The color was the deep blue of early summer, filled with promise. When she closed her eyes, she thought she could almost feel the power of the mountains looming up behind her in the distance.

She needed to return. Her nights were still haunted by images of what had happened in the throne room of the Bhorg. She remembered, in her sleep, what the power of the mountains, coursing through her veins, had felt like. She felt an urgent need to reconnect with that power, which she tried to dress up in her mind as a sense of obligation. But at the same time, she knew that the real reason was to feel the rush of cold energy and strength again.

But could she make it back through the mountains alone? Did she want to try the road alone? Nearly everything that had happened in their lost little valley had involved these three men. She realized, that with Kustaa gone, there was no one in all the realms she was closer to than them.

She wasn't entirely certain that was a very comforting thought, but it was true nonetheless.

Turid and Vali had kept themselves cold and aloof while raising her, perhaps under orders from the strange, frightening man who had left her with them in the first place. It may not have been their fault, and she probably owed them the benefit of the doubt. But because of all that, there was no real comfort in the thought of returning to the House of the Fallen Oak. She had dismissed that idea long ago.

The valley, though. She knew she needed to return there. She had been developing some suspicions about the wild old man of the mountain who had appeared so benign during their random-seeming little visits.

His face returned to her each night, in the midst of her torture and confusion. She couldn't have said why, really. In the moment of each of their meetings he had appeared like nothing so much as a half-crazed old mountain hermit. She knew she had felt like she was merely indulging him whenever they had spoken.

But now, with his face the only real image that brought peace to her troubled heart, she had started to wonder if he might not be more.

She would have to find him, somehow, and ask him face to face.

She sighed. That would have to happen. She needed to know how to control the power that she had felt. With all the dark revelations concerning the man she had called Tsegan, and then ... what had happened to him after ... there was no one at all she could go to for help. The book Tyr had stolen from the body and given to her later was no help at all. And she was even more certain now that the library in the tower of the ruined fortress of Alden's Tor was completely useless; a collection of ridiculous charades and superstitions that had nothing to do with the power she had felt.

If she was going to learn how to summon and channel the power of the mountains again, she would be on her own unless she could find someone else to guide her.

And there was no one else to do that in any of the Broken Kingdoms or Kun Makha besides, if what the Utan sorcerer had said was true. If those mysterious foes from the ancient history of her people had really spent over a century hunting down and destroying anyone with these abilities, there would be no one to help her.

If Wapa, hunched alone and frightened in his mountain home, was truly more than he seemed, he would be her only chance of finding help.

Her back stiffened. She didn't want to leave her real friends; not now. Wapa and the mountain valleys were so distant, both in travel and in her mind. She wanted to believe that they could wait. But the old man's words haunted her. What if the Utan were coming? What if she was the only one who might possibly hope to stand against them?

Perhaps she could go with the others back to Chagua's home, and then when Eirik was ready to return to the Bhorg, he and Tyr could escort her up into the mountains on their way. The three of them, once they returned from the islands, could go together.

Who knew; maybe Chagua would be returning with them! That would seem fitting, and warmed her heart even further.

But not for long. The cold of the mountains eased back into her chest, never letting her forget the power she had wielded, nor the many responsibilities she knew would come with it.

She stood there in the warmth of the courtyard, the smell of salt in the air, the soft sounds of the horses settling into their stalls coming to her from the stables. And still, the cold remained, settled deep in her chest; a constant reminder of what had happened, and a promise of what must happen next.

She pulled open the door to the tavern, letting the warmth and soft rush of noise wash over her, and tried to smile.

*****

The Oar House was stuffy, but the smell of pipe smoke and the sea gave the atmosphere a fresh, open taste that she found both strange and comforting. Even Turid would have approved of the tavern's cleanliness. This was an establishment that catered to the wealthier townsfolk of Hamon and their guests.

She peered into the swirling blue gloom and found Eirik's hulking form looking uncomfortable at a small table in the middle of the room. He had shrugged off the fur mantle she had given him once she had retrieved her own clothing at the old house, and was staring morosely into a pewter cup that might, from his expression, have contained warm mud.

She had learned the big man found it much easier to avoid spirits if he had any other choice but water to hand. If there was no tea or juice, that hang-dog expression was soon to follow.

Tyr sat across from the big warrior, a matching cup ignored before him. When she approached, he looked up, a smile peeking through his beard, and leapt up to pull a chair for her.

She returned his smile and sketched a curtsy. "Why, thank you, my lord. But I hope you do not mistake me for nobility."

He blushed a little at that, shrugged, and returned to his seat.

"I can't stay here much longer. What kind of tavern offers nothing but mead, ale, and spirits?" Eirik's growl was low, and he looked as if there was a thundercloud sitting on his grizzled brow.

"We can take a walk along the piers, if you'd like." She said, craning her neck to look for Chagua. "I don't need to spend any more time indoors than necessary."

The islander was at the long bar, speaking with two big men whose clothing was a bit finer than seemed to be the average in Hammon.

"Who's Chagua talking to?" She indicated the conversation with her chin.

Eirik didn't look up, but Tyr turned to follow her gaze. "Merchant captain, at a guess? He's not dressed like a sailor or a local, that's for sure."

The man had a jerkin of soft tan hide with a wide-sleeved tunic beneath. The clothing reminded her of the oyathey that had occasionally come through the Fallen Oak. The man's skin was pale, though, clearly marking him as fyrdar.

Chagua returned and collapsed heavily into the remaining chair, a mug of something frothy in one big dark hand. He cast a quick glance at Eirik and then grunted with a shrug.

"I've booked passage with Captain Stig aboard the Ausa. She's bound for Shawmut tomorrow and then heading farther north along the coast. I should be able to find a deep water ship in Sowaset or Raonoq."

A silence settled over the table, and a sudden wash of alarm rose up in Maiara. She had not yet made up her mind about her next step. What if the decision had already been made for her?

"Passage for one?" She tried to sound casual, but heard the break in her voice all the same. She ignored the flush she felt rising in her cheeks.

Tyr perked up also, looking first to her, then to Eirik, and then to Chagua, waiting for a response.

The big islander looked at her with a flat, stony expression. He looked tired, more than anything.

Tired and alone.

When he spoke, the tone of his voice belayed the words. "The captain may have mentioned that he has a few more berths available."

She thought she should feel relief at that. Obviously, there would be room for all of them, if they wished to accompany their friend on his journey.

Tyr grabbed his cup and took a casual sip, very nearly hiding the surprised choke as the water hit his throat.

Eirik was staring into his own cup, the muscles of his jaw clenching and unclenching, setting the grizzled beard squirming. His voice was gruff and distant. "I'm not certain I can go with you, Chagua." He looked up, and she knew the pain she saw there was genuine. "Astrigir's wounds are fresh and deep. It will take all of Einar's cunning to undo the damage that old man set in motion. Even with all that has passed, I don't know if I can deny his call now."

Tyr shook his head. "He's got all the hearth guard who weren't in the Bhorg. They'll return now. And the survivors. And the Shadows always thought that they were loyal. You told the king you thought they could be convinced to join his cause."

"Those aren't the types of men and women you necessarily want to join your cause." Chagua put his cup down and wiped at the froth on his lip. "But they're loyal, or at least they've always believed they were." Tyr's voice had taken on a plaintive tone, and she felt her heart breaking for him. Obviously, he had felt the same way she did, and didn't want to see their little group break apart.

But as she listened to Eirik's words, a greater certainty had arisen in her own heart. She knew she could not set sail for the northern islands now. She, too, had responsibilities that could not be denied.

"We believed we were being loyal, too, after a fashion." Eirik's voice had turned bitter. "Look what we nearly accomplished. I can't leave the kingdom to a bunch of murderers and cutthroats who thought they were loyal when they were conducting their butchery."

That obviously bothered Tyr even more than the idea of their all going their separate ways now. "No. You can't do that to yourself, Eirik, none of us can, or we'll drive ourselves mad. The blame begins and ends with Tsegan ... or whoever the old man was."

But even as he said it, she knew it wasn't true, and the guilt that was always surging just beneath the surface threatened to rise up and drown her. She sat back in her chair as a hollow feeling opened up in the pit of her stomach. They all owed a terrible debt, no matter what their intentions had been. And paying it was going to rip them all apart.

Eirik's eyes were dark as he stared across the table at the boy, but they softened as he spoke. "You know that's not true, Tyr. We will all spend the rest of our lives paying for our naivety, no matter how far we run." He sighed, looking back down at the cup of water and then pushing it aside with a sneer.

They all sat silently for an uncomfortable length of time, and then Chagua spoke in a soft, broken voice that had them all leaning in to hear. "None of you can come with me. Our actions here require each of us to follow a different road of atonement, now. I must return my sword to the islands and answer for what I have done." His black eyes were shining with unshed tears that unnerved her as she realized what he was saying. "You, Saemgard, must return to your king. You are too valuable an asset to him now to deny him, especially after the part we all played in your kingdom's present state."

And then he looked toward her, and he opened his mouth to pronounce his sentence upon her as well.

"I must return to the mountains." She met his gaze, and then each of the others' in turn. She saw confusion, doubt, and fear in all of them, but pressed on. "My road rejoins the greenway and will take me back to Alden's

Tor." She looked away, knowing the words she needed to say, but also knowing that if she looked at them while she spoke them, what she might see there could break her. "You all saw what happened. You know what I've become – well, at least as much as I know myself." She shook herself but pressed on. "I have to understand it. I haven't ... felt it ... since that night."

The others looked surprised at that, but Eirik's bright grey eyes were locked on hers from beneath heavy brows. "You can't do ... what you did, again?"

The tone of his voice made her nervous, and she felt the sudden urge to squirm in her chair. She fought it down but nodded. "I've tried, but it's as if there's nothing there."

His face tightened. "We need you. Einar needs you. They'll be returning, and when they do, the only person who could hope to stand up to another of the old man's ilk here is you."

Tyr nodded. "You heard him." His own voice was low. "They spent lifetimes making sure there is no one here who could do what you did."

Even Chagua, whose face looked more hopeless and haggard than it had a moment ago, agreed. "You are the bulwark against these people, whoever they are. A great part of my challenge as I return home will be to convince the islands they must prepare for war. We have been caught up in a massive web set to trap entire kingdoms. The failure of this one strand will not deter our enemies. They are coming."

"The Utan." Tyr sank back in his chair. "You heard him."

Eirik shook his head. "It doesn't matter who they are. We know what they are capable of, and we know their intentions." He turned to Chagua. "You owe the fyrdar nothing, but the rest of us have no choice."

It was Chagua's turn to shake his head, setting the thick snakes of snarled hair swaying. "We all heard him. There will be safety for no one. They come for the fyrdar, they come for Kun Makha, and they come for the islands. They will be satisfied with nothing less."

Eirik's head turned slowly back to her. "Which makes it all the more urgent for you to master the power you wielded in the Bhorg that night."

She nodded. She had felt, all through the developing conversation, the avenues of her life closing before her. Hearing her own thoughts echoed out loud by these men had proven more painful than she would have expected.

"I need to begin up in the mountains. I need to return to the valley, go through his things, and see what else there is up there that might help me."

Tyr's gaze shifted from Eirik's to Maiara's and back. "So she goes up into the mountains alone?"

A part of her was offended by his incredulous tone. But another part of her was very thankful for the words.

Eirik's eyes never shifted from hers. "I must return to Einar in Connat. Chagua must return to his people." Then his gaze slid to the boy's. "You have not yet chosen a path."

That seemed to catch Tyr by surprised. She knew it caught her by surprised. But—

Tyr's eyes darkened and he looked away. His face twitched as if a score of emotions were boiling just beneath the surface. When he spoke, it was in a soft, muttered tone. He stared down at the table. "I must return to Connat."

She could feel the older men looking at her, and she tried to keep up a brave front. With those few words, Tyr had sealed her fate. She would be alone when she returned to the valley.

And yet, there was something in Tyr's eyes, behind the guilt and the frustration and the wavering resolve. That something seemed to promise something more than his words might indicate; some other outcome, if it was given free rein.

Eirik slapped the table and made them all jump. He threw back the contents of his cup with a single dash and almost hid the reaction that flashed across his face. Then he smiled. "It'll be summer by the time we reach the greenway on our return. The journey up into the mountains will be safe and quick. I think Einar can spare two old war hounds for a few weeks. Long enough to see you safely established at Alden's Tor, at any rate."

Chagua smiled, now, too. Although the strain was still evident in his eyes. "I cannot think of a more formidable trio. I feel nothing but pity for any mountain bandit that might think to test your resolve."

She forced a smile onto her own face as she nodded, although it wasn't thoughts of mountain bandits that had caused the flush of relief when Eirik made his offer. She had been thinking of the huge, misshapen skull that still resided on a side table in the common room of their winter home.

Tyr smiled, too, but the expression was forced and brittle. "The valley was completely safe. And when you return, you'll be more than capable of looking after yourself."

The smiles froze at that, and the glances slid away from her.

None of them were comfortable with what had happened in the throne room, she knew. And she wondered, even if she was able to recreate that power in defense of the kingdom, if they would ever be comfortable with her again.

She had never felt more alone, sitting at that table with three men who, she had no doubt, would lay down their lives for her if that was ever necessary.

And then something else clicked in her mind.

An outsider. Fallen from high station. Rising up to become the protector the realm required.

She felt the weight of the old man's doctored Burdren Saga pulling at her mind.

It had never been Eirik Hastiin.

She felt the truth of the realization, pushing down on her chest. Whatever else the old wizard had done to the text, those parts were real.

She felt that in her bones. And they did not refer to the big saemgard. They referred to her.

She wanted to cry as she felt the weight of it settle in her gut.

Instead, she raised her head, looked at them all, these men who had been willing to give up so much for her and for the false dream they had all been sold.

She raised her glass in a light-hearted salute, her head cocked to one side, and smiled.

For more information on Zmok Books at:

https://www.wingedhussarpublishing.com

About the Author

Craig is from Bedford New Hampshire where he does his best to warp space and time to fit far more activity into each day than anyone, including his wife, thinks would be advisable. During the day Craig teaches Theatre and Literature courses to the intrepid students of Milford High School. After hours Craig actively pursues kickboxing and mixed martial arts, and is one of the two hosts of the wildly mediocre and not-too-horrible general gaming podcast The D6 Generation. He is husband to a remarkably supportive wife and father to clearly the smartest, cutest, and most promising three year old on the planet (an entirely objective assessment). Craig plays games whenever he can find the time and the opponents, ranging from his recent favorite, a classic South American dice game called Perudo, to whatever the local tabletop war-game flavor of the month happens to be. And in all the voluminous free-time this schedule allows, Craig writes. Craig has written over six novels and several short stories for various genre tie-ins. In addition, he has written *Legacy of Shadows*, the first in a multi-volume series.

Legacy of Shadows

By

Craig Gallant

Exerpt

Prologue

The white dwarf was a distant glowing ember floating in the void, barely brighter than the scattered diamonds of the galactic disk beyond. The forgotten star bathed the system with the last emissions of its final, quiet eons of death. Orbiting the dying sun were the charred and lifeless remains of its children, their black and fractured orbs absorbing the feeble light, giving back almost nothing in return.

Aside from these last fragments, the system had died over a billion years ago. The millennia-long paroxysms that had claimed the planets' atmospheres were long extinguished. What life might once have thrived there was less than a memory for the vast celestial engine that continued to spin, oblivious to the tragedy that had claimed it. It was a catastrophe that had destroyed countless similar suns, and would destroy countless more as the inexorable forces of entropy marched down through time.

The largest remnant spinning though the silent parade, a dull and melted sphere, had once been the core of a massive gas giant before its voracious parent had devoured its heavy atmosphere. The relic wobbled along in an erratic orbit, still reeling from the grievous deathblow. Had any sentient being felt tempted to visit the dark corpse, it would have taken inordinate skill and stamina to keep station with the dead husk for long. The moon-sized craft that orbited the planet did not suffer the weaknesses or limitations of sentience, however.

Blacker than the most brutalized planetary remains in the system, the shape appeared more a hole in the star field beyond than something concrete and real. It's blocky, utilitarian shape was unmarred by the violence that had claimed its current home. The ship had kept its vigil for eons. Civilizations had risen and fallen out in the wider galaxy while it followed its silent, purposeful course through the ages.

Deep beneath the vessel's matte shell, whispers of thought flashed through ancient crystal matrices. There was no awareness behind these whispers. There was no conscious direction behind the thoughts. Patterns and duties set thousands of years ago continued in the silence of the giant hull. Translucent frameworks flashed in slow, steady rhythms as the cadences of the galaxy beyond were tasted, compared, and stored in memory stacks nestled in the heart of the sentinel.

Without warning, the hull vibrated with an imperceptible motion detectable only from the thin layer of celestial dust that shivered free, glittering in the faint light of the distant, dying star. A dim red light formed a rectangle beneath the dispersing motes. A hatch receded, dwarfed by the impenetrable darkness behind. The crimson glow brightened, and then was eclipsed by a spindly shape the matte black of the vessel itself. An armature pushed a bundle of tubes, dishes, and wires through the faint cloud of debris, bringing the instruments in line with the dull metal core of the planetoid below.

Time meant little within the echoing silence of the dead system. The insectile limb hung still and silent for what might have been an age.

Without warning, the instruments stabbed downward. Gravitic power relays and crystalline conduits flashed with a brilliant pulse of intense green light. For a moment, the flank of the giant machine leapt out of the darkness, its structure outlined in fierce jade glory. Massive doors and hatches were scattered across its huge surface, vanes and bulbs protruded here or there following no perceptible pattern. There was no sign of a window, sensor array, or lens of any kind along the entire, colossal length.

A beam of coherent light pierced the remnant atmosphere of the planetoid below. The column struck the slagged sphere in the middle of a wide field of melted craters. The dull surface, greedy for a taste of heat and light, absorbed everything the beam could provide. The lance of energy struck deep into the incredibly dense material, seeking out its core, interacting with ultra-rare elements that had been smelted down in the cosmic furnace of the system's death. Naturally-occurring matrices of heavy metals came alive within the crust of the planet, and the entire orb rang like the largest bell ever struck. Countless vibrations rippled through the material of the planet and were cast out into space.

Waves and particles of a million varieties spread forth, each following the esoteric rules of its type. Some wrapped themselves around the various dead bodies of the system and returned at once to their point of origin. These were ignored by the hulk floating overhead. Many stretched forth their ethereal fingers, and would not return for hundreds or thousands of years. The sentinel was infinitely patient. Some special few flew outward at staggering speeds, passing tachyons and luxons in their haste to reach the far corners of the galaxy.

The blazing column vanished without fanfare, plunging everything back into endless night. The planet below was silent and dark once more, save for a single glowing crater that quickly cooled and disappeared into the gathering black. Aside from the dim crimson glow from the open hatch, the entire system was dead once again.

The armature drew its bundle back through the hatch. Vague hints of movement within followed, shadows cast out into the void, and then a second shape emerged. A silvery orb slid out into the night and came to a smooth halt.

Again, an unknowable length of time crept past. When echoes of the swiftest waves began to return, the orb shivered. There was no other sign that some of the most powerful elements in the galaxy had been harnessed to a coherent, measured purpose.

The orb was withdrawn, the dull red light eclipsed once again as the hatch closed. Deep within the sentinel, whispers of thoughts returned. Ancient patterns were followed. The paths of the net cast from the dead system were studied rote, mindless precision. Data was separated, weighed, measured, and stored for some possible future purpose. Nothing had been found.

There was no frustration at this lack of progress. There was no acknowledgment of empty eons sloughing by, except as yet another data point to be catalogued.

Colossal locks slid back into place, securing the huge hatch.

The leviathan had been created for a very specific purpose. It was a hunter, built to scent a particular prey, possibly the most dangerous prey the galaxy had ever known. Every system within the enormous hulk confirmed that this prey had not been detected. None of the ancient parameters so much as hinted at the prey's stirring.

But the sentinel was patient. It was singularly devoted to its purpose, neither restlessness nor anxiety designed into its temperament. Deep within the massive hull the last stray components settled back into their cradles. Power slowed to a trickle as its fiery heart was banked once again, its full potentiality relaxing into a quiet, wary rest.

The dust began to settle once more over the dull black hull, and the dead system was plunged once again into the deathly stillness of a crypt.

Craig Gallant

ZMOK
BOOKS

Printed in the US